AUSSIE YARNS

AUSSIE YARNS

A COLLECTION OF SHORT STORIES AND POEMS

JOHN McAULAY

Cover by leading Australian bush artist TOM McAULAY

ISBN: 978-1-956515-50-3 (Paperback Edition)
ISBN: 978-1-956515-51-0 (Hardcover Edition)
ISBN: 978-1-956515-49-7 (E-book Edition)

Library of Congress Control Number: 2021918510

Book Ordering Information

Phone Number: 315 288-7939 ext. 1000 or 347-901-4920
Email: info@globalsummithouse.com
Global Summit House
www.globalsummithouse.com

Printed in the United States of America

CONTENTS

A Legend Is Born

'C'mon, man. Stretch those fat little legs of yours, or we won't get to the waterhole by dark.'

'It's all right for you, you miserable old Scottish git! I gotta take two steps to your one.'

The friendly ribbing continued as the two old friends trudged along the dusty track, kicking up puffs of dust from their boots. The sun sank towards the hazy horizon in front of them, and a cooling breeze started to rustle through the scrubby trees. Matilda, the old cross-bred bitch who accompanied them, padded along in her customary position a few yards behind whoever was trailing as if to make sure no one got left behind. They were a tired and hungry trio as they gazed ahead to the clump of trees that indicated their destination, the well-known Combo Waterhole.

It was three long days since they had left the last homestead and probably two more before they reached Dagworth Station, where they hoped to get some work during the shearing season. Jobs were hard to come by in these wide expanses, and the graziers were not noted for their hospitality. Their supplies were running low, and if they were turned away from Dagworth, they would be in big trouble.

'I'm starting to think we should have headed east, rather than come to this godforsaken place,' Scotty McBride mumbled as he hitched his swag up on his shoulder. 'There's too much walk and too little work for my liking.'

Paddy O'Day always seemed to play the role of the optimist to balance his friend's dour nature. *Must be his Irish heritage*, he mused. Anyone who was brought up to believe in leprechauns had to be an optimist. 'Yair, well, we weren't doing too good there either, were we? At least the jobs on these big places last a while when you get one. I reckon we're ahead of the rush too.'

Optimistic old bastard, Scotty thought. 'Well, I hope you're right, my friend. We'll be right out of tucker by the time we get there, and it's a long way to the next one.'

*　　*　　*

They pitched camp on the bank of the waterhole, put the billy on, and stretched their weary limbs as they waited for it to boil. It was time for a spell and mug of tea before they set about knocking up a damper to go with the last of their corned beef. They were dozing off, when a low growl from Matilda woke them and they looked around for the source of her concern. And then they saw it.

A few sheep had come to drink after a long, hot day, scrabbling to find a feed on the drought-stricken plains. The two friends looked at each other and, without a word, moved to circle around behind them. Then they rushed them from both sides. The wethers panicked, floundered in the muddy edge, and then scattered – all but one; in the rush, he was knocked sideways onto his back in the water, and weighed down by his fleece, he struggled to regain his feet. The agile Scotsman was on him in a trice and triumphantly dragged him up the bank.

Probably because of his strict catholic upbringing, Paddy's thought immediately sprang to the eighth commandment, 'Thou shalt not steal'. But hunger and self-preservation are strong primal forces, and the thought of a nice mutton stew allowed him to overcome his reservations, as he helped Scotty drag the unfortunate animal back to their camp.

As darkness finally descended, the two travellers sat watching a stew bubble on the fire, while two legs of mutton sizzled and spat on sticks suspended above the flames. They would provide them with cold meat for the next few days, and by then they should have reached the homestead. Matilda lay munching on some bones when she suddenly sprang to her feet and ran barking back along the track.

Peering into the gloom, the two mates saw a lone stranger approaching and called her off. A gaunt figure stumbled into the camp and dropped his swag on the ground. 'My name is Heinrich,' he said with a heavy German accent. 'Do you mind if I join you?'

'Not at all, mate,' Paddy offered. 'Rest your bones, and I'll get you a mug of tea. You can join us for a feed then, complements of Dagworth Station. Paddy's my name, and this here's Scotty.'

Scotty McBride was a lot less effusive in his welcome, merely giving the stranger a curt nod. He had learnt to be suspicious of anyone he didn't know. This newcomer might be all right, but then again he could be trouble. If nothing else, he would be a competitor for the available work on the station. Still, it was an unwritten law of the bush that you shared, and shared alike, with your fellow travellers. So it turned out that the three of them were soon tucking into their best feed in days and yarning about their experiences.

'How long have you been out here, Fritz?' Paddy asked, hoping his choice of a nickname didn't offend the German.

Heinrich stared into the flames for a minute before he replied. 'Sometimes I think, my friend, too long. Many bad things have happened to me in this country. It is hard to come from a strange land and fit in here.'

'We all come from a strange land, as you put it, Heinrich,' Scotty said as he poured himself more tea, 'but I suppose we at least speak English or, as I like to call it, Scottish. It must have been harder for you.'

'It was.' Heinrich kept his thoughts to himself as he recalled his early days in the colony, battling prejudice while he tried to find enough work to keep body and soul together. Many times he wished he had never left Germany, but his circumstances there meant he had no option.

Paddy broke the silence. 'So where have you been in Australia, Fritz?'

'Mainly down south, but I had a bit of trouble there, so I've come up here, hoping for better luck. Not finding much, though.' Once again, he decided not to confide all of his experiences to these strangers. He didn't trust anyone after what had happened to him in Sydney. For the umpteenth time he recalled the disaster that befell him not long after his arrival from Germany.

Returning to his lodgings at night, he stumbled over a badly injured man lying in the gutter. He was bending over him trying to help him, when he was accosted by a policeman who had been summoned by a witness. His poor English prevented him from giving a cogent explanation of his story, so he was taken in for questioning. The not-too-sober witness identified him from a line-up, and that was all it took to have him convicted of robbery with violence. He had spent the next seven years in jail, where all he gained was a better grasp of English and a manic fear and hatred of authority.

On his release, he found himself unable to cope with living in the city any longer. The sight of a policeman walking towards him in the street almost caused him to pass out with fear, and the years of abuse he had endured in prison had left him suffering from claustrophobia and an irrational fear of people. Now, as he recalled all of those horrors from the past in the presence of two strangers, he started to shake violently.

'I'm sorry. I must go to sleep now,' he stammered as he climbed to his feet. He picked up his swag and headed off along the bank to find a place for himself. 'Thanks for the feed!' he shouted back over his shoulder.

'Funny bastard,' Scotty mused.

'Seemed to get the shakes at the mention of the past, didn't he?' added Paddy. 'I wonder what he's been up to.'

*   *   *

Scotty had them up before dawn as usual next morning, and they set about making tea, eating the leftover stew, and packing up their gear. There was no sign of life from the German's camp, so they decided to let sleeping dogs lie, so to speak, and head off on their own. 'He would catch up if he wanted to,' they supposed.

'We'd better hide the carcass of that sheep before we go, Paddy, just in case someone comes snooping around. Give me a hand to carry it over to that heap of logs. We can cover it over with some branches, and no one will ever find it.' They did just that, covering it with the skin and then a mound of branches until it was invisible. A quick wash in the waterhole, a billy of water on their fire, and they set off, warm sun on their backs, bellies full of stew, and a roasted leg of mutton each in their tucker bags. A final glance back along the bank showed no action yet at the other camp.

'Lazy bastard,' Scotty observed. 'He won't be hard to beat for a job. Still, I reckon we should leave the track and take that shortcut through the bush that we heard about. It's supposed to be a few miles shorter, and he probably doesn't know about it. C'mon, Matilda, let's go waltzing.' As usual, he headed off at the front of the trio, with Paddy whistling, 'Danny Boy' behind him and Matilda running to catch up after having one last sniff of the sheep's carcass.

* * *

The sun was well in the sky when Heinrich struggled out of bed. He eyed the empty bottle nearby and remembered why his head felt like it did. Last night's trip back to his unhappy past had left him panicky and sleepless, until he used up the last of his precious supply of rum. Now, on top of everything, his head pounded, and he had to move on. A glance along the bank told him his fellow travellers had left. He would have to try to catch them up to apologise for his rudeness last night.

It was then that he heard horsemen coming from the direction of the station. They emerged from the scrub into the clearing, and his heart missed a beat. Three men in uniform and a stockman rode over and inspected the campfire of the previous night. He hoped they might carry on along the track, but no such luck. They came straight over to him. The senior trouper addressed him.

'What's your name, friend, and what are you doing here?'

'My name is Heinrich Rommel, sir. I am on my way to the station to seek work,' he managed to get out, as he put his hands in his pockets to hide their shaking. His head was splitting, and he felt he couldn't stand the presence of these uniformed police much longer.

'We're looking into the theft of some sheep, Mr Rommel. You haven't taken any, have you?'

A black cloud descended over Heinrich's mind, and he couldn't speak. He shook his head.

'Speak up, man,' the inspector said. 'Have you seen anyone stealing sheep around here?'

Again he shook his head and managed to mumble 'No, sir'. All the memories of his years in jail came flooding back to him: his wrongful conviction, the years spent in the cold, friendless, and cruel jail, and the nightmares that had haunted him ever since. He knew he had done nothing wrong, yet he feared for his life. In a fit of despair, he slumped to the ground.

A call from the stockman caused them all to look in his direction. He had gone to see why his dog was barking at a heap of logs. He dismounted and started pulling branches off the heap and took only a few seconds to drag out the skin of the sheep that had been the subject of the previous evening's meal. The find meant nothing to Heinrich, but when the inspector's gaze returned to him and found him staring morosely at the ground, he certainly looked guilty.

'Do you know how this skin got here, Mr Rommel, by any chance?' he asked. 'It looks pretty fresh.'

Terrified now, Heinrich fought for an answer in his foggy mind. Obviously, the two men who fed him last night must have hidden it there. *It is my neck or theirs*, he decided, so he summoned up his courage and addressed the inspector.

'When I came last night, two men were camped over there at that fire. They were cooking mutton and invited me to share it. I didn't know it was stolen, sir. They were gone when I woke up this morning. They must have hidden the skin before they left. Surely you passed them on the road. They were going to seek work at the station too.'

The inspector slowly dismounted and indicated to his men with a nod of his head to do likewise.

'Unfortunately for you, Mr Rommel, we passed no one on the road this morning. All we seem to have here is you and a stolen sheep. You will have to come with us, I'm afraid. Seize him, men!' he barked.

Pictures of cold cells and cruel warders flashed in Heinrich's mind as the troupers advanced towards him.

'I didn't do it!' he screamed. 'I didn't do it, but I know you won't believe me. I'm not going back to jail. Please don't put me in there again.' By now he was wailing and backing away from the approaching troupers. He tripped over a log and sprawled on the ground, just as they made a rush to grab him. With an anguished wail, he sprang to his feet and rushed into the waterhole, screaming as he went. 'I'm not going back in there! You'll never take me alive!' With one last maniacal laugh, he plunged under the water and didn't come up.

The crowd on the bank was dumbstruck, and it was some time before the inspector could convince his men to strip off and search the waterhole. His body was never found.

*　*　*

Four days later, Paddy O'Day and Matilda struggled into Dagworth Station. He listened with alarm to the reported suicide of the German traveller who had been accused of killing a sheep.

'Apparently, he had tried to lay the blame at the feet of two fellows who had shared a camp with him the night before,' the squatter explained. 'You didn't happen to see a couple of travellers on the road, did you, Mr O'Day?'

Paddy's Irish blarney came to the fore now, and ignoring the ninth commandment and feigning a look of total innocence, he bore false witness against his neighbour saying, 'No, sir. I saw no such couple.' In spite of this further violation of his religious training, he silently gave thanks to the Lord for several events that resulted in his denial appearing plausible.

The first was the unfortunate demise of his friend and long-time travelling companion, Scotty, who was bitten on the bum by a brown snake while attending to a call of nature two days ago. Paddy saw no other option than to lay him in a gully and cover him with rocks to keep predators away and then hurry on to the homestead to report the death. This final matter, he now decided, should be left undone.

The second lucky event, though it didn't seem so at the time, was that he became lost. Scotty had always been the leader and navigator on their travels, so Paddy had spent two days wandering aimlessly around in the scrub until he came back onto the track. Fortunately, as events had turned out, this indicated he had come along days after the unfortunate events at the waterhole.

And finally, he felt lucky that the last of his mutton had become flyblown yesterday and that he had thrown the potentially incriminating evidence away before reaching the homestead. Now he stood before them, devoid of incriminating evidence and in possession of a convincing story. Only two dead men, who could do him no harm, and his Lord above, who might ask him some awkward questions in a later life, knew the real story.

*   *   *

Many years later, Banjo Patterson would put together various aspects of these occurrences to write the words of a famous song. He got one aspect totally wrong. The dour, old Scotsman who actually stole the sheep could in no way be called 'jolly', nor could the unfortunate German who refused to be taken alive. No, the only jolly swagman was the one who assisted in the felony, ate his share of the stolen goods, got away with it, and went on happily, waltzing around the countryside with Matilda, totally unaware of his role in creating a legend that has become our most treasured unofficial anthem.

A Legend Is Born Explained

The origins of Australia's most famous ballad have been hotly disputed since it was first put together in 1895. A few facts seem indisputable.

1.   Banjo Patterson wrote the original words, though they have been altered over the years to arrive at the version sung with gusto at sporting events today.

2.   Christina Macpherson helped him put his words to the tune, adjusting them to fit the tune where necessary.

3.   The tune was not original, but her version of a tune called 'The Craigeelee' was purportedly heard by her in Victoria and played from memory to Banjo while he was visiting common friends on Dagworth Station near Winton.

4.   No one seems to be sure just what inspired his lyrics, but several events may have been in his mind at the time.

5.   A German swagman or shearer called Hoffmeister, who helped burn down the Dagworth shearing shed full of sheep during a strike, shot himself soon after, possibly to avoid capture. At the time, he was being pursued by the owner and three troupers!

6.   At another time, a shearer did drown himself in the Combo Waterhole but was not involved in the strike or sheep stealing.

7.   During his visit, Banjo and the owner discovered a fresh sheepskin at Combo while riding around the property.

Being a bush poet, Banjo would have put all of these stories and experiences to good use and invented his own story to make the lyrics more interesting.

I have often wondered why a swagman described as 'jolly', would suddenly become so depressed that he would commit suicide. If the song had said, 'Once a severely depressed swagman with paranoia about being arrested camped by a billabong', I could have understood his actions. Obviously, Ms Macpherson would have had issues fitting those words to the tune, so he sacrificed believability on the altar of necessity and described our future national hero as 'jolly'.

There are also several explanations for the use of the term *Waltzing Matilda*, but none of them make much sense. The most common belief is that it referred to their swag being called *Matilda*, a German term for their greatcoats. Waltzing Matilda meant carting it around the countryside, also of German derivation. Others claim it refers to their water bag, or even their billy. But why always use a capital letter for a swag or a billycan? No, I think it was his dog!

'A Legend Is Born' is my much more plausible story of what could have really happened.

Oh, and by the way, the following are the original words penned by Banjo. Not up to the same standard as 'The Man from Snowy River', but he was distracted by his flirtations with the very presentable Ms Macpherson!

WALTZING MATILDA

Oh there once was a swagman camped in a billabong
Under the shade of a Coolibah tree
And he sang as he looked at the old billy boiling
Who'll come a waltzing Matilda with me

Who'll come a waltzing Matilda my darling
Who'll come a waltzing Matilda with me
Waltzing Matilda leading a water bag
Who'll come a waltzing Matilda with me

Down came a jumbuck to drink at the water hole
Up jumped the swagman and grabbed him in glee
And he said as he put him away in the tucker bag
You'll come a waltzing Matilda with me

You'll come a waltzing Matilda my darling
You'll come a waltzing Matilda with me
Waltzing Matilda leading a tucker bag
You'll come a waltzing Matilda with me.

Down came the squatter a riding on his thoroughbred
Down came policemen one two three
Where is the jumbuck you've got in the tuckerbag
You'll come a waltzing Matilda with me

You'll come a waltzing Matilda my darling

You'll come a waltzing Matilda with me
Waltzing Matilda leading a tucker bag
You'll come a waltzing Matilda with me

But the swagman he up and he jumped in the waterhole
Drowning himself by the Coolibah tree
And his ghost can be heard as it sings in the billabong
Who'll come a waltzing Matilda with me

A Farmer's Wife

It was a quiet day at the Quinalow Hotel. A few old stagers hunched over their beers at the bar, while a couple of groups sat at the tables. Jack the barman was unstacking the glass washer, when the swing doors of the pub shot open and George Barlow rumbled over to the bar.

'Geez, George, you look cranky! What'll it be?' inquired the bartender.

'Give us a schooner and a rum chaser, mate, and you can line up another one behind it if you like,' George rasped as he slumped on the nearest stool. He couldn't believe what his wife had just told him. *Twenty bloody years we've been married*, he thought. *I thought I knew her inside out, and now this happens!* He was aroused from his thoughts by a shout from the table behind him.

Jack sat the two drinks in front of him. 'Must be a bit serious, mate,' he said. 'What happened? Tanker driver run over your dog again?'

'Nah. Nothing like that, mate. Trouble with the old girl, that's all,' he mumbled after he had gulped down half his beer.

Jack was incredulous. 'Not Mandy, surely?'

'Yep. Bloody Mandy. I'm as shocked as you are, mate. Thought I understood her pretty well. Then she pulls this one on me.'

They were interrupted by a shout from one of the tables. 'Hey, George! Come and join us. You look like you could do with some company.' Looking around, George saw one of his neighbours and a stranger sitting there. He dragged himself to his feet and slumped into a chair at their table.

'You'll probably wish you'd left me on me own, Barney. I won't be much company today, I'm afraid,' he said as he drained the last of his beer and swallowed the rum in a gulp. 'Bring these blokes another one of whatever they're having, will you, Jack?' he flung over his shoulder in the direction of the bar. Barney noticed his glance fall on the stranger at the table.

'George, this is my brother-in-law, Charles Chambers, from the city. He's up here to see if I can help him sort out a bit of trouble he's having,' Barney volunteered.

'How're you goin, Chilla?' They shook hands, one smooth and white and the other suntanned and rough. 'Well, I hope you can fix up his problems pretty quick, Barney, cos then you can have a go at mine, but I don't like your chances.'

'Yes, well, you sure don't look too happy, mate. Looks like you've lost your best bull and found a bloody billy goat. I thought you'd be happy as a pig in muck after I saw in the paper what you got at the sale last week,' Barney joked, trying to lighten things up a bit.

George retrieved their drinks from the bar and plonked them on the table. 'Bloody hell, Chilla! What's that muck you're drinking? Looks like dishwater!'

'Well, actually, it's a lemonade shandy. I'm driving, you see,' Charles explained.

'Don't have to worry about that out here, mate. The worst drink driver around here is the old sergeant, so he wouldn't be game to put the bag on anyone else in case they dobbed him in to his superiors. Anyway, here's cheers!'

'Yes. Bottoms up,' said Charles, taking a sip of his shandy.

'So what's happened to you to make you so cranky?' Barney asked. 'The old girl ran off with the mailman or something?'

'Might as well have,' George replied, knocking off another couple inches of beer. 'At least I could understand that. Happens all the time these days, and no one hardly blinks. No, what she's done is worse. She's gone and bloody resigned.'

'What do you mean resigned?' Barney asked incredulously. 'She's never had a job, has she? I thought she always just stayed at home with the kids.' He caught Charles's eye and nodded in the direction of the bar. The newly christened Chilla got the message and went to fetch another round. 'What's she resigned from, the bloody Country Women's Association or something?'

'No, mate. Worse than that. She says she's not going to do the few jobs I ask her to do around the place from time to time. It's nothing much mind, but she says if I want them done, I can hire a worker to help me, cos she's not gonna do 'em any more.'

'Bloody hell, mate. What brought this on all of a sudden? It's not like Mandy to not want to be involved in the running of the place. She going through the menopause or something?'

The conversation slowed a bit as Chilla deposited drinks on the table for the two of them, while he nursed his half-drunk shandy away from George's uncomplimentary stare.

'Wouldn't know about that, Barney. Not something we'd talk about really. Maybe you're right. What do you reckon, Chilla?'

'Not in my field of expertise either, I'm afraid,' Charles spluttered, not really understanding the question. 'Could be, I suppose.'

'Anyway, that's not the cause of her revolution,' George continued. 'You're right, though, about her being involved. She's always wanted to be part of everything, and she's so bloody good at it all. Where the hell does she think I can find someone to take her place? It'd take me years to train someone up, and all that she's learnt would be wasted. Why, only last month she did an AI course. Cost me $300, and she was away from the farm for two whole days too.'

George lubricated his throat again, and Charles was almost tempted to get a word in by asking what an AI course was but wisely held his tongue, guessing correctly that George would not have been impressed. The question also crossed his mind that if she only did a few odd jobs, how come he was going to miss her so much? Anyway, he appreciated the chance to forget his own problems for a while as he listened to George's story.

'What do you think of that, Charles?' Barney laughed. 'How would Celia go poking her arm up a cow's arse?'

'Is that what you have to do? How gross!'

'All part of the job, Chilla, and at least they wear a glove these days. Never used to, eh, Barney? One arm used to turn green in the mating season.'

Barney laughed again. 'You'd better not go into any more details, mate. Charles's complexion is taking on the hue of an AI technician's left arm.'

Charles was feeling a little queasy, so he was pleased when George returned to his story.

'You know, Barney, no one can rear calves like her,' he went on, 'and if anything on the place gets sick, she seems to be able to fix it. Whether it's the kids or a cow or even the bloody chooks, she always knows what to do. Good with all animals, she is. Broke in that horse I bought cheap last year, you know. Now the kids ride it at pony club. Gives her a ton of fun looking after them all.'

'Yair, it's funny that', said Barney, 'some people are good with animals and others are good with machinery. Very seldom good with both, though.'

'Well, that's the odd thing about Mandy too,' George responded. 'She's pretty handy with that side of things too. Remember that pump that was causing me trouble last year? All those smart arses from The Pump House couldn't fix it, but she did. Hasn't missed a beat since. That's what I mean. She's too bloody handy to just resign and leave me up in the air, and that's not to mention what it would cost me to pay someone to do these little jobs.'

Barney took advantage of the break in the conversation to buy another round of drinks, and while he was away, George turned his attention to Charles. 'So what do you do for a crust, Chilla? Something out of the sun, eh?'

'Yes, well, actually, I'm an accountant with the taxation department,' he answered, rather self-consciously.

'Bloody hell, mate!' George exploded with a laugh. 'You should have warned me up front about that. Never know what little secrets I might have given away. I'd better slow down on the beers a bit before I get too talkative, eh?'

'There's no need to worry on that score, George. I'm here on family business and left my "work hat" at home.' By now Barney was back, and he threw a couple packets of chips on the table.

'Not for me, thanks, Barney. That bloody old deserter at home's got me on a salt-free diet too.'

*　　*　　*

Meanwhile, on a beautiful sunny afternoon, two women were sitting at a sidewalk table at the cafe around the corner from the pub. Sister-in-laws, Celia Chambers and Judy Hodges, were enjoying a coffee and a slice of carrot cake as they chatted about all sorts of things, from kids to climate change. Eventually, the subject got around to the reason for the Chambers' visit.

'I've really enjoyed our little chat, Celia,' Judy said. 'I'm so glad Charles suggested a drive in the country.'

'Yes, me too. I don't know what made him think of it, though. He even pulled out of his regular golf game. He must have an ulterior motive, but if he has, he's not letting on.'

Judy had no idea either. Barney and his sister hardly kept in touch these days, much less visit each other, and she knew for a fact that Charles hated visiting the farm. *Not his cup of tea*, she thought. And now he had suggested taking Barney to the pub when he hardly ever drank at all, other than wine, and he wouldn't be doing that in this pub.

'Maybe Barney will find out,' she mused. 'If he does, I'll let you know. Ooh, there goes Mandy Barlow. She's our neighbour. Yoo-hoo, Mandy! Come and join us.'

'Hello, Judy,' Mandy said as she drew up a chair. 'You seem to be having fun. I think I just might join you.'

Judy made the introductions and signalled for the waitress to order more coffee. 'Our men have gone to the pub to discuss some secret men's business, so we're cooling our heels waiting for them. What are you up to?'

'Well, I've just done the grocery shopping, paid a few bills, and now I'm on my way to buy some blades for the motor mower,' she replied.

'Good heavens!' Celia interjected. 'Wouldn't your husband do that?'

'God, no!' Mandy laughed. 'I tried that once, but he brought the wrong ones home. He thought it was a Victa, but we've had a

Rover since we were married. Not surprising really. He's never used it since the day we bought it.'

'Aren't you good?' Celia said. 'I'm afraid I wouldn't even know how to start ours.'

Judy joined in the laughter. 'Me either, Celia, but Mandy's a special case. She does everything on the farm. George doesn't know how lucky he is. By the way, I thought I saw him heading towards the pub too a while ago.'

'That'd be right,' Mandy said. 'Probably gone to drown his sorrows. We've been having a bit of a barney, if you'll excuse the pun. He's not real happy with me at the moment. I just told him I'm resigning and that he should start looking for a replacement.'

'You're not going to leave him, are you?' Judy asked incredulously.

'Good heavens, no! Nothing like that! I just don't want to spend all my time working on the farm any more. I want to do something for myself for a change.'

Celia had been quietly observing this exchange between the other two, and it brought to mind the problems she was having at home too. Charles had been particularly difficult lately, becoming more bossy and demanding all the time. She was determined not to let him rule the roost. She now entered the discussion.

'Well, good for you, Mandy. These men think we shouldn't have a life of our own. Charles has been wanting me to get a job lately. Blow him. I enjoy my spare time, and he thinks rearing kids and running a household count for nothing. What would you do with yourself, though, Mandy? Quinalow doesn't exactly appear to be a hive of social activity.'

'That wouldn't be a problem for me, Celia. That's what's causing the problem. I need more free time for my new hobby. Judy probably doesn't even know about it yet. I've been keeping it quiet, but for some time now, I've been writing short stories.'

'How clever!' Celia exclaimed. 'How did you get into that?'

'Well, I've always had the interest, so I did a correspondence course in creative writing. Other than that, I've just taught myself. It's not all that hard really. You could do it.'

'Oh, I don't think so.' Celia chuckled. 'But I do admire your confidence. Is there any money in it?'

'I certainly hope so, one day. That's what I've been telling George anyway. I thought if there were a few dollars in it, he might be more agreeable to giving me time off farm work. When he found that my first published story was worth a thousand dollars, he couldn't get over it.'

'Good heavens, Mandy!' Judy gushed. 'Neither can I! How long did that take you to write?'

'Oh, I don't know. Probably only a few hours once I got started. Coming up with an idea can take ages,' Mandy replied. Then, gathering up her gear, she continued, 'Anyway, I must keep moving. Lovely to meet you, Celia. See you at the fete next Saturday, Judy.'

With that, she scurried off to complete her business in town, leaving the other two to continue their wait for their men to return from the pub.

'What a marvellous woman!' Celia mused. 'She makes me feel so incompetent.'

'Don't feel bad about it. She makes everyone I know feel the same. She's a brilliant mother, great community worker, and she practically runs the farm. Now she's a published author as well. I'm afraid I don't measure up too well against her standards.'

'Nor me either,' Celia agreed. 'But she's got me thinking now. The trick seems to be to find something that interests you and make an effort to do something about it. I like cooking and cake icing. I think I might see if I can create a little business for myself. You never know till you try, I suppose.'

'Good for you. I guess if I have an interest, it is probably gardening. I wonder where the local florist gets her flowers,' Judy mused.

*   *   *

Back in the bar, Barney and Charles were continuing to pump George about his problems with Mandy.

'So what brought all this on then, George?' Barney asked for the second time.

'Bloody technology, that's what.' He took a long pull on his beer, while he recalled the good old days before all this modern technology invaded his life. He used to be able to go out the back paddock and escape for a while, but then, for safety reasons, she said, he now had to carry a mobile phone. Gone was any chance of peace and quiet. If it wasn't some mate or anyone else ringing him, it was Mandy telling him something that had gone wrong back near the house. She used to just fix it herself, but nowadays she rang him and called him home.

He'd even tried turning the bloody thing off, but that led her to think he had had an accident, and she would then come tearing out in the ute to look for him and give him such an earbashing that he wouldn't try that again. And then they bought a computer. What a mistake that turned out to be!

'It all started when she decided the kids had to have a computer for their schoolwork, bloody con act if you ask me. They spend more time playing games and sending emails than doing schoolwork, and God only knows what they get up to on it when we're not watching. The other thing is they used to spend a lot of time helping on the farm before we got it. Hardly ever see them outside these days. They'll probably end up like Chilla here working in an office.'

Charles cringed.

George continued. 'The next thing we had to do was put all our books on to a computer program. I couldn't say too much, cos Mandy has always done the books, ever since we got married, but at least I could understand 'em then. Never look at 'em now. Just leave it up to her.'

Charles suppressed a smile. *I bet their accountant and tax agent are pleased,* he thought to himself, while Barney thought, *How lucky George was!* His missus could barely write out a grocery order, let alone do all their bookwork.

'Anyway, I thought she was spending a lot more time on it lately but didn't think to ask what she was doing. Used to be up half the night sometimes. Don't know how she could do it and still be up in time to milk the cows next morning, but she did. Tap, tap, tapping away. Kept me awake too, half the time, but I never complained. Wish I had of now. Might have prevented what's happened.'

If the other two thought they were at last going to hear what was causing all his troubles, they were wrong. 'My shout,' he said to the barman as he passed him. 'Gotta have a leak, and for God's sake, give Chilla a proper beer this time, eh?'

As George moved off, Barney turned to Charles. 'Sorry, we haven't been able to get on to your problems yet, Charles, but we've got to hear the rest of it now. You don't know Mandy, but she's the hardest-working, most friendly, and cooperative person you could find. You've probably worked out for yourself that George doesn't appreciate her. Their place will fall apart if she really is resigning, as he puts it. He'd better pull his head in and do whatever she wants him to by the looks of it.'

'That's okay, Barney. I'm enjoying this, and you never know, I might learn something useful in how to deal with women.'

'Or how to not deal with them, more likely,' Barney mused, as he awaited the return of George and the next round of beers.

'She'd been cheating on me, you know,' George continued as he settled back into his seat. 'Oh, not like that,' he said when he saw their jaws hit the floor. 'Mandy wouldn't be interested in anything like that, believe me. Always too tired for some reason. No, she's been doing a course by correspondence for months now, and I never even knew. Paid for it by computer, so I didn't notice the money going for it, and that's what she was doing, tapping away all night. Now she's got a bloody Diploma in Creative Writing, or some such thing, and thinks she's a bloody author. Apparently some magazine printed a short story of hers and she actually got paid for it. Didn't bank it in the farm account either, but that's beside the point, I suppose.

'So anyway, now she thinks she can make more money writing bullshit stories than we can on the farm and tells me to milk my own bloody cows or find someone else to do it. She's resignin'. I ask you, what should a bloke do with her?'

Charles dragged his thoughts back to the present in time to realise it was his shout, so he headed off to the bar, taking his half-empty glass of heavy with him. In some ways, he wished his wife had been here to listen to all this, which would make her complaints pretty trivial by comparison. He wondered if Barney would give any advice or just let his mate ramble on. He didn't have to wait long to find out.

'Well, if I was you, I know what I'd do, mate,' Barney offered. 'I'd say, "Go your hardest, Mandy, cos if you can make a quid sitting on your bum, go to it." You never know, George, she might have a real talent for it, and be able to make big money out of it. Any silly bugger can milk cows and fix pumps. Get yourself a worker, man! You two haven't had a holiday for ages either, and if you buy her a laptop, she can even keep working while you're away.'

George was a bit taken aback by Barney's tirade. He hadn't really been asking his advice, just having a bit of a whinge actually. They all drank in silence for a while, each with his own thoughts.

Charles was giving serious consideration to a whole new approach to his own situation. He and his wife had been having a few problems lately, and he had come all the way out here to see if her brother could talk a bit of sense into her, but listening to George's ravings and then to Barney's advice had given him a few ideas as to how he could fix things up back home. Funny where you picked up helpful advice sometimes.

Barney, on the other hand, was thinking, *Poor old bloody Mandy. Slaved her guts out for this ungrateful bugger all their married life, and now he begrudged her the opportunity to do something for herself.* Listening to all this had given him a new resolve to never let himself fall into the trap of not appreciating his wife, and he made a mental note to encourage her to do something for herself too.

George was starting to wish he'd stayed home. He wasn't really asking this supposed mate to lecture him on his family relationships. But some of what he had said did make some sense. He was right in saying they hadn't had a holiday since the kids were little, and his father was still alive and able to look after the place. And while he thought it was probably just a flash in the pan, they had paid her $1000 for her story. *Maybe she could do one a week, and I would only have to pay a worker half that. Hmmm. She could turn out to be the best cash cow on the place. Maybe I shouldn't have flounced out in a huff the way I did. I'll have to find a way to fix things up with her.*

Looking at his watch, he thought, *If he left now, he'd just be in time to catch the florist before she shuts.*

'Sorry, fellows, gotta go,' he said, rising to his feet. 'Got some things to do in town. Thanks for the yarn, Barney, and nice to meet you, Chilla.' And with that, he shoved his battered old hat on his head and was off.

'Well, I'll be blowed,' Barney said. 'I don't know whether I offended him or what. He didn't seem too upset. Matter of fact, he left with a smile on his face. I wonder what the old bugger's up to. Anyway, Charles, you were about to tell me why you wanted to see me when George interrupted us. What can I do for you?'

'Not a thing, thanks, Barney. I only thought I had a problem, but you and George showed me what I needed to know. If it's all right with you, I think I'll see if I can avoid the cops and head home. We'll all be out to see you for Christmas. Thanks for the talk.'

And with that he was gone, leaving Barney wondering what it was exactly that he had said. He wished he could remember. It might come in handy at home some time.

*   *   *

It was Christmas Eve, and once again Judy and Celia were enjoying coffees at the Quinalow Cafe, though this time in the air-conditioned interior. As promised on their previous visit, Charles had brought his family to share Christmas with the Hodges. Also again, the boys had headed for the pub for a couple of beers on a hot day, leaving the girls to kill an hour or so over coffee. After placing their orders, Judy opened the conversation.

'Well, here we are again, eh? I really enjoyed our little girl's day out last time you came up, and I know Mandy did too. I've asked her to join us. She should be here soon. I think George is going to the pub again too.'

'I don't know what those three got up to last time, but it sure made a big impact on Charles. He's a changed man these days,' Celia said. 'You know how we were arguing at the time? Well, on the way home, we had a big discussion, and he encouraged me to pursue my own interests, instead of getting a job. He said he would do a bit of overtime to help our budget. He was being so nice, so I told him of my thoughts about starting a little cake icing business from home.'

'Goodness!' Judy exclaimed. 'What did he think of that?'

'He loved it. He helped me to set up a web site and introduced me to a friend of his who is a marriage celebrant. She was able to turn a lot of business my way, and in no time at all, I was being kept very busy.'

'Good for you. Maybe it will grow into something bigger one day,' Judy said.

They paused for a minute while their coffee and cake was delivered. Judy thought how much better Celia looked. So much more confident, and Charles seemed to have loosened up too.

'Actually, it already has,' Celia resumed. 'She and I are in the process of setting up a business in the New Year to provide all of the services for a wedding, from celebrant, flowers, cars, reception, the whole deal, including the cake, of course.'

'That's just marvellous, but how will you cope? You've still got kids at school, and Charles to look after.'

Celia gave a wave of her hand. 'I'll do what other working women do. I'll get some help in the house. Of course, I'll have to give up bridge and the book club, but time enough for that in my dotage. For now, I'm as excited as a pup with two tails, and I can't get over how supportive Charles has become. But tell me, what have you been up to?'

'Well, actually, I've been busting to tell you,' Judy replied. 'My story isn't as grand as yours, but I've been busy too. Remember I told you the only thing I was good at was gardening? Well, I told Barney I was thinking of trying to earn some money out of it, and he suggested I should go to the seminar held every year at the Carnival of Flowers in Toowoomba. So I did, and like you, I became inspired.'

'Good for you!' Celia enthused. 'What are you going to do about it now?'

'Barney's building me a big organic veggie garden, using George's cow manure from the dairy, and I'm going to sell what I grow at the Cabarlah Markets. I probably won't make much, but it will be great fun, and tax free, too, I imagine. Don't you tell Charles, will you?'

Celia laughed. 'Of course not! His mob don't get to see all of mine either.'

Just then, the door swished open and a hot and flustered Mandy joined them at the table.

'Whew!' she gushed. 'Hot as hell outside but beautiful in here, isn't it? Hello again, you two. We meet again. Are your men around at the pub again?'

'Hello, Mandy,' Celia said. 'Yes, afraid so, but after what happened last time they went there, we actually suggested it this time. What about George? Has he joined them?'

'Probably,' Mandy replied. 'I left him at the rural store buying himself new boots. First time he's ever done that. What on earth did they drink last time they were here, Judy? Whatever it was, George came home a changed man that day. Would you believe it? He actually bought me a bunch of flowers to apologise for his attitude to my writing.'

Judy and Celia looked at each other in surprise. 'How strange!' Judy said. 'We were just saying before you came that we have both experienced the same thing. You already know about my gardening venture, but just wait till Celia tells you her good news. I guess we may never know what brought it on, but all three of them seem to have turned over a new leaf.'

'Well, George certainly has,' Mandy said. 'Judy may not have told you yet, Celia, but he actually employed a man on the farm, and we took a trip to New Zealand. Mind you, we spent most of our time talking to farmers and looking at cows, but it opened his mind to new ideas. We're increasing our herd size and changing the feed system as a result. I think we might start to make some money out of the place at last.'

'So what happened to you then?' Celia asked. 'Did you get the sack?'

'No, not really, but the new guy's taken over a lot of my old jobs, leaving me much more time to write. I'm thinking about starting a novel.'

'That's marvellous!' Celia gushed. 'Well, whatever brought on this change in their attitudes, it's given us three a whole new life in the process. I hope they're all enjoying their session today. Heaven knows what exciting developments may come out of it!'

The three of them happily nattered away for another hour until their recently remodelled husbands came rolling around the corner and asked to be driven home, just in case the old sergeant happened to be out on the prowl. They had been equally amazed at how much easier to get along with their wives had become recently and were also at a complete loss as to what had brought on the change. Each of them felt privately smug at their own personal contribution, but in reality, all of the credit was due to one woman's decision to stand up for herself, and that woman was *the farmer's wife.*

'A Farmer's Wife' explained

I have come across some women like Mandy over the years but doubt any of them ever discovered the escape passage that she did. They're probably still rearing calves, fixing pumps, and waiting for that holiday to arrive.

The following poem is one that I wrote years ago for a mate who was getting married. It inspired the story.

A Farmer's Wife

There's something you will need to know,
now you have tied the knot.
As time goes on, as you will see, you'll have to learn a lot.
To become the wedded partner in our comfy little nest,
May not turn out to be the lifestyle you had guessed.

Now as the groom, I made a pact to love and not to harm her,
But the problem is, as you well know, I'm
through and through, a farmer.
And I will need a hand sometimes, in a business that's depressed,
To do some jobs, to help me out. A few. I'll do the rest.

If you can get the cows in while you're on your way to town,
And shift the fence, and check to see if that old cow's still down.
Don't forget to fill the car, and pick up the seed I bought.
(I don't know what I did before I found this bonzer sort!)

If you could do the milking, for an hour or two at most,
You'd still have time to mow the lawn,
peel spuds, and cook a roast.
As you're the smart one of us two, it's you who would be best,
To help the kids with homework. That's all. I'll do the rest.

The automatic washer will save you lots of time,
So you can do the vacuuming, mop dirt, and dust and grime.

And ironing's done one-handed, so the other hand is free,
To do the bookwork for the farm. You're good at it you see.

There are so many jobs on farms, where a bloke just needs a hand.
 From drafting cows, to fixing pumps, to carting loads of sand.
 I know I must take care of you and not leave you depressed,
 So after you have done that lot, you stop. I'll do the rest.

You really need to preg. test. You watch, I'll show you how,
And if you're careful with the gears, I'll teach you how to plough.
 A woman's patience is required to rear the calves on suckers,
 And horses broken in by girls, seldom turn out buckers.

I'm not much good at gardening cos I don't have a green thumb.
 The garden is all up to you, but call me, and I'll come.
 There are so many jobs around in which you are the best,
So you should handle all of them, while me, I'll do the rest.

Do I complain when I come in, and breakfast's running late?
 No. I simply read the paper while I am forced to wait.
 It just means that this morning, you'll have less time to do
The jobs I've listed for you, and there's more than just a few.

Now I'm not a wife abuser, and I know it's only fair,
 To even out the workload, and for me to do my share.
 That's why, when you have done those
 things, and met my last request,
Why don't you put your feet up, dear? Relax. I'll do the rest.

BERNIE

Bernard Ballantyne was a lucky man – and he knew it. He propped himself up on his elbow and turned to admire the sleeping form beside him. Early morning sunlight filtered through the window of the fifteenth floor of the apartment they shared in the central city residential tower. Double glazing kept the sound of traffic to a gentle hum, and the aroma of imported coffee wafted in from the automatic coffee maker in the adjoining kitchen. It was time for a quick cup of coffee, a swim, and twenty minutes on the treadmill before the ten-minute stroll to work.

His mind returned to the naked form beside him – Susan Hardacre. What a girl! Not only beautiful, but clever, funny, a good cook, and a wonderful lover. He watched the sensual rise and fall of the sheet as she breathed and thought of the unbelievable delights that it covered. He listened for the whisper of her gentle breathing, noticed the barely perceptible flutter of her eyelids as some dream flashed through her mind, and wondered if it was about him. He hoped so, because all of his dreams were about her.

He was eight years older than Susan and had enjoyed several relationships and subsequent break-ups before they even met. One or two of them were quite serious, but none of them were like this one. Recently, he had started to wonder if, at last, he had found his lifetime partner. She was still very young, but he was certain she felt the same way. He promised himself that he would create a romantic situation soon and ask her to marry him, any day now.

But not today! Today was a workday, and they should both be getting their morning activities under way. He tickled the tip of her nose with his finger. Still asleep, she brushed it away. He tried again. This time it worked. She broke into a dreamy smile, reached up, and kissed him. 'Good morning, darling,' she said. 'You'll never guess what I was just dreaming about.'

'Well, by the look on your face, it was something pretty good. Do you want to tell me?' he replied, giving her a little nibble on the ear.

She rolled over to face him, reached under the sheets to cuddle him, and whispered in his ear, 'I'll do better than that. I'll show you.'

Bernard did a quick calculation of time, mentally cancelled the swim and the workout, if necessary, and said, 'I was hoping I was part of it. Now what was it we were doing exactly?'

*   *   *

Strangers who passed him in the street on his walk from Admiralty Towers to the Riverside centre probably wondered what was behind the dreamy smile on his face, as he fondly remembered the aborted exercise program that morning. 'Win lotto or something, Bernard?' a workmate asked as they floated up to the twenty-ninth floor in the lift.

'Better than that, Richard,' he replied. 'Much better. I think I'm in love.'

'What, again? How many times does that make it? Five, six?'

'Ah, but this time it's different. This time I think it's for real, and forever. But you wouldn't understand the way you flit from flower to flower, pollinating everywhere, but never staying long. Susan is the real thing. Next weekend she is taking me to meet her parents. None of the others ever did that.'

'Well, whoopee! That should be fun. What does her old man do?' Richard asked.

In reality, Bernard wasn't quite sure. 'Well, they own a property out near Mitchell, so I suppose, they run cattle or sheep, or something. I'll let you know when I come back, if you cover for me on the Monday. Apparently, it will take the best part of a day to get there, so the round trip will take three. Just shows you how serious I am this time, doesn't it?'

'Well, good luck, mate. I hope you hit it off with the mother-in-law!' Richard laughed.

'You know me,' Bernard said with a smile. 'I'm sure the old Ballantyne charm will win her over, but from the little that Susan has let on about her old man, he may be a bit more of a challenge. Apparently, he's a bit of a rough old nut.'

*   *   *

Those thoughts were also on Susan's mind as she placed a call to her mother. Bernard was through and through a city slicker, who had not the foggiest idea about rural people in general, let alone someone like her father. Old Bob was a genuine bushy, tough as nails, who called a spade a bloody shovel and could not abide fools or show-offs. Bernard was neither of those in her mind, but she was a bit worried about the two most important men in her life to hit it off.

'Susan, dear, it's so good to hear from you! You must be ringing from work. Do be careful, dear. You don't want to get into trouble.' A call from her daughter was a rather infrequent pleasure these days, and Peggy Hardacre wondered what had brought it on, particularly at this time of the day.

'No, it's all right, Mum. There's something I wanted to talk to you about and I didn't want Dad or Bernard listening in.' Susan paused for a second to gather her thoughts.

'Don't tell me you're having a baby!' Peggy blurted out, before Susan could get a chance to explain.

'No, relax, Mum. Nothing like that. As you know, and I hope Dad doesn't, Bernard and I have been living together for about six months now, and things have become very serious between us. He's the most wonderful person I've ever met, and I think he's going to ask me to marry him,' Susan explained.

'That's marvellous, darling. You'll have to bring him out to meet us some time.'

'Yes, well, that's why I rang actually, Mum. I wondered if next weekend would be all right. We could come out on Saturday and return on Monday if that suited. You wouldn't have to go to any trouble or anything. Bernard is a very down-to-earth guy. There's just one little problem, though, Mum.'

'Yes, I'd already thought of that, dear,' her mother interrupted. 'I've never told your father about your domestic arrangements. You know him and his old-fashioned ways. I just don't know if he would accept the idea of his little Susie sharing a bed with a man before you were married.'

They contemplated the problem for a while. Peggy knew Bob was out of step with reality and was refusing to move with the times, but there were a few attitudes from the past that he clung to with a fierce determination, and this was one of them. 'Never happened in my day,' he would say. 'If you wanted to live with someone, you married them first. Too much of this bed-hopping going on these days, if you ask me.' Knowing his attitude, no one ever did ask him, but that didn't stop him laying down the law whenever the subject came up.

Susan was well aware of his attitude and had sworn her mother to secrecy when she confided in her some months ago – a secret she was confident Peggy would keep, just like the one that she had kept from her father all their married life. Peggy had experienced a few 'live in' romances herself before she fell for the charms of the good-looking young grazier at her sister's wedding.

Peggy broke into their thoughts. 'What do you think we should do, Susie?'

'I'll explain the situation to Bernard and tell him he'll have to go bachelor for a couple of nights. I'm sure he'll understand, and I know he is keen to make a good impression on Dad. We'll worry about bringing *him* into the real world later on. After they've got to know and I hope, like each other first. Sound good?'

'I'm sure that's a good idea, darling. You can stay in your old room, and I'll put Bernard in the spare room. What time can we expect you?'

*　　*　　*

The weather had not been kind of late on the western plains, and Susan could tell Bernard was less than impressed with the scene that he was seeing for the first time as they sped along the Warrego Highway. He didn't keep his feelings to himself either, constantly wondering aloud how anyone would want to live in such a godforsaken place. To Susan, though, it was home, and she once again enjoyed the sights and smells of the bush.

'Well, here we are, darling. Mitchell, on the beautiful Maranoa River. I can't believe you've never been further west than Toowoomba. What do you think?' Susan asked, somewhat worried what his answer would be, if he was honest.

'To be honest, dear, I think every kangaroo in Queensland must have committed suicide on the Warrego Highway. I lost count when I hit three figures. Going on the lack of grass in the paddocks, I can't say I blame them. What do the livestock live on?'

'Trouble is, you're seeing it at its worst,' she replied. 'When it rains, everything springs into life, but even now, you'd be surprised at how well they do on this country.' Susan had worried a little at his likely reaction to the land of her birth. You had to be born to it to appreciate countryside like this.

'I bet it doesn't make these roos spring back to life,' he said, swerving to avoid yet another rotting carcass. 'How much further?'

'Twenty more Ks along the highway, then about ten in from the front gate, all dirt, I'm afraid. How do you think the BMW will go on the bulldust and ruts of a rural road?'

'Good question. I just hope we don't arrive with one of these roos poking through the windscreen,' Bernard replied, braking sharply as a mother and joey shot across the road ahead of them.

*　　*　　*

They came to a halt in front of the house and were enveloped by a huge cloud of dust sucked in behind them from the road. Susan jumped out and hurried to embrace her mother while Bernard ruefully surveyed his dust-covered 'beema' for any damage. Finding none, he joined them.

'Mum, this is the man I've been telling you about,' Susan said proudly. 'Bernard, this is my mother.'

'I'm so pleased to meet you, Mrs Hardacre,' he said, grasping her hand in his and then giving her a peck on the cheek.

'I'll bet you are, after surviving that terrible track of ours. I keep telling Bob to fix it, but it's good enough for his Toyota, so he doesn't worry about anything else. Oh, and please just call me Peggy.'

'Will do, Peggy, and thanks for inviting us,' he said as he picked up their bags.

'Don't be silly,' she said with a wave of her hand. We've been bursting to see you both. Now come along. Bring your things in and we'll have a cup of tea. Dad will be back in a minute. Just putting some hay out for the weaners.'

She noticed they had been thoughtful enough to pack two bags, and as Susan took hers into one room, she ushered Bernard into another. 'I'm sorry about this,' she said. 'I know Susan will have explained the situation with Bob. You'll just have to pretend you're a bachelor for a couple of days,' she joked.

'No worries, Peggy. We really appreciate what you've done for us. But I love your daughter, so it won't be easy,' he joked back at her. They heard Susan and her father meeting in the kitchen. 'I'm dying to meet him. He sounds like a real character.'

'I hope you still think that on Monday,' she mused as they went to join the others.

'Dad, this is Bernard,' Susan said as they entered the room, 'and this is my father, Robert, Bernard.'

'What's this Robert business, Susie? Bob's the name. Pleased to meet you, Bernie,' he said, enclosing Bernard's soft, white hand in his big, rough paw. 'Been bursting to meet you ever since Peg told me you were coming out to see us. Only way we can get to see our daughter these days. Just us two oldies rattling around in the house these days. Want a beer?'

'Well, Peg suggested a cup of tea actually,' Bernard offered.

'Bugger the tea at this time of the day. That's what you have with a cornmeal sandwich for lunch. Leave that to the womenfolk. Come out on the veranda and I'll grab a coldie,' said Bob, pushing his new acquaintance through the screen door with one hand, while he adroitly pulled a bottle of his homemade brew from the fridge with the other. 'It's my own brew. I think you'll like it, but it's got a kick in it like a cow with sore teats.'

As the boys settled into the squatter chairs on the veranda, Peggy put the kettle on.

'Do you think you should go with them, dear?' Peggy worried. 'Goodness knows what your father will say to Bernard if he gets him on his own.'

'No. Let them go, Mum. They have to get to know each other eventually, for better or for worse. You and I can have a nice cuppa, and I'll tell you all about him. He may not appeal to Dad too much, but I bet by the time we go home, you'll think he's all right anyway.' But they were both inquisitive enough to take their tea to some chairs near a window where they could listen in to the banter on the veranda.

'Bloody nice car you've got there, Bernie,' Bob said, nodding in the direction of the dust-covered BMW. 'Would've cost a bit. Must be good dough in this share business, eh?'

'Not much to start with, Mr Hardacre, but—'

'Hey, none of this "mister" bit, son! Just call me Bob, and I'll call you Bernie, if that's all right. Not one for flash names. Now, you were saying—'

'Yes, well, if you can climb up the corporate ladder a bit, the money is good, and you can also make a bit on the side trading shares if you're careful. The big payday comes when you become a partner.'

'Never had anything to do with shares,' Bob mused. 'Thought you were in the livestock business when Peg told me you worked for a stockbroker. Told her it could be handy. Always on the lookout for some cheap wethers, I said.'

The womenfolk struggled to suppress their giggles in the kitchen.

'I'm afraid I won't be much use to you there,' Bernard offered. 'I don't know the first thing about rural matters. I was born and raised in Brisbane, and I don't think I've even seen a sheep until today.'

'We'll fix that up tomorrow, Son. I'll show you around the place while the two women catch up on all the gossip and cook us a nice lunch. You ever ridden a horse?'

'Never, I'm afraid.'

'No matter. We've still got one of the kid's old ponies here. Slow as hell, but good for first-timers. Be a new experience for you, eh, Bernie. Just hold on a minute till I get us another beer.'

'Yes, I'd appreciate that, Mr . . . sorry, Bob,' Bernard replied, dreading the thought of making a fool of himself in front of the man who he hoped one day would become his father-in-law.

With his hand on the doorknob, Bob turned and appraised his prospective son-in-law. 'Never know, Bernie. You might find you like the look of life on the land when you've had a look around. Always a job here if you want it,' Bob suggested with more hope than anticipation in his mind.

With less than unrestrained enthusiasm, Bernie replied, 'Thanks, Bob. You never know.'

They then settled down to knock off a long line of coldies over the next hour or so. Finally, a call from the kitchen sent Bob ambling off to change.

*   *   *

While Bob was in the shower and Peggy was busy in the kitchen, Bernard and Susan had a few moments to themselves, and he followed her into her bedroom.

'So this is where you lived before I found you and took you home with me,' he joked, giving her a quick squeeze. 'Pretty small bed, but I wouldn't mind getting by with half of it for a while tonight, but I suppose old Bob would hear a sleepwalker.'

'Probably, but I'm surprised that you didn't notice both our rooms have windows opening on to the side veranda,' Susie said. 'Now an enterprising country boy would have worked that out straightaway. Oh, and we don't have to lock them out here either,' she offered with a wink.

'I'll probably be prowling around a bit anyway,' he said. 'I don't think your father's home brew is sitting too well.'

*   *   *

Bernard's eyes sprang open to the raucous sounds of a rooster's crow. *Hell, I must have slept all night, and now dawn is breaking.* He wriggled away from the sleeping form beside him, put his pyjamas on, and crawled through the window. As he crept in the semi-darkness back to his own window, Bob rounded the corner from the front and greeted him jovially.

'G'day, young fella. You're up early for a city slicker.'

If nothing else, Bernard was quick on his feet when it came to getting caught out. 'Yes, well, I think the silence of the bush must have woken me. I'm not used to that where I live. I thought I'd just pop out here and watch the sun come up. It's a wonder anyone can sleep through that rooster crowing, though,' he said, privately thanking it for waking him in time.

'Well, he won't be causing us any trouble tomorrow morning. We've got to knock his head off afterwards. Peg's going to cook us a nice roast lunch to celebrate your visit. Now you'd better get your work gear on, son. I've got the kettle on for a quick cuppa, then I'll show you around the place before it gets too hot.'

*　　*　　*

'Now hold the bugger still, Son. Keep his neck stretched on the block, and don't let go.' Bernard hoped Bob didn't notice how much his hands were shaking. He'd never done anything like this before, and he turned his face away as the axe descended in a blur and the rooster's head flew across the yard. The body started thrashing and kicking and Bernard lost his tentative grip. The beheaded rooster flopped and bounced at their feet, splattering them with blood, until Bob put his boot on him until he was still. 'Told you to hang on,' said Bob with a laugh. 'Now you know where that old saying 'running around like a headless chook' came from, eh? Come on, we'll take him over to Peg. Women's work, plucking and cleaning them.'

Bernard's thoughts returned momentarily to how this poor bird's crowing had saved his bacon earlier, and now he had repaid him by assisting in his execution. *How on earth am I going to force myself to eat the poor creature?* A quick wash under the garden hose and they were off to saddle up for a bit of a gander around the place, as Bob put it.

'Better put a hat on, young fella,' he said, 'or you'll get sunstroke.'

'I didn't think to bring one, Bob, but I'll be right. We won't be gone long, will we?' Bernard asked, hoping his first lesson on a horse would be short and painless.

'Nah, not long, but you still need a hat. Here, put this, one of Peg's, on,' he said, taking a pink creation from the rack beside the back door. For a moment, Bernard thought of refusing to embarrass himself, but looking around and seeing no one was watching, he decided to put up with it and plonked it on his head. He just hoped the old bugger wasn't taking him for a ride in more ways than one.

*   *   *

They arrived back at the yards some three hours later. Bob had talked incessantly as they rode, yapping on about breeds and lambing percentages and microns and parasites until Bernie thought he would scream. His legs ached, and his bum was rubbed raw from his unnatural seat in the saddle. Also the pink hat was proving totally ineffective in shading the tender skin on his face. He left Bob to unsaddle the horses while he minced his way painfully to the house, hiding the hat behind him until he could put it back on its nail. He needn't have bothered. Mother and daughter had seen it all from the kitchen window and, as he came through the door, they were almost as red in the face as he was from suppressed laughter.

'How'd it go, Bernard?' Peggy asked with a smile. 'Know all about sheep farming now? My, you look a bit sunburnt! You'd better have a shower and I'll put some aloe vera on your face. Get me a bit from the garden, will you, please, Susie?'

*   *   *

They sat down to dine on Bernard's early morning saviour, he with his pink face shining under a liberal plastering of aloe vera and Bob still trying to fill in any gaps that might remain in his education on livestock management. But while he had been changing, some mischievous thoughts had been forming in Bernard's mind.

'I just want to say how much I enjoyed our ride, Mr . . . sorry, Bob,' he said. 'How about you and Peggy paying us a visit in Brisbane soon so I can return the favour and show you around the city?' Susan almost choked on a mouthful of rooster and had to gulp some water to regain her composure. *What on earth is he thinking?* she wondered. *How could they continue to hide their living arrangement?* But a sly wink from Bernard showed that he knew what he was doing.

'Unfortunately, I live in a one-bedroom apartment, so I can't offer you a bed, but I'd be happy to shout you a weekend at the Marriot Hotel just around the corner. I'd like to show you a few things too. Ever been on a sailing boat?'

'No. Can't say I have,' Bob replied, chomping with relish on a drumstick. 'That would be great, Bernie. We haven't been down to the big smoke for years. Peg could give the shops a bash. Buy a new hat or something, eh, pet?'

Although it was delivered with a poker-straight face, Bernard was sure he was having a go at him, but he'd keep. He returned to the task of struggling to digest a respectable portion of his, trying hard to keep the thought of his untidy demise from his mind.

Bernard spent an uncomfortable night, alternating between lying on his raw bum and his sunburnt face, but at least there was no thought in his head of nocturnal wanderings. After a Bob-inspired breakfast of fried mutton chops and eggs, he and Susan loaded their gear in the car and said their goodbyes.

Bernard gave Peg a peck on the cheek and then jumped behind the wheel quickly to avoid another bone-crushing handshake from Bob. Giving him a wave instead as he approached from the stables, he called out, 'Thanks for having us, Bob. Just let us know when you can come to town and I'll organise some entertainment.' *You bet I will,* he thought to himself, as he tried vainly to wriggle his backside into a more comfortable position on the cushion that Susan had purloined on his behalf.

'Bye, Mum. Bye, Dad,' Susan said, planting a kiss on them both. 'Do try to get down to see us.' Then she climbed in beside her man, and they crawled off down the track, trying to avoid the worst of the potholes.

'What a lovely young man!' Peggy effused. 'I think Susie is lucky to have found him.'

'Yair, I suppose he's all right. Real bloody city slicker, though. Pity she couldn't have found a good country bloke, but that probably went out the door when she went to work in Brisbane,' Bob offered. He was privately disappointed that his last chance to find a son-in-law to take over the place seemed to be fast going up in smoke. Whatever good attributes this young Bernie might possess, potential sheep station manager was not one of them.

'Well, I think she's lucky. Life on the land isn't what it used to be, is it?' she mused.

Bob gave her a searching look. He was aware of her growing frustration at their circumstances and was sure she would love to escape to an easier life in town.

'No, I don't suppose it is, but it'll do me. Don't you go getting any fancy ideas, old girl.'

*　　*　　*

The occasion was right, the ambience was great, and Bernard had made the decision. He and Susan were dining at the city's top French restaurant to celebrate the twelfth-month anniversary of their first date. He whipped an elegant little box from his pocket, flipped open the lid, and flashed the sparkling diamond ring in her eyes. 'Susan, darling, I think the time has come. I've never been more sure of anything in my life. Will you marry me?'

Obviously, the proposal didn't come as a complete surprise to Susan, but she had not anticipated it tonight, and it left her breathless. She let him put the ring on the appropriate finger, gasped at its magnificence, and then leant across the table and kissed Bernard gently. 'Of course, I will, darling,' she said. 'You've just made me the happiest girl in the world.' And the couple at the next-door table, who could not help but observe the whole episode, applauded quietly and offered their congratulations.

*   *   *

Bob and Peggy Hardacre agreed to use the much anticipated trip to Brisbane to make the announcement of their youngest daughter's engagement. Bernard organised everything and was looking forward to repaying Bob for his hospitality on the farm. *All of it*, he thought to himself.

They gathered at the same French restaurant, where, because the menu was in French, Bernard offered to order for everyone, including drinks. Being out of his safety zone, Bob didn't argue when Bernard insisted he forego his beer and open the evening with a champagne toast. The bubbles did their trick, so he also didn't protest at the suggestion he should then join them in a well-credentialed bottle of red. He thought, *It's nowhere near as good as a cold beer*. But after his second glass, when his face was almost reaching the same rosy colour as the Pinot Noir, he ceased to care.

The entrees arrived and he munched his way through his without much enthusiasm. 'Very tasty, Bernie. What the hell was that?' he asked, pushing his plate away.

'Deep fried frog's legs, Bob,' Bernard replied, watching his face carefully and pleased to see him swallow quickly a couple of times. 'Good, weren't they? Susan and I just love them.'

Trying to give Bob time to recover, Peggy jumped in with 'Well, I enjoyed them, Bernard. Certainly different. It's time we got out of our rut and tried different things, eh, Bob?'

But Bob was busy washing his mouth out with some plonk and didn't answer.

After another glass or two of wine, the party was warming up, and Bob, at least at this stage, was feeling no pain. So ambivalent had he become that he tucked into the main course with gusto, and without enquiring what it might be. As he wiped up the last of the gravy with a piece of bread, much to Peggy's embarrassment, Bernard politely asked, 'What did you think of that, Bob?'

'Well, to be perfectly frank, Bernie, and now we're practically family, we can be frank, can't we?' he slurred. 'It wasn't as good as a big T-bone. Bit mushy for my taste, but it wasn't bad, I suppose. Had a funny taste, though. What was it?' The wine was really starting to have an effect, and he was starting to ramble on.

This was the moment Bernard had been waiting for. 'That was the specialty of the house, Bob. Poached lamb's brains, with truffles in a goose liver sauce.'

Bob sprang to his feet and looked around for a toilet door with a little man on it. 'Might just take a walk,' he mumbled as he staggered off.

'Don't be long,' Bernard called after him. 'Dessert will be here in a minute.'

As he disappeared into the toilet, Susan was feeling sorry for him. 'That was a bit cruel, darling. We should have ordered him something more basic. Poor old Dad probably just wasted all his expensive food and drink.'

'I was just trying to broaden his horizons. You seemed to enjoy it, Peggy?' he said, pretending innocence.

'Mum probably enjoyed it for the same reason you did,' Susan chided. 'To see him squirm.'

'Don't worry about him, dear,' Peggy said. 'I like trying different things, but he certainly doesn't. I think you can safely cancel his dessert, though, Bernard.'

Noticing the toilet door opening, Bernard closed the discussion with 'Well, I hope he's feeling better before we go sailing tomorrow.'

*   *   *

Recognising him for the tough old bushy that he was, Bernard wasn't at all surprised at his appearance on time and looking not too bad at the marina next day. As he hopped out of his cab, Bernard gave him a wave.

'Over here, Bob,' he called out. 'Come and hop aboard. Meet Richard. He works with me and has offered to take us out on the bay for a bit of a sail. Pull up all right this morning, did you? Looked a bit seedy last night.'

'Yair, I'm okay. Not used to all that plonk, though. Should have stuck to beer. How're going, Dick? Don't mind if I call you Dick, do you? I'm not one for fancy names.'

'No, me either, eh, Bernie?' Richard said with a wink at his friend, as he grimaced under Bob's handshake. 'Dick's just fine.'

'Hope you don't need any help from me,' Bob said as he settled himself in the nearest seat. 'Never been sailing before.'

'We'll be okay, Bob. You just sit wherever you like and keep your head down,' Richard responded as he pushed off from the mooring.

The trip down the river was uneventful, and the fresh breeze had brought a bit of colour back to Bob's complexion. When they hit the bay, the breeze picked up and the boat started to lean into the wind. 'Here, better put this on, Bob, just in case you fall overboard or something,' Richard said, handing him a life vest. 'Just keep your head down. We don't want to get it knocked off when we come about, do we?'

'This is great, Richard,' Bernard enthused. 'Are you going to take her outside today? Bob would probably love to see the open ocean.'

But, in fact, Bob probably wouldn't. His recently regained complexion had reverted to its previous grey colour, and now he was starting to take on a green tinge. He made a dive for the rail.

'You all right there, Bob?' Richard called. 'He looks a bit crook, Bernard. Do you think we should go back?'

'No, give him a bit longer. See if he finds his sea legs.'

But he never did and hardly left the rail at all. Bernard played the concerned son-in-law-to-be role to perfection, showing concern, making suggestions, and finally calling to Richard, 'I think we'd better head home, mate. Bob seems to have picked up some sort of a bug. Have to take him outside some other time.'

The trip back up the river passed very slowly for Bob who seemed to have lost all of his usual vitality. He refused all offers of hospitality other than a bottle of water. He was even quiet when they were back on terra firma and hardly spoke to Bernard on the way back to the hotel. Bernard was starting to think he might have gone a bit too far and was glad Peggy was in when they reached their suite. Bob headed into the bedroom for a good lie-down.

*　　*　　*

'Sorry to bring him back in such a poor state, Peggy,' Bernard said as he deposited Bob back at his hotel. 'Seems to have picked up a bug or something. Never seen anyone throw up like that on a calm day before. Still, I suppose it could just be that he's not used to it.'

'Yes,' Peggy whispered to him after Bob had disappeared. 'Much like riding a horse, I suppose. Takes a bit of getting used to, doesn't it?'

Bernard thought he detected a note of amusement in her response and the hint of a barely concealed smile on her face. Was she awake up to him? He hadn't even confided in Susan that he was determined to get his own back for the uncomfortable weekend he had spent at Mitchell. Anyhow, it had worked, and Bob now felt about as good as he had after his first farm visit. He would probably recover more quickly than Bernard's raw bum had too. He thought it wise to change the subject.

'So what did you and Susan get up to while we were braving the waves, Peggy?' he asked conversationally.

'We had a great time, thanks, Bernie. We went shopping, and I bought a new hat.' She searched his face for a sign of amusement. Was that a barely concealed smile? She continued, 'A lovely pink one, actually. You'd love it. Perhaps you might like to borrow it sometime.'

He watched the smile on her face turn into a giggle, and they both had to hurry out of Bob's hearing before they hugged each other and laughed their heads off. He may be in for a tough time with his father-in-law, but he sensed that he and Peggy were going to get along just fine.

'Bernie' explained

Putting aside all the back-play between Bernard and his prospective father-in-law, there is a hidden intrigue in this story. Why, you might well ask yourself, would someone in Bernard's position want to get married? He has it all: an interesting job, plenty of money, a great pad, and a live-in lover. He's obviously seen the world, played the field, and seemingly lacks nothing in life. Why change?

Fortunately, there is a primitive urge in most of us to settle down with a life partner, breed the next generation, and provide ourselves with something to look forward to in old age. Marriage is a bit like superannuation really. You put a bit aside while you can afford it to provide for a more comfortable and interesting old age. Like surviving on the pension without any other income, going through your old age without family can be done but with much less pleasure.

Many young people today are finding this out to their mortification when they pass the child-bearing age and suddenly realise, while they always meant to have a family, they were so busy enjoying the fruits of their single lives, that they failed to provide against loneliness in their old age by creating one. Sure they've seen the world, enjoyed a great career, and become financially well off, but in their personal lives, they have become bankrupt.

Projections indicate that today's young people can expect to live twenty or thirty years, and in many cases more, after retiring. For what? They will have seen everything, done everything that money can buy, except one, and no amount of time or money will enable them to do that. Don't envy the young and their self-centred live for the day lifestyles. Pity them for the barren, lonely future that faces them – unless they are as smart as Bernie and recognise when they are on to a good thing, fathers-in-law (and mothers-in-law) included.

MARRIAGE

Relationships are okay, I suppose. They're better than none at all.
Partnerships are better still, till they finally hit the wall.
But the way of life, if you're game to try,
that's better than all of this,
Is to take the plunge, tie the knot, and live in eternal bliss.

What was that? Did I hear a chuckle, or even a whispered 'boo'?
Possibly came from some married bloke,
made game by a drink or two.
More likely it came from some single
girl, intent on playing the field,
Or a bachelor guy enjoying his life, and determined to never yield.

Well, that's okay, for the present, at least.
I'm jealous of all you can do,
With money to burn, no kids to attend,
you can travel and party too.
No worldly cares or problems, infringe on your carefree life.
Considering this, why change it all? Why
look for a husband or wife?

I'll tell you why, if you'll listen. The answer is simple but true.
Here's some timely advice, given freely,
from this old married man to you.

Too soon you'll have reached age thirty,
your free-wheeling life worn thin.
You'll realise now you should settle down,
for a family life to begin.

The carefree life of a single, might be just the thing for a while,
But when wrinkles appear and your hair
goes grey, marriage wins by a mile.
As you slowly sink into middle age, life will be dull and boring.
If you're too old for grog, too fat for sport,
and no longer get fun by whoring.

But if you marry and breed some kids,
they'll fill your forties with fun.
Your heart will burst with sorrow and joy.
You'll be constantly on the run.
The thrill of watching them grow and
mature will fill your life with joy,
As women and men, they slowly appear,
replacing your girl and boy.

And when the sixties creep up on you, and
your grey hair turns to white,
If you're still alone with no family, it's
too late to regret your plight.
But if you're surrounded by all your kids,
together with their spouses,
With *their* kids now sitting on your knee,
as you visit all their houses,

It's only then that you'll understand, the message that I'm giving,
On how important the future is, as you
ponder the life you're living.
Now Peggy and Bob have reached the stage,
when their hair is turning white.
Young Bernie and Sue fill their sixties with
fun. Get married, and do what's right.

BEST FRIENDS

'Put it up for ten to finish.' The blades bit into surface of the river in perfect unison. 'One, two, three, four—C'mon, put your back into it number five—seven, eight, nine, ten! Easy oar! Well done, girls! Have a bit of a breather and suck it in.' Coach Bill Shakespeare wheeled his motor boat around and headed for the boatshed, leaving the crew wallowing in his bow waves. Muscles aching and gasping for breath, the crew touched their craft around and followed him home.

When they had put all the gear away and changed back into their uniforms, the coach called them all together. 'Listen up, girls. Head of the river is now only three weeks away from this Saturday, and while you've been getting steadily better, we still have a lot to do. Unfortunately, the weekend after next is Easter, and we can't afford to miss training for a week's holiday. I want to organise a training session every day. Is that going to be a problem for anyone?'

Silence reigned. They had all fought too hard to make the team to let anything stand in their way now. However much inconvenience and pain a gruelling week's training would cause, they knew he was right, and they were prepared to give it all they had to improve their chance of taking out the title.

Staying back would create a particular problem for three of the crew who were boarders, as the school would be closed. Two of them had relatives, who lived nearby and could put them up, but Kathy Woodrow didn't, and she voiced her concern to the coach. Fortunately, Sally Morton overheard the conversation and suggested a solution.

'Kathy, I'm sure Mum and Dad would love to have you stay at our place. We've tonnes of room, and my brother can drive us to and from training. He's at uni and seems to have lots of free time on his hands.'

'Are you sure it would be all right, Sal? You'd better ask your parents first, but if it's okay with them, I'd love to,' Kathy said.

The two girls had barely known each other before they were thrown together in the crew at the beginning of the year and were still not all that close. They came from completely different backgrounds and other than rowing, had few common interests. Kathy came from a grain-and-cattle property near Roma, while Sally had always lived in Brisbane, where her father owned an import business. But circumstances sometimes throw up strange results, and when they made plans as the holidays drew near, they found they got on very well together.

*　　*　　*

'This is your room, Kathy. Chuck your gear on the bed and we'll go for a swim before lunch,' Sally said as she drew the curtains and opened the window.

Kathy joined her to look out over the pool set into the hillside and the gardens and driveway flowing down to the imposing front gate. 'This is the most marvellous house, Sal. You must really love living here.'

'It's all right, I suppose, but it's pretty lonely sometimes, and there's not much to do. Mum and Dad are always at work, and now Nigel is at university, we don't get to see much of him.'

'Well, loneliness and boredom aren't a problem at our place,' Kathy replied as she rummaged through her bag looking for her swimsuit. 'With a brother and two sisters in the house and a property to run, boredom is never a problem. Just hang on a minute while I jump into these togs, Sal. I don't want to get lost on the way to the pool.'

'Just go down to the kitchen when you're ready, Kath. I'll go and get into mine.'

Kathy tiptoed down the staircase, admiring the artwork and floral decorations as she went. Hearing a kettle boiling, she pushed through a door to her left and found herself in the kitchen, where she came to an embarrassed stop; busy at the bench, with his back to her, stood a young man. Acutely aware of her near nakedness, she spun around to escape back upstairs, but she was too late.

'Hello, there. Don't rush off. I'm Nigel. Sal told me we were going to have a house guest. Would you like a cup of tea or coffee?'

Kathy stopped with her hand on the doorknob but felt she had no option but to respond. Blushing furiously, she turned to address the smiling apparition across the room. He was tall, with blond wavy hair and the most incredibly blue eyes she had ever seen. Brought up in the bush and boarding at an all-girls' school had left her ill-prepared for the social situation in which she now found herself.

'That would be nice. Thank you,' she managed to stammer. 'Tea, please. I'm terribly sorry for barging in, dressed like this. We're on our way to the pool.'

Nigel turned back to his tea-making task, giving Kathy a chance to slip on to a chair at the breakfast bench. 'Don't mention it. Sal gets around like that all the time. Milk and sugar?' The disarming smile and friendly manner in which he plonked the mug in front of her eased her concerns, and she thrust her hand across the counter.

'Thanks, Nigel. I'm Kathy. Sally tells me you're at uni. What are you studying?'

'He'll probably tell you arts or law,' said Sally as she entered the room, 'but really I think his main interest lies in the parties and female students. Oh, and rowing, of course. He's the one who got me interested in it. I don't suppose your hospitality extends to making me a cup, Nigel?'

'Not after you gave away all my life secrets like that. Make your own. I'm going to change and join you for a swim. Don't tip my tea out. I'll be back in a minute.'

Kathy watched him disappear and then turned to her new friend. 'You didn't tell me your brother was so gorgeous, Sal. He's terrific.'

'Oh, he's all right, I suppose. A bit up himself, though. Thinks he's God's answer to the opposite sex. You keep your eye on him, girl, or he'll try to sweep you off your feet.'

'And who says I'd mind?' Kathy joked. 'But I don't think a naive little bushy like me would appeal to someone like him. I'm sure all his girlfriends are much more sophisticated than me.'

'Oh, I don't know about that,' said Sally as they gathered up their towels and headed out the door. 'Anything in a skirt appeals to him.'

They almost bumped into Nigel as he bounded back into the kitchen, wearing nothing more than a towel around his neck and the briefest pair of budgie smugglers. Once again, Kathy blushed bright red and tried to hide her embarrassment as she hurried out of the house.

*　*　*

For the first time in days, Nigel joined the family for dinner that night. An hour of splashing and small talk in the pool had broken down all the inhibitions that Kathy had suffered earlier, and they chatted and joked away like old friends. Sally was amused at how easily her brother had won her over. *Good old Nigel,* she thought, *a great one with the girls.* But she hoped he didn't take advantage of Kathy's inexperience.

For her part, Kathy's thoughts were centred on more than Nigel's flirtations. She was still somewhat uncomfortable in the sumptuous surrounds in which she found herself. The Mortons were one of the city's top families. Alex Morton was a leading light in the business world, and Penny Morton was heavily into the social scene. *How different to my own rather humble and down-to-earth family situation on our cattle property in western Queensland!* She just hoped she didn't make a fool of herself in their company.

'So, Nigel,' Alec said as he helped himself to some more beef, 'what do your lefty mates at uni think of these boat people, now that another lot has had to be rescued? Do they still think we should welcome them all with open arms?'

'God, you're an old redneck, Dad!' Nigel responded. 'Don't you have any compassion for the poor buggers who drowned?'

'I do wish you would watch your language, dear,' Penny interposed. 'Especially when we have a guest here.'

'Oh, I can assure you I hear much worse than that at home!' Kathy gushed and then wished that she hadn't, as Penny's eyebrows shot up.

'Well, I just wish they'd stay back where they come from,' Alec said. 'We're getting swamped with them. I don't like the way the men get around wearing dresses and the women cover themselves from head to toe. It's just not Australian.'

'You're just going to have to get used to it, Dad,' Sally cut in. 'We're a multicultural society now. Did you know that one of our girls rows in a hijab?'

'What? Well, that's the dizzy limit, that is,' Alec said, reaching for the wine. 'I think we should look after our Australian culture first, before we cater for the perverted customs of foreigners.'

Nigel took up the battle. 'That's a bit rich coming from you, Dad, given your attitude to our original Australians. You're never too keen to give them any credit either.'

'More than they deserve most of the time. Anyway, you just make sure you don't get mixed up with any of those types at uni. We don't want you turning up here with some burka wearer,' Alec said, jokingly, or perhaps he was serious.

Kathy was becoming increasingly uncomfortable with the conversation. She didn't have a racist bone in her body. How could she when her own much loved adopted brother back home was part aborigine? Charlie was two years elder than her, and she had always worshiped him. Thank goodness she hadn't confided this information before she had an insight into Alec's attitude.

Still, it took all sorts to make the world, and the Mortons were very good to her during her stay. They made her feel very welcome, and Nigel went out of his way to transport them to training and back each day. He also took them shopping and to the movies, and by the time she left, Kathy and he were getting on very well. *Too well,* Sally thought but didn't say it out.

'Thank you so much for having me, Mrs Morton,' Kathy said as she packed her bags into the boot of Nigel's car for the trip back to school. 'I'm really looking forward to Sally coming home with me for the June holidays. We can't keep up to the standards she's used to here, but I reckon we can guarantee she won't be bored.'

'Which is what I would be if I stayed here,' Sally added. 'Bored stiff. And I'm so looking forward to learning to ride a horse.'

*   *   *

'Here we are, Sal. Time to give the horses a bit of a spell. Your bum too, I expect. Just tie Jess to that tree and take the saddle off. You can do mine too if you like while I put the billy on.' Kathy gathered up a few sticks, lit a small fire, and filled the billy from the creek.

'What a marvellous place this is!' Sally gushed, as she flopped on to the ground and stretched out in the shade of the Coolibah tree. 'You're so lucky to live on such a glorious property.'

'I don't know about that, Sal. Our place doesn't stand up too well against your mansion, and it isn't always this pleasant either. You should be here in the summer. Oh, and by the way, that's our pool over there if you feel like a dip before lunch,' Kathy said, indicating the nearby stretch of water in the river. 'At least I can guarantee, you won't be hijacked by a half-naked brother like I was at your place.'

'More's the pity,' said Sally.' I wouldn't mind if Charlie sprang out of the bushes in his Speedos.' Kathy was a bit shocked at her friend's flirtatious nature, but she said nothing, and Sally went on, 'How come you never told me that your adopted brother was an aborigine?'

'Well, it never came up, I guess, and in the family, we don't even think about it. He's always just been one of us as we grew up, and now he and Dad run the place just like any other father and son would.'

'Don't get me wrong, Kath. I think he's great. It just seemed a bit strange, that's all. How did it all come about?'

Kathy poured tea into their pannikins and unwrapped their sandwiches. 'Sit up and get some of this good billy tea into and I'll tell you. Watch out. It's pretty hot. No milk, I'm afraid.' She settled down with her back to the tree. 'It's a simple story actually, and quite sad,' she went on. 'Charlie's mother had worked for Mum and Dad for some years when she became pregnant and produced Charlie. She wouldn't ever tell who his father was, but Mum always suspected a good-looking young stockman who left about the time of the big announcement. Poor little Annie had no family to turn to, so she stayed on and Mum helped her with the baby. I came along a couple of years later, and then, when Charlie was four, Annie was killed when she came off a horse.'

'Oh, that's awful!' Sally exclaimed. 'Poor little Charlie.'

'Yes, well, that's what Mum thought, so she just reared him as one of her own, and eventually adopted him formally. He's always been my brother Charlie and Mum and Dad treat him as a son, just like the rest of us.'

'What an incredible story!' Sally mused. 'Your parents are wonderful. I can't imagine mine doing something like that, especially Dad. I'm so embarrassed now when I think how he carried on that first night you spent with us.'

'Don't worry about it, Sal. Charlie is quite comfortable with his aboriginal heritage. Actually, he's proud of it. Reckons he's got the best of both worlds. He's very intelligent too, you know, and could have gone to university if he'd wanted to, but all he ever wanted in life was to help Dad run the property. Followed him around like a shadow when he was just a little nipper.'

When Sally made no comment, Kathy looked at her and found her gazing dreamily into the water. 'Penny for your thoughts,' she said.

Sally turned her attention back to her friend. 'I was just thinking how different your family is to mine. All Mum and Dad think about is business, making money, and social climbing. Nigel, too, for that matter. Family comes a poor third or fourth. But in your house, family is everything. You all seem so much more relaxed and able to enjoy the simple things in life. You don't know how lucky you are, Kathy.'

'Oh yes, I do. But I don't want to spend my whole life here like Charlie. I want to spread my wings, marry a genius, and live in a big house like yours one day. My sisters do too. Charlie's one of a kind really.'

'He sure is, and so good looking too,' Sally ventured.

'Hey, steady on there, Sal. I'm beginning to think you've got the hots for him,' Kathy said, as she jumped to her feet and used the last of the tea to douse the fire. 'Come on, give me a hand to pack up. They'll be sending out a search party for us soon.'

Thoughts were racing through Sally's head as she tightened the girth and swung into the saddle – thoughts that she decided to keep to herself for the time being.

*   *   *

They arrived back at the homestead just as Kathy's father and Charlie rode up from another direction. Harry Woodrow dismounted and handed the reins of his horse to Charlie. 'Can you look after them for me, Charlie? I need to make a phone call before the shops shut. G'day, girls. Have a nice time?'

'Lovely, thank you, Mr Woodrow. I'm really glad I've had this chance to learn to ride. Sore bum aside, it's the best way to explore the place.' Then, turning to Kathy, she said, 'Why don't you go and help your mum with dinner, Kath? I'll help Charlie with the horses.'

Anxious thoughts now raced through Kathy's mind, and like Sally, she kept them to herself, changing the subject with 'Okay. But out here we still call it 'tea'. Dinner is what we had at the river. See you soon.'

But Sally had already joined Charlie leading the horses towards the stable and probably didn't even hear her.

*   *   *

As the Greyhound bus headed east along the Warrego Highway at the end of the holidays, Kathy decided it was time to broach a subject that had been niggling away at her for the last few days. She turned to her friend who was staring sightlessly out the window and said, 'Sal, I hope you know what you're doing in getting so friendly with Charlie.'

Was that a tear in her eye as she turned to answer? 'Kath, I think Charlie is the nicest young man I've ever met. He's just so natural. Not up himself like Nigel and his friends.'

'Hey, steady on there! He's all right, I suppose, but there's nothing wrong with Nigel. I thought he was marvellous to us over Easter. I really enjoyed his company, and I like the way he has high aspirations for his future. Charlie has no ambition at all. Just wants to work for Dad forever as far as I can see.'

'Whoa, boy! Steady on there, old girl. Here I am all mixed up about how I feel about your brother, and it looks like you're more than a little bit interested in mine. What a hoot!'

'That's a bit different, Sal. For a start, I didn't flirt with Nigel like you have been with Charlie, and second, he's really my adopted brother. Have you thought about what your parents will think when they find out he is part aboriginal? I don't imagine they will be too happy.'

'They won't find out, Kath,' Sally replied, taking hold of her hands and staring imploringly into her eyes. 'At least not from me. You won't tell them, will you, Kathy? Please? You've seen my father in full flight on the subject, and Mum's only marginally less racist than him.'

'You're making it a bit hard for me, Sal. I think the world of Charlie, and I'm not ashamed of him in any situation. You shouldn't be either if you really like him.'

It was a tear that she had seen, because now several more formed, trembled on Sally's lids and then fell over the edge and rolled down her flushed cheeks. 'I know,' she murmured, 'and I will tell them when the time is right but not yet. Promise me you won't until I've had a chance to.'

'Of course, I won't if that's the way you want it. That's what friends are for. Anyway, once you get back to town, you'll probably forget all about Charlie.'

'Maybe you're right, Kath,' Sally conceded, but she couldn't get him out of her mind at the moment, even when she tried to envision the look of abject horror on the faces of her parents if they knew how she felt about him.

And how about Kathy and Nigel? Who would have thought a shy country girl like her would be attracted to a know-it-all playboy like him? Still, she did seem to have stars in her eyes when it came to her future. If only she knew how barren and uninteresting that so-called upper-class lifestyle could be! Not a patch on the two weeks she had just spent in the bush.

*　　*　　*

Over the course of the rest of that year and all of their final year at school, the two friends became inseparable. Kathy spent all of her boarder's weekends and most Sundays at Sally's place, who, for her part, could hardly wait for the holidays to come so she could return to the Woodrow property – and Charlie. Her original infatuation had developed into something else, and he seemed to be just as smitten with her. They were soulmates, enjoying the same pastimes, dreaming of a future in the bush, and perfectly comfortable in each other's company. Only one thing marred their friendship: while Sally's parents knew she was friendly with Kathy's brother, that's all they knew, and for now, all she wanted was them to know.

But not all of the action had been happening at Roma. Kathy's time spent with the Mortons had given her ample time to socialise with Nigel, who had more than a passing interest in her too. Not that he neglected his other social life when she was at school, but they became quite good friends. Eventually, they started leaving Sally at home on some of their outings. She started to wonder what they got up to.

Both were enjoying their budding teenage romances, and in other circumstances might have continued to do so, but then everything blew up following the Christmas holidays after they finished school. As usual, Sally spent most of them at Roma, where her friendship with Charlie developed into something more serious. The Woodrows treated her like a daughter, their girl's sister, but their adopted son was another matter altogether. He and Sally were totally besotted with each other, and as the day for her return to Brisbane approached, they were distraught at the prospect of being apart. Together they plotted a solution.

*   *   *

'You can't be serious, Sally.' Mrs Morton was mortified. 'What do you mean defer university for a year? Of course, you can't. You've always wanted to follow Nigel into law, and the sooner you start, the sooner you finish. Whatever gave you such a silly idea?'

Her reaction was just what Sally had expected. For weeks she had put off the confrontation with her family, wondering if perhaps she was letting her emotions get the better of her. But then fate played a role when Harry Woodrow's horse stumbled, pitching him off and smashing his knee as he landed. It would require a complete reconstruction, which would keep him on crutches for weeks and off a horse for months.

She heard Charlie and Mrs Woodrow discussing how they would keep the place running in his absence.

'I could help you with the cattle, Charlie,' Mrs Morton was saying, 'but I can't leave Carli on her own, and she still has to do her schoolwork.'

'You can't do that, Mum. I'll see if I can find someone to come in when we need him, and I can look after things on my own most of the time,' Charlie suggested.

'I suppose I could ask Kathy to defer uni for a while. She could look after Carli and I could help you.'

'Don't do that yet, Mum. Give me a day or two. I'll think of something.' But he didn't have to. Sally did it for him. That afternoon, as they tended to the horses after work, she shared her thoughts with him.

'I hope you don't think I'm rude, Charlie, but I overheard you and your mother discussing your labour problems, and I had an idea. Let me come out and help you. Between us we could handle it, and you know how much I love living and working here.'

'No way, Sal. You've got to start uni soon too. We'll be all right. I'll find someone to fill in for a few months.'

'But that's the point, Charlie. I don't want to study any more. I'm sick of it, and I just love this country life. Whatever happens here, I'm going to look for a job out here somewhere. It would be perfect if I could start here, and I could help your mother with Carli's schooling too. Please Charlie.'

What she didn't tell him was that her feelings for him were making it impossible to imagine a happy life in the city without him. Although he had never said as much, she felt sure he was more than a little interested in her too. A life in the bush would be nice, but sharing it with Charlie would make it wonderful. She had made up her mind.

*　　*　　*

'It's not a silly idea, as you put it, Mum. I have absolutely no desire to do more study at this time of my life. Lots of kids defer uni to go travelling overseas for a year. I don't want to do that. I just want to spend a while working in the bush, and it just so happens, I have a chance to repay the Woodrows for all their kindness to me over the last couple of years.'

Sally then explained the situation to her mother, being careful not to mention Charlie too much and portraying her role more as a governess than a jillaroo. She was determined and persuasive, withstanding the anticipated onslaught from her father, and was packing her bags, when another idea came to her.

'Mum, if you really wanted to be nice, why don't you let Kathy stay here while she's at university? Then, during the holidays, we could swap over. Wouldn't that be nice?'

So that's what happened, although Sally was pretty sure she wouldn't be spending too many holidays back in town.

*　　*　　*

In fact, her next visit didn't come until the following Christmas, and even then, she wished there was some way she could avoid it. She was not looking forward to the confrontation that was bound to follow when she told her parents her news.

'You're what?' her mother exploded. 'Getting married to a jackaroo? Have you gone mad?' To which her red-faced father added, 'I told you we were silly for letting her go living out there. It's all your fault, Penny. You've always been too soft on her.'

In spite of the fact that she knew what was coming, Sally was still shocked and disappointed at their reaction. 'Steady on there, you two,' she said, with as much force as she could muster. 'Stop blaming yourselves for my decisions. I'm nineteen now, you know, not nine. I make my own decisions, and I want you to hear me out.'

Her mother sat sobbing quietly in her hands, while her father poured himself a double Scotch. Both were speechless as they tried to come to terms with this latest escapade by their fractious daughter. She took the chance to launch into the pitch she had been preparing for days.

'Please hear me out before you interrupt,' she started. 'Now I know this has come as a shock to you both, but I've been telling you for years how much I love living out there. It's a terrific lifestyle and exactly what I want to do with my life. You won't understand because you've never experienced it, but believe me, I've got absolutely no desire to come back here.'

'But, darling, what about university?' Penny pleaded.

'No interruptions, Mum. There's a lot more to come yet, and Dad, do stop pouring yourself Scotches. I want you to have a clear head to hear what I have to say.'

He glared at her for a moment but said nothing and slumped into his chair, while Penny sat wringing her hands and looking completely inconsolable.

Sally proceeded. 'Over the past twelve months, the friendship I had developed with Kathy's brother has grown into love.' Alec slammed his glass on the table and flopped into a chair. Sally ignored him and concentrated on her mother. 'We absolutely adore each other, and we want to spend the rest of our lives together out west. He is the most marvellous person I have ever met, and when you get to know him, you will think so too.'

Penny could contain herself no longer. 'But, dear, Kathy's a nice girl, and I'm sure her brother is lovely too, but the Woodrows are not up to our social standing. You would be lowering your standards if you married into that family.'

Sally stared at her mother in disbelief. 'Mother, that is a perfect demonstration of why I love country people and want nothing to do with your city life with its social-climbing society. It's just not me. Not any more. Out there, everyone is equal, and there is no class bullshit.'

'Watch your language, my girl,' Alex interjected. 'You've become very course living out there. No wonder your mother is concerned, and while I'm at it, how can this boy hope to support you? He's only a jackaroo, isn't he?'

'No, Dad, he's a stockman and has practically run the place on his own since Mr Woodrow's accident. One day he'll take over when his parents retire, and he's saving up to buy some land of his own too.'

Mrs Morton heaved a deep sigh. 'Well, I suppose you should bring him down to meet us, Sally. Your father should have a talk to him about his prospects. We might be able to help you financially.'

Sally left them pondering while she went to the kitchen for a glass of water. When she returned, she sat down in front of them, took her mother's hands in her own, and moved on to the next unpalatable bit of information for them.

'I'll do that, of course, but there's something else you need to get your heads around before then. I've never told you that Charlie was adopted by the Woodrows when he was about two years old. Not only is he not their natural son, he is part aboriginal.'

Her mother's hands were snatched back and flew to her throat. Her father sprang from his chair and stood staring down at her, face glowing. 'What are you saying, young girl?' he shouted. 'Are you telling us you want to marry a bloody Abo?'

Sally rose up, drew herself up to her full height, and stared back into his florid face. Then, in a voice that she managed to keep calm in spite of her inner rage, she said, 'That's exactly what I'm telling you. With or without your blessing.'

Alec had great difficulty in controlling his urge to slap her. Penny had returned to gently sobbing into her handkerchief, and Sally waited for the tension to settle before she proceeded.

Eventually, her father broke the silence. 'Well, you won't be getting that from me,' he said. 'Not to marry some layabout Abo and breed a tribe of little piccaninnies! You can both go to hell as far as I'm concerned!'

Sally surveyed the distraught scene in front of her: mother now crying loudly and father heading for the Scotch bottle.

'That's exactly the reaction I expected from you both,' she said in a calm voice. 'And it's why I haven't told you before. I knew your bigoted attitudes to class and race would set you against him, so I waited to see where our friendship went in case it came to nothing. But the more I got to know Charlie, the more I got to appreciate him for what he is – a wonderful human being.'

She headed for the door but turned before she left to deliver one more bit of information for them to digest.

'Oh, and something else for you, Dad. Unlike you, he will make a marvellous father. You see, Charlie and I are expecting.' She slammed the door as she left, leaving Alec Morton to tend to his wife, who had collapsed in a dead faint.

*　　*　　*

Sally left them to digest the situation and spent the night at a friend's house, returning next day when she knew her father would have gone to work. She found her mother looking pale and defeated and nursing a cup of coffee in the solarium. She felt sorry for the distress she had caused her. Maybe she could make her come around, but she imagined her father was a hopeless case.

She sat down across the table. 'Mum, look at me. I'm still Sally. Remember, your daughter. I didn't set out to disappoint you and Dad. It just happened, and I'm so sorry you can't accept Charlie into the family.' Penny said nothing, so Sally continued, 'I've never been interested in the things that you have been, but I didn't know I would find my future living in the country. I just love it, and I hoped you might be pleased that I had found a happy future for myself, no matter where, or with whom. Apparently not, so I will just have to accept that and move on without your support. I'm sorry.'

A strained silence hung in the air as Sally waited, and Penny wondered what she could possibly say to her obviously totally committed daughter. What a shame that she was going to waste her life on some young man who could never provide her with a decent lifestyle! It looked like they were going to lose a daughter without gaining a son-in-law, as the saying went, but there was no way she could support such a union. Thank heavens Nigel had his feet on the ground, having just finished his degree and started a career with a big firm. Vaguely she realised Sally had gone into the kitchen, and she heard the kettle boiling.

Suddenly a new thought struck her. Lately, she had noticed that Nigel was getting overly friendly with Kathy Woodrow, especially since both of them had moved out a few months ago. She would have to speak to Alex about it and nip that relationship in the bud. She wasn't going to lose both her children to the Woodrows, that's for sure.

Her thoughts were brought back to the present by the door opening, and who should come into the room laughing and holding hands but Nigel and Kathy.

'Okay. Where is she?' Nigel asked. 'Where's that horse-riding, cow-poking little sister of mine?'

'Hello, Mrs Morton. We couldn't wait to come and see her, could we, Nige' Kathy gushed.

Penny indicated with a nod in the direction of the kitchen, where they could find her. *Fancy calling my son 'Nige'. How cheap and low class it shows her to be! Perhaps it would be better to leave them to get on with their excited chatter without me for a while.* She grabbed her purse and car keys from the hall and took off.

*   *   *

All the excitement of the reunion evaporated when Nigel and Kathy saw the look on Sally's face and noticed the tears in her eyes.

'What's up, Sis?' Nigel asked, as he took over the tea-making duties. 'We thought you'd be pleased to see us. You look like you've got some bad news. What is it?'

'Well, good news, bad news. Depends which way you look at it, I suppose. I think it's good. Mum and Dad think it's the worst possible, and I'm afraid it's going to be very embarrassing for you, Kathy. Not the news. Just their reaction to it.'

Nigel handed her a mug and said, 'Here, take your tea and we'll go into the sitting room. You can tell us all about it. I just heard Mum go out in the car.'

Sally told them her news and what her parents' less-than-graceful reaction had been. She was ashamed of them, feeling very sorry for herself, and even more so for poor Charlie.

'What's Charlie going to think, Kath, when he finds out my own family won't accept him because of his aboriginality? Your family did, and it shouldn't make any difference. He's the most wonderful person I know.'

Kathy put an arm around her friend. 'Don't worry about Charlie. He's suffered worse slurs than that in his life. He's learnt to ignore them and get on with his life.'

'There's worse than that to come, I'm afraid. Mum thinks your whole family is below the social standard for her daughter to be associated with, much less marrying into. I bet they'll be having a quiet talk to you any day now too, Nigel. About you and Kathy. Especially now.'

Sally noticed the stricken look Kathy gave Nigel and was pleased with the way he moved quickly to her side. Turning her to face him, he took her in his arms and spoke over her shoulder to his clearly embarrassed sister. 'Sal, we want you to be the first to know. We've been living together since we left here months ago. Mum and Dad are so self-occupied they wouldn't know, and you can see why we wouldn't tell them. They can go to hell as far as I'm concerned. We love each other, and that's all that matters.'

Kathy freed herself from his embrace and went to hug Sally. 'I'm so pleased for you and Charlie, Sal, but I'm afraid it's never going to meet with your parents' approval. What will you do if they don't accept your marrying him? And then there's the baby too.'

Tears welled into Sally's eyes as she slumped into a chair. She had worried all along about everyone's reaction to Charlie. If only they weren't so bigoted!

'I've made up my mind, and I hope you two will back me up. Charlie and I are getting married as soon as we can, and we'll stay on the property in the second house where the head stockman used to live. It's been empty since he left and Charlie took his job. We'll be all right.'

'We'll back you all right, Sis,' Nigel offered. 'You never know. One day we might join you. Do you need a good lawyer on the place?'

Kathy gave him a playful punch on the arm. 'Speak for yourself, Nige. I don't want to live out there again. There's too much for me to do in the city, thank you very much.' But she was quietly excited by what he had said. He'd never hinted at marriage before.

Sally didn't know whether to be excited or concerned for her friend. Kathy was rather naive in many ways, and she wasn't sure that Nigel was an ideal future, marriage material. *Anyway, maybe nothing would come of it in the end, and in the meantime, I have my own problems to consider.* It looked as if she had no chance of changing her parents' minds, so she and Charlie would have to go ahead without them. At least the Woodrows would support them.

She would try one more time when her mother came home. If that didn't work, she would pack up her possessions and move permanently to Roma. Nothing was more important to her now than Charlie and their baby.

*　　*　　*

Sally and Charlie sat in the coffee shop from where they could keep their eye on the bus terminal across the street. They had overcome the disappointment of the Mortons' reaction to their news and were looking forward to their simple wedding at the homestead in a few days' time. Mrs and Mr Woodrow had been marvellous about it. They had helped to make all the arrangements and had refurbished and furnished the manager's cottage for them.

Nigel had readily agreed to take the place of her father in giving away the bride, and naturally Kathy was to be bridesmaid, and then disaster struck.

When Nigel told his father of their plans to attend the wedding, he had blown his top completely. Alex and Penny had no intentions of reconciling with their daughter, who was hell-bent on ruining her life and wasting all the opportunity they had given her, and they were not happy at Nigel's obvious support for her. During the argument that followed, he had inadvertently let slip the fact that he and Kathy had been living together for months and were also considering marriage.

For Alex, that was the dizzy limit. Here was his only son and heir, a young man with the world at his feet, intent on marrying that silly, young Woodrow girl when he could have had his pick of the field. Well, he may not have been able to stop his hot-headed daughter, but he wasn't going to let the same thing happen to Nigel. He knew how to put him in his place.

*   *   *

'You can't be serious, Dad!' Nigel exploded as he sprang from his chair.

'Never been more serious in my life, Son. We stood by and let Sally ruin her life. We won't do the same with you. Unfortunately, the decision is up to you in the end, but what I have just told you is our final decision. If you don't break off this relationship with the Woodrow girl, you will be totally disinherited. All of our estates will be left to charities, and I'm sure you would realise, we're talking about quite a few million dollars here.'

The blood had drained from Nigel's face, and he slumped back into the chair. 'I can't believe you'd be so vindictive about this,' he managed to say. 'Why do you hate the Woodrows so much? I'm sure they're decent people, but you and Mum seem to be hell-bent on painting them as some sort of social lepers. They seem to love Sally more than you do, and you thought Kathy was all right too until she and I fell in love.'

'Fell in love, my eye! She's nothing more than your current bit of fluff. You'd better forget all about her if you want to stay part of this family, young fellow. Your mother and I are dead serious. It's her or us and your inheritance.'

*   *   *

The bus glided to a halt and passengers started to alight. 'Come on, Sal. Let's get this over with.' Charlie helped her up, pulled on his Akubra, and headed for the door.

Kathy ran towards them as they crossed the street and hugged her friend for a long time, quietly sobbing on her shoulder. Charlie collected her luggage and put it into his Toyota. The bus took off for Mitchell, and the two friends came hand in hand towards him.

'G'day, Kath. It's good to see you. Sorry about what happened.'

'Thanks, Charlie. I guess I had to find out what he was really like some time, though. I'm sorry, Sal. I don't mean to be nasty about your brother, but I really thought he loved me more than that.'

Sally opened the door and slid into the middle seat. 'You don't have to apologise to me, Kath. I've always had my suspicions about him. He's too much like his father for his own good, I'm afraid. Nothing and no one is more important than the almighty dollar to them.'

Kathy climbed aboard and Charlie started up and headed for home. 'Well, you could have knocked me down with a feather when he told me of Dad's ultimatum,' she said. 'It was a case of the money or the box, and it didn't take him long to make up his mind which was more important to him. So here I am. No man, no money, and nowhere to call home.'

'You know you always have a home here, Kath,' Charlie said. 'Mum and Dad are really looking forward to your visit.'

'I won't be staying long, though. I've got to get on with life, so I'm thinking of moving to Sydney, or even going overseas. First things first, though. We've got to make you two respectable first before that growing bump you're carrying around there turns this wedding into a threesome.' Her jocularity broke the tension, and the three of them chatted away on the trip to the homestead.

*　　*　　*

'Ladies and gentlemen,' Harry Woodrow tinkled a spoon on his glass to gain attention and rose to his feet, 'having just had the privilege of giving away this very beautiful bride, and being the father of the groom, I am granting myself the right to speak on behalf of both sets of parents here today. Also, as the best man is even harder to get a few words out of than his best mate, Charlie, I guess I can also take over his role too and propose the toast to the newly-weds.'

The gathering chortled and the best man blushed but looked mighty relieved. Harry took a pull on his stubby.

'Naturally, we are disappointed that Sally's family couldn't be with us today, but weddings aren't about us oldies anyway. Our role is to be spectators at the ceremony, to wish the stars of the day well in their new life, and to pick up the tab when all you freeloaders have drunk all our beer and gone home.'

A round of applause gave Harry time for another swig before he continued.

'Since the day we met Sally a couple of years ago, she has always felt like one of the family, and now she has officially become one of us. We are all delighted to have her. She has fitted in so well here that it's hard to imagine that she only learnt to ride a horse when she came here for the first time, and now she's taken over my job like a veteran. Probably just as well, I suppose. I keep falling off all the time anyway.'

Once again he wet his whistle while he waited for the jibes to cease.

He went on, 'Anyway, we think she's just bloody marvellous and far too good for this layabout young bloke she has married today.' Charlie looked embarrassed, and Sally gave him a hug, a peck on the cheek, and whispered something in his ear.

'Hey, steady on there, Sal. Just be patient, will you? I've got a few more things to say yet. Seriously though, really, you're a very lucky girl. I might be biased, but I think Charlie will make a great husband and father, and after today's ceremony, in that order too, I'm pleased to say.

More laughter allowed Harry to drain his stubby and knock the top off another one.

'Now before I propose this toast, there's something serious Lorna and I want to tell you. It's probably something that should have been done long ago, but we figured better late than never, and today's celebration seems like a good time.

'As you all know, we officially adopted Charlie when he was four years old and his mum died. He was born in this house and has always been treated as if he was our natural-born son.'

Harry's mouth was getting dry again, so he took another sip of beer. The crowd sat in silence.

'I'm sure everyone in this gathering already knew that.' Another pause. Another sip. 'But what I am about to tell you will come as a shock to all of you, including you, Charlie.' He stole a glance in his direction and saw the strain of confusion etched on his face. 'Son, as well as your adoptive father, I'm also your natural one.'

All eyes were on him as he paused to watch their reactions. They were stunned. Total silence reigned. Tears welled into his eyes, and Lorna rose to stand by his side. She put her arm around him and helped him out.

'We know this will come as a shock to all of you, but we hope it makes no difference to how you view us as parents,' she said. 'Harry told me before Charlie was born. I forgave him, and we have always treated Charlie as one of our own, even before his mother died.' Looking at his shocked expression, she went on, 'Charlie, you've always been our son, and you always will be. We both love you dearly.'

Then, seeing that Harry was still overcome with emotion and unable to continue, she went on, 'Come on, everyone. Lighten up, charge your glasses, and let's drink a toast to this marvellous young couple.' Then, raising her glass and smiling radiantly in their direction, she shouted, 'To Sally and Charlie and if my grandmotherly instincts are correct, little Charlie too!'

To which they all replied, 'To Sally and Charlie and Charlie II.' Harry drained his stubby before he went to hug his son and daughter-in-law.

*　*　*

Epilogue

Sally stood at the back door of the homestead, coffee in hand, watching the goings-on in the horse yard from a distance. The excited banter of her two boys carried back to her as they battled to attract a fair share of their father's attention.

'Watch me, Dad. Did you see how Dancer cleared that hurdle?' Charlie Jr was now six years old and the spitting image of his dad. *Only to look at,* Sally thought. He rattled off more words in an hour than Charlie did in a week. She smiled to herself. That quiet, self-conscious nature was the thing which appealed to her the most. He was the original strong silent type. How she loved that man!

'Don't let him go yet, Dad,' pleaded little Harry. 'He's a bit frisky this morning, I think.' Four-year-old Harry was still learning to ride, and he lacked his brother's daredevil attitude to everything. *Much more like his mother,* Sally decided. *So level-headed and sensible. Just like the grandfather after whom he is named.*

How honoured and proud Harry Woodrow had been when they told him what his new grandson was to be called, and, as things turned out, how fitting! Little did anyone suspect at the time that he would be dead in less than two years – the victim of cancer. Sally wondered at the time if Charlie would ever get over the shock of losing the father who had given him so much during his life, and whom he loved and respected so dearly. And the giving hadn't ceased with his death either. After providing for Lorna's future and making sure his three daughters were taken care of, he handed the property over to Charlie and Sally.

As any man of the land knows, one of his biggest concerns is always what will happen to the place when he's gone. Harry went to his grave secure in the knowledge that Charlie and Sally would take over the family heritage as he had from his father, and even at this stage, he was pretty confident little Charlie II would carry on when his turn came too.

Hungry wails from the front bedroom brought her thoughts back to the present. It was feeding time for the latest arrival to their family – little Samantha. She took her cup back to the kitchen and went to fix her up. A quick nappy change and then she was happily guzzling away at her mother's breast. As Sally gazed lovingly at her daughter, her thoughts turned to her best friend Kathy. *Poor Kathy.*

Being dumped by Nigel for the Morton family fortune seemed to have had a deep psychological impact on her. She seemed to be unwilling to trust men any more. While she had become a very successful artist, she had never settled into a long-term relationship, and now she lived on her own in the Blue Mountains. *I must see if I can help her when she comes up for Sam's christening,* Sally thought. *She's missing out on so much, not having a husband and a family of her own. I feel so sorry for her, and without her, I would never have met Charlie or had these three wonderful kids.*

The sound of little boots pounding up the hall brought her thoughts once more to the present. 'Mum, Mum, guess what! I rode Sonny out in the paddock on my own. Dad says I can go mustering with him and Charlie next time.'

'Well, that's lovely, Harry, but I wish you'd kick your boots off before you come inside.'

'Why, Mum? You let Dad do it.'

Sally couldn't help smiling at him, especially as she could hear another pair of little boots, and a pair of much bigger ones now also coming noisily up the hall. 'That's different love,' she said. 'He's special.'

*   *   *

'I'm off, Mum. Want anything else when I'm in town?' Charlie II, or Junior, as they had come to call him over the years, breezed into the kitchen.

Sally moved the tray of biscuits from the oven to the bench. 'No, thanks, dear. Just Aunt Kathy. Don't go mucking around with your mates and miss meeting the bus, will you? Here, take a few biscuits to munch on the way.'

'Wouldn't say no to that, Mum. You'd better throw in a few extra too, please. I'm taking little Charlie III with me for the drive.'

She wiped her hands on her apron and followed him to the front door, waving as father and son piled into the Toyota and took off in a cloud of dust. *What a pair!* she thought. Just like her Charlie and Junior were twenty years ago. Her glance passed across to the manager's house, recently refurbished again to accommodate Junior and his ever-increasing family. Perhaps it was time to talk to Charlie about estate planning. One day in the not-too-distant future, they would have to move on and let Junior have his turn at running the place. How lucky they were to have him!

Sally went to the spare room to open the window and let some fresh air in. The action brought back memories of that first time Kathy had come to stay with her in Brisbane when they were schoolgirls. How much water had flowed under the bridge since then, but they still remained best friends!

She still blamed herself in a way after all those years, because she was sure it was Kathy's experience with Nigel that had prevented her from marrying and having a family of her own. *What a bastard he had been to her! And now he is reaping his just desserts, facing court on embezzlement charges. Serve him right. He had ruined Kathy's life.*

*   *   *

Sally opened the door as the Toyota pulled up in the shade of the big tree in front of the house. 'G'day, Kath. It's good to see you again. We're so pleased you could come up for Harry's wedding.'

The two middle-aged women clung to each other for several moments.

'That's what best friends are for, Sal,' Kathy murmured. 'And thanks for sharing your family with me. I really appreciate it.'

'Don't be silly, Kath. You know you've always been part of our family, and always will be. Now come in out of this heat and tell me what you've been up to.'

'Not much, I'm afraid, but wait till you see what I've brought for the kids.'

Arm in arm, the two best friends chatted away as they went inside.

'Best Friends' explained

This story sets out to encourage the reader to explore their personal values, especially in respect to racism, bigotry, and family relationships. The obvious differences between the Mortons and the Woodrows challenge us to review our own attitudes to these aspects of our lives.

All too often, our efforts to gain short-term self-satisfaction result in failure to place sufficient thought into our long-term futures. Marriages and families are postponed, while we chase personal pleasure or the holy dollar, or both.

When we consider these two best friends, I guess it depends on an individual's personal preferences as to which lifestyle is best. Being a bit of an old romantic at heart, it is probably clear which of the two I think came out on top. But in spite of all that contrived to drive them apart over the years, the friendship forged through their schooldays survived and grew.

True friends, like marriages, can prosper in spite of, or even because of, the fact that they have completely different personalities and backgrounds. Diversity adds to the tapestry of life and encourages the development of well-rounded people. What a shame there aren't more Kathys and Sallys around!

Best Friends

It's not hard to see when you look at this pair,
They both share a love that is, sadly, too rare.
Developed from friendship and forged through the years
Of childhood, adulthood, in good times and tears.

Overcoming the trials of life when it's rough,
Helped build up their characters, gentle but tough.
Put steel in their backbone and love in their heart.
Not lost, only strengthened, by years spent apart.

Fate had decreed that their paths seldom crossed.
On life's stormy seas, they were savaged and tossed.
That time in between when they drifted apart,
Never dimmed for a minute, the love in their heart.

One was destined to end up as a wife.
The other to live a more solitary life.
But as time slipped by and they neared life's end,
They still reached out to their very best friend.

BETRAYED

Retirement was not turning out to be the bed of roses that Kelly Sharpe thought it would. The last few years of his work at the sawmill had seemed endless, as he and his wife planned their long-awaited trip around Australia, making up for all those grinding years of work and family responsibilities. Then, when they were only two months into their trip, his wife had contracted pneumonia and died, leaving Kelly bereaved, lonely, and looking for a purpose in life.

The first thing he did was return home to the town where he had spent all his life. At least he knew everyone and had lifelong friends to relieve his loneliness. The second was to buy a metal detector. Much of his time in the timber industry had been spent around the ranges where gold had been discovered and mined a century before. He had heard plenty of stories of an El Dorado as yet undiscovered, just waiting to make someone rich. Armed with his new piece of technology, he started making long forays into the bush and up the creeks and gullies, whose banks still showed signs of the gold-mining days of old.

One day, as he followed a gully pushing its way up towards the crest of the hills, it dawned on him that he seemed to be on a reasonably well-worn track. This surprised him a bit as there were not many animals in this section of native forest, particularly so far from water. Then, as he pushed his way past a lantana bush, there was the answer – a rocky pool. Even more surprising was the evidence of human visitation. The grass and weeds had been worn down through constant use, and to his utter amazement, several drums and big plastic bottles were stacked on one side.

The worn track continued to wind past the pool and disappeared into the scrub further up the gully. Kelly started to follow it, taking care to avoid noise, in case he came upon someone up to no good. Just off the top of his head, he couldn't think of any reason for someone to be around here, unless they were trying to beat him to the mother lode. Less than fifty metres in, he suddenly had his questions answered; in an open area that had obviously been manually cleared, there stood row upon row of bushes, waist high, and obviously well tended. Kelly had never seen it before, but he knew what he was looking at – marijuana, maybe a million dollars' worth.

Even an old bushy like Kelly knew that to be found anywhere in this area would not be a smart thing to do, so he hurried back down the track to his vehicle and headed home, still shaken at what he had found. Only after he had brewed a pot of tea and was sipping a cup on his veranda did he give some serious consideration as to what to do next.

Probably the smartest thing would be to say nothing and make sure he found a new set of gullies to prospect in. No one need ever know that he had seen anything. Smarter still might be to park his detector in the shed and take up fishing or gardening for a hobby. On the other hand, he couldn't stop his mind wandering to the fact that sitting there unprotected was something worth a million dollars. What if he'd come across a bag of money or a box of gold, just waiting to be picked up by a lucky finder? Would his honesty still force him to report the find, or would temptation get the better of him?

Of course, the difference was that he could spend or bank the money, and cashing in gold wouldn't be too hard, but what could he do with a truckload of marijuana? From what he knew of it, growing the stuff was easy, and the crooks generally only got caught when they were trying to convert it into cash. No, even the thought of having more money than he'd earned in his entire life couldn't tempt him to entertain the thought of stealing the crop. Besides the fear at the thought of getting caught, as a good law-abiding citizen, he guessed he had no option other than to report it to the authorities, making sure his name was kept out of it, if possible.

He didn't know whether it was greed, fear, curiosity, or a combination of all three that led him to decide to hold off reporting it for the time being. Setting aside the first two, curiosity saw him head back there the next day, nervously watching to see he wasn't followed. Parking his truck well off the road up a forested track, he cut across the country till he came to a spot where he could see the waterhole without being seen himself. With nothing more pressing to do with his time, he figured he would man his stake-out till someone showed up to water or harvest the crop, and then he would probably have to pass his find on to the police.

It took a couple of days, but on the third day of his watch, he heard a vehicle pull off the road and some time later, a young man emerged from the bush at the waterhole. He started carting water up the track to where the well-hidden plantation lay. Creeping closer, Kelly reached a spot where he could see him more clearly. His heart missed a beat. He knew him!

He was one of the young fellows he had coached years ago in junior football teams, Dale Simpson. Even worse, he was the son of Bob Simpson, a fellow worker for many years and one of his best mates. That threw up a whole new dilemma for him. He was basically a good kid, working locally, and obviously had been somehow sucked into the drug scene that Kelly knew now pervaded all areas of society. Surely he was only helping out a mate by watering the plants for him. *He couldn't possibly be involved in the drug trade, could he?*

If Kelly's mind had been in turmoil before as to what to do about his discovery of the plantation, now he had the added complication of the fate of some friends to consider. If he went to the police, the boy would probably end up in jail, and he doubted that he deserved that fate. On the other hand, if he ignored the situation, Dale could get sucked into even more trouble in the drug scene. He often read of murders and disappearing people associated with the drug trade. Finally, he took the decision any good family man would take and arranged to meet with Bob Simpson.

*　　*　　*

It was an awkward matter to discuss with his mate of many years, and Kelly was not surprised that Bob had been very upset when he heard the story. His face was ashen and he had to sit down. Fearing he might be having a heart attack or a stroke, Kelly was starting to doubt the wisdom of confiding in him, but after a while, he regained his composure and they started to discuss what to do next. Bob asked if he could have a day or two to think it out and promised to call on Kelly when he had come up with his decision, which seemed fair enough. It was, after all, his son who was involved.

True to his word, he arrived on the third day, bringing a very contrite-looking Dale with him. Their explanation was much as Kelly had suspected. Dale was only a mild user of the drug and had agreed to help out his local supplier by watering the crop in return for some free cannabis. But he was switched on enough to know that in the eyes of the courts, he would still be in very serious trouble if he was turned in to the police.

It was his father, Dale said, who had come up with a suggestion that might serve them all well, even though it involved a fair bit of pain for the family. Not as much pain as a conviction for drug offences, though. Dale would totally destroy the crop and then head off overseas for a year to somewhere the owner of the crop wouldn't be able to find him. When he came back, he would have to relocate to Western Australia or some other locality well away from the people he had become involved with.

Kelly didn't particularly like the idea, as it meant he would be implicated in the event. It also left his mate, Bob, in danger if some drug Lord came looking for Dale and discovered their relationship. Reluctantly, he agreed to go along with it provided he was there to see that Dale went through with the plan of completely destroying the crop, and he arranged to meet at the waterhole in two days' time.

*   *   *

Kelly left early and parked in his secret spot before going overland once again to reach the ridge near the waterhole, without being observed, where he waited for the appointed hour to arrive. The sound of a vehicle heralded the arrival of Dale, who wended his way up the gully and reached the appointed spot on time. He looked a bit nervous but settled down to await Kelly's arrival. The fact that Kelly came in unexpectedly from the side seemed to rattle him a bit, and when he spoke, he seemed to be a bit loud, which Kelly put down to his nervousness.

'Bloody hell, Mr Sharpe! You frightened the shit out of me,' he almost shouted.

'G'day, Dale. I'm glad you kept your word. Are you ready to go?'

Dale didn't answer but took off along the track so fast old Kelly had trouble keeping up with him. Bursting into the clearing, he was met, not by Dale, who had disappeared, but by a menacing-looking bloke of Italian extraction, sneering and levelling a handgun at his chest.

'G'day to you too, Mr Busybody,' he rasped in a thick Italian accent.

The blood drained from Kelly's face, and he raised his hands as he had seen them do in these circumstances so often in the movies.

'What's this all about, and where's Dale gone?' he managed to get out.

'Well, the fact is, Mr Busybody, that good young fellow Dale is probably halfway back to his truck by now. Back to his girlfriend, in fact, who will swear, if she has to, that he's been in bed with her all morning. "Didn't leave me alone for a minute," she'll say. "Couldn't possibly have been out to the "farm" and back." See, she likes her bit of free pot, almost as much as Dale in the cot,' he smirked, clearly amused at his bit of rhyming humour.

'So who are you, and how the hell did you get here?' Kelly asked, trying to get his captor to relax a bit.

'Just who I am don't matter to you, Mr Busybody, and how I got here either but "when". Now that's a different story. You see, I've been around this scene a long time. I guessed you might come early to suss out the scene, so I came even earlier. I' been here since daylight. Heard you come too, and watched you waiting for young Dale. Just in case, you understand.'

He kept the gun levelled at Kelly's chest but seemed to be ready to talk, so Kelly kept firing the questions.

'I assume you own this lot, eh? Must be worth a fortune down in the city.'

'Down in the city, yeah. Okay. Probably a million at least, maybe more, when it's ready, that is. Until then, Mr Busybody, it ain't worth nothing. Just a headache, keepin' snooping old codgers like you away, and employin' useless young dope heads like Dale to keep it growin'.'

Kelly was not altogether surprised that Dale had betrayed him. Even as a kid, he was never quite as trustworthy as the other kids in the teams, taking the easy path whenever possible and tending to hang around with the wrong crowd. But to hand Kelly over to the drug gang when all he was trying to do was help him, well, he could hardly believe it had happened. Drug dependency could cause otherwise decent people to do unbelievable things.

'I suppose Dale told you I was only trying to help him?' Kelly asked.

'Yeah. But lucky for him, he's not that silly. I can't believe you thought we would just let him get away with stealin' our crop like that. We'd have got him, no matter where he went, and he was smart enough to know that. Smarter than you, I'd say, Mr Busybody.'

Kelly had to keep this cocky little crook talking as long as he could. 'What happens to him now?' he asked.

'He's joined the ranks of those who owe their lives to us. He won't say nothin', and his old man won't neither, if he wants to ever see his son again.'

There was only one question left in Kelly's mind, and he didn't think he wanted to hear the answer to that. But it had to be asked.

'What about me?'

'Well, Mr Busybody, when you've finished asking all them very interestin' but very useless questions, you and me are goin' for a long walk in the bushes. And I mean a long walk to somewhere where no white man has probably ever been. More important, none will ever go in the future neither. Sadly, only one of us is comin' back. Bad luck for you, Mr Busybody. That's gonna be me, but you've lived a pretty long life, and we all got to die sometime. Now that's enough talk. Let's go, and don't you try nothin' funny, Mr B.'

Right on cue, a figure in a tracksuit stepped from the bushes, also armed with a handgun, but this one was aimed at the drug dealer.

'Hello, Tony,' the newcomer said. 'Good to see you again. You can throw the shooter into the middle of your "farm", mate. You won't be needing that.'

'Garry bloody Gledhill!' Tony blurted out. 'How the hell did you get here?'

'I think I can start answering some questions now, instead of asking them, Mr Tony,' Kelly butted in. 'Detective Gledhill is here because, the more I thought about it, the more I didn't trust Dale to keep his bargain. So I contacted a friend of mine in the police force and told him to send the drug squad along, just in case. If Dale did as he said he would, they would help him to avoid going to jail over it. If he didn't turn up, they would go looking for him. The third possibility also occurred to me, that he would run to his bosses and ask them to sort it out for him. This bloke is here to cover that contingency too. Lucky for me, eh, Mr Tony?'

'But how did you get here without me hearin' you? I've been here since daylight, man.'

'Tony, Tony, you and I have crossed paths before,' the detective said. 'I know how you think, so I came out last night and camped further up the gully. Not the best night I've spent, but worth it to get the drop on you, old mate.'

'Who you got with you, Garry? That usual slimy sidekick, Peters?'

'Nah. I left him home, Tony. Which is just as well for you as it turns out. If Jeff was here, you'd have the cuffs on by now and heading down that track towards five to ten behind bars. No chance at all to discuss any alternative options if Detective Peters was here,' he said with a wink.

The hairs rose on Kelly Sharpe's neck. These two knew each other pretty well by the looks of things. He couldn't believe the scene that was unfolding before him.

Panic left Tony's face and was replaced with a slimy grin. 'What kind of options you got in mind then, Garry. You know the boss back in the big smoke can be pretty generous to anyone that helps him. How does a quarter share in the crop sound?'

'Nice try, Tony, but you're in a bit more trouble than that. Here you are standing in the middle of a patch of very suspicious bushes, with a witness and a fugitive helper that I can track down. You haven't got much to bargain with, mate.' The detective stared down the increasingly nervous Tony, who was starting to ponder the alternatives of a stint in jail or giving away his boss's drug crop.

'Righto, mate. You got me. Half the crop, paid in the usual way.'

'The usual way' meant to Kelly that this bloke was on the take and had obviously had previous dealings with him or his mob. Now he really was in trouble. His saving angel had turned out to be a devil and had even more reason to see him dead than the drug dealer.

'Fair enough, Tony, and you know better than to try to double-cross me, don't you? Oh, and by the way, you can go and find your gun, because you still have to clean up here,' he said, nodding in Kelly's direction.

As Tony went to retrieve his gun, they all heard a noise that they quickly realised was a chopper zooming in low over the scrub and preparing to land in their clearing. The big red seven on its side showed it came from Channel 7.

'Back where you were, Tony,' said Gledhill, levelling the gun at him again. 'I'm afraid there's been a change of plans. I'm taking you in. Turn around while I cuff you. I may not get rich, but I'll be a hero instead.'

Tony was no hero. He submitted to the handcuffs being put on but screamed above the noise of the chopper, 'I'll squeal, Garry! I'll tell them you were gonna take a bribe!'

'Who do you think they'll believe, Tony? A drug dealer, an old fossicker who had no right to be here anyway, or a respected member of the drug squad? No chance of that, sticking old mate. Without proof, it's your word against mine, I'm afraid.'

The landing chopper made further conversation impossible, so they all stood at the side of the clearing till it settled, and then the door opened, and out stepped, not a reporter, but Inspector Peter McAdam.

'Well done, Garry,' he said. 'They told me back in the office where to find you, and these TV fellows kindly gave me a lift when I told them there might be a story in it. And what a story, eh, by the looks of this lot!'

Kelly Sharpe stood quietly to the side, letting the tableau play out in front of him. He made no effort to tell the inspector what had taken place, even as Tony was led away who was yelling obscenities and trying to implicate Gledhill in a conspiracy to accept bribes.

Inspector McAdam ignored him completely and addressed the detective. 'I'll tell you what we'll do, Garry. You give these TV people a short interview, and then the chopper will take you and your prisoner back to town while the camera crew do some filming of the site. It can bring you back for your car then, and I will go with them on their return flight.'

'Sounds okay to me, Inspector. Where do you want me to stand, boys?' asked Garry, after he had handcuffed Tony in the chopper and shut the door on his tirade.

The inspector approached Kelly at last. 'You must be Mr Sharpe. Peter McAdam's my name. While they're busy here, perhaps you could show me the waterhole that led to this drug farm being established.' The pair of them headed off down the track, leaving Garry Gledhill perjuring himself in front of that night's TV viewers. When they were well out of sight and earshot, Kelly turned to his friend and said, 'Geez, Pete. For a while there, I thought you might have left it a bit late to turn up, but as it was, it worked out just right. Early enough to save me from a bullet in the head, and late enough for Garry to hang himself out to dry. You were right about him, though. He had no hesitation in using the situation to his advantage.'

'I've been aware of his connections with the drug gangs a long time now, mate,' the inspector said. 'When you contacted me to let me in on your plan, it was a perfect opportunity to let him prove once and for all whether he was bent or not. If he was straight, he would save you and arrest the drug man. If he wasn't, he would use the fact that he was on his own to do a deal for himself. All I had to do was make sure his boss sent him out alone. The rest was up to him.'

Arriving at the waterhole, they sat on a log for a while to give the chopper time to leave. Kelly reached into his shirt pocket and handed the inspector the palm-sized recorder he had hidden there. 'Here you are. You'd better see if it all worked. If not, it will only be his word against mine and the dealer's.'

Inspector McNabb pressed play. 'G'day, Mr Busybody' came across loud and clear in Tony's thick accent. They listened to the whole episode, the inspector almost dumbstruck at the audacity of the detective's brazen attempt to extort drug money, and even more so in his complicity in planning to have Kelly done away with.

'That should see him put away for a long time, and he won't be the most popular bloke in the prison system either,' he said. 'Just give me a minute to arrange for his arrest when he lands, will you? And then I want to know what made you call me. After all, your original intention was to get young Dale off the hook, wasn't it?'

The inspector's phone call gave Kelly time to ponder on that decision, one which undoubtedly saved his life. There was just something about Dale that he felt he couldn't trust. He'd mentioned to one of Dale's friends that he might be intending to go overseas, and the friend thought that would be unlikely because he knew for sure he didn't have a passport. Then there was his insistence that Kelly come alone, even though Bob offered to go with them. All things considered, Kelly thought the risk was too much, and he still wasn't too pleased about circumventing the law either.

In the end, he decided to contact Peter McNabb, a lifelong friend and a man he knew he could trust. If Dale had been true to his promise, Peter would put in a good word for him, and he probably would escape jail. If not, he deserved what he got. Then Peter hit on the idea of using the sting to test out Garry Gledhill by sending him out alone to test his honesty, something that had been under scrutiny for some time. Kelly had been supplied with a recorder, and the TV crew organised to provide cover for Kelly's rescue if things went wrong.

*　*　*

That afternoon, as he sat drinking tea on his veranda, the reality of what he had let himself in for finally sank in. He shuddered at the thought of being forced far into the scrub by Tony and the inevitable consequences. Probably, if he could have his time over, he would have just reported his find and stayed well away while justice took its course. But he had always liked those shows on TV, and it gave him a trill to think he had been part of one. Relieved the boredom of his lonely life for a while too, but he sure was pleased it was over.

Besides, there was just something about those rock formations that had formed that waterhole in the gully so far from a creek that aroused his fossicker's interest. First thing tomorrow, he would take his metal detector back there. You never know. Maybe there was a cool million to be picked up in that gully, legally.

'Betrayed' explained

The inspiration for this yarn came to me when I was chasing some noxious weeds along the bank of a creek on our property. Over the years, I have always wondered whether any of the local townies might have planted a few strategically located bushes where they would be safe from detection.

Now let's get this clear: I wouldn't know a cannabis plant if I fell over it, but If I came upon a scene like Kelly did, I guess I'd know what it was. And like him, I'm sure I would do the right thing and report it to the police.

However innocuous this practice of drug cultivation may seem to be, the other end of the trade leads to greed, crime, corruption, and death. So next time you're out for a bush-walk and you stumble on to a healthy looking stand of shrubs that look like they shouldn't be there, get out of there before a 'Tony' takes you for a one-way walk up a lonely gully.

A Little Patch of Green

In every tract of native scrub across this wide brown land,
From Cape York's towering jungles, to West Australia's sand.
Down every track, by every creek, a common sight is seen,
In man-made clearings everywhere, a little patch of green.

Hidden far from where we go, to keep the coppers out,
Tendered by the owners and watered through the drought.
Protected by bad men with guns who'll kill to guard their plot,
The crop is marijuana, which we all know as pot.

Ten thousand acres sown to wheat will hardly pay its way.
A thousand head of cattle, or five thousand bales of hay.
Tomatoes, sugar, pineapples, of all the crops you've seen,
None are half as profitable, as that little patch of green.

Harvested when time is right, and gone to city streets,
More work for all the ambos and coppers on their beats.
Fodder for the dealers, and lifeblood of the users,
First time kids and addicts, and other drug abusers.

All the pain and horror for their father and their mother,
The scourge of drug use gets a hold and quickly claims another.
While hidden in the forest, where it's hardly ever seen,
Grows another crop of druggies' gold, a little patch of green.

BLIND LOVE

The two girls chatted away happily as they stacked the freshly baked bread into the shelves at the Goondiwindi Bakery. Julie had come to quite like her feisty young assistant. At first, she thought her rather cheeky, but Polly's cheery personality and fun-loving nature had won her over, and now they were the best of friends.

'So how was your weekend, Polly?' Julie asked. 'I hope you behaved yourself with the new boyfriend of yours.'

Polly gave her a sly look. 'Well, now that's for Roger and me to know and you to wonder about, isn't it? At least I wasn't sitting at home watching "The Bill" like you, was I?'

'Touché! You're spot on actually. I lead a pretty boring life, I suppose.'

Thinking now that perhaps she had been a bit too smart, Polly felt sorry for her friend, who seemed to be too shy when it came to men. Although she was a few years elder, Julie didn't seem to have many friends in town, and certainly not a boyfriend. Perhaps she could introduce her to some of her circle.

'You'll have to come out to the river with us this weekend, Jules,' she offered. 'Have you ever waterskied?'

'Not yet,' Julie replied, 'but I'd love to try sometime. You'd better check it out with Roger first, though. He mightn't appreciate your bringing a chaperone with you.'

'Oh, he'll be okay.' Polly shrugged. 'He'll agree to anything to keep in my good books.'

'Yes, I bet he will,' Julie mused, half to herself. 'I wonder why.'

They were distracted by the sound of the door opening and turned to watch a young man walk tentatively towards them with a white cane prodding the floor in front of him. Dark glasses hid his eyes, but he seemed to be looking straight ahead as he reached the counter. Julie took in his immaculate appearance, dressed as he was in checked shirt, moleskin, and RM Williams boots. As she came towards him, she also took in his lean muscular body, youthful good looks, and the tentative look on his face.

'Excuse me, sir,' she said. 'Can I help you?'

The young man turned towards her. 'Thank you, miss. Is this the bakery? I'm afraid I'm not too good at finding my way around yet, but I thought I could smell fresh bread from the footpath.'

'You did very well then,' she replied. 'This is the bakery all right, and I'm the salesgirl. Can I get you something?'

He gave her a tentative smile. 'I'd love a cappuccino and a slice of apple pie, please. Is there somewhere I can sit down?'

'There sure is,' Julie said as she moved around the end of the counter. 'Here, let me show you to a table. Just over here to your left. There you are, sir,' she said as she pulled out his chair. 'I'll bring your order over in a minute.'

The young man continued to stare sightlessly into space, while Julie busied herself putting his order together. *What a shame!* she thought. He was just the sort of guy who would normally have set her heart fluttering. He didn't seem to be disfigured in any way, and his tentative demeanour led her to assume he hadn't always been blind. As she set his tray on the table, she was still wondering what his story could be.

'There you are, sir. I've brought you a bowl of sugar instead of those silly little packets we're forced to use these days. I'm Julie,' she offered. 'If you need anything else, just call out when you've finished and I'll help you find the door. You should be right then next time you visit us.'

He turned towards her as she spoke and gave her another engaging smile. 'Thanks, Julie. I'm sorry to be such a nuisance, but I guess I'll get the hang of things eventually. By the way,' he said, poking his hand in her direction, 'I'm Tom. Tom Mathews.'

'Well, I'm pleased to meet you, Tom,' she replied, shaking his offered hand. 'Would you mind if I sat down and had a talk for a few minutes? I've been on my feet all morning and need a break,' she said, and without waiting for a reply, she flopped on to the other chair at the table. 'You must be new around here?' she queried.

'Yair, well, I used to work on a cotton farm at St George before an accident did this to me,' he said, indicating his glasses. 'I still live there with my parents. I'm just in town for a couple of weeks to get treatment at the hospital.'

Julie watched as he fumbled for his cup. 'How ever do you manage to get around on your own?' she asked.

'With great difficulty at this stage, I'm afraid. The fact that I used to come to Goondiwindi a fair bit before the accident helps. I can sort of visualise the main street pretty well.'

'And our nice fresh bread did the rest, eh?'

That disarming smile again. 'That's right. I've been in here a few times over the years too. Have you been working here long?'

'Only a few months. I came here with my boyfriend, but he's moved on looking for greener pastures on the coast. I like it here. The people are friendly and I enjoy my job, so I decided to stay for now.' They sat in silence for a couple of minutes while Tom demolished the extra-large slice of pie that Julie had served him. A customer entering the shop brought their discussion to a close. 'I'll have to get back to work now,' she said. 'Just call out when you're ready to go and I'll show you to the door.'

Polly was right on to her when she returned to the counter. Julie shushed her and pushed her to the other side of the room before saying in a whisper, For goodness' sake, Poll! Keep your voice down! You'll embarrass him!'

'What do you reckon about him now, Jules?' she whispered.

'Well, as well as being drop-dead gorgeous, he has a voice like Mel Gibson, and he seems such a nice person.'

'What a pity he's blind then!' Polly whispered. 'Wouldn't be much good on waterskis, would he?'

'You're awful, Polly. I just feel so sorry for him. Anyway, we'd better get stuck into getting those sandwiches made, my girl. The lunch crowd will be in soon.'

A few minutes later, Tom called on Julie to help him to the door. 'That was great coffee and pie. Thanks, Julie,' he said.

'I'm so pleased you found your way into our shop, Tom. Are you going to come again?'

'Sure thing,' he replied. 'Just keep those bread smells coming out the door so I don't go in the butchers by mistake. And thanks for your help, Julie. I really appreciated our little talk.'

Julie opened the door for him and he tapped his way on to the footpath. 'I'll keep the kettle boiling, so to speak. See you again, Tom.' And he was gone.

*   *   *

Her thoughts often returned to their meeting for the rest of the day. He had made quite an impression on her, and she was looking forward to seeing him again. The hours seemed to pass slowly next morning, and she found herself hoping it was him every time the automatic door opened as a customer entered. Polly smiled to herself as she noticed her fellow worker's jumpy state.

'Well, it's almost ten o'clock. Do you think he'll come again?' she asked.

Julie hadn't confided in her at all about Tom and didn't want to let on she was at all interested. 'Think who'll come again?'

"You know who I'm talking about. Him with the stick, of course. Don't try to tell me you haven't been thinking about him all morning. I've seen you watching the door.'

'Aren't you a little smarty-pants then?' Julie shot back. 'Actually, I have been thinking about him a bit, and as a matter of fact, I do hope he comes back. He seems so shy and lost. Life must be terrible for an active young bloke like him since he lost his sight. I wonder what happened to him.'

'Well, you'll be able to ask him yourself in a minute,' Polly whispered, nodding towards the door. 'He's just about to tap-dance his way in again. I'll make his coffee.'

Smiling broadly, he approached the counter. 'I hope that's you there rattling the cups, Julie,' he said. 'If it is, I'll have the same as yesterday, please, including a chat, if you're not too busy.'

'Actually, It's me, Polly, sir. Julie's gone to the coast with her boyfriend,' she teased.

'Don't be so cruel, you little meanie!' Julie shot back. 'I'm here, Tom. Do you want me to show you to your table? You seem to be right at home today, though.'

'No, thanks. I think I'll be okay if the same table's free.' He started to make his way across the room.

'Off you go then,' Julie said. 'I'll bring your order over in a minute and let this little smarty run the shop for a while, if she can.'

While Polly finished making the coffee, Julie cut a slice of pie that was twice the normal size and added a good helping of whipped cream. Then, with a wag of her finger at Polly, she took the tray to Tom's table.

'There you are, Tom. I'm sorry Polly was so cheeky. It wasn't very sensitive of her, I'm afraid.'

'No worries. I may have lost my sight but not my sense of humour. I'm sure I'll have to put up with worse than that.'

'You must have had to learn so much to be able to cope,' Julie said as she sat down. 'You seem to be handling it so well, though. I don't know how you find your way around. Where are you staying while you're in town?'

'With my grandmother in River Street. It's handy to the hospital and only two left turns and three blocks from here. The white stick does the trick. Everyone seems to give me a wide berth. I'm looking forward to going home, though, but I'll miss coming here.'

I'll miss you coming here too, Julie thought to herself but merely asked, 'So when do you leave?'

'Sunday,' Tom answered as he got stuck into his pie. 'My cousin's taking me.'

'Well, you make sure you come every day till Friday, won't you? I'll organise a freebie for you as a regular-customer discount.'

And he did, regular as clockwork at ten o'clock. Once she became more used to his blindness, Julie found their conversations much more relaxed. He had a quirky sense of humour, interesting stories to tell, and a smile that melted her heart. To her surprise, she found she really liked him, so much so, in fact, that she found herself wondering if anything more could come of their friendship. She had never had anything to do with a disabled person before. Could she imagine having a full-on relationship with someone who couldn't even see her?

On Friday morning, Polly noticed that Julie had taken extra care with her appearance and was hurrying through her work as ten o'clock approached.

'Is lover boy coming again today then?' she asked.

'Don't be so cheeky, you,' she replied. 'Tom's a great bloke. You're just jealous because he doesn't talk to you.'

'He would if you let him.'

'You wish, and he is coming today, but this will be his last visit, and I have a little surprise for him.'

'Ooh, that sounds interesting!' Polly purred.

'Get your mind out of the gutter, Poll. I just enjoy his company, that's all. I'll miss his visits when he goes home.'

Polly noticed the sad look in her eyes at the thought. 'If I didn't know better, I'd say you were falling for him, Jules. Doesn't it worry you that he's blind?'

'Not any more, but it is a bit awkward. I don't know whether I could handle it if our friendship went any further than a cup of coffee in the shop. Still, that's not likely to happen anyway, is it?'

'You never know. From the way you've been fussing around this morning, there's something going on between you two,' Polly said. 'Do you want me to disappear when he comes in?'

'Just the opposite actually!' Julie laughed.

*   *   *

Right on the dot of ten o'clock, he came through the door and confidently approached the counter. 'Who's that banging the cups today?' he asked.

'Just me, I'm afraid, Tom,' Polly replied. 'Lover girl's just popped out the back to get something. She'll be back in a minute. You'll just have to cool your heels and talk to me instead.'

'Oh no, he won't,' Julie said as she came through the back door and went to stand with Tom, giving Polly a slap on the bottom and a 'don't you dare' look as she passed. 'Hello, Tom. I've got a little surprise for you, seeing as this is your last day. I'm off duty tomorrow.'

She picked up a bag from the counter and taking his arm, led Tom towards the door. 'How about we leave Ms Cheeky on her own for a while so we can go somewhere a bit more private? I've got two coffees and some fresh biscuits, and my car is parked out front. Are you on?'

Julie thought he seemed a bit hesitant, but they were already outside and heading towards her little red Barina. He recovered his composure quickly enough to joke, 'Would you like me to drive?'

'Not on your life, mate!' She laughed. 'I've seen you trying to find your way across a room, remember?'

She felt pleased with the fact that they had got to know each other well enough over the last few days to allow a bit of leg-pulling without any embarrassment. Maybe it was premature, and she still wasn't sure she could handle his blindness too well, but she had a funny feeling that there was something special developing between them. She had to find out. Perhaps an hour or so on their own would help clear her confused feelings.

Tom broke into her thoughts. 'Where are we going? My newfound sense of direction tells me we're heading towards the river. We're not going swimming, are we? I didn't bring my togs.'

'Well, we could go skinny-dipping, I suppose, but it wouldn't be much fun for you, would it?' she joked. 'No, we're going to a lovely little bench overlooking the water. I often spend my lunch hour there.'

'Sounds great.' Tom was silent for a while and seemed to be pondering on a problem. When he spoke, he sounded nervous. 'Julie, I just wish I had got to know you before, you know, when I was normal. It's strange to get to know someone who is only a voice. I've absolutely no idea what you look like, but I have built up a mental picture. Sometimes I wonder how far off the mark I am.'

While she searched for an answer to this, Julie parked the car, led Tom to the park bench, and handed him his coffee. Finally, she answered him.

'Tom, it must be very difficult for you. I've been trying not to feel sorry for you, but I can't help it. You're so brave about your condition, and it doesn't seem to have left you at all depressed or bitter. I'm sure I couldn't have handled it half as well.'

Gazing sightlessly over the river, he said nothing, but Julie noticed the strained expression on his face. She took his hand and placed it against her cheek saying, 'Tom, I want you to feel my face. I want you to get your mental picture right. I can see you, and I want you to see me too, even if it has to be by touch.'

His hand trembled as it traced a line down to her chin and up the other side. He gently touched her nose and her eyes, eyes that she kept closed as he explored her face. Her body tingled all over at his touch. She could feel her heartbeat rise and blood rush to her face. The cool fingers moved down to her throat and back to her chin, which tilted upwards at the touch. Her lips parted and she gasped as she felt him lean closer. And then he kissed her, slowly, sensually.

Abruptly, his hand was withdrawn and Julie felt him pull away from her. Her eyes sprang open. 'Bloody hell, Julie!' he blurted. 'I can't go on like this any longer.'

Her eyes sprang open in alarm and she saw that his face was wreathed in anguish. His chest heaved as he sucked in a couple of deep breaths and tried to compose himself.

Julie was alarmed. 'Tom, whatever is wrong with you? You look like you're having a heart attack. It can't have been that bad, could it? I was quite enjoying myself.'

'That's just it, Julie. So was I, and I shouldn't have.'

'Why Tom? What's wrong? Tell me,' she pleaded.

He slowly turned to face her, whipped off his dark glasses, and with an angry flourish, threw them in the river. Julie found herself staring into gorgeous blue eyes, which seemed to return her gaze unflinchingly. Tom took her hands in his, and with a tremble in his voice, he explained, 'Julie, promise me you will hear me out with what I have to tell you. Then if you want to, just hop in your car and go home. That's what I deserve, but with all my heart, I hope you don't.'

By now Julie was starting to panic. She just couldn't understand what she was seeing and hearing at all. 'Whatever's happened to you, Tom? Of course, I'll listen, but I can't imagine what's got into you.'

'It's a long story, Julie, and one I'm ashamed of, but I've come to like you too much to let it continue. You see, the fact is, I'm not blind at all. It's all been an act, and now I wish the whole thing had never happened.'

Julie stiffened, and she pulled away from him as she took in this startling admission.

'What?' she shouted. 'I don't believe you! Are you telling me that you could see all the time? Was this whole charade just your way of having a bit of fun at my expense?'

Tom was obviously distressed and unable to face her, returned to staring out over the river.

'It's worse than that I'm afraid, Julie,' he mumbled. 'I want to tell you everything, right from the start, and then I'm going to ask a big favour of you. I'm going to ask you to forgive me so we can still be friends.'

He stole a sidelong glance and was pleased to see that at least she was still there and seemed to be prepared to listen. She said nothing but sat wringing her hands, tears welling into her eyes. It broke his heart to see it, but he managed to continue.

'I am who I said I am. My parents own a cotton farm at Dirranbandi, and my cousin and I work on the place. We were due for some holidays, and my gran, who lives in town here, had to go to Brisbane for an operation. We offered to house sit for her till this Sunday.'

'So you are going home on Sunday then? Good,' she spat at him.

Tom swallowed hard and went on, 'We were getting a bit bored one day, when my cousin wanted to bet me I couldn't get you into the sack before we went home.'

Julie gasped but said nothing.

'He'd been in your shop one day and told me what a good sort you were. Of course, I didn't take him on because I knew I would lose. I've lived in the bush all my life, Julie, and never had much experience with girls. I knew I could never just front up and ask you out, much less get to sleep with you. But I looked through the window one day and saw how beautiful you were. I spent hours trying to think of a pick-up line to approach you with.'

'You could have tried "Hello, I'm Tom. Would you like to go out with me?" That would have been simple enough.'

'Believe me, I've wished hundreds of times since that I have had done just that, but I didn't, and it's too late now.'

'You can say that again. Whatever made you come up with such a crazy idea?' Julie asked.

Pleased that she was at least giving him a chance to explain himself, he continued, 'One day I watched a movie on telly about a blind bloke who fell in love with his nurse, and I came up with this stupid idea of getting to know you. I borrowed one of Gran's sticks, painted it white, and, well, you know the rest.'

He waited while she digested this explanation. Obviously she was upset, and quite understandably so. She still stared out over the water, unable to bring herself to look at him. He mustered up the courage to continue, 'Well, that's not quite true either. You probably don't know all the rest at all. You see, as I got to know you, I realised how stupid I'd been because I wanted our friendship to continue, and I couldn't keep up with the blind story forever. I realised I was going to lose you.'

Another quick look. Still no reaction. Still the vacant stare, but this time, a tear running down a flushed cheek. He felt terrible for the turmoil that was obvious in her face, but at least she was still here. Emboldened by that fact, he reached over and took her hands in his.

'Julie, please look at me.' Slowly, she did. 'Today, when I kissed you, and you kissed me back, I knew I couldn't keep this going any longer. I had no option but to risk everything by telling you the truth.'

'Well, that was a change for the better,' she whispered.

'I know. I'm truly sorry. I know I don't deserve it, but I'm asking you to forgive me. To let me start again. I want us to be friends for the right reasons. More than that really. I think I'm falling in love with you, Julie,' he blurted out.

Julie stood and walked to the riverbank, leaving a wretched Tom sitting disconsolately on the bench, feeling very contrite and sorry for himself. *What a stuff up!* he thought. If only he'd never come up with that stupid idea! Obviously she was upset, and why wouldn't she be? He guessed it was all over now, but at least he hadn't gone home without telling her. At last, she came and sat next to him. He stared at the ground while he waited for her to say something.

'Tom, I really don't know what to think. Strange as it seems now, I was starting to fall for you too, and when you kissed me, I realised how much I had grown to like you. In spite of what you did, I think I still do, but I need time to get my head straight.'

'I understand,' he said. 'I really do.'

Julie stood and started gathering up their rubbish. 'I'm going back to work now. Come and see me on Sunday before you leave. By then I might know what to make of all this. Relationships have to be based on trust, not lies. I just don't know at this stage if I can accept what you did, Tom.'

Tom was shattered as he watched her drive off. It looked like he had lost the first girl he had ever been really interested in, and it was all his fault. Julie's mind was also in a turmoil of deceit, attraction, excitement, and doubt. They both had much to think about over the next two days.

Tom sat munching on a biscuit and sipping his now-cold coffee after Julie had driven off. He was shattered.

*   *   *

On Sunday morning, he left his cousin to finish packing and drove the Toyota around to the shop. He wasn't looking forward to the coming confrontation with Julie and was resigned to leaving on bad terms, but he was determined to give it one last go to get her forgiveness. There she was behind the counter, just as she had been on that first fateful day. Was that a hint of a smile on her face?

'Can I help you, sir?' she asked. 'I see you've found your way to the counter.'

He tried to gauge from her voice whether she had forgiven him, but the lack of expression on her face left him none the wiser. He decided to press his luck.

'Yes, and I see my table is vacant too. Can I have the usual, please, and a few minutes' talk with the best-looking girl in town?'

'With pick-up lines like that, you certainly don't need a white stick to help you,' Julie said, this time with a smile.

Polly pushed her way into the conversation. 'Oh, that'd be me, but I'm sorry, sir. I'm too busy at the moment. This other girl has done no work this morning. She's spent all her time looking out the door for some reason.'

Julie gave her a shove. 'That's enough of your cheek, Pol. Just bring the gentleman's usual order to his table. I'll help him find his way. Just put your hand on my shoulder, sir, and follow me.'

The butterflies left his belly as Tom followed her to his table. If she was going to send him on his way, at least it wasn't going to be a slanging match. Maybe she'd even give him a second chance to start afresh. He wouldn't stuff up next time. She was something special, and he had a feeling they were going to part on friendly terms.

'I can't tell you how happy I am that you've taken my stupid prank so well, Julie,' he said as they sat down. 'It's more than I expected, or deserved. I'm really sorry.'

'So you should be, you clown. You made me look like a complete idiot.'

'Don't think that. There's only one idiot around here, and that's me. What I did was unforgivable. I just hope and pray we can put it behind us and start again.'

Julie felt sorry for him. He looked so miserable. He'd obviously suffered terribly, and she decided the time had come to let him off the hook.

'Don't feel too bad, Tom,' she said. 'I've got something to tell you too.'

Once again, Polly interrupted them. 'There you are, sir,' she said, placing coffee in front of him. 'No sugar bowl today, I'm afraid, now that we know you can tell the little brown packets from the blue ones.'

'Thanks, Polly,' he said. 'You're the second-best sort in town.'

'Well, that's a matter of opinion. It's not what my boyfriend thinks. Don't keep her here too long. I can't run this place on my own, you know.'

They waited for her to leave, and then Julie returned to their conversation.

'Tom, I listened to your story yesterday. Now I want you to listen to mine. I'll admit I was offended at what you did, but then I started to think about why you did it. I found I could sympathise with your shyness. I was in the same boat once, but working in shops has helped me to overcome it, and that's an opportunity you've never had.'

'You're right about that,' Tom butted in. 'I've only ever worked on the farm.'

'Then I realised that we all tell lies from time to time,' she continued. 'In fact, I've told you one too.'

'Don't tell me you're married,' he blurted out.

'No. Nothing like that, but remember I told you I'd come here with my boyfriend? Well, actually I've never had a real boyfriend, much less lived with one. I guess I was trying to keep a bit of distance from you. It's a habit I've got into as a way of fending off unwanted advances, I suppose.'

'Well, it didn't work too well in my case, did it?' Tom laughed.

'No. And I'm glad it didn't now,' she said as she reached across the table and took his hand. 'Over the last week, I've come to really like you. So much, in fact, that I've made a couple of bets of my own.'

'I hope they're better than the one I made,' Tom said, still embarrassed and chastened at what he had done.

'That remains to be seen. It's all up to you. I bet myself that if I said I wanted to spend a few days on a cotton farm to see how they work, that you'd be prepared to ring your mum to ask if you could bring a visitor home with you.'

Tom had a grin from ear to ear. He could hardly believe what he was hearing. 'Well, you've won that one already!' He chortled.

Julie went on, 'I also bet she'd trust you to only bring someone nice like me, so she'd say yes. Put your phone away. I'm not finished yet. Finally, I bet myself that we might move on to bigger and better things one day,' she finished, giving his hand a squeeze.

'I don't have to ring anyway,' he said, putting his phone back in his pocket. 'I just know she'll love you, almost as much as her silly son. Double your bets, Julie. You're about to collect.'

'Actually, your mother had better say yes. See that bag over there?' she said, indicating a suitcase behind the counter. 'It contains a week's supply of work gear, and that new girl who came in while we were talking is my replacement for the next seven days. If you go without me now, I'll have to find some other young farmer to show me around.'

'Now who's teasing who?' he chided.

'Oh, and by the way, you can collect that bet off your cousin.'

'What?' he almost shouted.

'Well, you will get me into the sack, so to speak, but it will be in your mother's spare room, and you won't be in it with me!' She laughed, as they rose.

She gave him one of her most radiant smiles, removed her apron, and went to give some final instructions to Polly.

Tom never took his all-seeing eyes off her. *Maybe not this visit*, he thought to himself.

'Blind Love' explained

One of the wonders of the written word to me has always been — where do novelists and playwrights get inspiration for their stories? I find it impossible to sit down with a blank sheet and come up with a concept, plot, and storyline. Generally, some experience or yarn prompts a short story or poem, but this one is an exception. It came from nowhere. Maybe my wife is right. You do need to have a twisted mind to come up with a plot like this. Oh, and unlike most of the poems in this book, which were written some years ago, 'A Little White Lie' was written specially.

A Little White Lie

I'm sorry, Mum.
It's not my fault, that there's felt pen on your chair.
It must have been the fairies, cos I wasn't even there.

Oh, thank you, Granny.
Just what I wanted, another pair of socks.
They'll go down really famously with last year's cotton jocks.

Hello! Is that you, dear?
The traffic's bad and I'm running a bit late.
(Really caused by drinking beer with my drunken mate!)

I'd like to dear—
I'd love to take the kids to the park to play,
But work comes first. This tender's one I just have to get away.

A visit from your mother?
Of course, I don't mind having her. How long can she stay?
Oh, what a shame to hear the old dear can't stay another day!

Honestly, hand on heart,
We stand here, married fifty years, and like I always said,
She's more beautiful today, than the day that we were wed.

Now here's your chance,
Hands up, all you heroes, who haven't told a lie.

I'll take your word for it, you know. I'm a trusting sort of guy.

Oh oh! What's this?
No hands up. Don't worry. It's like I always thought.
Just like Tom and Julie, it's all right till you get caught!

DREAMTIME

Shadows crept slowly across the gully as the sun slipped silently behind the trees on the far side of the creek. Soon nightfall would envelop the scene and destroy for yet another day any chance they had of success. But that was the whole point of the exercise, wasn't it? Patience and persistence. These were the skills he wanted to teach the boy, and they could only be learnt by tempering occasional success with lots of failure.

They lay together side by side under the lignum bush, the old aboriginal man and the young white boy. Nothing was said and not a muscle moved as they waited patiently for the dingo to come up the gully, as he must have done many times before. Joe's old twenty-two calibre hand-me-down rifle lay stretched out in front of him, ready to be brought up to his shoulder with next to no movement. He had been taught to use it as a small boy and was quite sure that if he could just get one shot away, it would be the end of the wily old male dingo that had been causing them grief for months.

Just last week they had found one of the station dogs torn to shreds out past the horse paddock, and had no doubt who was the culprit. Calf losses had also increased in the paddocks close to the homestead, and their carcasses all showed the same killing methods and eating habits. Dingo attacks were part and parcel of rearing livestock in these parts, but when they became as cheeky and destructive as this one had, the only solution was to seek him out and destroy him. Now, as shadows descended into darkness, they both sensed that today was not going to be the day that they would return triumphant to the homestead with his scalp.

Still, that was not surprising really, as he probably holed up in the scrub miles from where they lay in ambush. Dingos travel many miles in search of food and will not always follow the same pattern on a regular basis. What made them so confident this time were the fresh tracks that old Toby had noticed only a few days previously when out looking for a stray horse. He had made a point of taking young Joe out in the daylight to show him what he had found.

Paw marks around the waterhole in the creek were easy to see, but only the experienced old full-blooded aborigine could work out where he went from there. Guessing he might be heading in the direction of the homestead, he scoured the banks for the most likely track out, and reasoned he probably followed the gully that ran into the creek upstream from the waterhole. Sure enough, some fifty yards up the gully, he found a clear print on a patch of bare dirt. It was clear to Toby but completely invisible to Joe until it had been pointed out to him. After that, they found many other signs that led them to believe this was a regular path for him when he was hunting in the area.

'Him no come today, mate,' Toby said as he stretched his aching old legs and stood up. 'We most better get home or missus will have my hide. Anyway, my belly says it's teatime.'

'I better not argue with your belly, Toby. He's too big for me to fight,' Joe teased.

'You a cheeky young fella.' Toby laughed as he gave him a gentle push in the back. Then they retrieved their horses from a nearby patch of scrub and rode home in the gathering gloom.

*　　*　　*

As he had grown up on the station, Joe, alone amongst the four Henderson kids, had developed a loving relationship with the old man who had lived on the place all his life. Born in the black's camp sometime in the late 1800s, he had never left Boggabilla, working from when he was a small boy for many years as a stockman, and more recently as a handyman. His family had all moved away or died over the years, and he now lived a lonely but contented existence in a small cabin behind the homestead.

Contented that is, if you ignored the constant friction between Toby and the stockmen who lived in separate quarters near the stockyards. As it happened, all of them were of part aboriginal heritage, commonly called 'half-castes' at the time in the middle of last century. Back then, aboriginal ancestry was not something to be proud of, and those of mixed blood went to great lengths to emphasise the white part of it, while doing their best to ignore their aboriginal ancestors.

For this reason, the stockmen continually chucked off at Toby because he was the only full-blooded aborigine on the property. He, in turn, was proud of his heritage and would return their barbs with 'I might be a blackfella, but at least I am a proper blackfella, not like you half and half blackfellas.'

To keep the peace, many years ago, it was decided that Toby would have separate quarters, and even eat alone in his own little room. That was until Joe became his best mate as a little nipper, sitting on his knee while he ate and listening to the tales of his ancestors. Over the years they became inseparable.

One day, when the boss had gone to town and the men were all enjoying a rest day, Joe finished his schoolwork and went to see if Toby would take him fishing before dark. He couldn't find him, so he searched up towards the yards. There seemed to be some sort of a commotion going on behind the men's quarters, with much laughter and shouts of excitement. The sight that confronted Joe as he looked around the corner of the building would stay in his mind forever.

Stretched between four star pickets driven at the corners of a meat ant's nest was Toby, stripped naked, and writhing in agony as the ants crawled over his body, biting as they went. The stockmen jumped on to the nest, stirring up more of the swarming ants, to join the fray while Toby stoically gritted his teeth and tried not to move. All the while, the men jeered and teased him, saying, 'This is just an initiation ceremony, Toby. Didn't your ancestors tell you? You can be the new chief of the meat ant totem. King Toby, King of the meat ants!'

Joe ran helter-skelter for the homestead. 'Mum! Mum! Come Quick! The men are killing Toby! Quick! Bring the gun!' he jabbered away at her, telling her what he'd seen while he helped get the shotgun from his father's office. His mother could hardly believe what he was telling her, but she had realised that the men had been getting more cheeky lately, especially when the boss was away. As they ran back to the yards, she wondered what she could possibly do if the men ignored her bluff and turned on her and Joe.

She needn't have worried. As she rounded the corner of the building, she let off one barrel into the air and yelled, 'Stop that *now*, or I'll shoot the lot of you!' Taken by surprise at her sudden appearance and the report of the shotgun right behind them, they needed no further encouragement and took off in all directions. Within seconds, as the noise and smell of gunpowder still hung in the air, all that remained of the scene was a white-faced mother, a much relieved Toby, and Joe, already springing into action with his pocketknife on the rope tethers.

After a bath in salty water and some liberally applied calamine lotion, the embarrassed old man recovered quickly. The men stayed well out of sight, not even coming in for tea, and spent the night terrified at having to confront the boss next morning. Joe's mum made Toby's favourite meal that night, and as an attempt at apologising for the actions of the other employees, he joined the family at their table. He was thankful for their kindness but was pretty uncomfortable about it and was happy to return to his own little room the next day, where his hero, saviour, and mate joined him.

'Toby,' Joe asked one day, 'why do the men pick on you about being a black man?'

'They don't understand, young Joe. They all brought up by white folks. No one tell them the old stories. They don't know the dreamtime.'

'Tell me about those stories, Toby. I won't laugh at them.'

So he did. Night after night, they would sit at the fire in front of Toby's hut while he told him the tales of his ancestors and myths and legends of the dreamtime. The bond between them became as close as that between a father and son. Old Toby never forgot how Joe had rescued him from the ant's nest.

*　　*　　*

The day arrived sometime later when Toby was able to repay the favour. Joe had taken his rifle and headed out to the scrubby ridges at the back of the property to see if he could come across any sign of the dingo that was still causing trouble around the place. In mid afternoon, his horse arrived back without him, and everyone knew something bad could have happened. Of course, the pony might have just broken free from being tied up while Joe did something on foot, but quite naturally, their fear was that he had taken a buster and was hurt, or worse.

They knew the general direction in which he went, but he could be anywhere in a ten-thousand-acre paddock. Before they all spread out to cover the most likely areas, the boss called Toby over.

'Listen, Toby, you have a better chance of finding him than us, particularly if he is hurt and can't answer our calls. Before we all muck up any tracks he's left, you go on ahead and see if you can see where he went. You know how to call us if you need us.'

'Okay, boss. I'll find him.'

He sat on his horse on top of a rise, surveying the area in front of him. The time they had spent together over the years gave him a good insight into how Joe would think, and he headed off in the direction of a spot that they had once decided was where the dingo most likely hung out during the day.

Riding parallel to the scrub it didn't take him long to come across the tracks that he knew belonged to Joe's pony. Following them was another matter. The rough terrain meant signs were few and far between, and there were several alternative tracks he could have taken. After some time spent backtracking and searching, he found where he had entered the scrub. From there on, the thick bush made tracking easier as broken branches and the softer earth allowed Toby to speed up his progress, but he was worried that approaching darkness would call an end to the search before they found him.

Then, as he ducked under a low branch, he saw Joe lying just off the track. Dried blood covered his face, caused by a nasty gash in his head. Obviously, he had been travelling at speed and not seen the branch in time. Toby checked the unconscious boy and realised he needed help to get him home. Unslinging his rifle, he fired three shots into the air, which was the prearranged signal that he had found Joe and needed help. From then on, another shot every few minutes guided the other searchers to the spot. While he waited, he could do little for his young mate except nurse him in his arms and call on his ancestors to keep him alive till help arrived.

*   *   *

Car lights lit the landing strip as the Flying Doctor took off to deliver their patient to hospital in Toowoomba. The medicos had diagnosed a possible skull fracture and kept him sedated for the trip. His mother went with him and promised to ring through a report next morning. Toby was inconsolable. The one person left in the world who meant anything to him could die. He spent the night sitting in front of his fire, mumbling to himself and talking to his ancestors.

The call came at breakfast time and the family all gathered around the phone to get what they hoped would be good news. And it was. X-rays showed no permanent damage had occurred, and Joe was now conscious and telling them what had happened. The boss went straight out to tell Toby the good news, but he already knew. As he dozed in front of the dying embers before dawn, his old father had come to him from the dreamtime.

*   *   *

Crack! The shot echoed up and down the gully. The old male dingo dropped like a stone, shot cleanly through the head. The old black man squeezed the boy's shoulder as they rose stiffly from their hide. 'You got him, Joey. I told you he come tonight.'

'You been talking to those ancestors again, Toby,' he replied. 'That's cheating.'

'That's why you lucky you got me for a friend, young fella, and not one of them other half-caste blokes, eh?' he said.

They returned to the homestead in triumph with the dead dog strapped on Joe's pony. The boss was very proud of his son's tenacity and courage, but no one was more proud than Toby of his young protégé and mate. He was quite certain that one day, long after he had gone to his ancestors, Joe would be the first white man to find his way into the dreamtime, and they would meet up again to sit in front of a fire and tell tales of their days chasing dingos in Boggabilla.

'Dreamtime' explained

The genesis of this story is based on fact, and the boy could have been me if my family had stayed out west a few more years. In fact, we moved to a large cattle property near Injune when I was a toddler and left a couple of years later.

The animosity between the only full-blooded aborigine on the place and all of the mixed race stockmen was real, as was the friendly relationship, which developed between him and me, or so I have been told. As there were no other children living there, he was my only friend, and I his. As he was quite old at the time, he would have gone to meet his ancestors many years ago. This story is for him.

DREAMTIME

'How'ya going, Son?' he asked, as he ruffled up my hair.
A timid little toddler then, he gave me quite a scare.
His skin was black as blackest coal, his features grim and fierce.
That day I made a lifelong friend, the full-blooded Jacky Pearce.

He lived on Warrinilla as his forebears always had,
The last surviving tribesman from before their lives turned bad.
He made the big transition to the white man's way of life,
And now he lived alone with them, no family, kids, or wife.

Ostracised by all of those with mixed blood in their veins,
Exploited by the grazier in his quest for fiscal gains.
Left to make the best of life that circumstance decreed,
He pottered around the garden now to earn a bed and feed.

He and I became good mates as I followed him around.
I listened to his dreamtime tales, absorbed, without a sound.
I joined him while he ate his tea inside his little shed,
Then left him to his lonely thoughts, a dog, his mate, in bed.

It's many years since that took place and Jacky has passed on.
His spirit's in his dreamtime where all his kin have gone.
I hope my time as his young mate gave him some days of joy,
And that he still remembers well, that blond-haired little boy.

FIONA'S SURPRISE

Henry Roberts parked the Toyota in the shade of the pepperina tree near the back door, flopped into the old squatter's chair on the porch, and kicked off his boots. He hooked his hat on the wall peg, sauntered into the kitchen, and put the kettle on to make a cup of tea. Well, not a cup of tea, a mug of tea actually. He hated the old-fashioned custom of serving tea in fancy little cups and saucers. His mug held at least two and a half cups, including a good four or five spoons of sugar. He gave it a good stir and went looking for Nora.

He found her cleaning the windows in the spare bedroom. The freshly washed and pressed curtains lay on the new quilt on the bed, and the sparkling dressing table was adorned with freshly picked flowers. At first, he wondered what had got into her, and then he remembered – their son and his family were coming to stay for the long weekend. *Bloody hell! I wasn't looking forward to that one little bit!*

'Going to a bit of trouble there, old girl, aren't you?' he asked. 'Probably still won't be good enough for Ms Fiona, though.'

'Well, we've got to try our best.' Nora gave the window a final rub. 'I know you find all of them a trial to put up with, but Peter is our son, she is his wife, and Harley and Mercedes are our grandkids. I do wish you would try harder to get along with them.'

'You know I try my best, but it's pretty hard for a bloke like me. Why Peter had to latch on to a greenie snob like her at uni I just don't know.' Henry recalled the first time Peter brought her out to meet them, and how she had criticised him for chopping down a bit of useless scrub to plant some pasture. 'And look what she's turned him into – a bloody environmental scientist no less. Why couldn't he get a proper job? He could be running this place by now if he'd played his cards right, instead of sitting on his bum in some air-conditioned office, telling all us poor buggers who are trying to produce something what we're doing wrong.'

'He was never interested in staying here. You know that,' Nora said as she treaded the curtains on to their rod. 'He couldn't wait to get away and find something else to do with his life. Not everyone wants to spend their lives struggling on the land, you know. Now stop whinging and give me a hand to put these curtains back up, and I hope you washed your hands.'

Henry knew not to push her too hard criticising Peter. She'd swoop on him like a magpie with a nestful of babies if he did. Mothers were like that, he guessed. Very protective of their kids, especially the sons. *Yair, funny that.* She wasn't backward in criticising their daughter Susie, though. She had been a bit of a tomboy as a kid, and still was, even though she was now married with a family of her own.

It brought a smile to his face to think of how different she was to Peter. Married to a local grazier, with three scruffy adorable little kids, they were the pride of his life. His thoughts returned to Peter's perfect pair. Harley – yes, he was named after his father's favourite toy – was twelve years old. Probably because of the examples set by Peter, his hobbies included birdwatching and chess, but he showed no interest in sports or any form of physical activity and spent most of his life indoors playing video games. Poor little bugger. These visits to the bush must be absolute purgatory for him, and it wasn't really his fault.

And then there was little Ms Mercedes – yes, named in honour of the car import business run by Fiona's father. She was ten, going on twenty. Very intelligent and full of confidence, she was a miniature version of her mother. Between them, they knew exactly how to twist Peter around their little fingers, which they did quite regularly. Both were spoiled beyond redemption and had absolutely no respect for him or Nora.

He knew Peter was trying to do the right thing by insisting they all pay an annual visit to the farm, but these occasions were invariably uncomfortable for all of them. They sometimes ended in a slanging match that took the next twelve months of separation to get over. It wasn't a good situation, and Henry promised himself that he would try really hard to do better this time. *Here's hoping,* he thought, as he plonked his mug in the sink and went back to work.

Meanwhile, Nora was also fretting about the forthcoming family get-together. Their total lack of empathy for rural life didn't grate on her like it did on Henry. In fact, she was quite pleased that Peter had built a career for himself away from the farm. Life on the land no longer held the charms or financial rewards of previous times, and with education now so much more important, they were certainly better off living in the city. She just wished they could all get on better.

*   *   *

In the city, Fiona decided she was going to give it one more try. 'Peter, is it really necessary for us to visit your parents this year? You know how upset everyone gets, especially your father, and it's getting worse every time. I'm sure they feel the same too. It would be doing us all a favour if we made an excuse and stayed home.'

'We go through this every year, Fi, so you know my view. Mum and Dad are the kids' grandparents, so we owe it to them to get to know each other. Maybe as Harley and Mercedes grow older, they will get on better, and when they leave school, I promise we'll drop the custom.'

How he wished things were different! He had never really fallen out with his father, just drifted apart over the years. Ever since he decided to go to university instead of returning to the property when he finished boarding school, they had lost the tremendous rapport they had enjoyed when he was younger. His decision to work for the government didn't help, particularly in his chosen profession of environmental protection. He now had the feeling that that his father considered him as something of a parasite, sucking the lifeblood from all the hard-working productive parts of society, especially farmers.

Things only went from bad to worse when he married Fiona. She was more than indifferent to rural life. She hated it with a passion. The only daughter of doting and very wealthy parents, she had been indulged all her life and was never forced to do anything she didn't want to. Perhaps this had resulted in her being a bit self-obsessed, but she had many good qualities too, ones that his parents never got to see. Maybe they should be spending more time visiting, not less.

'Come on, Fi,' he said, giving her a quick squeeze as he picked up the paper and went to sit in his favourite chair. 'Cheer up. It's not that bad, and we'll only be there for a couple of days. I'll talk to the kids and see if I can convince them to be a bit more cooperative and friendly. *And* I'll take a couple bottles of red to ease *your* pain. I know Mum really looks forward to this every year, so how about you make a special effort for her sake, eh, and mine?'

Actually, I didn't mind Peter's mother, she thought, as she stood watching through the window for the kids to come home from school. Although they had very little in common, she was a nice old thing and did her best to build a loving relationship with the children, tried too hard, if anything. Sometimes she suspected she was glad Peter had made a life for himself away from the land, and even sounded almost jealous of Fiona's city-based lifestyle. Perhaps she could use this visit to see if she could find some common interest that would enable them to become more friendly.

She moved over and sat on Peter's lap and gave him a friendly peck on the cheek. 'For you, darling, of course I will. I'm going to try very hard this time, and I'll talk to the kids too. Oh, and don't forget to take a bottle of Bundy as well as the wine. I don't think Gramp would think much of a nice shiraz after work.'

Peter put the paper aside and turned his attention to his beautiful wife. 'Thanks, Fi. I'd really appreciate that.' And just as he turned to give her his full attention, the front door banged, and they jumped to their feet as Mercedes and Harley burst into the room.

*　　*　　*

Covered in dust and full of tired travellers, the car pulled into the shade of the pepperina tree beside the Toyota. One by one, they – Peter, Fiona, Harley, Mercedes, and Fiona's pride and joy, her pedigree poodle, Landsdowne, Jessica's pride or Jessie for short – alighted, stretched, and headed for the house. While the humans held on till they went inside, Jessie squatted and relieved herself near the tree and then trotted aristocratically up the steps behind her owner.

A battered old blue cattle dog, who hadn't even bothered to herald the arrival of the visitors, now dragged himself away from his spot under the tank stand, ambled over to the tree, and gave the wet patch of ground a very thorough examination. After a thoughtful look in the direction of the departing fluffy backside, he retreated to his cool, resting place. *Hmmm*, he thought, *very interesting*. And then he went back to sleep.

*   *   *

Things are going very well, so far, thought Nora, as she cleared away the last of the dishes and ran water into the sink. They all seemed to be trying so hard to get along that she could hardly believe her eyes. By this time last year, everyone had already been offended by some thoughtless comment or another, and the atmosphere could be cut with a knife. Now, as she listened to the drifting conversation from the dining room, she couldn't get over the fact that it was even sprinkled with occasional laughter. *I wonder if it would last,* she pondered.

'Here, Mum, let me wipe up for you,' said Peter as he appeared beside her. *That is another first*, thought Nora, but in line with the new spirit of courtesy being displayed tonight, merely said, 'That would be lovely, dear.' A strained silence followed, as both searched for the right thing to say. Should they bring their thoughts into the open, or keep dodging around the elephant in the room as usual? Finally Peter took the plunge.

'Have you been putting Valium in the gravy, Mum? Everyone seems so friendly in there. Fiona's even got the old man sampling red wine, much to the kids' amusement.'

Nora wondered if this was the moment she had been waiting for. The friction that existed between Peter and his father had been a bitter disappointment for her, and she longed to get to know and love his kids but had long ago decided that it was a forlorn hope. Henry was just too stubborn and set in his ways to cope with change and too proud to back down from the views he had adopted over the years.

'Penny for your thoughts,' Peter said, jolting her from her reverie.

'I'm sorry, dear,' she said. 'I was miles away.' She tried to collect her thoughts and work out the best way to approach the subject. 'Peter, I'm just so disappointed that we don't have a more normal relationship any more. Seeing you and your family for only a couple of days per year doesn't allow us to get to know each other at all, and even those visits haven't been too much help. I know Dad's a bit hard to get on with, and he seemed to find fault with Fiona right from the start.'

Standing behind her, Peter saw the sadness reflected in her sagging shoulders and her premature grey hair. She was still only fifty-five years old but looked much elder. He put the tea towel down and gave her a hug, noticing a tear roll down her cheek and plop into the sink.

'Here, dry your hands on this,' he said, handing her the towel. 'Let's go and sit on the back veranda for a while. We need to have a talk.'

And talk they did, putting years of silence and frustration behind them. They opened their hearts to each other, full of regrets for the past and finally, hope for the future. At last, Nora could see a brighter future for them all, provided, they agreed, Henry and Fiona hadn't come to blows back inside. They hurried back, ready to play their usual pacifier roles, but were dumbstruck by the sight that confronted them.

Fiona had gone to take Jessie for a toilet break, as she put it, while Harley and Henry were poised over a chessboard, with Mercedes coaching her granddad on his moves. They were chortling and joking together, and Nora could hardly believe her eyes. Until, that is, she noted the now-empty wine bottle on the table, and the ruddy glow on Henry's face. *Just think*, Nora mused, *all it took was a few glasses of wine over dinner to break down all the resentment and distrust that had kept them apart.* Peter gave her a wink, as he quietly opened another bottle and poured some into his father's glass.

And then Fiona struggled through the door with Jessie in her arms. 'That old blue dog kept following us around. I thought he was going to attack her.' *Hmm. I wonder,* thought Henry, but he said nothing.

*   *   *

As another glorious dawn started to filter in through the kitchen window, it found Henry and Nora enjoying their normal early morning cuppa and discussing the previous night. Henry seemed a bit subdued for some reason and had even put an extra spoon of sugar in his mug to build his energy up a bit.

'I was so pleased to see you getting on well with the kids last night,' Nora offered. 'Peter and I had a good chat too. I think this visit may be a lot better for everyone.'

'Well, I'll let you know if that's right later on, but I'm doing my best. Matter of fact, I'd better go and kick young Harley out of bed. I'm taking him out for a bit of a surprise, and we need to make an early start.' With that, Henry drained his tea and went to wake Harley, being careful not to disturb his parents. 'Come on, Harley. Get your gear on, grab your binoculars, and get a bit of breakfast into you. I'm going to show you something special today.'

*   *   *

Henry and Harley chatted amicably as the old Toyota rattled and bumped over the rough track through the back paddock until it stopped at a gate in the boundary fence. 'Righto, young fella. Shake a leg. Let's through, and make sure you shut it properly. I don't want to have all the neighbour's cattle in my place.'

They drove on another mile or so until, emerging from the trees, they reached the edge of a huge body of water. 'There you are, Harley. This is what I wanted to show you. Some years ago, my neighbour built this irrigation dam, and since then waterbirds have found it and made it their home. Get your glasses out and see what you can find.'

Harley was beside himself with excitement. 'This is terrific, Granddad!' he exclaimed. 'They're everywhere! I'll call out what I see and you write them down for me, please. Boy, won't Dad be jealous when I show him our list! And we won't tell him where it is, will we?'

They spent two hours, sighting, recording, and moving to new sites. They found fifteen different species of waterbirds alone. Pelicans, heads under water and tails in the air, fished the shallows. Blue cranes and spoonbills stalked around the edges, prodding the mud in search of crustaceans, closely followed by magpie stilts looking for leftovers. Flocks of ducks glided in to land amongst all the activity, while cormorants sat drying their wings in trees long ago killed by the rising water levels.

But it was the black swans that most fascinated Harley. Their large nests made from reeds and grass sat virtually on top of the water, with mother perched precariously on top of them. Cygnets that had already hatched scurried between them watched over by their graceful parents.

Binoculars swinging from target to target, Harley was thrilled to bits, calling out species and hassling Henry to keep up with his recording. 'This is far and away the best place I've ever been, Granddad,' he enthused. 'Do you think I could come back on the holidays?' And Henry smiled slyly to himself as he wrote. *You just had to hit the right spot,* he decided. *He might make a man out of this young fellow after all.*

'Come on, mate. We'd better head home, and I know where there's an emu's nest along the way. Did you know that the male emu hatches the eggs and then looks after the chicks till they leave home?'

'Much like humans in some cases,' mused Harley, still concentrating on the swans. *Probably speaking from experience, poor little bugger,* thought Henry.

*   *   *

Back at the homestead, Nora was up to her elbows in flour when Mercedes wandered into the kitchen. 'Hello, Grandma. What are you up to?' she asked, sidling up to look into the big mixing bowl.

'Good morning, dear. I'm making a batch of scones for morning tea. Do you want to help me?'

'I wouldn't know what to do, Grandma. I've never seen anyone make scones before. We buy ours at the bakery,' she said as she hoisted herself up on to a high stool from where she could watch.

'Well, that wouldn't be much good out here.' Nora chuckled. 'Our nearest bakery is about two hours' drive away. They'd be stale by the time we got home. Just watch while I mix the dough and then you can cut out the scones and help me put them in the oven.'

While the scones were cooking, Nora thought to herself, *I'm on a winner here. The poor little thing loves cooking, and has obviously never had a chance to do any at home. Maybe this is the missing connection I have been searching for.*

'How would you like to make some pancakes for Mum and Dad's breakfast all on your own?' she asked. They set to with gusto, and when Peter and Fiona eventually emerged, they sat down to a pile of pancakes and maple syrup, complements of their very proud daughter and a smugly contented grandma.

*   *   *

Nora introduced Mercedes to another new experience, wiping the dishes. Henry and Harley arrived back in time to polish off the last of the pancakes, while Peter prepared to pack the car for their visit to his sister and her family, and Fiona took Jessie for her morning toilet break.

The old cattle dog met them at the steps and followed them at a distance, carefully inspecting each of their stopping places. This activity was starting to upset Fiona, who kept trying to shoo him away, especially as Jessie seemed to be coming increasingly attracted by him. She strained at her leash, to no effect, while he merely kept following, sniffing, and gazing after the pretty little poodle as she was whisked back inside. He took a final whiff and padded off back to his tank stand. *Hmm,* he thought once again, *very interesting. Nearly there.*

*   *   *

Henry was out and about the next morning before sunup. Rounding the corner of the house on his way to the shed, in the gloom, he came upon a scene that at first amused and then scared the daylights out of him. His old dog and Jessie were locked in what could only be described as a loving embrace. He was going for his life, with a grin from ear to ear, and Jessie seemed to be enjoying herself too. *Fiona would have a fit, and undo all the good that had come about yesterday.* He couldn't let that happen.

Creeping along the side of the house, he found the cause of the problem. Obviously feeling the heat last night, Peter must have opened the bedroom window a bit, not much mind, but enough for a pretty little poodle to squeeze through if driven by lustful urges. When he returned to the scene of the crime, the old dog was already heading back to his bed, while Jessie whimpered at his feet, as if to say, 'I'm sorry. I just couldn't help myself', which of course was correct. The law of nature rules. Exactly what the old dog thought as he drifted off into an exhausted sleep.

Henry scooped Jessie up, carried her back to the window, and pushed her through. Then he silently lowered the old sash window to the sill, removing any evidence of her escape. 'Good luck, Jessie,' he whispered to himself. 'You're going to need it in a few weeks' time when Fiona takes you to the vet to find out why you're putting on so much weight.' He knew neither of the culprits could tell anyone what had happened, and he was bloody sure he wasn't going to. Not even to Nora.

*   *   *

Together they waved as the car with its five passengers drove away from the house. They both heaved sighs of relief and headed inside to have a cup of tea to ease their taut nerves. All in all, though, it had been a very successful weekend. They had built bridges to their grandkids and repaired the strained relationship, which had developed with their son over recent years. As for Fiona, well, while Nora held hopes that she might be coming around too, Henry knew that might change in a few weeks.

As for the old dog, well, he watched the departing car from his spot below the tank. *Hmm*, he thought, *sometimes daydreams do come true. Very exciting*. And then, exhausted by his nocturnal activities, he drifted back to sleep.

'Fiona's Surprise' explained

In some ways, old Henry Roberts was actually looking forward to Fiona's visit. That was before he and Nora decided to try one last time to reach out to their estranged family. Now he had to put out of his mind the idea of having a shot at his daughter-in-law's personal pride by suggesting she should try a new diet he could recommend.

A mate of his had recently sent him a poem involving an impressionable blonde, much like Fiona, he thought. It even featured a French poodle like Jessie. Anyway, the decision to improve family relationships had put paid to that, and they had built some bridges that were well worth the effort.

Maybe they wouldn't be so great when Jessie produced a heap of fluffy little blue pups, but that would be a battle for another day.

Hmm. Interesting.

DOGGY DIET

Around the fire the crowd all stood, enjoying a beer or two.
A lump of steak, two bits of bread, it's a joyful thing to do.
The stories flow, as the night wears on, getting taller and taller.
As the pile of empties grows in size, and
the Esky stocks get smaller.

'You've lost a lot of weight,' she said. 'So what's your secret diet?
I want to lose a pound or two. If it sounds okay, I'll try it.'
With long blonde hair, and big blue eyes, innocent as they come.
As we all know, those features show, a sheila who is dumb.

'You may not like it,' I started out, 'but it sure does do the job,
And the beauty is it's really cheap. It works. You'll save a bob.'
The big blue eyes, they opened wide, and she gave a trusting look.
'Oh, tell me please,' she begged of me. I had her on the hook.

'The answer, it is simple. Take notes. I'll tell you how.
Just go on down to the rural store, and buy a bag of chow.
Don't look like that. It may sound bad, but it's really very tasty.
Have a try, before you buy. Don't make a plan that's hasty.

To make it work, eat nothing else, just dog chow, day by day.
Carry some where'er you go. That's the easy way.
Each morning, fill your pockets, with enough to last till night,
And whenever you feel hungry, just have another bite.'

'I must confess,' I added, 'that I ended up in strife.
Although I lost a lot of weight, it nearly cost my life.
I ended up in hospital, on life support, they tell me,
But time heals all. I'm fit again, and slim, as you can see.'

'I thought as much,' the blonde said. 'It's poisoned you for sure.
Humans can't eat dog food. It simply isn't pure.'
'Not right!' I shouted. 'It's packed with all things good.
If I thought it would poison me, do you really think I would?

I lost the weight, and my health improved.
My hair turned black and glossy,
But I roam at night, I bark a lot, and my
nature's turned quite bossy.
My new friends are all canines, and I've started chasing bitches.
That's what put me into bed, with broken bones and stitches.

She was a sexy little poodle, with pink ribbons in her hair.
We were the very best of friends. I loved
her, and chased her everywhere.
She ran in front of a great big truck. I didn't hear it come,
'Cos I had stopped, and shut my eyes,
as I stooped to sniff her bum.'

I'd gone too far, I know it. The blonde had seen right through me.
It looked as if she wasn't dumb. She'd caught on I could see.
Until she said, for all to hear, 'You lie! Your little girlie
Could not have ribbons in her hair, *cos it would be too curly!*

FOR OLD TIMES' SAKE

Jock McLean was going back to school. The thought amused him slightly as he drove his hire car away from the airport and headed along unfamiliar roads in the direction of his old boarding school at East Brisbane. New six-lane highways now traversed what had been barren industrial areas when he first flew into Brisbane to commence his higher education fifty years earlier. Gone also was the dusty, undeveloped town of the 1950s, replaced by blocks of high-rise offices and apartments as far as the eye could see. He marvelled at the transformation as he climbed the imposing arch of the Gateway Bridge and stole a sideways look across the city to Mount Coot-tha in the west, and to the islands of Moreton Bay to the east, while ahead of him stretched uninterrupted development rolling away to meet up with the Gold Coast beaches.

It felt strange, coming to the school from the east, rather than the old familiar route along the tramlines on Shafston Avenue. How many times during the four years of his 'incarceration' had he travelled to and from the city on those old rattlers, swept away by progress some forty years ago? And now, as he approached the main entrance, he could scarcely believe he had come to the right address. Towering brick and tile edifices had replaced the old weatherboard and iron-roofed buildings of his day, and most of his memories of the past had been obliterated, lost forever in the march to modernity.

As a boy in his early teens, Jock had been equally gobsmacked at what to him was a bustling metropolis, so far removed from his former life in the bush, that he wondered if he could ever adjust to the changed lifestyle presented by a boarding school with hundreds of students. All of his life had been spent on his family's sprawling cattle property in central Queensland, punctuated only by the very occasional holiday on the coast. From the quiet and rustic seclusion of a home education with his younger siblings, to be thrust into sharing his life with dozens of strangers in an alien environment a thousand miles from home was to test his mettle and adaptability for some time. In retrospect, he sometimes wondered just how different his life would have been had he not been forced against his wishes to gain the broader perspective on life that his boarding experience had given him.

Given a say in the matter, Jock would never have thought of going on to secondary education, let alone in a boarding school so far from home. He had always been a typical country kid, relishing the solitude and wonderful lifestyle that life on a cattle property provided for a young fellow, and would have been perfectly happy to join the mustering camps as soon as legally able to do so. However, his father had attended this school in the 1930s and was determined his sons would follow in his footsteps. So he had and, after a difficult settling in period, enjoyed a reasonably happy time at school.

That was, as Jock now recalled, until he was sent home in disgrace and expelled from the school, just weeks before he was due to sit his final exams. Just as his experiences over the next fifty years were to prove, life is not always fair and just. Perhaps if he had been intent on going to university, he would have been more upset, but, truth be told, he had no higher ambition than to return to the property, so he simply found himself mustering a couple of months earlier than planned.

These thoughts ran through his head as he sat looking out over the grounds. He hadn't really thought about these things for ages, and had not retained much interest in the school for obvious reasons. His life, while probably rather mundane, had nevertheless been a happy one, married to Sally with three grown-up sons and now a tribe of grandkids. As his brother had never been interested in working on the land, and following his father's untimely death in his fifties, Jock had assumed ownership and control of the business. His main concern now was to work out a transition to the next generation.

All of these thoughts welled up in his mind as he slowly cruised out of the school precincts. Tomorrow, he would be meeting up with many of those classmates, most of whom he had not seen for fifty years. He now started to ponder what had become of them over that time. No doubt some would have died, some he knew had enjoyed great success in sport and business, and at least one, justifiably, was in jail. Then it hit him. *What had become of the girl involved in that incident? Anna!* While he would never forget her, he hadn't thought about her for years.

He and Anna had become the closest of friends over the last two years he was at school. Standards of those times, plus Anna's strict Greek upbringing, meant their relationship remained platonic, but they enjoyed a deep and abiding friendship, which, in other circumstances, would have blossomed into full-blown love. The sexual attack, and his subsequent expulsion, meant this was not to be, and he had never seen her again. He had got on with life, and he fervently hoped she had too.

Recalling his friendship with Anna brought back memories of their times together. Two years after he had come to Brisbane, Anna's family had bought the cafe near the school tram stop, and renamed it 'The Athenian' after the birthplace of her father, Con Pippos. Jock still remembered the first time he saw Anna when he called in for a milkshake on the way home from sport. Her glossy black hair, sparkling brown eyes, and flashing smile made left him weak in the knees. A smile crossed his face as he thought of all the reasons he had manufactured over the following days to go to the tram stop and to visit 'The Athenian.'

To the consternation of Anna's father, Jock had not been the only schoolboy to appreciate her obvious charms, but he was the only one who turned fascination into friendship. As the months rolled on, they became great friends, and to a limited degree Jock was accepted into the family. But there was always an element of wariness, particularly with Con. He became increasingly concerned that if the friendship turned to romance, his plans for a traditional wedding for Anna to a 'good Greek boy' might not eventuate. And then it happened.

Frustrated at being continually spurned by Anna in favour of 'that oaf from the bush', as he often referred to Jock, Alec Jackson, the school captain, had taken an unusual opportunity when it presented itself and tried to molest Anna as she walked her dog in the neighbouring park. Unluckily for him, Jock had arranged to meet her in the park and arrived just in time to save her. In a frenzied reprisal, he gave him a hiding in excess of what might have been called justifiable, landing the molester in hospital for several days. Even after all those years, the recollection of that day gave Jock a sense of exhilaration that he had not felt for decades.

Unfortunately for Jock, Jackson enjoyed the benefits of coming from an old school family, his father being a member of the Board of Governors. His word was accepted over that of the little Greek cafe worker, and Jock, rather than being hailed a hero, found himself in danger of being charged with grievous bodily harm. Only his expulsion from the school saved him from further action. Perhaps it was true justice that Alec Jackson was now serving time for fraud. One lie too many, it seems.

As he drove towards the city, he came to the spot where the tram stop had been and paused for a moment to absorb the memories of the place. He still had visions of hoards of schoolboys clambering aboard, much to the consternation of the other travellers, or most of them, anyway. *The girls from the convent up the road didn't seem to mind*, he recalled with a smile. Then his gaze sought the site of his old haunt, 'The Athenian.' He was amazed. It was still there, still a cafe, and still proudly displaying its Greek name.

Nostalgia was on top of Jock's mind this weekend, so he couldn't resist the temptation to park the car and go for a look inside the cafe, maybe even have a milkshake for old times' sake. Nothing much had changed. Sure, a hotbox full of the usual fried foods now fronted the shop, and an espresso coffee machine shared the back bench with the milkshake maker, but the same booths still lined the side wall, and ceiling fans slowly stirred the humid air. What circumstances could possibly have allowed this relic from so long ago to have survived the changes that had overtaken everything else?

Even the girl who served him jolted his memories. Although not as pretty as Anna had been, she was obviously of Greek extraction, probably related to the current owners, and therefore explaining why nothing much had changed, including the name. Silently sipping his milkshake in one of the wooden-seated booths, Jock closed his eyes and evoked pictures of those happy times when he was almost part of the furniture. He could see Anna's brilliant smile, hear her mother's broken English as she busied herself in the kitchen, and picture her father toasting every special family occasion with ouzo.

He was wakened from his reverie by a woman's voice calling to the girl from the kitchen, followed by the slap of the swinging door as she came into the shop. Jock's senses raced. She was the image of Anna's mother from all those years ago, perhaps a bit slimmer, but with the same hair and posture. And then she smiled in his direction, and he knew.

*   *   *

'Anna?' the name fell from his mouth as he rose to his feet and moved towards her. 'Pardon my asking, but is your name, or probably, was your name Anna Pippos?'

A frown of non-recognition crossed her face, but good manners replaced it with a timid smile as she replied, 'Well, yes. That was my maiden name, but I'm afraid I have to ask who wants to know?'

'Look again, Anna. It's me. Jock.'

Her jaw dropped, and remembrance coupled with shock passed across her face. She came from behind the counter, and they stood in the middle of the room, appraising each other in silence for a few seconds before they hugged and then pulled apart. Neither was quite sure what to do or say next. Jock broke the awkward silence by saying, 'Anna, you haven't changed a bit. I'd have known you anywhere, but I must admit seeing you in the cafe helped a bit.'

'I can't believe this,' she replied. 'After all those years. And you look so good too, so tall and suntanned. Maybe it's being out of your school uniform that does it for you.' She stepped back to appraise him more fully. 'We really must sit down and catch up. What are you doing here? How long can you stay? Who told you I was still here?' she gushed.

'Hey, steady on there. One question at a time.' Jock smiled. 'Come and join me in a milkshake, or maybe a coffee would be better.' And he led her back to the booth.

Anna took the seat opposite him and sat gazing at the handsome man who was smiling broadly at her obvious shock at seeing him. With thumb and forefinger, Jock pretended to raise a cup to his lips.

'Oh sorry! I'm so rude. Maria, would you bring two coffees, please? And meet an old friend of mine. Maria is my niece, Jock, Tony's eldest. You remember Tony, don't you?'

'Anna, I remember everything about you and your family. I will never forget the kindness you all showed me, and the very special friendship we had either.' The memory of their times chatting and laughing together as teenagers were still vivid in his mind, and he found himself wondering if her recollections were as happy as his. Perhaps she had forgotten about him long ago, and his presence here today was embarrassing her, but he had to know.

'Many times throughout my life I have wondered what happened to you and what might have been, had circumstances not forced us apart so abruptly. It took me a long time to get over what happened back then, and to accept the fact that you and I were destined to go our separate ways. I know we were young, but we had something special going for us before I was unceremoniously sent back to the bush.'

'I'm so sorry, Jock,' Anna said, taking his hand in hers. 'It was my fault that you were sent home. My parents were so thankful for what you did for me, and so frustrated that they could do nothing to save you.' She noticed the dark look that swept briefly across his face, but he lowered his gaze, so she went on, 'I wish I could have kept in touch, but they decided to send me back to the family in Greece to recover from my ordeal. By the time I came back, I was married to one of Dad's "good Greek boys".' They both smiled derisively at the memory of Anna's father and his desire for a big Greek wedding. 'Nick and I took over the cafe when Dad died. I've run it alone since he died five years ago. What about you? Did you marry?'

Jock forced his mind back to the present. 'Sure did, although it took a while. Potential brides are a bit thin on the ground where I come from, and none of them reminded me of you, but I eventually married a governess called Sally. We have three grown-up kids who have all made lives for themselves away from the property.' Was that disappointment he saw in her eyes at the word 'have'? 'We live in the same house I was reared in. I suppose life has been pretty good to me on the whole.'

Two more cups of coffee and a plate of Greek cakes later, Jock suddenly realised he would have to leave for his reunion dinner, but neither of them could resist the chance to meet up again the next day for another trip down memory lane. Anna wanted to show Jock the sights of the city, and he was just enjoying her company so much that the years of their being apart seemed to melt away.

*   *   *

They spent the day touring the city, Jock marvelling at what progress had done to the Brisbane of his memories. The shipyards he had rowed past were now covered in high-rise unit blocks, and pedestrians swarmed all over Queen Street, where trams and trolley buses had once disgorged him and his mates as they enjoyed their infrequent trips to the picture theatres. By the time they finished dinner at a top hotel, they had rekindled their teenage friendship to the point that both of them hated the thought of Jock's intended departure the next day.

They sat together in the car in font of the cafe. 'Maria, I can't tell you how much I've enjoyed seeing you again. It feels like we've never been apart.' She stared at her hands folded in her lap, and he thought, *How sad she looks!* 'What's wrong? You seem upset.'

She turned to face him, and he saw more clearly the look of abject disappointment on her face. 'I haven't had so much fun for years, Jock. It brought back so many fond memories of our friendship when we were kids. Thank you so much.' She turned her gaze back to her lap, but not before he saw tears well into her eyes.

Jock took her hands in his and pulled them to his chest, forcing her to bring her gaze to his face. 'There's something else, isn't there? What is it?'

Fighting to control her emotions, she whispered, 'Jock, you're married.'

The depth of her feelings for him hit him like a sledgehammer. Their one day together had rekindled all of the passion from fifty years ago. He too had been aware of their attraction but had restrained himself for the very reason she had raised. She was right. Sally and his whole life were waiting for him back out west.

'I know,' he replied softly. 'I wish it could be otherwise, but it can't. We each have our own families to consider. Maybe fate has played a cruel trick on us. Although we have enjoyed this reunion, perhaps we would be better off if it had never happened.'

'Don't say that, Jock. We both know we can't return to the past, and nothing can come of our little sojourn together. We've had fun, and now we must let go once again. I wish we could have a bit more time, though.'

'Well, unfortunately, I have to leave tomorrow, Anna, but let's keep in touch by phone, eh?' Jock suggested.

Anna picked up her bag and opened the door. 'Under the circumstances, I don't think that would be a good idea, Jock. I should be going now. Some of us have to work tomorrow.' It was a weak attempt to lighten the atmosphere, but he saw tears again glistening in her eyes as she gave him a peck on the cheek and fled inside.

*   *   *

He spent a sleepless night. No matter how hard he tried to drag his thoughts back to Sally and the property, they kept straying to the wonderful woman his sweet young Anna had become. They had so much in common and were so relaxed in each other's company, and he dreaded the thought that he would have to leave her behind yet again. He was proud of the fact that he had always put his family first in every thing he did. He knew they all loved him, but they had all left home except Sally, and even she now spent most of her time pursuing her latest hobby of painting. Just last year, she and a female friend had toured the galleries of Europe for two months, leaving him at home with just the stockmen for company. By morning, he had made a decision, booked out of his hotel, and rushed back to the cafe.

Anna had also been reviewing her situation, realising that her life would not be the same again following their brief time together over the last couple of days. Nick's untimely death had left her lonely and depressed, and the seven-day grind in the cafe was starting to wear her down. The last couple of days with Jock had lifted her spirits for the first time in years, yet she knew he would have to return to his family. For the second time in her life, having found the man she could really love, she would have to let him go.

As she struggled to keep her mind on the job that morning, Jock burst through the swinging door to the kitchen. His face showed the tension he felt.

'Anna, we have to talk,' he blurted out, 'but not here. Let's go for a walk in the park.' They could hardly control their emotions in the crowded shop, so they said nothing until they had crossed the road and entered the park. This was something that Anna had not been able to do since she had been attacked there, but Jock's strong presence made her feel safer than she had ever been as they walked hand in hand to the seat by the riverbank where Jock put his idea to her.

'Anna, meeting you again is the best thing that has happened to me for ages, and I don't want it to end. I don't know where this will lead, but I know I want to find out and not have us just walk out of each other's lives again. Maybe we will find that what we have found is nothing more than wishful thinking from the past, and we will be able to return to our normal lives as if we had never found each other again. But we have to find out, for old times' sake. I want you to come away with me for a few days where we can be alone together, away from families and business worries, so we can really get to know each other again.'

He waited to see her reaction, but all he saw was her mind racing to sort her thoughts, so he went on, 'I'm due to fly to Rockhampton today to attend the bull sales, as you know. Come with me, Anna, and we can head off to an island where no one will know us. Let's just spend a few days enjoying ourselves. I guarantee to bring you back safe and sound by Friday. Our families will never need to know. Just for old times' sake. What do you say?'

Confused thoughts raced wildly through Anna's mind. Jock's reappearance out of the blue had rattled her and tipped the quiet and boring life into which she had slipped since Nick's death on its head. She had barely thought about where her future might lay, much less about any member of the opposite sex. But it was her conservative upbringing that now made her apprehensive about his suggestion.

'Jock, that would be lovely. It really would, but my family would die of embarrassment, and even worse, you're still married. Are you prepared to risk everything for a few days that may only prove our chances as a couple died fifty years ago when we were driven apart?'

This very thought had occupied much of Jock's thinking through the night. Instinctively, he too had ruled out the idea as Sally and his family had always been his first consideration. If it meant risking all that he had worked for all his life, then, once again, he would probably walk away from Anna and head back to his life in the bush. But that decision may never need to be made, and for once in his life, he was determined to do something just for himself, for a change.

'You and I have given our lives to our families, Anna, families that would not have existed if we had stayed together back then. I think they owe us a favour, a chance to reminisce, and to enjoy each other's company one more time, and the good thing is, they need never know. We won't tell anyone where we're going. Come with me, Anna, for old times' sake.'

*   *   *

Monday, 6 October 2009
(a staff reporter)

PLANE CRASH KILLS TWELVE

Queensland's worst air disaster for twenty years claimed the lives of ten passengers and a crew of two when a small commuter plane crashed into the sea while trying to land on Hamilton Island yesterday. A freak gust of wind caused it to drop suddenly on its approach, and to nosedive into the sea. A spokesman for the airline said there was no way anyone could have survived the impact. All twelve bodies have been recovered and relatives have been notified.

*　　*　　*

Sally McLean was devastated. Even now, days after Jock had been buried in the family plot on the property, she still could not believe what had happened. As her family busied themselves in the house, she sat on the veranda, where she and Jock had shared so many hours, and stared unseeingly at the garden gate, still half-expecting him to come swinging through it with his dog at his heels.

What made it harder to accept was the fact that she couldn't understand at all what he had been doing on a plane flying to Hamilton Island. When he last called her from Brisbane, he was on his way to the bull sales in Rockhampton. *What on earth could have induced him to change his plans and go to Hamilton Island, of all places? He hated the sea!* All that their enquiries had turned up was that he had traded in his Rockhampton ticket for a return one to Hamilton Island. *Why was a complete mystery, and destined to stay so forever?*

Equally devastated was Anna's family who were also at a loss as to how she came to be on the plane, as they thought she was spending a few days at a health farm on the Sunshine Coast. They knew she had never really recovered from their father's death and had been a bit depressed of late, but they had absolutely no idea why she would have suddenly taken off for Hamilton Island without telling anyone. They tried to console themselves with the thought that perhaps she had decided to make a break from the past and start a new life for herself.

Neither family ever found out about the reunion of the 'Romeo and Juliet' duo of high school days. They had died holding hands on their way to re-explore their childhood friendship, 'for old times' sake'. After being separated by circumstances for fifty years, they had taken their final trip to eternity, together.

'For Old Times' Sake' explained

Ain't young love grand? No matter what experiences life throws at us later in life, we never forget those first nervous, tentative steps we took into puberty all those years ago when girls changed from being the enemy to the quarry, to be pursued with much planning and thought, but with very little success.

I write here of the decade of the 1950s, just before the flower power 1960s removed all of the innocence of youth forever. Young readers of today will probably not believe the timidity and caution with which young teenagers approached courtship. Locked up in single-sex boarding schools, interaction with the opposite sex was very restricted, and consisted of lots of letter writing and unfulfilled lecherous thoughts.

Surveys now indicate that today's kids are losing their innocence in such matters before they reach high school. Are they better off than we were? When you indulge in all the adult activities before you leave school, what's left to keep you excited for the next sixty or seventy years?

Anna and Jock were typical of the young people of the times. For whatever reason, most of those early romances never reached fruition, and everyone got on with their lives, but, given the right circumstances, would that puppy love still survive the ravages of time?

CHASING SHEILAS

As I sit here now aged sixty, cogitating on my past,
Drawing on those recollections of what pleasures were back then,
Trying hard to bring to memory all those joys that didn't last,
Like those passing young romances, all
the thrills come back again.

Now the middle 1950s were quite different from today.
Adolescence didn't start till you were fourteen years or so.
We were innocent and naive in a childish sort of way,
And the only word that mothers taught their girls to say was 'No'.

We were the human version of a kelpie chasing trucks.
If we ever got to catch one, then we'd know not what to do.
When it came to chasing sheilas, we all
showed great zeal and pluck,
But like a kelpie out at Boulia, our chances were but few.

Our only source of contact was by writing through the mail,
So instead of doing study, we wrote letters by the score.
We romanticised and plotted from within that rotten jail,
Of how we could meet up somewhere,
hold hands, and talk some more.

Now modern youths today just ask the sheilas, 'Do you do it?'
They don't have to plan and wonder if their chances are okay,

And if the answer's no, they just say, 'I always knew it,'
As they go in search of someone else who's more inclined to play.

But I think we were quite lucky as we put up with frustration,
Cos we still enjoyed the chase, our testosterone still flowed
To extend the expectation of that sensual sensation,
Till we were several years or so down lifetime's lengthy road.

Like that kelpie chasing truckies, the best part is in the chase.
When you catch one, expectation simply turns to pain and dust.
It's more fun if all those sheilas travel at a certain pace,
That ensures you never quite catch up to satisfy your lust.

FOUND

Andy Thompson never ceased to be amazed at the feelings of well-being and relaxation that hiking through the state forests gave him. For a bloke who had been born and bred in the city and had never really worked anywhere else in his life, he seemed to be inexorably drawn to the bush whenever his busy life allowed. His father had not been that way inclined, and it was not until he joined the scouts as a twelve-year-old that he had his first experience of camping and bushwalking, and from day one, he loved it.

He had encouraged his own kids to go with him when they were old enough, and while the girls found the whole idea too strenuous and boring, his son took to it like a duck to water. Now he was twenty and about to head overseas to do a postgraduate degree in his chosen career in environmental management. This would be their last time camping together for years, so it was with mixed feelings that they plodded along the rough tracks through the forests that covered the rolling hills and ranges in the Conondale National Park.

Today Andy headed off to skirt the western boundary of the Park where it abutted several privately owned cattle properties that had been settled in the previous century. He had been told of some spectacular views from the higher points, looking towards the faraway Great Dividing Range a hundred kilometres away. They pushed on doggedly into areas seldom visited by even the most intrepid bushwalkers.

They stopped for lunch and a cup of tea under the overhanging branches of an old box tree. As he gathered up some twigs for a fire, Andy stumbled over an unusual boulder – unusual not only in shape, but also by its very presence – there on a sandstone ridge. He brushed the leaves and rubbish off it and was amazed to see that it was actually some sort of marker with writing etched into its rough surface. After giving it a quick clean with a bit of their precious water, he was able to make out the inscription.

Ken Patterson
1918–1938
Loved Erin

Although he could not be sure after the passage of almost seventy years of time, Andy didn't think it looked like a gravestone, situated as it was amongst the roots of the old tree. *More like some sort of memorial stone*, he figured. But what it was doing out in this rugged area of native forest, he had no idea.

'Hey, Jock,' he called to his son. 'Take a look at this.'

Together they examined the stone, searching for a clue as to what it might signify or why it was there. Nothing came to mind, other than the obvious fact that it was some sort of memorial to a young man who died at the age of twenty, the same age as Jock, and the more obtuse fact that he loved Erin, the ancient name of Ireland. What a puzzle! Father and son discussed the find over their break.

'I know it was common practice to bury people where they died in those days,' Andy remarked, 'but I just don't think this stone marks a gravesite. What do you reckon?'

'No, I tend to agree, Dad. Not so close to a tree that must have still been big, even back then. It just doesn't make sense, but I guess we'll never know.'

'Well, that may be so, but I'll tell you what. I'm going to do my best to find out. I have no idea how to go about it, or even why I want to, but I'm going to give it a go. I wonder where I should start.'

Jock squatted at the stone, scratching the moss and dust from the letters with the point of his pocketknife. 'Well, if we're right in assuming this isn't a grave, he must be buried somewhere else, probably not too far away. I'd try the local cemeteries first, and there's always the Register of Births, Deaths and Marriages. Good luck, but after all this time, I don't like your chances.'

*   *   *

The following weekend saw Andy scouring the headstones in the nearest cemetery, and it didn't take him too long to find what he was seeking – a simple headstone on an old decrepit grave, with an inscription that told him little more than he already knew.

Here Lies
Kenneth William Patterson
Born 10.8.1918 Died 16.10.1938
Accidentally killed

Andy spent some time looking for further clues amongst the other graves, but without success. *Ken seemed to be the only Patterson in the place, so he was obviously not part of one of the local pioneering families. He must have been an itinerant worker or visitor to the district, so where to from here? Because he died as the result of an accident, maybe it would have been reported in the press. My next visit on Monday would be to the archives of the old Brisbane Courier of 17 October 1938.* His luck was in again.

Brisbane Courier
17 October 1938

A young stockman was killed yesterday when his horse bolted into scrub on the property where he worked. The manager of Yednia Station said it appeared that the rider was wiped out by a low-hanging limb and suffered a fractured skull. His name is being withheld while an attempt is made to locate relatives.

Andy was familiar with the name of Yednia Station. It still existed, and he passed the entrance to it on the way to all his favourite hiking haunts. A phone call to the current owners revealed that they had only owned the place for about twenty years, and were not aware of the story of the tragedy that had occurred nearby seventy years ago. Fortunately, one of the owners, a Mrs Saunders, was a bit of a history buff, and she promised to see what she could do to help Andy in his quest to find out the full story of Ken Patterson and the stone at the foot of the tree.

She rang him back a few days later.

'Hello, Andy. It's Mary Saunders from Yednia.'

'G'day, Mary. Thanks for calling back. Have you come up with anything yet?' he asked.

'Well, as a matter of fact, I have. I found an old local man whose father worked on Yednia in the 1030s, and he is familiar with the event. He told me a bit on the phone, but I suggest you and I should sit down with him sometime, and even take him up to see the stone you found. He was not aware of it, but he does seem to know a lot about what happened. Can you come for lunch next Saturday?'

'I'd love to, and could take you both to the site. This is exciting, Mary. He just might have all the answers we're looking for.'

*   *   *

Toby Tomkins proved to be a frail old fellow, who declined the offer of a trip to the mountains but was more than happy to tell all he could remember of the death of Ken Patterson. Mary and her guests sat sipping a beer on the veranda of the old homestead as Toby related the story of the accidental death of the young stockman. It went like this:

'Back in them days, this was a big station, with five thousand heads of cattle and about ten or a dozen stockmen and rouseabouts. It wasn't fenced like it is today, so most of that national park up there in the mountains was part of it. It was a rough country to manage, and the blokes who worked it were pretty rough too. Above all, they had to be great horsemen, able to break in and ride the brumbies that bred in the ranges. They didn't have much to be proud of, other than their horsemanship, and they continually challenged each other to prove who was best.'

'Well, I don't know much about horses, Toby, but I've spent a fair bit of time walking up there. It's pretty a rough country, all right,' Andy interrupted.

'Yair. You're not wrong there, mate,' Toby continued. 'Anyway, into this group one day came a young bloke looking for a job. He worked hard and kept up with the others most of the time but was not as gung-ho when it came to showing off in the rodeo ring. They were constantly taunting him with the latest mongrel horse, but as the months rolled on he never rose to the bait.' He paused to wet his throat. 'There was another thing that set him apart from the rest. That was the relationship that developed between him and the pretty young Irish governess in the homestead. Her name was Erin O'Keefe.'

'Aha!' Andy interrupted again, 'that explains the word *Erin* on the stone. It doesn't refer to Ireland but to Erin the sweetheart. I wonder what happened to her. Anyway, sorry for the interruption, Toby.'

'Yair, well, the story is that they were going to get married, but then the accident happened. All the ribbing eventually got to young Ken, and he felt he had to prove himself as a man before he could marry Erin. Against his better judgement, he agreed to prove his manhood by riding the worst rogue horse on the place, a terrible old mongrel called Gundagai.'

'Another beer, Toby?' Mary asked him.

'Thanks. Another slice of that cake would be nice too. Not used to home cooking these days. Anyway, Erin was beside herself with fear, but knew she dared not try to stop him. She wished him well and said a few Hail Marys and he mounted the snorting, rooting old brumby being held by the other stockmen. When they let him go, he took off for the hills where he had been born. Perhaps his worst fault was he was hard-mouthed. When he got the bit between his teeth, no rider was strong enough to pull him up. Nothing was going to stop him reaching the safety of the scrub, so Ken had no option but to hold on and hope exhaustion would wear him down eventually.'

Andy was rapt and hanging on his every word. Mary returned with the beer and cake.

'As time passed, the jokers back at the yards started to worry that their prank had gone wrong. It was starting to get dark, and there was no sign of Ken or the horse. But if Ken had come off, there was no chance the old nag would come back to the homestead. Anyway, there was nothing they could do now. They would have to wait till daylight to mount a search. Unless, of course, Ken walked back during the night, which was what usually happened.

'My dad told me that when he went for tea, he saw Erin kneeling in the dust at the stockyards, and he reckoned he could hear her sobbing from fifty yards away. He never forgot it and never forgave himself for the part he had played in goading young Ken to take that ride.'

Andy and Mary could sense from the emotion in Toby's voice that his father must have somehow passed on the deep feelings of guilt he had to his son when he told him the story years later. 'I'm sure he had no idea what might happen, Toby,' Mary said. 'These things occur in life, and we can't go on blaming ourselves, and even less, to pass it on to the next generation. Have another beer, Toby, and tell us about the stone.'

'Well, actually, Dad never mentioned anything about a stone to me. Maybe he never knew about it. But he did tell me that, sometime during the night, Erin saddled up her own horse and headed off in the direction the bolting horse had gone. No one ever found out how she knew where to go, but somehow she found Ken out in the bush and managed to bring his body back home on her horse. Just as dawn broke and the boys were about to set off on the search, Erin came walking across the paddock, leading her horse, with tears making tracks down her dusty cheeks. The memory of it haunted Dad for the rest of his life.'

The three of them sat for a while, transfixed by the mental picture each of them conjured up of the devastated young girl and her dead lover. While the mystery of the stone remained unsolved, they realised that Toby had told them all he knew of the Ken Patterson story. Obviously the station owners had seen to his funeral at the local cemetery. Toby's father thought Erin would have moved on soon after, and no one had ever heard of her again.

*　　*　　*

Andy had run into another dead end. He suspected that only one person could enlighten him about the stone in the bush. Probably she was dead by now, and, even if she was still alive, all he had to go on in searching for her was the name Erin O'Brien, probably changed by marriage over the years. It looked as if his search for the last bit of the story would remain a mystery.

As the months passed, Andy had forgotten about his quest, as other events closer to home took over. Sadly, his grandmother was dying, and, as her husband had passed away some years before, his mother would soon be orphaned. One day, as the end grew near, the old lady called Andy's mother to her bedside. Invigorated by a larger shot of morphine than usual, she took Kelly's hand in hers, and with tears in her rheumy old eyes, she told her a secret that she had never suspected.

'Kelly, dear, there's something I must do before I die. No, don't try to humour me. I know I haven't much time left,' she said, alarmed at the grief on her daughter's face. 'I know this will come as a shock to you, and I'm terribly sorry that I haven't told you before, but the fact is, dear, Dad and I adopted you when you were a baby.'

Kelly was absolutely shattered by the news, particularly the fact that she hadn't been told until she was more than sixty years old. But she had enjoyed a happy life with her adoptive parents and managed to avoid showing her disappointment to her mother. She assured the old lady of her love and that the news of her adoption made no difference to their relationship. She died in peace, happy to have at least tried to right the wrong that had worried her for years.

Kelly was intrigued by the fact that she had absolutely no idea where she had come from before her adoption. Her parents were told nothing of her birth or mother's name, other than the date, 12 May 1939. That was how it was done in those days, and she now assumed she would have no chance of tracing her history. Her family was all aware of her predicament and decided to see if they could help. Jock was a whiz on the Internet, and Andy had contacts in government departments, so between them, they set out to see if they could trace her birth mother.

When the letter from the Children's Services Department arrived on Andy's desk, he couldn't believe what he read. He was not a great believer in coincidence or in spirituality, but the information he now contemplated just blew his mind. Had some inner sense caused him to embark on this search when he stumbled over that stone in the bush? Surely not, but what other explanation was there for that feeling of compelling interest that struck him as he contemplated the life and death of Ken Patterson? He read the details from the letter again.

> Born to Erin Anne O'Keefe and Kenneth
> Patterson, a daughter on 12 May 1939.

> Adopted by Mrs and Mr Barlow on 20 May
> 1939 and christened Kelly Leanne Barlow.

Ken Patterson and Erin O'Keefe were his mother's natural parents and his grandparents! *What would Kelly think of this development? She had always been a bit circumspect about the search since her adoptive mother's death and was still unsure if she would want to make contact in the unlikely event that could ever locate her birth parents. Now, with this development, would it influence her to be more inclined to try to find Erin O'Keefe, if she was still alive?* He certainly knew it made him more interested than ever, but it would have to be his mother's decision. Besides, Erin was born eighty-six years ago and would more likely than not be dead by now.

Before he visited his mother on the way home from work, he thought he would try one long shot at finding out if Erin was still alive. And what a long shot it was! *If* she was alive, and *if* she still went under her maiden name of O'Keefe, and *if* she still lived locally, she just might be on the electoral role. But he had to admit that the chances of a young Irish girl staying unmarried in the 1940s or divorcing in later years were pretty slim, and he had no idea where to go from there.

Once again, Andy was shocked by the coincidence of it. Of course, it may not be their Erin O'Keefe, but there was a fair chance it was, because the one he found lived in a Catholic retirement village. Perhaps, before he told his mum, he would make one more phone call to the village. 'Yes,' the manager said. They did indeed have an Erin O'Keefe as a resident, an elderly lady who had been there for years. Other than that, she would divulge no other personal information.

Kelly was as shocked as he had been when he told her what he had found out. She was aware of his search for the story behind the Ken Patterson stone and could barely credit the turn of events that now connected their family to it. She was now just as keen as Andy to meet Erin, so they arranged to go together to the village, provided, of course, Erin was prepared to see them. Andy wrote a long letter to the matron and asked her to break the news to Erin. The response was immediate, and positive.

* * *

A few days later, Kelly held the frail little old woman in her arms for a long time, as they sobbed and whispered in each other's ears. Andy stood respectfully aside as the two women tried to make up for the sixty-seven years that circumstances had held them apart. Nothing could make up for those years of loss, but he was pleased to see that they both appreciated the chance to try. There could be no stronger bond than the one between mother and daughter, heightened in this case by the tragic circumstances that led to the separation. Finally, over a cup of tea, they heard the full story.

'Your grandfather, Ken, was the most marvellous man ever born. You would have been so proud of him if you'd known him. So level-headed for such a young man. He was also very good looking, much like you, Andy,' she said, with a twinkle in her eye. 'So different from all the other workers on the station and the only one I was ever attracted to.

'Of course, I was a simple, young, Irish girl of eighteen but knew straightaway that he was the man for me. We used to sneak out into the bush whenever we could to be alone together, and in spite of my catholic upbringing, nature took its course and we became lovers. We were only weeks away from leaving the station at Christmas to get married and make a future for ourselves somewhere else.'

Tears glistened in her eyes at the memory. *If only we had left sooner, how different my life would have been!*

'I will never know how those other yokels talked him into riding that brumby. I have been haunted all my life by the thought that he did it for my pride rather than his. He didn't have to prove anything to me. I had a terrible premonition that it was going to end in disaster, and was not surprised when he didn't come back. Heart broken as I was, I just knew that I would find him if I looked, so I set off in the dark and something led me straight to where he lay. Of course, he was dead. We sat together for a while as I cried my heart out. Eventually, I managed to get his body on my horse and walked home.'

Erin was having trouble controlling her emotions. She took a couple of deep breaths, gently blew her nose, and sipped her tea while she composed herself.

'I'm so sorry, Erin. Bringing this up again must be very sad for you. Would you rather we stopped?' Kelly asked, but Erin shook her head and continued.

'No, I'm all right. The station owners arranged a funeral and headstone, but, of course, my name wasn't mentioned. I left and moved to town and then found out that I was pregnant. Kelly, I'm so sorry I put you up for adoption, but I had no option in those days, you see. No family, no money, and no support. I had to give you the chance to have a decent life, and I hope you did.'

Kelly moved to put her arm around the old lady and to reassure her that she understood. 'What you did was very brave, and you should have no regrets about it from my point of view. I had a very privileged life with my adoptive parents, not even aware that they were not my birth parents till recently when my mother died. It's you who suffered all these years, and I want you to know just how much I appreciate what you did for me. I want you to be part of our family now, and I want to call you 'Mum'.'

Tears of relief rolled down Erin's wrinkled old cheeks. She eventually composed herself and continued the story. 'I never did get over my romance with Ken and eventually entered the church where I have spent the rest of my life. Some years later, I had a simple commemorative stone made and set it at the base of the tree where Ken and I used to meet, and where you were conceived, by the way,' she said with a chuckle and gave Kelly a hug. 'Oh, and by the way, Andy, you should have scratched a bit harder on that stone. It actually reads '*loved* by *Erin.*'

'Well, I'll be blowed,' Andy responded. 'One day soon I'll take you there if you like, and you can show me.'

*　*　*

And so that's what happened. After a few months of getting to know her new extended family, Erin decided she was ready to visit the site of her romantic days with Ken. After putting flowers on his grave in the cemetery, Andy drove as close as he could to the old box tree, and he and Kelly pushed Erin the rest of the distance in a wheelchair. It was a long trek and it obviously tired her out. After scratching the stone a bit harder, Andy did indeed find a small 'by' etched in the surface, endowing the inscription with its full meaning.

Then, feeling that Erin would appreciate some time alone with her memories, Andy and Kelly headed off along the track to look at a rock formation Andy knew of, leaving Erin sitting on the ground, leaning against the tree, her hand caressing the stone, and a faraway look in her eyes.

And that's exactly how they found her when they returned twenty minutes later, hand draped over the stone. Kelly knelt beside her to gently wake her from her siesta but found to her horror that she was not asleep. She had passed away. A faint smile played on her lips, and she looked composed and happy. She had finally come back to her lover, and had nothing left to live for.

Their lives had come full circle. She was back with her Ken, and in the loving presence of their daughter conceived all those years ago on this very spot.

Here lies
Erin Anne O'Keefe
12.5.1939 to 20.10.2008
Loved by Ken
And their family

Kelly had been heartbroken at the loss of her mother, whom she had only known for such a short time. Due to yet another stroke of extraordinary luck she was able to purchase the plot in the cemetery next to the grave of her father and Erin who had been buried there with all of her new family in attendance. The mystery of the stone under the tree had been solved, and the long saga of Ken and Erin's lives had closed.

'Found' explained

This story is based on a poem my father wrote when he was a young man working on a cattle property in the mountains near Kilcoy in the 1930s. It was probably loosely based on the death of his friend and fellow stockman at the time when thrown from a horse.

While this is all fiction, dotted all over Australia are similar little headstones, indicating the last resting place of our pioneers who died in the bush and were buried where they fell. You come across them in all sorts of places, on roadsides and creek banks and scattered around the rural properties and national parks. In most cases, we will never know who they were, what they did, or how they died.

This is a yarn for all of them. Maybe they were drifters who had no family or friends and were given a decent burial by a compassionate stranger. But maybe, just maybe, they had an Erin waiting for them somewhere, heartbroken, mourning the loss of a lover. I just found this poem very moving.

HIS LAST RIDE

The young man entered the stockyard
with a grim-set smile on his face,
And balefully eyed the big roan horse as
it pawed up the dirt in the race.
The horse was already saddled, surcingle and girth done up tight,
But he lingered yet in the stockyard in the hope of catching a sight

Of the blue eyed girl, his only love, who
would come to bid him goodbye,
While the sun sank slowly westward, in the sullen summer sky.
And in his mind there lingered yet a day not long gone by,
When they said he was a coward if he didn't ride Gundagai.

Now Gundagai was an outlaw bred, a killer of the meanest sort.
To try to ride him was, all knew, a gamble
with quick death fraught.
He had promised her he would never ride a killer such as this,
But the jeers of the bush folk led him on,
and she gave her consent with a kiss.

All at once she was there beside him, fair features and golden hair,
Her pale face trembling with awful doubt,
midst the dust of the stockyard there.
But she knew, for him, 'twas the only
way his lost honour to redeem.

To have his name marked down in gold on
the scroll of the bushman's realm.

She spoke not, but her eyes said more than
ever her lips could have said.
'You know, Ken, life without you is not
worthwhile.' Then sadly she bent her head.
He stooped and kissed her gently. For an
instant, he paused and then
Climbed briskly up on to the race, as she
whispered, 'Goodbye, Ken.'

When all was set, he gave the word for the boys to open the gate.
Out of it bounded the big roan horse, a bundle of fury and hate.
He rooted and snorted and squealed, he
bucked and reared and shied,
And was lost to sight as he topped the hill,
as he made for the ranges wide.

The summer night came quickly on, and
the evening light grew dim,
As, kneeling there in the stockyard dust,
pale-faced, she prayed for him.
The stars shone out and he came not back,
so she went out for him to seek.
Her pale lips quivered with pain and fear,
while tears rolled down her cheeks.

She found him out there in the ranges, by
the aid of the stars and the moon.
Old Gundagai had another killed and
turned a woman's life to ruin.

Bill McAulay 15.10.1936
(Age 19)

Most of the poems he wrote at the time were very emotional and sad, expressing the lonely life he led, living on his own miles from civilisation. The loss of his mate by accident obviously affected him very deeply, as this little poem reveals.

THE RELIC

It hangs there unused, on a nail in the wall.
It had been abused, as I can recall.
Hanging there covered in cobwebs and dust,
Memory it stirs, of a man one could trust.

Still showing signs of the sweat from his brow,
And the faint hoof mark of an old bally cow.
It recalls busy scenes mid stockyard and dust,
And a friend who has gone where everyone must.

It's a link from the past, I cannot forget.
A link with a friend, the truest I've met.
As I enter the door, my eyes always fall,
On a battered old hat, hanging there on the wall.

Bill McAulay 15.3.1938

Okay. So I've got carried away reading some of my father's poems, but there is one more which has nothing to do with 'Found', but it blows my mind to think that a young bloke in his teens who left school at twelve to work on a farm could teach himself to write poetry like this. I'm sure he wouldn't have known what alliteration was, but he used it often, and his ability with words to create imagery and convey a picture is brilliant.

Incidentally, he went on to become chairman of the local Shire Council for twenty-five years and was awarded an OBE by the Queen for his service to the community.

Evening in the Bush

The fiery sun had set and all was quiet and still,
As slow and timid as a cat, the moon crept o'er the hill.
The evening breeze had murmured and whispered as it went,
And on its gentle passing, I caught its own sweet scent.

The hint of hidden flowers, heads bowed in peaceful sleep,
In some secluded secret place, where shadows softly creep.
The moon climbs slowly higher, while starlight twinkles out,
Like embers glowing in a fire. God's campsite, without doubt.

The huge trees gently swaying, before the evening breeze.
The possums all out playing, no more the hum of bees.
Afar a dingo howling and searching for its prey.
Upon the hill an owl hoots, then blinks and flies away.

The rung barked trees all standing, as if in silent prayer.
I watch a luckless moth land in the spider's cunning snare.
A horse bell gently tinkles, a cow lows for her calf.
The clouds roll in and wrap the moon in a silken scarf.

Dewdrops start to glisten, on leaves that quietly nod.
I sit here and I listen. I have had a glimpse of God.

Bill McAulay 5/5/38

HIJACKED

The Woolworths store manager usually made sure someone went with him when he took the day's takings to the bank, but today everyone was so busy he decided to go alone. It was against company policy, but in all the years he had been doing this job, he had never had any trouble. Why would today be different? He stacked the bags of cash in his briefcase and headed for the car park.

As he reached his car, he didn't notice the attractive young woman with a backpack walking towards him. Then, just as he blinked his door open, she tripped, spilling the contents of her shopping bag on to the road at his feet. She dropped to her knees, desperately trying to gather up oranges as they rolled towards the gutter and to return her other purchases to her bag.

'Here let me help you,' Gary offered, crouching down to pick up some of the items. He neither saw nor heard the man approach him from behind, before a savage blow to the back of his head sent him crashing to the ground.

'Forget the bloody oranges, babe. Just get in the car.' He picked up the dropped keys and briefcase, jumped behind the wheel, and they sped out into the traffic. A few blocks away, they parked at another shopping centre, transferred to a car stolen earlier, and headed out of Dubbo on the Newell Highway, heading north.

*　　*　　*

Two hours later at the Coonabarabran truck stop, Gary Johnson mopped up the last of his gravy with some bread, drained his coffee, and looked at his watch. He should be able to get through Narrabri before he put his head down for a few hours' compulsory break. That would land him back in Brisbane by daylight in time to drop the rig at the depot and get home before the kids left for school. He really missed his family on these long interstate trips.

These thoughts were still with him as he started to climb into his rig, when there was a call behind him.

'Excuse me.'

Turning and stepping back to the ground, he was confronted by a young woman wearing a backpack – a very attractive young woman, actually. He waited till she came over to him.

'Yair. Can I help you?' he offered.

She flashed him a hopeful smile. 'I'm sorry to worry you, but could you possibly give me a ride, if you're heading north, that is?'

'Well, I don't pick up hitch-hikers. It's against company policy, and the law, for that matter.' He saw a look of disappointment fall across her face. 'Where are you trying to get to?'

'Cairns eventually, but anywhere in between would be a start. Brisbane would be good. I won't be a nuisance.'

Gary was in two minds. He'd been in trouble once before for breaking company rules, but he had a long night-time drive ahead. A bit of company would relieve the boredom, and she seemed all right.

'Tell you what,' he said, 'I've got to pull up for a kip in a few hours, but I'll give you a ride until then. That should get you to Narrabri, or even Moree, if I'm feeling okay. How does that sound?'

'Terrific. Thanks very much. My name's Mandy,' she said, offering her hand.

'I'm Gary. I'll unlock your door,' he said as he climbed into the cab.

*　　*　　*

By the time they reached Narrabri an hour and a half later, Gary was enjoying her company so much that he was reluctant to drop her off just yet. But he was due for a rest break to comply with regulations.

'Listen, Mandy, I'm going to have to drop you off here, I'm afraid. I've got to get a few hours' sleep before I get to Moree, so I'll be pulling up at a rest area pretty soon.'

Her disappointment was evident. 'Oh, please let me stay, Gary. I'll curl up here on this big seat and have a nap too. I've enjoyed our chat so much, and you've still got such a long way to go. Please.'

He smiled at her girlish enthusiasm and in spite of his better judgement, drove on through town and pulled into the first rest area they came to.

Climbing into the sleeping compartment, Gary said, 'Just give me a couple of hours' kip and we'll go straight through to Brisbane. You should get some shut-eye too.'

'Okay. But I have to go to the toilet first. I'll be back in a minute,' she said, opening her door and climbing down to the ground.

Gary had just stretched out and settled down, when he heard the door open and shut again. Then the curtain was drawn back, and he opened his eyes to find himself staring down the barrel of a gun.

'What the—Who are you?' he shouted.

'Who I am doesn't matter, mate,' the young man said. 'What I want is the important thing, and that is for you to get back behind the wheel, and get us heading up that highway. Just keep your hands where I can see them, and climb out of there.'

As he emerged from the sleeper, Gary took in the full picture. There was Mandy, looking scared and jammed against the door, while most of the seat was taken up by a scruffy looking bloke in his twenties, wielding a lethal-looking pistol.

'What the hell's going on here?' he managed to get out. 'Where did you come from? Are you all right, Mandy?'

'She's okay. It's you who's in trouble, eh, Mandy. Smart little girl, she is, and a bloody good actor. Now if you want to stay alive, I suggest you start driving. Then we might answer a question or two for you. And don't try to get funny with us. We're already in a lot of trouble, so a bit more won't make much difference.'

As they headed up the Newell, Jacko, as the young man called himself, filled in the story. He and Mandy had got themselves into a bit of trouble in Dubbo, stolen a car, and dumped it at Coonabarabran. While Mandy was talking Gary into giving her a lift, he had slit the canvas wall on the other side of the truck, hid himself with the cargo, and waited until Mandy could organise a chance for him to get in the cab.

'So here we are, mate, me and you and little Mandy, heading for the big smoke. Talking of which, dig us out some of that good stuff you've got in that bag of yours, Mandy. I've been hanging out for one back in there. You sure took your time getting him to pull up.'

Soon the cabin reeked of marijuana smoke, and Gary wondered if he could keep driving.

'How long will it take to get to Brisbane, mate?' Jacko wanted to know.

'About six hours, I suppose, but if you keep smoking that stuff, we mightn't make it at all.'

'Aw, stop your whinging. Open the window if you're so touchy. You got any beer on board?'

'Don't be stupid,' Gary replied. 'I wouldn't keep a job long if I did.'

'Yair, well, I'm dying of thirst. Are there any pubs around here, other than in town?'

Self-preservation thoughts were running through Gary's head. Maybe if he could get one of them out of the cab for a minute, he could get a message through on the CB. Jacko must have seen him looking at the wireless. He grabbed the handpiece and ripped it from the unit. *So much for that*, Gary thought.

'We'll be coming to Gurley soon. There's one there, if they're still open.'

'Well, pull up when we get there, but keep the engine running, and don't try anything smart. And by the way, mate, it's your shout. Where's your wallet?'

*   *   *

Gary brought his rig to a stop just past the entrance to the pub, and briefly thought of trying to make a run for it, but another look at the gun levelled at him put that idea to rest.

'Here, babe,' Jacko said as he handed the weapon to Mandy. 'Just keep this on him, and if he moves a muscle, shoot the bastard.'

With that he lowered himself out of the door and headed back to the pub.

Any thoughts of talking Mandy into getting him out of his predicament quickly vanished when he looked at the sneering face on the girl who had seemed so friendly half an hour ago.

'Sorry about that, Gary,' she said. 'Desperate times call for desperate measures. Just play along with Jacko until we get to Brisbane, and he'll probably let you go home to that wife and kids of yours.'

Not now I can identify you, he thought to himself. Escape still seemed the best option, and Mandy didn't seem all that confident with the gun.

'Can I at least have a drink of water, now that we're stopped?' he asked, reaching for the water bottle that he always carried between the seats. He took a few mouthfuls, screwed the cap back on, and then brought it down with all the force he could muster on Mandy's forearm. He thought he heard a bone crack, but more importantly, the gun dropped to the floor. Gary was on it in a flash and whipped it up to aim it at the moaning girl.

'Get out!' he screamed at her. 'Move!'

She fumbled the door open and he pushed her out, and screaming to Jacko she fell to the ground. Gary hit the accelerator, and the big truck took off with a jerk. The door slammed shut and he was away. A look in the mirror showed Jacko running after him but falling further behind. He was free.

Still shaking from the ordeal, he pulled into the next rest area to gather his thoughts and decide what to do. No CB and he didn't carry a mobile. Then he noticed Mandy's backpack on the floor. Maybe she had a phone. He searched among the clothes and stuff inside. No phone, but packed in the bottom he found bundles and bundles of banknotes of twenties, fifties, and even hundreds. *There must be fifty thousand there*, he thought. *Obviously drug money or the proceeds of a bank robbery.*

Only one thing to do now, he decided. *Get to Moree as fast as I could, and report the whole incident to the police.* He just hoped it didn't hold him up too long, but he still had his rest period up his sleeve. But as he drove on, his thoughts turned to the two crooks he had left back at Gurley. He wondered what they would do now.

Stealing a car in a little dump like Gurley wouldn't be easy, but it was probably what they would do. Then he guessed they would chase him up the highway to try to get their money back. He wished now that he hadn't told Mandy which route he always followed, through Goondiwindi and Millmerran. They'd probably try to run him off the road. At least he still had their gun. Maybe they had another one. The sooner he got to Moree, the better.

But as he drove north, his thoughts turned to all that money sitting at his feet. *What if I just keep it?*

Jacko and Mandy weren't going to tell anyone about it. If he could get away from them, their next thought would be to keep clear of the law. The notes themselves were probably from drugs and therefore not traceable. *Who would it go to if I handed it in? The government? Probably. What would they do with it? Waste it as usual, most likely.*

He started to ponder what he would do if he kept it. His wages as a truckie were not that great, and his young family could make great use of fifty grand – for all the things they needed around the house, and the holiday they had been waiting years to take. The thought of keeping it was tempting, very tempting. Too tempting.

But what if they caught up with me before I got back to Brisbane? Is it worth the risk? Then the solution came to him. He could turn east at Moree and go via Warialda to Glen Innes and then up the New England Highway. *No way they would think I might do that, and if*

I drove through my rest time, I'd still arrive on time. It would be so simple. The decision was made.

He pulled to the side of the road, removed all the cash, hid it under his mattress, and threw the backpack out into the bushes on the side of the road. He picked up the gun to do the same, but then the thought of Jacko catching up with him made him think twice. Plenty of time to ditch it after he left the Highway, so he stowed it in the sleeper cab too, nice and handy, where he could reach it while he was driving, if necessary. He hoped like hell it wouldn't be.

The rest of the trip to Moree was nerve-racking, but no one came up behind him, and he relaxed as he slowed down on the outskirts of town. Then his plan fell apart with an unexpected development – a police roadblock. Two officers were flagging him down.

'Good evening, sir. Would you step down to the road, please?'

Gary did as he was told. 'What's the trouble, officer? I was under the limit, wasn't I?'

The policeman ignored him, instead said, 'Just turn and put your hands on the truck, sir, and spread your legs please.'

Gary complied. 'What's all this about?' he asked again. The second officer frisked him down and finding nothing other than his wallet, allowed him to turn to face them. The senior officer checked out his driver's licence.

'We have some questions to ask you, Mr Johnson, if you don't mind. Where have you come from today?'

'I left Melbourne yesterday afternoon.' Gary was getting nervous now.

'On the Newell all the way.'

'Yes.'

'When did you go through Dubbo?'

'Don't know for sure. About four or five o'clock, I suppose. Why?'

Again no answer.

'Have you stopped anywhere since then?'

'Yair. I had a feed at Coonabarabran.' By now Gary had given up asking questions and was starting to wish he had nothing to hide. But he had, and he was sure the cops were getting more and more suspicious.

'Did you happen to pick up a female hitch-hiker there?'

'Of course not. It's illegal. You know that.' He mustered up as much confidence in his voice as he could.

'Were there any other trucks like yours there at the time?'

'Not that I noticed. That's all? I've got a schedule to keep you know.'

The officer ignored him. 'Mind if we take a look in the cab, sir?' he asked.

By now Gary was really worried. 'Of course, I do,' he blurted. 'What are you accusing me of?'

'Let me give you a few facts, Mr Johnson. At 4.30 p.m. today, a violent robbery occurred at Dubbo. A young lady wearing a backpack distracted a Woolworths manager who was then attacked from behind and knocked unconscious.' He looked closely at Gary, whose mouth was so dry he couldn't have spoken even if he could think of anything to say.

'The perpetrators made their escape from Dubbo in a stolen car, which was subsequently discovered by a patrol car at a Coonabarabran truck stop. When questioned, the manager reported seeing a young lady with a backpack talking to a truckie. He thinks she may have gone with him, and his description of the truck fits yours. Now do you see why we're asking you some questions?'

Gary said nothing, not trusting his voice if he tried and not sure what he could say anyway.

The sergeant stared at him, waiting for a response. Getting none, he went on, 'Now we can have a look in your cab, with your permission, or we can take you to the station while we get a warrant. We only want to make sure our lady friend isn't hiding in there. Okay?'

'Go on then,' Gary managed to get out.

The other officer climbed into the cab. 'She's not here!' he shouted down. 'Bit of a funny smell, though. Could be cannabis.'

'Well, have a good look round while you're there. You don't mind, do you, Mr Johnson?' Gary shook his head and felt bile rise in his throat.

'Well, well, well. Look what we've got here' came the dreaded call from the cab, and an arm waved a bundle of notes in the air. 'Seems a lot of dough here for a truckie to be carrying around. Must be thousands.'

'Your money, Mr Johnson?' asked the top cop.

Gary thought quickly. Too late now to tell the truth. He'd just have to try and bluff his way through. 'Yair. I was going to buy a car on the way home, so I brought the cash with me.'

'Why would you pay for it when you've got one of these on board?' said the other cop as he stepped down from the cab and handed his senior a revolver wrapped in his hanky.

'That's enough for me,' the cop said, never taking his eyes off the now-sweating Gary. 'Cuff him, Tony.'

*   *   *

On his way to the police station, Gary had time to think and to work out what to do. Obviously he couldn't stick with his present story. They had the money, which any search at his bank would show wasn't his. They had a gun with his prints on it from when he had chased Mandy out of the cab. They had him in Dubbo at the time of the robbery, and at the truck stop with Mandy. No one had seen Jacko at all, and they seemed to have disappeared. He was in deep trouble, and he knew it. He decided his best option was to tell the truth. So he did, with a twist.

'So that's what happened. You can check the cut in my trailer and the disabled CB,' he concluded. 'Maybe the publican at Gurley saw what happened to them, but that's the last time I saw them.'

'Sounds like a tall story to me, Mr Johnson, but even if it's true, you're still in trouble. Failing to report a crime, that is, your hijacking, receiving the proceeds of crime, carrying an unlicensed firearm, destroying evidence, and lying to avoid arrest. That's one whole lot of trouble you're in, if further investigation does clear you of the actual crime.' Sergeant Osborne started packing his papers.

'There is one other thing I want to say,' Gary said. 'Okay, I admit I was tempted by the money at first, and I admit I hid it and threw her bag away. But after I did that, I changed my mind. As I came the last few miles into Moree, I decided it wasn't worth the risk. I was going to call in here and report what had happened if you hadn't stopped me.'

'What about the cock-and-bull yarn you told us then?'

'I panicked, I guess. You wouldn't tell me what you were on about. In the confusion, I went back to my earlier plan, I suppose, but honest, I had changed my mind.'

'No getting out of the fact you lied to us, I'm afraid,' the sergeant said, 'or the fact that you tried to conceal the crime against you.'

Gary tried to remember exactly what he had said when they stopped him. 'I lied about picking up the girl because I didn't want to get into trouble with my boss. So I could hardly report the hijack, could I?'

Sergeant Osborne sat for sometime, eying him suspiciously. They were interrupted by a phone call.

'Osborne. Yep. Yep. Is that so? Are you sure? Well, hang on to them till I get there, will you? About two hours.' He put the receiver down and turned back to Gary.

'Your luck might have changed for the better. The police in Narrabri are holding a couple caught trying to steal a car. Seems the girl fits the description of your hitch-hiker, and the bloke is known to us for dealing drugs and stealing. You might be off the hook after all.'

'Can I go then?' Gary asked hopefully.

'No way. You're staying right here till we get this sorted,' he said, gathering up his papers. 'You can ring your boss and family, but you've got a few problems to face yet. Like, how can we be sure you weren't going to keep the money? The fact that you hadn't driven past any stations since it happened might help you, but you'd better get your story straight before I get back in the morning.'

*   *   *

It was eight o'clock next morning, before a very tired-looking Sergeant Osborne came to let Gary out of his cell.

'C'mon, mate. Time for us both to go home,' he said.

'Am I being charged with anything?'

'Not this time. I've done enough paperwork in the last few hours to last me for a week. The good news for you is that pair admitted to everything after a bit of gentle persuasion. Tough little bird that Mandy, but lover boy knew he had no chance of talking his way out of it, so he dobbed her in. Said it was all her idea in the first place.'

They headed for the front office of the station. 'So I'm free to go? Am I?'

'Yair. Tony and I decided not to mention the little fib you told us about not seeing the girl. We reckon you'll have enough trouble explaining what happened to your boss and your missus anyway. And we all know you intended to pull in here and hand over the money and the gun, don't we?'

Gary took a quick look at his face to see if he was having him on, but the sergeant met his glance with an impassive stare.

'Thanks, Sergeant,' he said. 'I admit I was tempted for a while, though.'

'I bet you were, mate. I bet you were.'

As he gathered up his possessions from the counter, Gary wondered just why the sergeant had become so friendly all of a sudden – a bit different to how he had been last night. 'Temptation is a funny thing, isn't it?' he ventured. 'But I've learnt my lesson. Never been tempted yourself, Sarge?'

'Not on your life, mate. More than my job's worth. Bit like yours actually, eh?'

'I guess so,' Gary said as he shook his hand and headed out the door.

*　*　*

When Gary went to climb behind the wheel, he found the pillow from his sleeper cab on the seat. He threw it back on his bed, and there, staring up at him, were ten crisp $100 bills.

'What an old bastard!' he mused to himself. 'I wonder how much of the loot actually made it to the police station safe.'

He stuffed them in his wallet. After all he'd been through last night, he reckoned he deserved it.

'Hijacked' explained

All of us have at some time succumbed to temptation. Probably, if we are honest, many, many times, but the vast majority of these would be of minor and inconsequential nature – looking over the shoulder of the smart kid next to you at exam time, kicking your golf ball from under a bush when your playing partner's not looking, and even an extra spoonful of sugar when on a diet. Everyone does it, right?

But what if a really big temptation appeared in front of you? Something that could change your life forever, for the better, of course? It may not even be illegal either. Just something that you know you shouldn't do, but hell, the opportunity will probably never come up again! Would you do the right thing, or would the temptation to take advantage of the situation to set yourself up for life be too great?

As I write, this a very famous American golfer is becoming even more famous every day as one indiscretion after another is revealed by a succession of willing temptresses. Tut, Tut, Tiger! We wouldn't allow ourselves to be trapped by a wink and a sexy smile from a gorgeous young woman, would we?

TEMPTATION

I'd gone to the baker's shop down in the
town to pick up a loaf of bread.
The thought of flirtation with the opposite
sex had never entered my head.
The passage of time and a vigorous life had
left me quite old and uncouth.
No sexy young sheilas had made eyes at me
since the days of my faraway youth.

But as I considered with grave contemplation
the choices of wholemeal or white,
The pretty young sales girl made approaches
to me. It gave me a hell of a fright.
Without provocation or suggestion from me,
she said with a breathtaking smile,
'If you hang around a bit, you can ferry me
home. I knock off in a little while.'

Now I know I am guilty. The fault was all mine,
as I could have just run for my life.
At age sixty-eight, with four grown-up
kids, and at home, a lovable wife.
But from deep in the past those old feelings
returned, of man involved in the chase.
I just couldn't resist the thrill of it all, or
the come-hither look on her face.

Like a silly old fool, I fell hook line and sinker,
for that bonzer young sort who sold pies,
So I waited outside like a schoolboy's first date,
cos that come-hither look in her eyes
Had fired up a passion from deep in my soul,
that just forced me to join in the chase,
And next thing I knew, she slipped into my car,
and said, 'Hurry up, back to my place.'

But even at this stage, I could have reneged
and just dropped her off in the street,
And walked away from the chance that she
offered, but I couldn't control my feet.
They followed her in to the small flat she owned,
as past all the neighbours we crept.
Through lounge room and kitchen, to, lo and
behold, the room where my pick-up girl slept.

Her dazzling smile, as she kicked off her shoes,
made my poor old knees wobble and shake.
I just couldn't knock back this lifelong denied
chance of my first lucky break.
Her left hand reached out to unbutton my shirt,
her right turned the key in the door,
And next thing I knew, both my pants and her
dress were untidy heaps on the floor.

Then a sudden sharp pain hit the small of my
back, and I felt a cuff to the head,
As I woke with a start, and a fast-beating heart.
'You were dreaming again,' she said.
My seditious ideas of a one-night-stand
fling had cruelly all been betrayed,
Cos, instead of the sort with the come-hither
eyes, it was 'she who must be obeyed!'

LAST WILL AND TESTAMENT

Dr Prothero heaved a heavy sigh and dropped into the seat behind his desk. In spite of nearly forty years working in his profession, he had never ceased to become depressed when he had to pass on bad news to a patient. As part of his medical training, he knew that it was important to maintain a personal distance between himself and his patients. But the elder he became, the less possible it seemed to be. Now he had to deal with telling a lifelong friend that he only had months to live.

Bill Mathers and his family had been some of his first customers when he had set up his practice in town as a newly qualified doctor all those years ago. Their kids had grown up together, attended the same school, and played sports in the same teams. His wife, Alice, had become close friends with Bill's wife, Maggie, and he and Bill had sunk a few stubbies over many family barbecues. He and Alice had been his main support when Maggie had been killed in a road accident a few years ago. Poor old Bill didn't deserve that, and he didn't deserve the news he was about to get now either. *Oh well. Might as well get it over with.* He reached for the phone.

'Send Mr Mathers in, would you, please, Rachael?'

It was a pale and worried-looking Bill Mathers who took the seat opposite the doctor. His old chirpy disposition had long since gone. The look on his old friend's face as he shook his hand did nothing to allay his concern.

'Take a seat, Bill. How have you been going, mate? Those pills I gave you doing any good?'

'Not much, I'm afraid, Harry. Whatever I've got doesn't seem to be getting any better.'

Harry took a deep breath as he pretended to be reading the paper in front of him. He knew his mate pretty well and decided not to beat about the bush.

'Bill, I'm sorry to have to tell you this, but it's not going to get better – ever. Your tests show that the cancer has spread to your liver and a couple of other places. The specialist says it's inoperable. Sorry, mate, but I thought you'd want to know the truth.'

Though he had been half-expecting it, hearing it spelled out with such finality left Bill shattered; first Maggie getting killed, then an operation for prostate cancer, and now this. What had been a pretty good life for his first sixty years had now become a nightmare. Thank God the kids were all grown up and independent, and maybe Maggie's death was a blessing in disguise. The thought of leaving her behind to wander aimlessly through twenty or thirty years of widowhood left him cold. At least he could now spend his remaining time putting his affairs in order.

'You did the right thing, Harry. I guess it's not much fun for you to have to give me the bad news. I sort of suspected the worst anyway. How long have I got?'

'Probably six months. Maybe more. But you won't be able to go on living out on the farm on your own for too much longer. You'll have to find somewhere in town or move in with one of your kids. In the meantime, I'll give you some stronger pills that should help you to deal with the pain for some weeks, but they won't work forever. How about coming home for a drink after I finish here?'

'Thanks, Harry, for everything. You've been a wonderful friend, but I just want to go home now and try to get my head around what's in store for me.'

'Okay, but if there's anything I can do for you, just ask, won't you?'

*   *   *

Bill sat in the darkening room, sipping a Scotch. No use worrying about damaging his liver now. He briefly wondered if the heavy drinking bout brought on by the loss of Maggie was in any way responsible for his problems but quickly decided looking back was a waste of the little bit of time he had left. He forced his mind back to consider what had to be done.

The first thing he had to do was bring his will up to date. He hadn't had the heart to even look at it since Maggie's death, so it was completely out of date as they had left everything to each other. In the event of them dying together, their estate went to their three children in equal parts. If he now did nothing, that is what would happen, and that is what worried him when his thoughts turned to them.

He and Maggie had done their best to provide all the help and support they could for their kids, and were still being called on to get them out of their scrapes even though they were all in their thirties. In many ways, they were something of a disappointment to him, and now he wondered how well they would handle life without his guidance and help. Becoming suddenly quite well off might even make their situations worse, for various reasons.

Hugh was the eldest son, the one Bill always assumed would take over the family property when the time came for him to retire. He had been interested at first but eventually was attracted to the bright lights, bigger money, and easier lifestyle of the city. Bill had come to accept that he would be the last of his family to work the land. He couldn't blame the younger generation for leaving. Times had changed, and life on the land was not what it used to be.

Unfortunately, Hugh's ambition had got the better of him, and instead of being satisfied with reasonable success in the business world, he had recently overextended and had been forced into bankruptcy. His wife had been compelled to return to work, his marriage was in trouble, his kids had to leave their private schools, and his boat and flash car were gone. Bill was determined not to bail him out this time, as doing so in the past had only compounded his problems.

Daughter Kay was also in trouble for completely opposite reasons. Her failure lay in her choice of a marriage partner. He and Maggie had done their best to make her see through his false exterior but to no avail. The more they tried, the more she dug her toes in, and eventually they had to accept their son-in-law as part of the family. Now seven years and two kids later, the chickens were coming home to roost.

He had recently become violent to her and the kids, and Kay was sure he was having an affair with a girl from work. In spite of everything, including an offer for her and the kids to come home, she was determined not to leave her marriage. Bill was terrified that the situation could lead to disaster but could do no more to help his stubborn daughter and just as importantly, his two little grandkids.

Jason was their third and last kid, born after a break of five years, and probably spoilt because of it. He had led a wasteful existence since leaving school, never settling into a steady job, let alone a career, and spent most of his twenties drifting around the world with a series of girlfriends. He was now back in Australia, but Bill had recently found out that he had gone from bad to worse and was now a serious drug user and living in a squat in Sydney.

All of them, in their various ways, disappointed Bill as he pondered the fact that in a few months' time he would no longer be around to guide or help them. How would they handle his death, and even more importantly, what would they do when they suddenly found themselves quite wealthy if he passed his worldly wealth on to them? It was entirely possible that, rather than solve all of their problems, it could actually magnify them. He spent some time pondering on the potential outcomes, and the more he thought about it, the more worried he became.

Bill and Maggie had lived a fairly frugal life and had added to the property he had inherited from his father. They had also diversified into off-farm investments in the form of shares and investment properties and had paid out the last of their debt years ago. He guessed, altogether he might be worth somewhere between three and four million. Normally such a windfall could solve their problems for life, but Bill could see potential disaster ahead.

For a start, he could imagine Hugh using his share to pursue his aim of becoming mega rich rather than to get himself out of his current troubles. One million would probably enable him to borrow another ten, landing him in even bigger trouble than he was now. He needed some action that would jolt him out of his grandiose pursuit of fame and fortune and to force him to get his feet back on the ground.

On the other hand, Kay could do with a heap of money to get her out of the hole in which she found herself, if – and it would be a big *if* – she could keep it from the mongrel she had married. To do that, she would have to ditch him and start a new life for herself and the kids, but so far, she had seemed to be incapable of leaving him, even though he gave her plenty of reasons to do so. Then again, if she did divorce him, the courts would probably give him half of her money anyway, and Bill certainly wasn't going to let that happen.

As for Jason, just imagine what mayhem a million dollars landing in his lap would cause. It would go up in smoke, or ice, or some other drug. That would be the best outcome. At worst, it could kill him or turn him from being a user to being a dealer, leading him to spend his life in jail when he eventually was caught. No, his best chance was for penury and eventually maturity, to break him of his habit and lifestyle.

Bill pondered on these problems for a couple of days while he tried to decide what to do to wind up his affairs in the little time left to him. The thought did occur to him – why should he worry? He wouldn't be around to watch all the disasters unfold. That's what would have happened if he had been killed in an accident and didn't have a chance to alter his will. That would be the easy way out of his dilemma, but he wouldn't go to his grave peacefully if he didn't make one last effort to fix up the lives of his kids. Maggie would have expected it of him.

*   *   *

A plan had gradually evolved in his mind, and he had arranged to meet his two best mates to run the plan past them and to seek their cooperation. His accountant, Denis Barnes, and Harry Prothero arrived at the farm together and settled down on the veranda with a cold beer. Both felt a bit uncomfortable at the circumstances and the thought of discussing his death with Bill, but he made them feel more at ease with his attitude and philosophical acceptance of his fate.

'Let's get this straight from the start, boys. I'm not looking forward to what I've got coming, but let's be realistic. I've had a pretty long life, and a good one, and I've accepted my lot. Life hasn't been much fun since Maggie died, and I can't see it getting any better from here on, so let's just say it's a fact of life, or in this case, death, and get on with it.'

Neither of his friends said anything, so he continued, 'I've pulled you blokes in to ask a big favour of you. I want you to become executors of my estate, and in doing so, help me to solve some family problems that I won't be around to sort out myself. You've both been friends to Maggie and me for many years and know our kids pretty well too. It's them that I'm worried about.

'While I want them to be the beneficiaries of my estate, for various reasons I'm certain inheriting a heap of money at this point in their lives would destroy them. I have devised a scheme that may just give them the incentive they each need to turn their lives around, but it will require your help to make it work. Harry, you told me to ask if there was anything you could do to help. Well, I'm asking, and you, Denis, know my finances and the business world better than anyone else I know. Hear me out, and then tell me what you think.'

Bill went inside to get more beers, and when he returned, he explained to them what he was afraid would happen to each of his kids if he couldn't control their access to his estate and then went on explain what he had in mind.

'For starters, none of them are interested in the property and wouldn't have a clue on how to run it if they were, so the first thing I have to do is sell up and convert its value to cash. That shouldn't take long. Old Mick next door has been wanting me to sell it to him for years, and I did promise to give him first offer if I ever wanted to get out.

'To keep things as simple as possible, I'll also sell all my off-farm investments so the whole estate can just be invested on the money market. I reckon, after I clear everything up, there will be about $3.2 million left, and this is what I plan to do. I will stipulate quite clearly in my will that you two have complete authority to manage the funds at your discretion, and giving you authority to distribute it in accordance with my express wishes. None of them will be able to legally challenge whatever you do.'

'You seem to have put a lot of thought into this, Bill,' Denis said.

'I sure have. I just hope it works out. On my death, the three kids are to be informed of the contents of the will, and each of them given $20,000 in cash. They will share equally in the balance of the estate, subject to certain conditions. If any of them fails to meet their individual conditions, their share will be forfeited. Each of them can gain a draw on their entitlement on the first anniversary of my death, subject to meeting their first hurdle. They can get the balance on the second anniversary of my death, provided they can satisfy you that they have fulfilled the obligation I am placing on them. In the event that any of them fail to qualify for their share, it will be donated to a charity, which I will nominate in the document.'

'Gees, Bill. That's a bit tough, isn't it?' Harry asked.

'It may seem like tough, love, but I am adamant that my estate will not be the seed of their own self-destruction. I know I am asking a lot of you, but there is no one else I can trust to do this for me. What do you think?'

Harry and Denis sipped their beer for a while as they pondered what Bill had told them. They sympathised with their mate and what he was trying to do for his kids. What he was asking of them was a tall order, but they felt somewhat obligated to help him in this last wish.

'Can you outline the hurdles you're proposing to put in for them to meet?' Denis asked.

'Righto. Well, Hugh first. As you probably know, his business went bust when he overstretched. I want him to get his feet back on the ground. After twelve months, he has to have sorted out his bankruptcy and either started something else or found a solid job. Not too much to ask of him, but he should demonstrate that he has learned his lesson and show promise of a successful, sensible future.

'Kay's only problem is the absolute no-hoper she's married to. You may not be aware, but he abuses her and the kids, both physically and emotionally. She seems to be unable to leave him, but unless she does, she and the kids have no future. After twelve months, to qualify for her first draw, she must be divorced and living a long way from him.

'Jason's task is the hardest. He's a junkie, living in a squat in Sydney. Harry, I hope you can talk him into going into a rehabilitation clinic, which can be paid out of his share of the estate. He's not unintelligent, and given the incentive built into this plan, I'm betting he will respond favourably. After his first twelve months, he should be drug-free for some time, employed, and living a reasonable life.

'If they are still on track after two years, they can receive their third share of the estate. If they have lapsed, and in your opinion have not complied with my wishes, you will be required to donate their share to the nominated charity.'

After many questions and with some trepidation, the two friends agreed to help Bill with his last request. He set about converting all of his assets into cash and putting into place all of the legal documentation to empower his executors to act on his behalf. He went to his grave confident he had done all he could to ensure the safety and security of his family.

*   *   *

Two years later, Harry and Denis called the three beneficiaries to their final meeting. They were amazed at how well Bill's plan had worked, and at the changes that had taken place in the three kids. At first, they had been a bit miffed at having to jump hurdles to gain their share of their inheritance, but they accepted the fact that he was only trying to do his best for them, and the prospect of eventually losing their share induced them all to accept the challenge before them. By the end of the first year, they had all reached their targets and received their first payments.

Now as they waited for the meeting to start, they reviewed the current situation. Hugh had moved with his family back to the town where he was born and bought a news agency business. His kids now attended the school, where successive generations of Mathers had gone before them. He was president of the golf club and was a well-respected member of the community.

Kay had taken the plunge soon after Bill's death, leaving her husband and suing for divorce. When Hugh moved back to town, she followed, helping him to run his shop. With her part payment after twelve months, she was able to buy a house and had recently been seen dating a local farmer.

Harry Prothero had put a lot of time and effort into helping Jason overcome his drug problems. Working with a colleague in the city, they had managed to oversee his recovery, and he had now been drug-free for more than a year. He moved to Brisbane and had been working for an accountant mate of Denis for some time while he completed a degree part-time.

All of them were a credit to themselves, and to Bill's efforts to turn them around. They had overcome any resentment they had initially experienced at his plan of withholding, and even giving away their inheritance, but they still anxiously awaited the decision of the two executors.

Dr Harry opened the proceedings. 'Denis and I want to say how pleased we are that you are all here to take part in the winding up of your father's estate. When he first suggested his plan to us, we both thought it a bit kooky, but time, together with your cooperation, has proven him right. We know you all realise that what he did, he did with your best interests at heart. It has proven to be an outstanding success, and we congratulate you all on the changes you have made to your lives. Unfortunately, we also have some bad news for you, but I will let Denis handle that.'

Denis produced a bundle of papers from his briefcase and prepared to hand out copies to the three visitors. 'As you know,' he started, 'we were authorised to administer your father's will and to make judgements and payments in line with his wishes. We have tried to do that to the best of our ability, and you have all received some part payments over the last two years. Under the terms of the document, we have reached the time when the estate must be wound up, with each of you getting one third of the total sum, subject to our approval of your current situation.'

Denis let this sink in before he continued. 'As Harry said, we are delighted that our friend's plan worked out so well, and we will not have to deny any of you your share. Unfortunately, what Bill could not foresee was the upcoming world financial crisis. Just as most super policies have lost a lot of value in recent months, the value of the estate has fallen a fair bit. Your shares will now be worth a bit something less than they might have been when your dad died, but they still represent a very tidy sum. All transactions for the past two years are included in these papers, along with audited accounts from an independent source. We're sorry about this, but we did our best.'

Hugh broke the ensuing silence. 'I don't know about you other two, but I'm not too disappointed. What the delay will cost me has been more than made up for by what it forced me to do with my life. I've come to realise that money isn't everything, and I'll be forever grateful that Dad cared enough for us to do what he did, and to you two blokes for the roll you played in the scheme.'

He looked at Kay and Jason as he spoke and could see that they supported him. He couldn't believe the change in his brother since he had got on top of his life, and Kay was also the happiest she had ever been.

'Well, thank goodness for that,' Harry said. 'We have been worried that you might think we failed you, but it all seems to have worked out okay. I suggest we all duck out to the golf club and raise a few glasses to poor old Bill.'

'I'll drink to that,' Denis agreed. 'Your shout, Harry. Doctors earn more than accountants.'

'Now you tell me,' Jason joked, and they all headed off to celebrate the thoughtfulness and success of a man they had all loved dearly.

'Last Will and Testament' explained

There is a well-known adage – 'Money is the root of all evil', but few of us actually believe it, and we spend our lives trying to accumulate more of it, rather than less. But we probably also know of cases where the acquisition of wealth has ruined people's lives.

We also know that 'you can't take it with you', but it doesn't stop a lot of us from trying our best to do so. This attitude was probably more usual last century, as many retirees these days seem intent on employing the SKI principle, that is, spending their kids' inheritance on themselves.

The problem for today's beneficiaries is that the chances of at least one parent living into, or even past, their mid-eighties is very high, and by the time they get their hands on the family fortune, they will be retired themselves, with all of their productive, child-rearing life behind them.

As Bill demonstrated in this little story, much good can be done if their inheritance is handed on to them in a timely and thoughtful manner. He didn't manage to take 'it' with him, but he did manage to use it in such a way that his descendants would never forget what he did for them, and his 'footprints' will always be remembered.

This poem is one of my favourites. It was written after attending the funeral of a friend's very elderly father. It tries to express my view that the most substantial thing we leave behind us when we die is our impact on our family and friends left behind. Everything else will be dissipated and lost in time, but the influence we have over our kids will be, in turn, passed on to theirs and be part of the make-up of future generations forever.

FOOTPRINTS FROM HIS PAST

The congregation bowed their heads. The vicar read the text.
The grandkids were all overawed and wondered what came next.
The coffin was of polished wood, bedecked with crimson roses.
The relatives all wiped their eyes, and quietly blew their noses.

'We've gathered here', the vicar said, 'to pay our last respects.
To send the soul of this good man wherever God directs.
His time on earth has run its race, his three score years and ten.
He's gone to meet his mortal fate. It happens to all men.

His soul lives on in all our hearts, his body goes to dust.
We wish it could be otherwise, and yet we know we must
Accept that in life's rugged race, one feature always stays.
That we are granted one great gift, our stock of mortal days.

Now we can use those days on earth in one of two directions.
The choice is ours to always make the ultimate selection.
To live a good constructive life, contribute something useful,
Or waste the chances given us, be useless and abuse-full.

For in the end, when we pass on, we leave not much behind.
Our families and our friends and foes and folk of every kind.
It's in the hearts and minds of those that memories will last.
It's there we leave our legacy, the footprints from our past.

Those people feel the footprints that we leave on their lives.
They pass them on to their own kin, to husbands, kids and wives.
As years roll on, when we are gone, our cause for celebration,
Will be those footprints from our past on future generations.'

The vicar closed his notes and said, in tones, subdued, sincere,
'The man we honour thus today has shown he was here.
Throughout a long productive life his footprints freely fell,
And many people whom he knew still feel his vital spell.
His family understands the contribution he has made.
In towns and cities everywhere, their memories will not fade.
They all will feel the benefit as long as they all last,
Of everything he meant to them, his footprints from his past.'

OLD BLUE

Ted and Jenny McAlpine were at it again. The cause of all this angst was once again the future of their pride and joy, their number-one son, Jimmy. Although young Jim had three younger sisters, it was the son and heir that featured most often in their thoughts whenever they contemplated the future. After all, it was a well-known fact that girls all got married and moved away to live their lives and rear their kids a long way from the family nest, especially when that very nest was a desolate, drought-stricken sprawl of the mulga and saltbush country fifty miles from the nearest civilisation. But young Jimmy was different.

His dad had big plans for him and could hardly wait for him to grow up so he could take his rightful place as the right-hand man and heir to the family property, 'Bulldust.' Since he could walk, he had ridden and driven with his father over the dusty plains, mustering, fencing, and watering the herd of merinos that had been selectively bred on the place for nearly a hundred years. Now just when he was getting to be really useful, this silly woman was trying to spoil everything by insisting he get an education! *What does she think he's been getting so far?*

It's all the fault of that opinionated young governess the missus insisted on hiring a few years ago. Jenny had been doing a perfectly good job of home schooling them all as far as he could see, and he had let her miss the shearing and crutching so she could get on with it. Anyway, to keep a bit of peace and quiet, he had relented, and they had hired Penny McNab to take over the schooling duties. He had to admit, it was good to have Jenny back in the shed when it got busy, but now the chickens had come home to roost. Just when he got old enough to legally call an end to Jimmy's formal education, the two women had got their heads together and decided he should go to high school.

Penny had convinced Jenny that they had a genius on their hands and that to deny the boy further education would be a travesty of justice. Argue as he might, this was one he was never going to win, so he had to content himself with insisting that this 'broadening of his mind' would occur at the State High School in Cunnamulla, and not at some flash boarding school in the city. At least he would get a bit of proper work out of him on weekends and holidays, and the saving on fees would be welcome if it didn't rain soon.

So there it was. On the first day of the new school year, Jimmy drove the ute the twenty-five miles to the front gate and rode the bus another twenty-five to town. He signed himself in and set about the business of 'mind broadening' that his mother was so set on. And it must be said, he did it very well. Penny McNab must have been right to suspect he had brains and talent. In spite of the hours of travel and weekend work on the property, he finished his four years as school captain and with the highest academic result ever posted by a student from Cunnamulla.

This led to more trouble at home. That damn dynamic duo in the kitchen had now decided he should go to university no less and get a bloody degree. What good would that do him? They didn't need a solicitor on the place. They needed a stockman and potential manager, down the track. Then, when Ted died, he would own the place, just like his father, grandfather, and great-grandfather had before him, but not if his mind got twisted by all those academics in Brisbane.

But once again, he had to give way, calculating that university costs would still be cheaper than divorce. He did insist, however, that he had to do Agricultural Science, reasoning that perhaps he may learn something that might be useful back home and that learning about animals might remind him of his heritage and stop him straying too much. He also put him on a very skinny budget and promised him full ringer's award wages if he ever got sick of city life.

*   *   *

Jimmy spent the first year of his three-year course settling into his new life, learning the ropes and making friends. He quite liked the subjects, and he finished on top of his year, much to the delight of his mother and Penny but to the profound disappointment of his dad. Ted was proud of him in his own way and still remembered the good times they had spent working together before this blasted education bug had taken him over. All he wanted was to have him back home, but he was resigned now to having to wait for two more years.

Ted picked him up at the railway station when he came home for the holidays, and they yarned as they drove the fifty dusty miles home. He was surprised and a bit upset when Jimmy told him that he didn't really fit in down there, hadn't made any real friends, was lonely, and missed the property, especially his old dog, Blue. Not one to miss an opportunity, Ted's other reaction was one of hope that maybe Jimmy would throw it in and come home after all. But then he figured that he had invested one-third of the cost involved and that this would be wasted if Jimmy pulled out now. No, he must do what he could to help his boy in his time of need.

'Tell you what,' said Ted. 'When you go back next year, why don't you take old Blue with you for company?'

'Gee, Dad, that'd be great, but I'll need some more allowance to feed him.'

'Well, okay, but I can't give you much. Money doesn't grow on trees, you know.'

So that's what happened. At the end of the holidays, old Blue was put in the guard's van of the Westlander, and he went with his mate to the big smoke. There they enjoyed each other's company, and life became better for young Jimmy. He began to make friends and to spread his wings, which led him eventually to make a big mistake.

Egged on by a few of his new friends, he found himself one night at the casino, half-tanked and investing some of his very scarce dollars at the two-up ring. When his money ran out, his mates kindly lent him some more, and yet more, until he could hit a lucky streak. But he never did, and woke up next day with a headache and a debt of several hundred dollars.

As he sat drinking strong black coffee and staring absently at Blue, the germ of an idea came to him. He was smart enough to realise that his tight old man was no brain's trust and just might fall for a story if he thought he could make a few dollars out of it. The more he thought about it, the better he liked the idea, even more so when his creditors started putting the screws on him to come up with their dough. So in desperation, he placed a reverse charge call home.

'Great news, Dad! One of my lecturers is doing a research program involved in teaching animals to communicate with humans. One day he saw old Blue doing tricks I have taught him, and you know how smart he is! Well, Professor Francis thinks he can teach him to talk.'

'Well, blow me down, Son! Wouldn't that be something?' Ted enthused. 'He'd be worth a bit if he could talk. Keep at it, Son. We'll make a fortune out of him one day.'

'There's a bit of a problem there, Dad,' Jimmy said cautiously. 'To enrol in the professor's course will cost a thousand dollars for the rest of the year, and I know things are pretty tough back home.'

Dollar signs rattled in Ted's head like a poker machine. 'Don't you worry about that, son. I'll see the bank tomorrow and send you the money as soon as I can. You just make sure old Blue studies hard and learns to talk before some other mutt beats him to it. It's only the first one that will make the big money.'

*   *   *

So that's what happened. Jimmy repaid his debt and had some over to fund his new pursuits of wine, women, and song (but not two-up. He wasn't that silly). He pushed to the back of his mind the problem of eventually having to explain to the old man that old Blue wasn't as smart as they thought.

When the summer holidays came around again, Jimmy explained that he wouldn't be able to bring old Blue home with him as Professor Francis wanted to take him to his place so he could keep the program going. The good news was that it would only cost two hundred dollars for food and so on. Once again, Dad came good, which helped considerably with the end-of-term parties.

Ted spent many happy hours over those holidays, having a beer on the veranda with his now-mature young son, discussing what he had learned that might be useful on the place after all. He also let his mind wander about the prospects of owning the first dog in the world that could talk and how it could be their financial salvation.

The young student spent a lot of time worrying how he was ever going to get out of the tricky situation into which he had managed to place himself. One day, he would have to come clean about the con act he had perpetrated on his dad, but for now he was safe. Maybe something would turn up. In the meantime, he was quite looking forward to getting back to town and picking up old Blue from the mate who was looking after him.

*　　*　　*

The last year of his time at university was proving very pleasurable indeed for young Jimmy. Only one thing was spoiling it – lack of spending money. Finally, in desperation, he moved to stage two of the greatest talking-dog con ever thought up. He placed another reverse charge call home.

'Marvellous news again, Dad. Old Blue is the only one of his class to graduate at this stage, and he is now back living with me. We chat for hours about the good old days back on the property. He can't wait to have a yarn with you when we come home.'

'Jeez, that's great, Son!' Ted gushed. 'You look after him now, and when you've finished your course, we'll make a moxa out of him.'

'Ah, but I've got even better news, Dad,' Jimmy ventured carefully. 'Professor Francis thinks if he works with him one on one, he can probably teach him to read too. Just think of that. Trouble is, Professor Francis doesn't come cheap. We'll need another two thousand dollars, I'm afraid.'

Poor old Ted could see dollar signs in front of his eyes. It hardly seemed possible that you could teach a dog to talk, never less read, but he had to admit, they had shown they could do almost anything these days. Who would have thought you could land a couple of blokes on the moon and then bring them home again? So another trip to the bank, ostensibly to buy some sheep, and he was able to fund old Blue's further education.

*　　*　　*

December came around too soon for Jimmy. Not only did he have to kiss all his newfound independence (and many of his female classmates) goodbye, but he was now starting to focus his mind on how to handle an irate father when he arrived home with a much fatter, but no smarter, old Blue. He thought of canine laryngitis, but that couldn't last long, and it didn't solve the reading problem. When he eventually loaded old Blue into the guard's van and headed west, he was none the wiser as to how he was going to handle the situation. Then, somewhere between Roma and Augathella, he knew what he had to do.

Fortunately for his plan, Dad had left the ute at the garage for some work to be done, and Jimmy was to drive it home on his arrival. Old Blue dozed away in the back until they were well inside the front gate. Then with a heavy heart, but personal salvation uppermost in his mind, Jimmy removed the rifle always kept under the seat in case a dingo was sighted and took old Blue for a one-way walk into the bush.

Ted met him at the shed, beside himself with anticipation, only to find Jimmy but no dog.

'Dad, bad news, I'm afraid,' Jimmy said.

Ted was mortified. 'Hell! What's happened, Son? Where's old Blue?'

'Dad, he was just so excited at the thought of seeing you again. We talked about it all the way home. I even bought him a *Country Life* at Toowoomba so he could brush up on the wool prices and rural news. All the way from Cunnamulla he kept up a constant chatter about things he remembered from the past.

'When we got to the front gate he said, "Do you remember the day you left this open? All the sheep ended up halfway to town." And then, when we'd gone a few miles further, he said, "What about the day you drove the ute into the dam over there, trying to run down that wild pig?"

'I tell you, Dad, he never shut up, and then he said something that I bet you wouldn't be too pleased to hear. Just completely out of the blue, he said, "Tell me, Jimmy, is your old man still having it off with the governess every time the missus goes to town shopping?"

'What! Bloody hell, Son! I hope you shot the bastard!'

'Well, yes, Dad, as a matter of fact, that's exactly what I did,' Jimmy purred.

'Gee, thanks, Son. You won't tell your mum, will you?' Ted whispered.

'No, Dad. Never,' said Jimmy, as he threw his arm around his father's shoulders and headed for the house.

And, of course, he never did.

'Old Blue' explained

A number of years ago, a school reunion degenerated in the middle of the night to a joke-telling session. This story came from a well-known Brisbane barrister who had been born and bred in far western Queensland. With the assistance of a few glasses of amber liquid, it probably took him longer than my rendition takes to read.

Some of my more fragile readers never get to finish it, breaking down and sobbing uncontrollably when Old Blue takes his one-way walk into the bush. This unrealistic attachment to pets has never been part of my make-up, but the same can't be said for my spouse, who, by the way, fought long and hard, though unsuccessfully, for me to come up with a happy ending for this yarn.

Like Old Blue, pets need to be functional, free, cheap to maintain, and expendable when circumstances demand, as the following poem explains.

The Perfect Pet

I've always had a little problem with this spouse of mine.
There's times I must admit to all she just won't toe the line.
For thirty-seven years or more she's promised time again,
To never, never have more pets that cause me fiscal pain.

Before we even said 'I do', she had a bird and cat.
She'd started on a lifelong binge, it got worse after that.
Before she'd even proved herself and had a kid or two,
Her penchant for acquiring pets had caused us many a blue.

A sheep called Lamb-chop soon arrived, a little lamb at heel,
A big improvement on the cat, at least a future meal.
A clutch of little ducks, some chooks, as things looked up a bit.
I bought an axe and butcher's knife, she bit her bottom lip.

That's when we started making friends of people with more nous,
As one by one they trundled down to our little house.
They helped us solve a major tiff, stay married one more day.
They kindly loaded up our pets and took them all away.

She gave up buying useful things, returned to dogs and cats.
They bred like flies, she kept the lot, with coos and hugs and pats.
Our record for maintaining lines was the best in the nation.
As years rolled on, it reached into the seventh generation.

I sometimes wonder as I sit and contemplate our past.

Just how much money I have spent to make our marriage last.
If I had put my foot down in those early days instead,
Of all the tons of pet food that my loving wife has fed.

Of all the medications used, and visits to the vet.
Of all the purchased puppy things we simply had to get.
Of all the well intentioned rules that led to utter failure.
As we became the owners of the worst pets in Australia.

That brings me to the present and the numbers have reduced.
Our present line of neutered pets, not easy to seduce.
We're down to one decrepit dog and one demented cat.
From all the numbers I've endured, so I can live with that.

But she, the mother of all pets, had started to complain.
She thought that I should have a pet, that I'd have much to gain,
From knowing all the love they give, if only I would try.
'So how about it?' she had said. 'What is it you should buy?'

I gave the matter lots of thought, the whole pet inventory.
What is it that would calm my nerves,
become my pride and glory?
It must be cheap to buy and feed, with no need for attention,
And well behaved, with no bad traits or signs of proud pretension.

I found the answer on the farm while visiting our daughter.
The perfect pet, it cost no dough, it needs no feed or water.
Its numbers don't increase each year creating a large flock.
He caught my eye, I picked him up, I'd found my own pet *rock!*

The property's called Fairfield, so I had to call him Fairy,
Which tied in well you see cos our cat responds to Mary.
He sits upon my desk at home, he is my pride and joy.
A painted face that always smiles, he's such a lovely boy.

He never wanders out at night to feast on native life,

And to this day, he's never shown the need to find a wife.
He has no fleas, no worms or pains; he's free from all infection,
And best of all, unlike the cat, he follows all direction.

When I say sit, he does just that, until I tell him not to.
If I say stay, he always stays; he's smart, you'd think he knew
That if he does what he is told, he'll get an extra pat,
And always make his owner proud, I ask you how smart's that?

I haven't fed him anything since I first brought him here.
He doesn't need a coat or rug or other costly gear.
He makes no noise, he doesn't bite, no hair does he discard,
And best of all, I've never yet observed him foul the yard.

I hope he sees me out, my mate, be still here when I die,
And he will handle that event with courage; he won't cry.
I'll have to put him in my will and give my eldest son
The joy of owning fairy rock, the friendship, love and fun.

But if some ailment only known to lumps of lava stone,
Should strike him down before I go, and leave me all alone,
There'll be no visits to the vet, no needles drugs or pill.
I'll simply go to our backyard, *and chuck him down the hill!*

Several years passed before one day, purely by accident, and with a
bit of help from me, Fairy found a mate. Who would have thought
that rocks had hormones and knew all about the birds and bees (or
more likely in their case, the flowers and trees)?

FAIRY'S MATE

My Fairy Rock's no fairy any more.
He's heterosexual male, I know for sure.
The test I gave him proves he is not gay.
A lady's man. No boys for him. No way!

I found a mate for him the other day.
Stubbed my toe on her and noticed where she lay.
Her brilliance glistened in the morning dew,
And straightaway I thought of Fairy. I just knew.

I knew that they would make a breeding pair,
Though sexy looking rocks are pretty rare.
A pretty face, a healthy look, and wide from tip to tip.
A sure fire indicator of good rock-bearing hips.

To give a bit of privacy and help them on their way.
I sent them on a honeymoon in a drawer the other day.
They seemed to hit it off all right and made a lot of noise,
As they set out to breed a set of rocky girls and boys.

I took a peek this morning, but I didn't need to worry.
The bottom of the draw looked like a gravel quarry!
Little rocks abounded, all sizes, shapes, and colours.
They really are a lovely lot of little girls and fellas.

It suddenly occurred to me, while staring in my drawer,
That Fairy wasn't a good name for my rock anymore.
To make his name more macho was something I should do,
And to think up something suitable for the little mummy too.

The finance page gave me a clue as I read of the USA.
They seem to like their 'F' words too. I noticed some today.
Freddy Mac and Fanny Mae seemed to be well known,
So I named my two after them. Meet Fred and Fanny Stone.

Now they will be a model for a happy married life.
Proud as punch of all their kids, Dad Fred, and his new wife.
But I hope they can slow down a bit on all those bedroom capers.
I need to keep some drawer space spare
for all my poems and papers!

It is a rare occasion indeed that a problem with your pets can be turned to your advantage, but that is just what did happen to me recently. While stumbling around in the gully where I had found Fred, and wondering if I could hire a truck and bring him and his extended family home, I was amazed to come across a stone that must have been to uni with Old Blue. He could talk!

UNCLE JOCK

It's time to introduce you to the latest family member.
I found him down at Fairfield, when I went there in September.
He looked like any other stone, just a lump of lava rock,
But he said, 'Hey, hold on there, mate. I'm Freddy's Uncle Jock.

I haven't seen my nephew since you took him from the farm,
And I hope you haven't let the little hot head come to harm.
He's such a little bugger, and such a ladykiller.
I just bet he's found some sheila stone
and done his best to thrill her.'

There was no other option. I just had to tell the lot,
Of Fred and his mate Fanny, and how friendly they had got.
I wondered if this Uncle Jock could help me in my trouble.
If he could stop this randy pair, and burst their breeding bubble.

'The problem is', old Jock told me, 'that
all of us Rocks have habits.
We may have hearts of solid stone, but
we breed like bloody rabbits.
If we can't stop them, you, my friend, had better start to worry,
Cos the room you call an office will soon become a quarry.'

His warning set me thinking, and I had an inspiration.
Something that would suit all sides, a win-win situation.

I took them both, with all their kids, and
dropped them on our farm.
In a gully, near the road, where they could do no harm.

I'm waiting now, with bated breath, to watch their family bloom,
As pebble follows pebble, from that fertile Fanny's womb.
In years to come, they'll do their bit to ease my money worry.
I'll sell the lot to a concrete crowd as *a never-ending quarry!*

REMINISCENCE

The weak winter sun filtered through the window and warmed the bones of the old gentleman sitting in his wheelchair. In spite of his heavy jacket, his sheepskin slippers, and the crocheted blanket covering his legs, his frail body sagged under the combined stress of old age and an increasingly weakening heart. He looked forward without enthusiasm to another long day of boredom stretching ahead of him – another day exactly the same as yesterday, and the day before, and the day before that as well. *How long do I have to go on like this?* he wondered.

Ernie Myers had been a resident at the Jacaranda Retirement Village for more than two years now. Following the death of his wife, he spent a few months living with his daughter and her family but quickly realised that was not going to last forever. They needed their life, and his old-fashioned attitudes made living with them and their kids stressful for all concerned. He voluntarily entered his present accommodation, resigned to the fact that this was where he would end his days.

'Everything okay, Mr Myers?' asked the nurse as she popped her head through the open door.

'Yes, thank you, Jodie. Just soaking up some sun and thinking of the past, as usual. I just realised that today is the twenty-second of July, my wedding anniversary,' he replied.

'That must be very sad for you, I expect. How long were you married?' Jodie asked.

Ernie sighed and thought to himself how sad it was that everyone seemed to think a marriage ended when one partner died. As far as he was concerned, he and Abby were still as married as they had ever been. 'Sixty-two years today,' he replied. 'We didn't quite make it to our diamond wedding before my wife passed away.'

'I'm so sorry. You must really miss her,' Jodie said, with genuine feeling.

He turned to her with tears in his eyes. 'More than you could imagine, Jodie. More than you could ever imagine.'

Jodie crossed the room to give his shoulder a squeeze. She adjusted his blanket and refilled his glass.

'I'll just leave you to your thoughts, Mr Myers,' she said kindly. 'Just call if you need anything. I'll bring you your morning tea soon.'

'Thanks, Jodie, but I do wish you'd call me Ernie,' he said as she hurried out of the room to hide her embarrassment. Ernie closed his eyes and let his mind drift back over the years.

*　*　*

Abby was the most beautiful sight he had ever seen. As he drowsily awoke from the anaesthetic, there she was fussing over him, taking his pulse, and urging him to wake up. A starched white veil highlighted her pretty face, and her nurse's uniform accentuated her small, neat figure.

'Come on, Mr Myers. Wakey, wakey. No more of this lying around asleep in the middle of the day,' she joked.

In spite of the effects of ether and an appendicitis operation, Ernie could still hear the sound of her voice and recall her sparkling personality. He fell in love with her that day, and his stay in hospital became one of the highlights of his life.

Not only was Abby his first love, he had never really had a girlfriend at all. Since leaving school, he had worked on cattle properties well out of town, and as his only means of transport was a horse, his opportunities to socialise were few and far between. An occasional trip to town for groceries and the two or three trips to the railhead with cattle each year hardly gave him much of a chance to meet anyone. By the time he was in his twenties, he had become a very shy young man. And then he contracted appendicitis.

He could never really understand why Abby was as attracted to him as he was to her, but that is exactly what happened. In those days, even an operation like a simple appendectomy resulted in a lengthy stay in hospital. The fact that Ernie would have to look after himself when he got home induced the doctor to allow him to stay for a full three weeks. By the time he left, a relationship had developed between them that was to last forever.

A smile crossed his face for the first time in days as he recalled how Abby would come to him after lights out and draw the curtains around his bed. Then she would sit beside him, and they would spend hours whispering to each other. They found they had much in common, and by the end of Ernie's stay in hospital, they were great friends. *But not lovers,* he thought ruefully. It took two years of frustrated letter writing and occasional outings before they were eventually married and moved into a cottage on the property where he worked – just him and his sweet little Abby. Then they became lovers and stayed so for the next sixty years.

*   *   *

Ernie woke with a start. He must have dozed off as he reminisced about his past. His thoughts returned to those early days with Abby. *What a girl she was! And so much fun!* He still couldn't get over how she put it over the locals at the annual stockman's carnival.

It was their own fault. They insisted she come onto the organising committee. Probably thought she'd do all the work for them and keep out of the road when the big decisions were being made. Big mistake that was! It all came to a head when she insisted the bushman's contest, called The Augathella Fella, should be opened to women as well as men. 'What's the point?' they had argued. 'Women would only make fools of themselves.'

Finally, probably to get some peace and quiet, they agreed, provided she guaranteed she could find at least one female to enter the contest. Even if you have to do it yourself, they had joked, because Abby was about five feet four and weighed no more than seven stone. Fair enough, she had said, and they had all looked forward to her competing in the gruelling events against the toughest young men in the district. Well, the big day arrived, and there on the list of contestants appeared the name, A. Myers. The locals could hardly wait.

Ernie could still recall the look on their faces when he and Abby arrived at the showground towing a horse float and with a passenger in the back of the ute.

'Hey, fellas, come and meet my little sister,' he had called out to them. 'This here's Angela, but she's no angel. She's a jillaroo out at Quilpie and can ride, drink, and fight as good as any of you, I bet.' Their jaws bit the dust as the six-foot-twelve-stone Angela climbed down from the ute and cracked a few knuckles with a handshake that made them wince.

Ernie was chuckling away to himself when Jodie wheeled into the room with his morning tea.

'Penny for your thoughts,' she offered. 'You think up a dirty joke from the past?'

'No, nothing like that. I was just remembering how Abby put it over the locals when she entered my sister in the bushman's carnival not long after we were married.' Ernie filled Jodie in on how it had all come about.

'You see, they just assumed A. Myers was Abby, when actually it was my unmarried sister, Angela. They didn't know what hit them when the contest started.'

Jodie sat on the spare chair and asked, 'So what did they have to do?'

'Well, there were ten of them in it, nine men and Angie. First off, they had to load fifty bales of hay on to the back of a truck, against the clock, you see. She beat them all by more than a minute. Then they had to crutch ten sheep with hand shears. Some of the poor dills couldn't do it at all, and Angie beat the rest by two sheep or more. She used hand shears all the time where she worked.'

Ernie drank a few sips of tea and nibbled on a biscuit before he continued. 'The next task was to dig a hole and stand a strainer post. Well, one of the blokes was a fencing contractor, and he gave her a bit of a touch-up, but she still came second.'

'She must have been quite a girl,' Jodie suggested.

'Still is. She's worked on the land all her life. Still does. Anyway, the final event came, and everyone thought it might find her out. You see, it was a horse race over a mile, out to the main road and back, and she was heavier than most of the men in the field. But what they didn't know was that I'd borrowed the boss' big thoroughbred stallion. She ran them down over the final hundred yards and won going away.'

'Abby must have really enjoyed that,' Jodie said as she prepared to leave. 'You must have so many wonderful memories from your past, Ernie. You'll have to tell me more sometime.'

'Well, plenty of memories, all right,' Ernie replied, 'but not all of them are as happy as that one, I'm afraid.'

*   *   *

No, life wasn't all happy times, Ernie thought to himself. *It could also be totally cruel.* His mind slipped from some of the happiest times of his life to some of the saddest. If only he could have done something to avoid them, but even with the benefit of hindsight, the tragic and unhappy times could not have been averted. *That's what life was all about,* he supposed, *enjoying the good, putting up with the bad, and trying to live with the tragic.* He'd done them all and had reached the stage, where life no longer held any prospect of joy or despair, just memories. And now, after all the pleasure of recalling his early days with Abby, those memories turned to his darkest hours.

Poor little Johnny. How excited they had been when Abby found she was expecting their first child after they had been trying for a few years! Allison was their pride and joy – pretty, intelligent, and with her mother's bubbly nature. Life was great, and they tried hard to produce a little brother or sister for her, without success. Then, when Allison was five, a son arrived, and their world was complete.

For ten years they enjoyed their life on the property. Little Johnny followed his dad everywhere. Whenever he could escape from his mother's schooling, he would be out on a horse, helping the men to muster or take part in all the varied activities of station life. At home, he helped his mother around the house, and that led to disaster.

Ernie forced himself to push the memory from his mind by taking a drink of water and looking out the window at the gardener busily trimming a hedge. His accommodation here was very comfortable, and the grounds were immaculate, but it didn't measure up to the wide brown plains that had been his home all his life. Hell, he missed it, but he guessed he'd probably never get to see it again. He could still see it in his mind, though, clear as day – the sweeping paddocks, brigalow scrub, dusty stockyards, and grazing horses. And there in the middle of it sat their little house, rose garden in the front, veggies in the backyard, and there under the big tree in the corner, the woodheap.

His thoughts returned to the disaster that befell their family on that late October afternoon. His ears ached with the memory of Johnny's cry of anguish from the backyard. 'Mum, Dad!' he had shouted. 'Come quick! A snake bit me!' As usual, he had gone to fetch wood to fill the box beside their woodstove. It was his job, and he had done it every day for years without incident, and then this happened.

Ernie and Abby rushed to the back door and met him hopping on one leg and holding his other ankle. As was the recommended procedure of the day, Abby applied a tourniquet to his thigh, cut through the puncture marks, and tried to suck the poison out of his system. Together, they loaded him into their old car and raced for the hospital half an hour away. Abby's plaintive commentary from the back seat and Johnny's moans made him drive like a madman, and he screeched to a stop at the emergency entrance. They had done their best, but it wasn't good enough. Their boy was unconscious, and he never came around. His life was gone, and their lives were shattered. *Things would never be the same.*

As if to wrench him away from his tragic thoughts, Jodie came bouncing into his room again.

'Ready to go to lunch, Mr Myers? My, you look sad! What have you been thinking about now?' she asked. As she wheeled him to the dining room, he told her of Johnny's death. In spite of Jodie's obvious sympathy, he didn't feel any better and ate very little lunch. He was pleased to be taken back to the seclusion of his room, back to his reminiscences, back to the next great sadness in their lives.

Initially, he and Abby had been excited when Allison had told them she was engaged to this marvellous man, who worked in her office in Brisbane. It seemed a bit strange that they had not even met him, but their daughter had always been a level-headed girl, so they assumed she knew what she was doing.

They met him for the first time a few days before the wedding, and from day one they couldn't for the life of them see what attracted their daughter to such an overbearing and bombastic man. He was nearly ten years older than her and appeared to treat her more as a servant than an equal. If only they had met him earlier in the relationship, they might have been able to influence her to see through him, but by then it was too late. The die was cast.

The marriage seemed to work all right for the first few years, and they produced two little girls, but Ernie and Abby seldom saw them as they grew up. Once or twice each year, Allison brought them out to the property for a visit, but they never stayed long, and their father never came with them.

'We should have realised something was wrong,' Ernie mused to himself, but Allison didn't let on what was happening back home. Thank God she finally made the move before it was too late. He would never forget the forlorn sight of her when she arrived on their doorstep with the kids and a carload of clothes or the bruised and swollen face that crumpled into tears as she collapsed into her mother's arms. The mongrel had belted her up one time too many, and when he started to treat the girls in the same way, she knew it was time to go.

Andy and Abby had done the best they could for the little family, but their lives could never be the same without a father. Allison never remarried, and while the girls seemed to grow up without too many hang-ups, they would never know the pleasure of being part of a normal loving family.

Sadness wracked Ernie's body as he recalled this long-running saga. He was sure it played a big part in Abby's illness. He had become convinced that stress was a major cause of cancer, and he remained bitter to this very day over her lingering death. It just wasn't fair that such a wonderful person should suffer in such a terrible way.

He had done his best to help her right to the end and clearly remembered holding her hand as she took her last shuddering breaths. And then she was gone – lost to him forever, and leaving him now with nothing but memories. Through bleary eyes he looked at their wedding photo beside the bed. What a great team they had been! He picked it up and planted a kiss on her smiling face.

'Happy anniversary, love,' he whispered.

*   *   *

'Cuppa time again, Ernie,' Jodie said as she bounced into his room. 'Chocolate cake too. Your favourite. Come on. Wake up.'

She sat the tray on the table and turned to straighten him up, but he hadn't moved.

'Ernie. Mr Myers. Are you all right?' she asked. He remained slumped in his chair, chin on chest, and eyes closed. She touched his shoulder. He didn't move. Realisation dawned on her, and she felt under his ear for a pulse. There was none. He was gone.

Jodie noticed his frail old hands were firmly wrapped around his wedding photo. Looking more closely at his face, she could see tears still glistening in the corners of his eyes, and the damp stains where others had run down his cheeks.

'Goodbye, Ernie,' she said kindly. 'I think I know where you've gone to. I hope you find her.'

'Reminiscence' explained

Like Ernie, as we grow old, we spend more time looking backwards than forwards, probably because there is more of the former, and the latter is a bit problematic anyway. In reality, I suppose life would become pretty boring if it didn't have its ups and downs, and they all contribute to the tapestry of our lives.

In the end, though, when we reach Ernie's stage of life, memories are our only asset we have left that we can utilise. Hopefully!

The part of this yarn relating to the courtship of Ernie and Abby directly follows a real event. It happened, almost precisely as described, when my father was the patient and my mother the nurse over seventy years ago. They even produced a little Johnny, me, but thankfully I never had an encounter with a king brown.

Although Dad really was a shy young bushie, he had taught himself to write bush poetry, and I can visualise him poring over this poem under a hurricane light in his little house in the bush. I never thought to ask, but I bet he never dared to show it to my mother.

MY VISITOR

I can visualise her beauty, and her figure tall and slim,
As she goes about her duty, in those rooms so cool and dim.
There are tempos to be taken, and pulses too, I know.
There are pillows to be shaken, and patients asked, 'Did your BO?'

The flowers must be shifted, the quilts all folded up.
Patients must of course be lifted, that they might better sup.
Bottles must be taken, while others must be brought.
Thirsts there are to slacken, and diseases to be fought.

Tea is over, crowds come pouring in, their sick friends for to see.
As I listen, I keep wonderin', why no one visits me.
Perhaps I am not worth a cuss, and perhaps never will.
Yet, when I die, there'll be a fuss. They'll miss old cobber Bill.

Eight o'clock, and lights are out. All is quiet and still.
Two hours time, or there about, there's one who'll visit Bill.
She'll ask him how he was today, and why he's not asleep.
She'll wonder why he bids her stay, and why his pulses leap.

All night long he'll lay awake, plotting his golden scheme.
Thinking thoughts he mustn't speak, dreaming his lonely dream.

This second poem has nothing to do with the story really, but I
recently read of a bushman's contest called the Cunnamulla Fulla
and was reminded of the one I had written years ago called the

Augathella Fella, a better title in my view, but not if you're staging it at Cunnamulla, I suppose.

I have a good mate who has lived in my town on the coast for many years, but several times each year, he heads off for weeks at a time to visit his old home town of Augathella in Western Queensland. He suffers a lot of ribbing over what the possible attraction can be. After all, Augathella doesn't seem to hold too many delights for the average tourist. Once a thriving town in the wool boom years of the 1950s, today it is but a shadow of it's former self, but to someone who spent his youth there, it is still home.

THE AUGATHELLA FELLA

Bob's been to Augathella, he's been gone for weeks and weeks,
And I don't know why he goes there, what he sees.
Is it flies, and crows and sandflies, or a dust storm that he seeks?
It's time for explanations, time to level with us please.

So we'll go to Augathella, to this jewel of the west,
So we can share the benefits that it alone bestows.
To seek the vision splendid, with which that town is blest,
And to solve that tricky riddle, what he does, and why he goes.

So we head to Augathella, out into the setting sun,
Pushing roos and southern tourists off the track.
Past Dalby, Miles, and Mitchell, boy that trip is not much fun,
So it doesn't seem the scenery is making him go back.

So this is Augathella, eh? This jewel of the west.
No towering gothic structures or high rise units here.
No sweeping parks and gardens, and like I always guessed,
Just miles and miles of desert, with some houses drab and drear.

What to do in Augathella now we've sampled all the sights.
We must seek out where the action is that old Bob seems to yearn.
As we brush away the blowflies, and ignore the pig-dog fights,
It's to the 'Thella' bowl's club that we turn.

What's with this Augathella that keeps taking him back there?
What makes him leave us here and tend to roam?
It's surely not the scenery, or the township bleak and bare.
No, the answer is quite simple. Augathella is Bob's home.

Finally, another little poem that my father wrote some forty years after the first one. He was launching a campaign to build a community owned Retirement Centre, much like Ernie's Jacaranda Retirement Village. It took many years, but it now contains forty units providing the sort of care and support that make the twilight years of elderly people like Ernie comfortable.

A Place in the Sun

The old people were tired and lonely, their
role in life finished and done.
They mused to themselves that if only they
could find a place in the sun.
To relax and rest, now they're feeble, to be
cared for in their time of need.
Midst pleasant surroundings and people their
own age, who'd listen and heed.

When they talked again of the old days, of
things that they'd seen, things they did.
When bosses were scant with their praises,
and men worked a week for a quid.
They'd think of the battles they'd wagered,
'gainst, droughts and floods and fire.
Now all they sought was a place in the sun,
where they could rest and retire.

They found what they sought to enter,
this haven of comfort and joy.
In the Senior Citizen's Centre, we intend to build soon in Kilcoy.

RETRIBUTION

Alan Harper loved his dad with a passion. He was an only child, and now, at ten years of age, it was a pretty good bet he would remain so. That state meant he enjoyed his father's total interest and commitment, unspoiled by having to share it with any siblings. Oh, he loved his mother too, but the two males in the family had a special rapport that no female could share. They worshipped each other.

And then his father was killed, run down by a car thief trying to avoid arrest. Just like that. Here one minute, gone the next. No rhyme or reason. No justice. Just gone, leaving Alan and his mother alone, destitute, and inconsolable. They wondered if they could survive the future without him, and yet somehow they did.

While the next two years were hard, they managed. They learnt to put aside the emptiness in their lives and to adjust to his absence as best they could. As if to replace the bond Alan had enjoyed with his dad, he grew ever closer to his mum, trying as hard as he knew how to replace what had been so tragically ripped away from her. She was a lovely caring mother, and she deserved a better deal from life, but instead, she ended up with a far worse one incurable cancer. She was given only months to live.

Since Jed Harper had been killed, she had lost most of her appetite for life and was not all that distressed at the sentence on her own account. But for Alan's presence, she would have been quite ready to join her husband, as life held no great appeal for her any more. At times, she could, in fact, have welcomed it on her own account, but the thought of leaving twelve-year-old Alan behind, alone in the world, had kept her going. Now the decision had been taken from her. That was what was going to happen, and somehow, she had to do what she could to help him cope with another catastrophic loss in his short life.

She was already concerned at the change in him since Jed's death. Possibly he was absorbing some of her despondency, but his nature had certainly changed, and not for the better. He seemed more withdrawn and insular, more inclined to sit staring mindlessly at some drivel on the telly than to go and mix with his friends. Sports no longer held any appeal for him since his father wasn't there to watch, so he gave it up. Gradually, his circle of friends disappeared, and his sole companion in life became his mother – a mother who was about to leave him totally alone in the world. The thought of what that might do to him filled her with dread.

Only one possible solution came to her troubled mind. Her parents were both dead, but she did have a younger married sister who lived with her husband and three daughters on a farm. They were not all that close and rarely saw each other since she married and moved to the country. The fact that she had never liked her sister's choice of a husband didn't help either. Barry always seemed to be moody and temperamental to her, so unlike Jed, and family get-togethers had always been a bit of an ordeal. She knew for a fact that Alan didn't think much of him. But what else could she do but ask her sister Jane if she would take him into her home?

Jane's response did nothing to relieve her concerns. While she was naturally upset at her sister's impending death, when the conversation turned to Alan's future, she was disturbingly circumspect, saying she would talk to her husband about it and see what they could work out. This was hardly the loving response Alan's mother had hoped for, and indeed expected, but what else could she do? She and Jed had not been wealthy, but she had been left with their house and some insurance money, so she would be able to provide for his upbringing and education. Maybe it would ease Jane's concerns if expense was a problem.

Her anxiety was eased when Jane rang to say that, of course, they would take on the responsibility of looking after Alan and that she should not worry about it any more. She and Barry were making plans for his arrival and would be ready when the time came. This was great news and lifted a great burden from her mind, but she still sensed a strange and lingering concern at Jane's less-than-fulsome support. Still, it was the best solution she could come up with, and, just like his mother's impending death, Alan had no option but to accept his fate.

*   *   *

It didn't take long for Alan to realise the cause of the hesitation in his aunt's offer to accept him. His presence in their household certainly added to the tension, but it was obvious, even to someone as young as him, that it had existed before he came. In short, Barry Wade was not a very nice man. In fact, he was an utter pig. Brought up in a loving household as he had been, Alan couldn't believe the way he treated Aunt Jane and the girls.

He constantly ranted and raved at them, especially when he had been on one of his regular drinking bouts, and even became physically violent towards them on occasions. Aunt Jane sometimes showed the results of these attacks, and he had caught her crying quietly to herself at times. His cousins were intimidated by their father and seemed to have no love or respect for him. Now Alan's presence gave him more reason to fire up, and he became the butt of many of Barry's outbursts. His new life became a misery, one that he was forced to endure stoically, but he came to hate Barry Wade with a passion he had not felt for years.

By the time he was fifteen, Alan found himself constantly thinking of how he might escape. If he had anyone to run to, he would have, but there was nowhere to go, and living in the country made that task even more impossible. He also had come to love his aunt and felt bad at the thought of leaving her and the girls to endure their unhappy lives alone. Then something happened that tipped him over the edge.

Aunt Jane and the two young girls had gone to town shopping, and Alan was working away from the house when he cut his hand rather badly and headed home to bandage it. As he walked along the side of the house, he heard his fourteen-year-old cousin, Jessie, sobbing and pleading with her father in one of the bedrooms.

'Please don't, Dad. I don't want to do this.'

'You'll be all right, Jess. You know you're my favourite girl, don't you? You're a big girl now, and need to learn about these things. You'll get to like it, you'll see,' he crooned.

'No, Dad. It hurts, and it's wrong. I'll tell Mum!' Jessie wailed.

'She won't believe you, Jess. It's her fault anyway. Miserable bitch. If she was a decent wife to me, I wouldn't need to ask you.'

'No, Dad. Please. Not again. You promised me you'd stop after the last time,' she pleaded.

Alan could take it no longer. He went into the kitchen and started making noise as he searched for the first-aid kit. He slammed a cupboard door, and the discussion in the bedroom ceased. Barry came through the door, obviously unhappy at Alan's presence.

'What are you up to, you little pest?' he yelled at him. 'I thought you were supposed to be fixing that fence like I told you. What're you after here?'

'I cut my hand, Barry. Need to put some disinfectant on it and bandage it up. Won't be long.'

His uncle glared at him for a moment and then took a stubby from the fridge and headed out of the house. Alan made sure he took his time treating his hand and then made himself a sandwich. By the time he left the house, he could hear Aunt Jane's car in the distance and knew he had saved Jessie from further trouble, at least for the time being.

He was a shy fifteen-year-old boy, and at a loss as to what to do about the conversation he had overheard. There was no one that he felt he could talk to, including Aunt Jane, and yet if he did nothing, he had a fair idea what Barry had in store for Jessie. All he could do was to be alert for any time when Aunt Jane and Jessie were separated and Barry was around. He made a point of hanging around too. They had reached the point where they detested each other, and Alan wondered how it could possibly get any worse.

*   *   *

The day arrived when he found out. He heard Barry yelling out to him from the direction of the tractor shed. His cries were muffled, and he sounded desperate, so Alan hurried over to investigate. He could scarcely credit the scene that confronted him. Barry was pinned between the tractor and the barn door, his chest being crushed by the grille. The motor was running, so he had obviously gone to open the door and the tractor apparently had rolled forward. He must have turned around and tried to hold it off, but failed, and now couldn't push it back to free himself.

'Thank God you're here!' Barry gasped. 'Quick. Hop in and reverse this bloody thing off me. I can hardly breathe.'

Something clicked in Alan's mind – retribution. At last the bastard was getting his just desserts. For once, he wasn't in control – Alan was. Here he was pleading for help – Alan's help. He hesitated. In some macabre way, he was enjoying the situation and didn't want it to end. Then Barry did a silly thing.

Gasping harder now, he rasped out, 'Come on, you stupid bastard! Get this thing off me before it kills me. What are you standing there staring at?'

Alan didn't move. He just stood there watching Barry's contorted face, with memories of all the occasions he had abused him verbally and emotionally flooding back to him. He thought of poor little Jessie too, and Aunt Jane.

Drawing courage from the position of power in which he found himself, he went closer and eyeballed his distraught uncle.

'Before I get you out of this, Barry, you've got to promise to leave Jessie alone. You've got to stop bashing Aunt Jane too. I mean it.'

Barry exploded, 'What? You mind your own business, you dirty little shit! What I do is none of your business. You wouldn't even be here if I had my way. Now stop being such a little smart arse. Get in this bloody tractor and back it off me. I'll give you threaten me when I get free.'

Alan stared silently at him for a few seconds and then climbed into the tractor cab. Bulging, frantic eyes pleaded with him from a distorted, desperate face. Any compassion he had in his nature deserted him, as he sat grasping the gear lever. *Why hadn't the tractor done a proper job and killed the mongrel?*

'Come on. For God's sake hurry up, stupid! I'm dying here!' Barry wheezed.

Cold, dispassionate eyes stared back at him, devoid of sympathy and full of revenge.

'How right you are, you miserable bastard!' Alan muttered to himself. 'How right you are!'

Gritting his teeth, he shoved the tractor into first gear, released the clutch, and watched dispassionately as it jerked forward and crushed the life out of his obnoxious uncle. He felt no fear, no compassion, no regrets, and no guilt. His action was calm and collected. If he felt any fear at all, it was for his own cold-bloodedness and lack of emotion. Momentarily, he wondered what he had become, but it passed, and was replaced with a feeling approaching exhilaration at what he had done.

Leaving the tractor running and in neutral as he had found it, he ran to the house, calling as he ran, 'Aunt Jane! Aunt Jane! Come quick! Uncle Barry's had an accident!'

*　　*　　*

The funeral was over, the girls had gone to bed, and Alan and Jane were sharing a pot of tea. He might have been imagining it, but to Alan's mind, Jane already looked better, in spite of her bereavement. The haunted look had faded from her eyes. Worried and tired, yes, but not nervous or terrified. Not for the first time, Alan wondered if she knew about Barry and Jess. He suspected that she did but still couldn't bring himself to ask, especially now. Anyway, it didn't matter so much any more. At least it wouldn't happen again.

'Aunt Jane, you know you can count on me to help you run the farm,' he said. 'I can leave school soon, and I know how to do most things around here now.'

'Thanks, Alan. I appreciate your offer, but we won't be staying here. I'm a city girl really and have never been happy on the land. As soon as I can arrange it, I'll sell up here and we can all go and live in Brisbane. I can go back to teaching.'

'What about me, Aunt Jane? Will I be coming with you?' he asked.

'Of course, you will, Alan. I promised your mother I'd look after you, and I will, to the best of my ability,' Jane said, taking his hand and giving it a gentle squeeze. 'You can finish high school there, and go to university if you want to.'

'Thanks, Aunt Jane. I really appreciate what you've done for me since Mum died. You can rely on me to look after you, and the girls too, no matter what it takes,' Alan said with feeling. Holding her gaze, he calmly stated, 'I'd do anything for you. Anything.'

Jane looked thoughtfully into his serious grey eyes, eyes that contained so much sadness and suffering. But they were now also filled with a depth of steely determination that it almost frightened her. Was that also a hint of fear and uncertainty that she also detected? She took him into her arms and held him to her body.

'I know you would, Alan. Thank you from the bottom of my heart.' Jane thought she felt him relax against her. 'I appreciate everything you've done for me and the girls. I really do, Alan. Everything.'

Pulling back and placing her hands on his trembling shoulders, she looked again into those serious, loving eyes. 'You heard me, Alan. *Everything.*'

'Retribution' explained

I guess this story demonstrates the good and the bad sides of fatherhood, and the impact that both can have on a boy's development. But for the unfortunate circumstances that resulted in Alan being orphaned, he would have grown up to be a normal well-adjusted kid. As it was, plucked from an ideal family situation and plunged into a dysfunctional one, his character changed completely.

One of the biggest social changes of the last thirty or forty years has been the increased incidence of divorce, resulting in many one-parent families. In the vast majority of these, custody is granted to the mother, and the kids grow up without a male presence in the household. I'm sure the mothers do their best to cover that absence, but it is a situation that defies natural human instincts.

This little jingle was written one Father's Day some years ago.

FATHER'S DAY

Mother, Father, Sister, Brother. Which one would you be?
I'd rather be the father, than be all the other three!

I've done a few things in my life, some good, some fair, some bad,
But of them all, the best by far, is simply being dad.
It is the most important role, perhaps behind one other.
No dad can do the job alone. He needs a wife and mother.

To watch your sons grow into men and find their way in life,
Hopefully to settle down and find themselves a wife.
To see your daughters also wed to someone who is true,
Someone who will also learn to be a good dad too.

Too often now the sad fact is, that marriages don't last,
And kids are left with mum or dad, the other has been cast.
No matter how they try to fill, the hole that has been left,
The family that has no dad, is lacking, sad, bereft.

So here's to dad on father's day, a chance to pay him back,
For all he's done, for all of you, along life's bumpy track.
Imagine if he wasn't there, how life would be quite sad.
Then pop a cork, or flip a lid, and drink a toast to dad.

RUSTY

'At last,' he mumbled to himself through gritted teeth. 'At long bloody last.'

Rolling himself over to a sitting position on the side of his bed, Rusty eyed the first streaky grey lines of the approaching dawn that were visible through his open door. He tried to stand, but the piercing pain in his gut forced him to flop back down.

'Gotta do it,' he again muttered. 'If I don't, I'm a dead man.'

This time he forced himself to stay standing and stumble to the edge of the veranda. For the umpteenth time that night, he tried to relieve himself, but once again, nothing came. His bloated bladder sent shuddering pains up into his chest, and he reached for a post to support himself. Thinking he was going to pass out, he was about to struggle back to bed when he saw a light come on in the homestead kitchen.

'Thank God for that,' he whispered to the chill dawn light. 'The missus is up.'

Bent almost double, he hobbled across the backyard from his quarters to the main house and approached the back door.

* * *

Everybody knew how tough Rusty Dawes was. He'd proved it hundreds of times over his years spent in the harsh conditions of the giant cattle stations that straddle the Queensland or Northern Territory border. He'd been born on the veranda of one of them to a young quarter-caste domestic girl, his father being an itinerant Irish stockman who had moved on to Alice Springs, even before the blessed event of his birth occurred. Father and son never set eyes on each other. He was reared on the station until he was given a job as a rouseabout by a passing droving team at the age of fourteen.

Thus began a harsh life, eked out on droving trips and in mustering camps across the vast expanses of the Barkley Tablelands. His was a generation born to spend its life in a saddle, before road trains and helicopter mustering changed the way things were done forever. For the worse too, all his mates agreed. Not for them herds of terrified cattle galloping over the plains with a chopper up their bums. Of course, they still had to deal with them in the yards. No one had yet come up with a machine to toss and brand calves.

The only thing his father had bequeathed him, other than life itself, was his short stature and gaunt frame. This, coupled with the fact that he had learned to ride almost as soon as he could walk, was only natural that he would gravitate to the rodeo circuit. There, injury was ever present, and he suffered plenty of bumps and bruises. But in the bush, those things are left to heal themselves, and he had never been to a hospital nor had a day's sickness in his life. That was, up until today.

Today he was in agony. Today he couldn't pee at all, and he felt like he was dying. The problem had been getting worse for sometime now. At first, he had put it down to his latest buster. *Probably just bruised kidneys or something,* he thought, but over recent days, instead of getting better, it had got worse. A few years ago, he could knock bark off a gum tree with a full bladder. Now it was an effort to reach past the toe of his riding boots, especially on a cold morning. But today, even that was beyond him. He struggled to the back door and knocked as loudly as his debilitated state allowed. 'You there, missus?' he called out.

Robin Thompson dried her hands on her apron and hurried to the door. 'Coming, Rusty,' she replied, worried at what brought on this early morning call. Rusty was a bloke who always kept to himself and only ever came to the house at mealtimes. She was shocked by the sight of him that confronted her when she opened the door. 'Good grief, man! What's the matter with you? You look terrible.'

'Sorry, missus. I'm real crook. Can't pee. Don't know what's wrong, but it's killin' me,' he rasped between clenched teeth.

Robin put her arm around his shoulders and led him inside. 'Come in here and lie down, Rusty. I'll see what I can do for you.'

Rusty staggered to a chair and slumped on to it. 'Can't lie down, missus. I'll just sit here, if that's all right. Haven't got any painkillers, have you?'

'Sure. I'll be right back, but I think I'll ring the Flying Doctor first and see what he says.' She hurried into the office, leaving Rusty huddled on his chair, hugging his aching belly.

*   *   *

The next two hours dragged on horribly for Rusty as he waited for the Flying Doctor to arrive. Hunched under a blanket in the kitchen, teeth clenched in agony, the drone of the landing plane was music to his ears, but he knew his ordeal was far from over. The boss's Toyota soon pulled up in a cloud of dust, and the doctor hurried inside where Robin greeted her.

'Come on in, Doctor,' she said. 'I'm Robin. I think I spoke to you on the phone.'

'Yes, that's right, Mrs Thompson. I'm Kelly Saunders. Now, where's this poor man?'

'Right through here in the kitchen, and please call me Robin,' she said. 'I've been trying to make him as comfortable as possible, but he's in terrible pain. Do you think you can help him?'

'From what you told me on the phone, I think I can guess what his problem is. If I'm right, I'll have him fixed up in a few minutes,' she replied. As they entered the kitchen, Rusty tried to struggle to his feet. 'This is Dr Saunders, Rusty,' Robin said.

Kelly put a hand on his shoulder and gently pushed him back to his seat. 'Hello, Rusty. Don't try to stand up. Thanks, Robin. Rusty and I will just have a little talk, and I'll call you when I need you.'

The waves of pain sweeping through him momentarily paled into insignificance when compared to the nightmare sight that now confronted poor old Rusty. It had been embarrassing enough talking to the boss's wife about his problems, and he had worried for the last two hours about talking to a total stranger about it, even a doctor.

Now, removing his blanket and getting ready to inspect him was a very attractive young woman, who couldn't be more than twenty-five years old. In all of his fifty years, no woman had ever seen his private parts, let alone a young girl like this. How was he ever going to tell her about his problems? Kelly saw the fear in his eyes and guessed what was causing it.

'Rusty, my name is Kelly. I'm the RFDS doctor, and I think I can fix your problem pretty quickly. Mrs Thompson told me your symptoms, so I know what is needed. I want you to relax and let me help you. Okay?'

Another spasm hit him, bringing his attention back to his main concern. 'Sorry, miss. This is a bit embarrassin' for me. It's my peein', you see. I can't seem to pee, and it's killin' me.'

Kelly gently removed his blanket. 'Yes, and we'll have to find out what's causing that to happen later. But first things first. For now we've got to empty your bladder.'

'Yair, well, that's what I've been tryin' to do all night. It just won't happen.'

'So that's why you're going to have to let me help you, Rusty. Let me explain what we have to do. We've got to siphon it out of your bladder, just like you might do to transfer petrol from a drum into a car. Your tube seems to be blocked off, so we are going to have to insert a temporary one into your bladder. It's called a catheter, and it doesn't hurt much. I bet you've suffered worse.'

Her comforting words had done little to ease Rusty's fears. 'How you gonna do that? You gonna operate on me here?'

'No, Rusty. No operation, but it may be a bit uncomfortable. Still the pilot tells me you're a tough old bird,' Kelly said as she reached into her bag. 'What you have to do is let me pass this tube through your penis. You know. Your old fellow.'

Rusty nearly fell off the chair. 'What? I couldn't let you do that, miss.'

Kelly put the tube back in her bag and took Rusty's hands in hers. 'Look, Rusty,' she said. 'I'm afraid you have no option if you want to recover. You'll just have to shut your eyes and forget I'm a woman. It will only take a minute, and your pain will be all over. Now what do you say?'

His mind was in turmoil. *Why the hell did this have to happen?* This girl was young enough to be his daughter, if he had one, and here she was wanting to do something to him that he could barely get his mind around. But what options did he have? *Just lie down and die in agony like a cow in a bog. What a way to go!* Opening his eyes, he took in the sympathy on her face, the gentle hands holding his own, and gave her a nod.

'God, I'm in pain,' he said. 'I suppose you'll have to go ahead then, miss. Just don't tell anyone what you did, though, will you?'

Kelly gave his hands a squeeze. 'Of course not. Not a soul. Patient confidentiality. Just give me a minute to organise a room with Mrs Thompson. I'll be right back.'

*　　*　　*

Thirty minutes later, Kelly left her patient dozing and went through to the kitchen where she found Robin taking a tray of scones from the oven.

'Come and have a cuppa, Kelly. How is the poor old fellow going?'

Kelly pulled up a chair at the kitchen table. 'He's okay now. As I suspected, it was a blocked urethra preventing him from passing water. He's terribly embarrassed at having me attend him, though. I promised not to tell anyone what we had to do to relieve him.'

'The secret's safe with me. No one else needs to know. Now how about this cuppa, and would you like a scone or two? You must be starving after such an early call-out.'

'Yes, please. They smell delicious.'

The two women chatted about other things while they enjoyed the morning tea. Kelly had been reared on a property in New South Wales and, on completing her training, had volunteered for service with the RFDS. She loved the work and found she was able to relate really well to the down-to-earth country people who became her clients. She would need all of her charms for what she intended to do next.

'I'm rather worried as to what caused Rusty's problem. If we leave it untreated, it will probably happen again. Tell me, do you know if he's ever had a prostate test?' she asked as they packed the sink.

'Not really, but I would be surprised if he has. I have a feeling you might be the first doctor he has ever spoken to. Why?'

For a moment, Kelly wondered if it was ethical for her to be talking about one of her patients with a stranger like this but then judged in her own mind that Robin was as close to being family as Rusty was likely to have. Besides, she might need her support in what she was planning.

'Robin, he may have prostate cancer, or at least an enlarged prostate. If so, he should have treatment right away. Before I leave, I'm going to talk to him about it. I'll see if his acceptance of our recent bout of personal familiarity will extend to allowing me to do a digital examination,' she said, unable to hide a smile.

'Well, good luck with that, but if he needs to go to town for further tests or treatment, we will look after him. He's such a nice old fellow. Just like one of the family really. In the meantime, I'll take some morning tea to the boys down at the yards so you have some privacy.'

*　*　*

Rusty lay in a semi-daze, due to the sedative Kelly had given him. The relief her treatment had provided left him feeling weak after the hours of sleepless pain he had endured. He lifted the blanket and looked at the tube protruding from his weapon, with the last of the contents of his bladder slowly draining into the bucket beside the bed. *Bloody hell! How embarrassing, having that young girl doing that to me!* But it was worth it. He just hoped he never bumped into her again after today. And then, there she was.

'Hello again, Rusty. Feeling better now? My goodness! Look at that. Nearly half a bucketful. Would you like a cup of tea?' she asked, passing him the mug she had brought with her.

'Love one, thanks,' he replied, avoiding her eyes. 'I thought you'd gone home.'

'I can't do that till I've fixed you up. Can't leave you draining into a bucket for the rest of your life, can we? Besides, we haven't found out what caused the trouble yet, have we?'

Rusty propped himself up on his elbow and sipped his tea. 'What do you reckon is wrong with me, miss?'

Kelly knelt in front of him, forcing him to meet her gaze. 'I'm pretty sure your problem is a swollen prostate gland. Have you heard of that?' He shook his head. 'No? Well, it's a gland about as big as a walnut at the base of your bladder. The tube from your bladder to the outside world passes right through it. If it becomes swollen for any reason, it can cut off the flow. That's probably what happened to you.'

Kelly searched his face to see if he understood what she had just told him. She judged that he had but also saw the look of confusion that followed.

'So what can I do about that, Doc? Stop drinkin' or somethin'?' he asked.

'No. You could need an operation to either fix it, or even remove it if necessary. They can become cancerous and spread to the rest of your body, resulting in death. You really should do something about it, Rusty.'

Again she waited for the information to sink in. She was fully aware how confronting this all was for him and was determined to help guide him through the mental anguish he was suffering. Eventually, his next question came.

'How will I know if that's the problem?'

She plunged ahead. 'Rusty, I'd like to check that while I'm here if you're willing to let me. The test is quite simple and totally painless. It may cause you some more embarrassment, but I hope not. Just remember, I'm a doctor. This means no more to me than it does for you to castrate a calf.'

This even brought a wry smile to his face. 'I hope that's not what you're suggestin' is the cure.'

She gave him a warm smile, pleased that he was starting to be more relaxed with her. 'No. All I need to do is poke my finger up your bottom and feel to see if that old prostate is how it should be, or if it's grown too big for its boots. What do you say?'

Once again she was pleased to see a little smile playing around his mouth. He gave her the answer she was so anxious to get. 'After what you did to me before, that sounds like child's play. You'd better get into it, so to speak.'

Kelly giggled and gave him a playful slap on the hand. 'Cheeky! That's very sensible, Rusty. I'll just disconnect this plumbing system we've got going here first. Then I'll get you to roll over and face the wall. At least you won't be able to watch me this time, eh?'

*   *   *

Two weeks later, Rusty was admitted to the Mount Isa Base Hospital. Kelly's investigation confirmed her suspicions of an enlarged prostate, and he had been called in for further tests, starting with today's biopsy. He still felt uneasy about all that had taken place at the homestead, but no one seemed to be aware of the gruesome details. *So that young doctor sheila must have kept her word*, he thought.

Anyway, he didn't want to go through all that again, so, at Mrs Thompson's insistence, he had hopped on the mail plane, and here he was. He had no idea what indignities they intended to subject him to this time, but they said it required a general anaesthetic, so at least he would be unaware of what they were doing. *And,* he thought with relief, *the doctor this time was a man.*

He was roused from his thoughts by a white hurricane that swept into the room in the form of a bustling, loud, but friendly nurse. *She is about my age,* he thought, *and about as good looking too, but probably twice my weight.* Not anything like young Dr Saunders.

'Hello, Mr Dawes,' she boomed. 'Hilda's my name. I'm your nurse today. Can I call you, Rusty?'

'Yair, okay,' he replied. 'What's happenin', Hilda?'

'Well, I'm here to get you ready for the operating theatre,' she said as she ruffled around in the cupboard beside the bed. 'The orderlies will come for you soon, and the doctor will talk to you before you go under. You won't know a thing till they wheel you back in here. Then I'll be looking after you till you go home tomorrow.'

'Sounds good,' Rusty offered. 'What's next?'

'First up, I've got to shave you,' she said, setting a razor and shaving cream on the bed stand.

'Why?' he asked in all innocence. 'They're not gonna operate on my head, are they? I've had this beard since I was a teenager.'

'Not your beard, silly.' Hilda laughed. 'All that fluff around your old fella. Just in case they decide to operate or something.'

The blood drained from Rusty's face. *What other indignities am I going to be called upon to suffer? Why the bloody hell couldn't my problem just need me to take some pills or something?* All this concentrated inspection of his private parts by women was causing him no end of mental turmoil. Noticing his discomfort, Hilda gave him a friendly cuff on the shoulder.

'Hey, what's wrong, mate?' she asked. 'You're not going to get embarrassed with me, are you?'

'Too bloody right I am,' he blurted out. 'I'm not used to all you females handlin' my private parts.'

Hilda threw back the sheet and reached for the shaving cream. 'Good God, man. I've handled more men's weapons than you've had hot feeds. I've washed them, shaved them, and slathered them with ointment. I even had to hold one poor bugger's for him while he peed cos he'd broken both his arms. You don't have to be shy with me, mate.'

Rusty didn't know whether her tirade made him feel better or worse, but it looked as if there was no way out of his predicament. Besides, there was something about Hilda that struck a chord with him. He reckoned she'd hold her own in any of the droving camps he'd ever been on. She could almost be one of the boys.

'Well, you'd better get on with it then, I suppose. No offence, but at least you're not young enough to be my bloody daughter, like the RFDS doctor was.'

Hilda gave a chuckle. 'Well, thanks for the backhanded compliment, I think. Now drop your draws and I'll lather you up. You can hold Johnny Wonder out of the way if you like. Wouldn't want to slip and chop him off, would we?'

Rusty complied and then averted his eyes as Hilda began her task. 'Wouldn't matter much,' he said. 'He's not much use out where I live.'

'Don't be like that, Rusty. I take it you're not married then?'

'Nah. Never have been, neither. Wish I had been sometimes. Gets pretty lonely out there.'

Hilda thought about her own rather barren existence and felt sorry for him. 'You're not Robinson Crusoe there, mate, as the saying goes. I've missed the marriage boat too, I'm afraid.'

'That's a bloody shame, Hilda. I bet you'd make some bloke a great wife. Where do you come from?' Rusty asked.

'Born and raised in the territory, mate,' she replied as she cleaned up the excess cream from Rusty's crutch. 'I love the bush. You're lucky living on a station. I hate it here in town, but this is where my job is, I'm afraid. There you are now. That didn't hurt a bit, did it? Oh, and you can let go now, if you like.'

In spite of his ridiculous position, Rusty gave a chuckle. 'God, you're a cheeky bugger, Hilda,' he said.

*   *   *

Three hours later, when he opened his eyes, there she was hovering over him. As the anaesthetic fog lifted, and he was able to focus, he thought he detected a look of concern on her face as she fussed about his bed. The jovial smiling face of that morning had become all too serious. She saw him looking at her and smiled.

'Come on, you lazy old bugger. You can't stay asleep all day you know. Wake up, and I'll give you a sip of water.'

'I need more than a sip of bloody water, woman,' he rasped. 'You wouldn't have a cold beer, would you?'

'No beer for you for a while, I'm afraid, old fella, but if you can prop yourself up a bit, you can wet your whistle with a bit of water.'

Rusty tried to hoist himself up on to his elbow, but pain shot up into his guts, and he flopped back down.

'Bloody hell. What's happened to me?' he said through gritted teeth. 'I feel like I've been kicked in the crutch by a scrub bull.'

Hilda gently lifted his shoulders enough to give him a sip of water. 'I'll let the doctor explain the details for you, mate, but in general terms, you've had an operation. Apparently, the biopsy showed you needed some work done. Made good use of our shaving job, eh? How do you feel now?'

He sagged back on to the pillows. 'Bloody sore. What have they done to me?'

Hilda sat beside the bed, took his hand, and looked steadily into his eyes. 'Look, I'm not supposed to talk to patients about their cases, you know, but I don't want you worrying about it till he decides to pay you a visit. Apparently, your prostate was cancerous, so they decided to take it out. No big deal. You can do very well without it, but you're going to feel a bit crook for a few days. The good news is, it just might have saved your life. Now you just lie back there while I go and find the doctor. He'll fill you in on the details.' In a rush of white, she left him to his thoughts.

He was stunned. Never been crook a day in his life before this. Now it looked as if he'd never be the same again. He sure hoped he could keep his job. It was all he had in life, and without it, the future would be hopeless.

His thoughts returned to Hilda. What a terrific old battle-axe she was. Full of fun and good humour, and like him, with only her job to live for. He was quite looking forward to matching wits with her over the coming days.

*　*　*

Because of the isolation of his home, the doctor allowed Rusty to stay in hospital to recuperate for over a week. Hilda spent more time in his room than she needed to, and their friendship grew every day. She even visited him on her days off. They spent hours yarning about their lifetime experiences in the bush, swapping yarns, and eventually strolling around the grounds.

Finally, the doctor said it was time to go. Rusty was fit enough to fly back to the station for the rest of his recuperation. Neither of them was looking forward to his departure. Then their lives took a turn that they would not have dreamt of before they met. As she helped him pack his things, Hilda mustered the courage to put a proposal that had been on her mind for days.

'Listen, mate,' she said. 'I've got a suggestion to make to you. You can't possibly go back to work for a couple of weeks at least. Instead of lying around out at Boulia staring at the ceiling, why don't you come and stay at my place? I've got a spare room going to waste. What do you say?'

'I'd say that's very kind of you, Hilda. Are you sure it'd be okay? I'd be a perfect gentleman, of course,' he said, with a wink and a smile.

'Not too perfect, I hope. We're both too old to let inhibitions stand in the way of a good time.' She chuckled.

'Not much chance of that, eh, after what I've been through in recent days. We're already on pretty intimate terms, aren't we?' he joked. 'By the way, it'll give me a chance to see if you're a good cook. Boulia Downs has been on the lookout for one for ages. Do you think you're ready for a change of career?'

'You never know,' she replied as she hoisted his bag and headed for the door. 'I might be. Heaven knows, a no-hoper like you needs someone to look after him.' He gave her a playful slap on the backside, took her spare hand, and they headed for the car park.

'God, you're a cheeky bugger, Hilda.' He chuckled.

'Rusty' explained

My Macquarie dictionary tells me this is a 'didactic' story. That is one 'intended for instruction.' In other words, woven into what I hope is an amusing yarn about a real old bushie, it is a lesson for all of my readers who enjoy the privilege of vertical urination.

My own father died at a relatively young age from prostate cancer, which, if detected earlier, could have been cured. Embarrassment over the intrusive nature of the most common test often leads to us putting it off till next time, especially us older blokes who grew up before the permissive age left young people less paranoid about such matters.

Perhaps someone reading this could actually save their life, or that of a loved one. Now wouldn't that be something?

THE FINGER OF FATE

Life's too short to be embarrassed and shy,
Over problems that only relate to a guy.
Us blokes always tremble and baulk at the gate,
So that when we *do* act, it is sometimes too late.

The thought of exposing our most intimate bits,
To a doctor no less, scares us out of our wits.
All that it needs is a finger and glove,
With a 'roll over, mate', and a quick painless shove.

Maybe he'll find that your prostate's okay.
A sigh of relief, and he'll bid you good day.
But maybe he'll find it's a bit oversize.
To investigate further would be very wise.

So forget all the stalling, the backing and lying.
Those cowardly acts could lead to you dying.
Go do it today. Don't leave it too late.
Go visit your doctor, and his 'Finger of Fate.'

THE BUSHY AND THE BACKPACKER

'Have another one, Bazza?' Fred the publican, having guessed the likely response, plonked another pot of XXXX on the counter and sorted out the cost from the pile of change left from the previous round. 'What's dragged you into town this time, mate? Gonna try and pick up a sort at the B&S tonight, eh?' he said with a wink.

'Nah. Reckon I'm a bit long in the tooth for that these days, mate. Couldn't keep up with all those young sheilas any more. Thought I might give the poet's breakfast a bash tomorrow morning. Might see a few old mates there and pick up a good yarn or two.'

'Yeah. I heard they lifted the standard a bit this year. Bush poets and braggarts' breakfast now, no less. Might even try to get there myself if I wake up in time. See if all the bullshit yarns they tell are as good as the ones I've heard here over the years in here.' Fred chuckled. He moved on to serve his only other customer, a woman of indeterminate age, sitting on her own at the end of the bar, and stayed chatting to her.

Barry (Bazza) Armstrong sat with his beer and his thoughts, pondering on his lot in life and remembering the days when wild horses wouldn't have kept him from a B&S Ball. He would have danced and drank all night and been still on for a hair of the dog at daylight. Could have driven home and done a day's hard yakka then, if he needed to. Those days were gone. Now all he could manage was next morning's brekkie with the whacky old bush poets.

Mind you, he wouldn't mind putting in a bit of a show at the ball for a while. Might have a drink or two if he could find anyone he knew there, cast his eye over the modern young talent, and then leave it to them while he flopped into bed back at the pub. No hanky-panky for him any more. He'd missed the bus, by the looks of it. Forty-five years old and never been married. Never likely to be either by the looks of things. He'd had his chances years ago but let them all slip past.

Ah, well, he had his property and his dog, and had grown used to his solitary life now. Probably couldn't stand to share his life with a woman even if he could find one. Not much chance of that, though. Not in this dump of a town. Was a time when there was always a young teacher around, or a few nurses, but since they shut the school and the hospital, the only time you saw a bit of young fluff around was for the annual B&S when they flooded in from all over the place. Gone the next day, though. Didn't give a bloke much of a chance, did it? Especially if he was twice their age.

He found himself staring at his empty glass and gave it a bit of a rattle on the bar, dragging Fred away from his other customer. 'Why don't you come up and join us, Bazza?' he asked. 'There's someone here you should say g'day to.'

'Haven't got much option by the look of it,' Bazza growled. 'Not much chance of any service up this end of the bar.' Picking up his hat and change, he moved to where Fred had already sat another pot next to the lady.

'This here's Betty, Fred. Sort of one of them British backpackers you hear about. Flitting around the world trying to find themselves. This here's Fred, Betty. Never been anywhere in his life as far as I know, but he's never lost his self neither. This round's on me. Want another gin and tonic, Betty?' Chuckling at his own joke, he moved off to see if he could remember how to make a G and T. *Not much call for them out here in the bush,* he thought. *Lucky I still have half a bottle of gin left from last year's B&S and a couple bottles of soda water only a month or two past their use by date. Getting too flash for me these days. Even have to order in a supply of them alcopop things this year, but I reckon Bundy and Coke would still outsell them a hundred to one.*

'Pleased to meet you, Betty,' Bazza said, offering his hand.

'How do you do, Bazza?' she replied, returning a firm handshake. 'Is that really your name?'

'Near enough,' he replied. 'All anyone around here calls me. Barry Armstrong's the full, monica. From Muckadilla. I'm not much on accents, but I bet you're not a local.'

'You'd be right about that. Betty Thompson, from Salisbury in England. Have you heard of it?'

'Better than that, I've been there. Old Fred here thinks we're all as thick as him,' Bazza said as the barman handed Betty her drink. 'Went to England when I was a young fella on a farm exchange program. Spent a day or two around Salisbury. Liked your cathedral, and that Stonehenge is an interesting place. Buggered if I know how they built it, without a crane or forklift or something. Must have been strong buggers, those old poms. But tell me, how the hell did you come to end up in this godforsaken hole?'

In spite of her rather refined background, Betty found herself amused at Bazza's laconic manner and use of his natural outback language. 'Well, actually, Fred wasn't too far off the mark when he said I was a backpacker. Not your usual Swedish blonde with the long legs, flashy smile, and sexy accent, I'm afraid. It would make hitch-hiking a whole lot easier. But that's what I'm doing — hitching around Australia for a couple of months. I got this far on my way to Darwin when I heard there was something special going on tonight, so I've booked one of Fred's rooms, and I'm off to this B&S Ball, whatever that is. I understand the 'S' stands for spinster, so I figure I'm qualified to attend.'

'Yair, well, I fit the bill for the B bit too,' said Bazza with a grin. 'B&S Balls are supposed to bring all the young people together so they can make a few social contacts that might lead to them losing their singles title one day, but they don't always work. I must have been to twenty or thirty of them over the years, and I'm still qualified. So what do you do for a crust, Betty?' Bazza asked.

'A crust? Oh, I see what you mean. You Aussies and your idioms. Actually, I teach English at a girls' school and have done so for twenty years.' She took a sip of G and T and continued. 'That's why I'm here. Life was passing me by, so I decided it was now or never. I took some long service leave, bought a return ticket to Australia, and set out to see the world. I've been here for weeks now and am due to fly out of Darwin next weekend. What about you, Bazza? I take it you live around here somewhere.'

'Yair, about a hundred miless from here on a sheep property. Not much of a place, but it keeps me in tucker and an occasional beer. Only me and my old dog to provide for, and he don't eat much. Just an occasional roo.'

I wish I had more time now,' said Betty. 'I'd love to see how a sheep station works, if you were prepared to show me, but I don't know how long it will take me to get to Darwin, so I will have to keep moving, I suppose.'

Barry wondered what grandiose ideas she had about what a sheep station looked like and how his pretty ordinary outfit would measure up. 'Well, you'll just have to come back again and start at the other end next time, eh? Listen, Betty, I've got a bit of business to do while I'm in town, so I'll have to love you and leave you as the saying goes.' This attractive middle-aged woman had made quite an impact on him. He liked the way she seemed relaxed and comfortable with him and old Fred. He wouldn't mind seeing a bit more of her. Oh, well, nothing ventured, nothing gained, as the saying goes.

'How about I shout you a feed tonight? No good going to a B&S on an empty belly. You wouldn't last till midnight, let alone daylight. I could take you to it if you like. Couldn't trust your gentle self to the local boys without a bit of masculine protection, even if I couldn't fight my way out of a wet paper bag these days.'

'That would be lovely, Bazza. I'd really appreciate it, but let me buy dinner for you in return. Where should we go?' Betty asked.

'Not much choice there, I'm afraid. Only the cafe and the two pubs, but Fred's cook puts on a good steak and chips. Need to get in early, though, before all these youngies eat it all. How about we meet in the bar about half past six, eh? Oh, and you'd better put on your glad rags. These do's are pretty flash, you know.' Without waiting for a reply, Bazza put on his hat and sauntered out into the street.

*   *   *

Betty dressed in the best outfit her limited travelling wardrobe could provide and joined Bazza in the now-crowded lounge. Music blared, beer flowed freely, and excited chatter and laughter filled the room. She took the seat he had saved for her in the quietest corner and tried to continue their conversation from earlier in the day.

'I think we should leave it to them, Bet. Let's go into the dining room, where we might be able to hear ourselves talk,' he suggested.

And talk they did. Over a giant T-bone and a few drinks, they spent an enjoyable couple of hours, discovering a compatibility and interest in common things that surprised both of them. The battling bushie bachelor and the urbane, educated English teacher talked and laughed their way through their visit to the B&S Ball too, although both felt rather awkward and out of place in the crowd of much younger revellers they found there. At least Bazza managed to introduce Betty to the delights of Bundy and Coke. With a few of them on board, they trundled off back to the pub just as the real partygoers were getting stuck into it.

'You going to come to the poet's brekkie in the morning?' he asked as they headed to their rooms.

'Wouldn't miss it for quids,' she replied, pleased with herself at having picked up at least one bit of Aussie idiom. 'What time and where?'

'Brekkie at seven in the beer garden, and the whips will be cracking by about eight o'clock. See you there, Bet.' And he was gone.

Hmm. Whips are cracking, she thought as she closed the door behind her. *That's another one for me to remember.*

*   *   *

Like all true Aussie blokes, the night on the grog had no effect on Bazza, who enjoyed a couple of bacon and egg sangas, but Betty could manage no more than a cup of coffee and a slice of toast.

'Feeling a bit seedy, are we, Bet?' he asked. 'Why don't you try a bit of Vegemite on that? Pick you up a treat, it would.'

'Not on your life. I've been caught with that already. I don't know how it doesn't make you throw up. Still, to each his own, I suppose. I bet you wouldn't fancy kippers or devilled kidneys either.'

'Nah. A couple of fried mutton chops and an egg or two if the chooks are laying is my idea of a good breakfast,' he said, smiling as the blood drained from her already pale face at the very thought.

The bush poets and braggarts soon got under way, and Betty found she loved the humour and leg-pulling nature of their efforts. She was surprised when the compare said, 'I see old Bazza Armstrong here in the crowd. How about giving us one of yours, Bazza? We haven't heard from you for years. C'mon, drag yourself away from that good sort you've found and tell us the one about young Johnny Poole.'

Bazza was a bit reluctant, particularly with his suggested choice of poem, but Betty was excited and urging him to be in it, so he thought, *Oh, well. This'll see how thin skinned she is.* He stood out front, returned her smile of encouragement, and recited the following poem:

MATING GAMES

Knock, knock, knock, on the farm house
door, and she went to see who's there.
It was Johnny Poole from the farm next door,
with his father's favourite mare.
'We've come to see if it's okay to borrow you old man's horse,
To breed us a foal who can run a bit. We'll
pay you up front, of course.'

'My old man's not home,' young Mary
said, 'but I guess it'll be okay.
If you wait a jiff, I'll put on my boots,
and show you and her the way.'
Together they went to the mating yard, and
she brought out the colt from Regret.
'His dad was a champion and he is too.
He'll please your dad, I bet.'

'Yair, he looks all right,' young Johnny
said, 'but can he do the job?
He's only a colt, and pretty scared, since
the time he ran with the mob.'
'We'll sit on the rail where we can watch,'
offered Mary with a smile,
'And you can hold my hand if you like. My
dad won't be home for a while.'

Now young Johnny thought that his luck had
changed – for the better I might add,
Cos all that had kept them apart in the past,
was young Mary's cranky old dad.
As the colt and the filly out in the yard,
started to prance and cavort,
The pair on the fence was cuddling too –
Young John and the sassy young sort.

While down in the yard, the act was done,
and when the colt was through,
Young Johnny thought he'd try his luck,
saying, 'I can do what he did too.'
'Well, of course, you can, if you really
want. It's up to you, silly billy.
It seems a bit strange to prim girl like
me, but it *is* your father's filly.'

The crowd erupted into great peals of laughter and applause. Bazza cast an anxious look at Betty, but he needn't have worried. She was enjoying it along with everyone else and gave him a big wink as he returned to the seat beside her.

'That was terrific,' she enthused. 'I didn't know you were into poetry.'

'There's probably a lot of things you don't know about me,' he replied, 'and me about you too, for that matter.' They couldn't continue for the time being as the next act was being introduced.

'And now, we have the King of Braggarts, the one and only Smacka McBride, to spin you a yarn about the smartest dog in the world.'

A scruffy old bloke took the floor and said, 'These blokes were sitting around a campfire yarning, you see, when the conversation got around to who owned the smartest dog. "Well, I reckon mine's all right," one of them said. "Watch this." He called his dog over, sat five beer cans on a log, and said, "Go on, Butch, tell us how many are there." Butch looked at them and then went woof, woof, woof, woof, woof. "How about that?" he asked. And they all applauded.

'A second bloke spoke up and said, "I can beat that. Here, Tiger. Go and get my smokes for me, mate, and a light." Tiger trotted over to his bunk, ruffled around till he found his owner's smokes, brought them to him, and then, to their total amazement, pulled a twig from the fire and brought that to him too. They all roared laughing and agreed he was the winner.

'"Not so fast," a third man said. "My old Digger is smarter than that. Watch this." Looking into Digger's eyes, he said, 'One three-minute egg please, mate.' With that, Digger shot off. He put a billy of water on the fire, scratched around till he found the boss' clock, waited till the water boiled, then dropped an egg in, and sat looking at the clock.

'Right on three minutes, he took the billy off, tipped it over, and rolled the egg over to his owner. Applause started to erupt, but the boss said, "He's not finished yet." Digger arrived back with a spoon. Then, to everyone's amazement, he tipped upside down, balancing on his head, with his backside pointing to the sky.

'"Great performance," one of them said, "and he's obviously the smartest dog here, but what's with the standing on the head bit?"

'"Ah, well, that's the smartest bit of all," says Digger's owner. "You see, he knows I didn't bring an egg cup with me!"'

The crowd laughed their heads off, and Betty thought she might wet her pants. This was the best fun she'd had on her whole trip. *What wonderful people these country folk are! So different to the insular and stuffy rural gentry back in England.* She was sorry now that she had spent so much of her trip in the cities. This was where you found the real Australians, and she felt a real rapport with them, especially Bazza.

The show drew to a close, and her thoughts returned to her need to get to Darwin in five days. 'Thank you so much for all the fun I've had, Baz,' she said, 'but I must get back on to the road if I'm not to miss my flight. I wish I could stay longer, but it might take me a while to get a lift.'

Bazza had been giving some thought to that matter too. He couldn't remember when he'd had so much fun with anyone and was reluctant to see their time together come to an end.

'I've been thinking about that, Bet. Tell you what we could do. I know most of the truckies who travel this road. They go right past my place and generally have a feed at the local truck stop before they head off on the next big stretch. How would you like to come home with me, have a quick look over the place, stay the night, and I'll get you on to a truck tomorrow morning going straight through to Darwin? You'll be there in three days.'

'Baz, that's a marvellous offer!' she beamed. 'Give me five minutes to pack, and I'll be right back.'

Ten minutes later, they were tearing along the bitumen in Bazza's ute, swapping stories, laughing at the jokes told at breakfast, and wondering quietly in their own minds, *Just where this whole new friendship is leading?*

*   *   *

'Just be careful of old Woofer, Bet. He doesn't take to strangers too well,' Bazza warned, as they hopped out and headed for the house.

'He'll be right,' she responded. 'I love animals, and they can tell.' She was right. In no time at all, they were best friends.

'We'll just have a quick cuppa and Vegemite sandwich, and then I'll take for a run around the place,' he teased.

'Thanks, mate. Spread it on thick. I'm ready for anything,' hoping like hell, he was joking.

They spent an enjoyable few hours going from paddock to paddock. He taught her how to open and shut a cockie's gate, explained how the water supply came from thousands of feet below the surface, and even ran a few ewes into the yards so she could play with the lambs. She breathed in the oily aromas of the shearing shed and took a handful of greasy wool as a memento.

They watched the sun go down while they downed a couple of Bundys on the back veranda, and then ate a hearty meal of cold corned meat and salad. As she went to bed, Betty thought it had been one of the best days of her life. 'Matter of fact,' she mused, 'not one of, it was *the* best that she could remember.'

'Wakey, wakey. Rise and shine. C'mon, show a leg. The kettle's on, and I want to talk to you about something.' Bazza had spent a restless night. He too had been thinking about how much he had enjoyed the last two days and was not looking forward to waving Betty goodbye as she headed home. *What a bummer!* he thought. *Finally found someone I could really hit it off with and I'm never likely to see her again.* Once more in his life, it looked as if his chance was going to pass him by. By daybreak he had steeled himself to not let it happen again.

'Bet, I've got an idea to run past you. Promise me you will give me an honest response,' he said. 'If you don't like it, just say so, and I'll run you into the truck stop.' This wasn't coming easily for him, but he pressed on. 'I just want to say how much I've enjoyed your company over the last two days, and I was wishing you didn't have to leave so soon, and then I hit on an idea. How about you let me drive you to Darwin? I haven't had a holiday for years, and this place would look after itself for a while at this time of the year. What do you say?'

She didn't hesitate. 'Why, that's a tremendous offer!' Betty gushed, 'but I couldn't possibly impose on you like that. Mind you, I'm tempted to be selfish enough to accept. I was thinking last night in bed that I have never had more fun than in the last two days. I wish it could go on longer too, but I couldn't impose on you like that.'

'My motives are purely selfish, Bet. Nothing would give me more pleasure than showing you a bit more of our country, and getting to know you a bit better. A few days on the road would give us time for a real chinwag. Can I start packing the Toyota?'

Betty had to conceal a smile at the excitement on his face. 'You're on then, but you must let me share the cost. It's a great idea, and I think we can have so much fun. When do we go?'

'Soon as I pack some gear, put some juice in the Toyota, organise some tucker for Woofer, who, by the way, will enjoy the trip too cos he's never been to Darwin before.' And with that, he was off at a trot, excited as a schoolboy on his first date.

*   *   *

They spent a happy five days on the trip, camping overnight, sightseeing, and telling each other their life stories. They spent some time at the Stockman's Hall of Fame in Longreach, boated through the Katherine Gorge at sunset, and fished for barramundi in the Daly River. Betty was captivated by the beauty and raw charm of the Australian outback and loved every minute of their time together. All too soon, it was over, and they stood waiting in the terminal for her plane to leave for Singapore and London. They exchanged phone numbers and addresses and promised to keep in touch.

'It's a pity you don't have email, Bazza. We could communicate every day,' Betty suggested. 'You should buy a computer.'

'Bit too flash for me, I'm afraid, Bet. I'll just have to phone instead.'

'Passengers on Flight 201 to Singapore and London, your flight is now boarding through Gate 1.'

Betty reached for Bazza's hand. 'Bazza, I really must thank you once again for giving me the best time of my life. I just wish I could repay you somehow. Why don't you come to England and let me show you around there?' she asked hopefully.

It was what they weren't telling each other that made the moment awkward. Bazza was thinking, *Here I go again. Letting her walk out of my life like all the others in the past, but what can I do? She has to go home, and she probably only saw our time together as a bit of holiday fun. Never let on that it meant anything more to her anyway. Oh well. Back to the bush, I suppose.*

In turn, Betty was amazed at the effect this quietly spoken Australian bushy had produced in her. In all her forty-two years, she had never felt like this before about a man. Was she in love? How could she be, when she had only known him for a week? All she did know for sure was that she wasn't looking forward to returning to the lonely humdrum life that faced her back home.

'Final call for all passengers on Flight 201 to Singapore. Please board through gateway number 1.'

Betty gathered up her hand luggage, turned to Bazza, and said, 'Well, this is it, Baz. Please keep in touch. Goodbye.' Then blushing profusely, she reached up, kissed him gently on the cheek, turned, and scurried towards the door, trying to hide the tears brimming in her eyes.

Bazza stared sadly after her retreating figure. That kiss told him more than any words could have. She felt it too. There and then he made a decision.

*   *   *

Two weeks later, Betty was on the phone talking to Bazza, again. He had rung every day since she arrived home. 'Listen to me, Baz,' she said. 'It's great of you to keep ringing all the time, but you really must spin it out a bit. You'll have to sell half your sheep to pay the bill. I really do love it, though, and I am missing you so much. I wish I could see you again soon. Why don't you come – Just hang on a minute, Baz. There's some idiot ringing my doorbell. Don't hang up. I'll just get rid of whoever it is. Okay, okay, I'm coming. Keep your hair on.'

She flung the door open with an irritated flourish, ready to send her unwelcome visitor away. There he stood, mobile to his ear, and that big silly grin she had grown to love so much in their time together. She dropped the phone to the floor and rushed into his arms. They clung to each other wordlessly for minutes, while she cried quietly into his shoulder. Finally, he drew back, smiled into her tear-stained face, and said, 'G'day, Bet. How're been? Oh, and you won't be getting rid of that idiot too easily.'

'Bazza! It's so wonderful to see you!' Betty said, giving him another hug. 'But what are you doing here?'

'I'm here to collect on that offer you made to show me England,' he replied. 'Does it still stand, or have you got better things to do?'

She gave him a friendly slap on the shoulder. 'Of course, it does, silly. Where do you want to start?'

'How about in your kitchen?' he said. 'I'd kill for a decent cup of tea.'

*   *   *

Things were pretty quiet in the Augathella Hotel, with only the few regulars sipping their beers in a corner. Fred looked up from *The Country Life* as he heard a customer enter.

'Well, bloody hell! Look who's here, fellas. That well-known bloody international tourist, Mr Bazza Armstrong, has returned to grace us with his presence no less. Welcome back, mate,' he said, extending his hand.

'Thanks, Fred,' Bazza replied. 'It's good to be back, and I've got a surprise for you. Come in, Bet.'

She skipped in through the door, rigged out in some obviously new country gear.

'Good God!' Fred exclaimed. 'It's the little British backpacker. G'day, Betty. Where did you find her, Baz?'

'That's Mrs Armstrong to you, thank you very much. Show the lady a bit of respect, you boofhead,' Bazza said with a smile.

Betty reached over the bar to shake Fred's hand. 'Hello, Fred. It's nice to see you again.'

The barman was dumbfounded. 'I don't believe what I'm seeing here,' he said. 'Not old bachelor, Bazza. How did all this come about?'

'It's all down to you, mate. You introduced us, remember?'

'I sure do. I knew all along it would lead to this,' he said with a wink. 'Congratulations to both of you. This shout's on the house. What'll it be, Betty? Gin and tonic?' he said, slapping a beer in front of Bazza without asking.

'Not the way you make them, thanks, Fred,' she said, entering into the spirit of the day. 'Besides, I'm an Aussie now. Give us a rum and Coke, thanks, mate.'

Beaming from ear to ear at the unexpected good fortune of his lifelong friend, Fred reached for the bottle of Bundy. 'No troubles, Mrs Armstrong. The pleasure's all mine.'

'The Bushy and the Backpacker' explained

My 'sounding board' complained that I should have invented a younger Betty so they could have some kids, but I overruled her. I think at their stage of life, they ought to be able to devote all their time to each other and enjoying their remaining years.

Lack of a family was a price they had to pay for their unwillingness to take their earlier chances. To give them the opportunity to go back in time would have mocked the sentiments expressed in my poem which are that you have to take your chances when they come, or you will miss out.

Here's hoping Bazza and Betty find fulfilment back amongst the sheep and flies and dust at Muckadilla. I don't see Bazza fitting in to, well, in the Old Blimey.

Take Your Chances As They Come

Do what you do, do well, boy, the old-time song did say.
Another said, on sunny days, is when you should make hay.
The message I would give to you, from all I've learnt to date,
Is take your chances when they come. Don't leave your lot to fate.

There is a wide divergent range within what fate bestows.
Sometimes the very highest highs, sometimes the lowest lows.
We must accept our share of both, as through our life we ride.
Enjoy the good times as they come, take bad ones in your stride.

The measure of how people will recall us when we're dead,
Is not the way we've treated them, or even what we've said.
But how we handled all extremes, the good times and the bad.
Humility on happy days. Acceptance of the sad.

And we are even luckier if we can find the way
To garner something useful from what comes to us each day.
To ride the highs, survive the lows and always understand,
Our attitude to life will help us reach what we have planned.

So when a chance presents itself, enjoy it while it lasts,
And, using your experience to profit from your past,
Extract whatever benefits those chances offer you.
Take your chances as they come. Don't
waste them. They're too few.

THE LAIRD OF LANARKBURN

Dusk fell like a sullen blanket across the landscape. Clouds rolling in from the west blotted out the last rays of the setting sun, bringing on an eerie murkiness that quickly plunged the scrub into semi-darkness.

On the flat near the creek, preparations for the overnight camp were well under way, being handled in the usual efficient way that several months of practice had refined. Since leaving Bathurst in central New South Wales at Christmas, this procedure had been undertaken nearly every day as the travelling caravan threaded its way towards the faraway Palmer River goldfields in north Queensland. No one foresaw the tragedy that was about to unfold.

*   *   *

Stripped to the waist, the two young men circled each other warily, poking out jabs and feints as they each waited for an opening in the other's defence. The elder and taller of the two was Hugh McKenzie, twenty-two-year-old eldest son of the Laird of Lanarkburn. The shorter and stockier one was his twenty-year-old brother, Andrew. To the utter despair of their father, they hated each other with a passion, and this was not the first occasion they had sought to settle their differences down on the bank of the river, well out of sight of the manor house.

'I'm going to teach you once and for all not to call me names, you little twerp,' Hugh snarled between his gritted teeth.

Andrew planted a punch on his brother's ribs, stepped back, and replied, 'I'll call you whatever I like, you pompous poof.'

Forgetting his advantage in reach and height, Hugh rushed at his opponent, grabbed him around the waist, and they crashed to the ground, rolling, punching, kicking, and swearing, as each tried to get the upper hand. A headbutt from Andrew dropped Hugh on to his back, and Andrew flung himself on top of him. At the same time, he whipped a knife from a concealed leg holster and placed it against his brother's throat.

'One more move and I'll drag this from one ear to the other, you despicable bit of scum! You might be elder than me, but I'm more of a man than you'll ever be, and don't you forget it!' he growled into the face a few inches from his own. 'Now get back to that effeminate friend of yours, before I put this knife to better use, making sure the McKenzie clan doesn't breed any more of your kind.' With that, he sprang to his feet, sheathed his dagger, and stalked off towards his horse.

'I'll win in the end, you know!' Hugh shouted after him. 'Whatever you may think of me, I am still the oldest son, and one day I'll be laird. You'll be nothing. You might not like it, but that's the truth, so you had better get used to it.'

As he sprang into the saddle, young Andrew's face flushed red with frustration. What his brother was always keen to remind him of was the parlous position of the younger family members in the patriarchal inheritance system, which had ruled for centuries and still applied in this year of 1850.

He longed to escape, but he and his two young brothers were bound to the estate by loyalty to each other and their ailing old father. For now, he had no option but to control his discontent and wait to see what fate had in store for him.

As it turned out, he didn't have much longer to wait. The old laird failed to see out the following winter, succumbing to a bout of influenza. Hugh automatically assumed his position of laird and master of the whole family. His father was barely in his grave when he called his mother and brothers to the study.

'As you know,' he started, with a meaningful glare at Andrew, 'I am now the laird and, therefore, responsible for all of your lives. You, mother, will, of course, be very welcome to live out the rest of your life here with me in the manor. As for you three,' he indicated to his three brothers, 'I know you all hate the sight of me, so I see no point in trying to find positions for you around here. Accordingly, I am offering to give each of you two hundred guineas in cash, on the understanding that you will leave this Scotland and not return while ever I am alive. Refuse this offer, and I will still expect you to be gone from this estate within the week. It's up to you.' With that, he stomped off, leaving the rest of the family to consider his edict.

Andrew put his arm around his mother's shaking shoulders. 'Mother, can't you see? We have no option but to accept his offer and make our way in the world somewhere else. There's nothing for us here except frustration and bitterness.' She seemed totally unconvinced. 'If we're out of the way, maybe Hugh will settle down. Change his ways and marry a good woman maybe. He'll look after you, all right, and one day he might let us return, but for now we have to go.' For her sake, Andrew tried to sound more confident than he felt, as he watched her sobbing quietly into her handkerchief.

'But where will you go, Andy, and what will you do? And poor little Scott's only ten years old!' she wailed.

'William and I will look after him, Mother. I promise. At least we have some money behind us, enough to make a new start somewhere. I have been reading about the gold strikes in Australia, and I am of a mind to go there. It is a big new country, and they say newcomers are making fortunes there, one way or another. Plenty of our countrymen have already gone, so we won't be alone.'

So the McKenzie brothers migrated from Scotland as part of the rush of free immigrants to Australia, following the opening up of the inland to settlement during the first half of the nineteenth century, and particularly on the subsequent discovery of gold. The three young brothers left Hugh lording it over the family estates and rode the wave of eager newcomers who put their futures into the hands of this great southern land. It was the lure of gold that enticed many of them to brave the hazardous trip and primitive local conditions to try their luck in the goldfields of Victoria and central New South Wales. The McKenzies were no exceptions, landing in Melbourne and joining the rush to the alluvial fields of Ballarat and Bendigo.

*   *   *

Fourteen-year-old Scott ran panting into their camp, calling out as he ran, 'Andy, Will, the soldiers are coming! Quick, hide all our gold!'

The two elder brothers stopped what they were doing and stared down the road towards the settlement. 'It's not our gold they're after, Scotty. It's these blasted miner permits they're making us buy. Lucky for us, I bought one, or we'd all be dragged off to jail. Unfortunately, not everyone has. Some of the poor bludgers can't afford to eat, let alone buy a permit. It looks bad. I think there might be a revolution coming. That Peter Lalor is urging everyone to strike and stand up to the government, but you can't beat the law. Not with pickaxes against guns.'

'Do you think we should move on, Andy?' asked William, who had always been the more timid of the two. 'We've done all right here, and we could move to the fields at Bathurst or somewhere else and start again.'

'Yes, well, I've been thinking about that actually, Will. I'm getting a bit fed up with scratching around in holes all my life. With what we've found here and the rest of our money we brought with us, we could set ourselves up in business and let others do our scratching for us. But I wouldn't want to put money into this lot, that's for sure. It's going to blow up any day. Let's think about it for a day or two, eh?'

Their minds were made up for them in a most unexpected way. That night, as Andy was returning to the camp from a miner's meeting, he heard strained sounds coming from a hovel on the side of the track. He knew the owner, a vile pig of a man, who drank away whatever little gold he ever found and was detested by everyone who knew him. Now, as he paused to listen, Andy was surprised to hear a woman's plaintive cries for pity.

'Please, Mr Biggs, I've changed my mind. I should never have agreed to in the first place. Just let me go home. Please.'

'Like bloody hell!' the man snorted. 'We made a deal. Ten minutes with you for a loaf of bread. And you've had a free tot of rum. You can't back out now, my girl. Now get back on that bunk before I get rough.'

'No. Please. I can't do it, Mr Biggs. I thought I could, but I just can't!' she wailed. This was followed by a loud smack and the sound of someone falling to the ground. Andy could stand it no longer. He burst into the room and surveyed the scene before him.

Clive Biggs, with no pants on, stood menacingly over a young woman lying sprawled on the ground, clutching her head in her hands. She was sobbing violently, trying to scrabble away into a corner.

'What's going on here, Biggs?' Andy barked.

Biggs swung around to confront the intruder. 'Nothing of your concern, McKenzie. Just a private matter between me and Jenny here. I'd be pleased if you would mind your own business and get out of my house.'

Biggs moved menacingly towards Andy, reaching for a shovel as he did so. Andy backed off but made no move to leave. 'I'm not going anywhere unless she comes with me,' Andy said, nodding in the direction of the frightened girl. 'Make yourself decent, man, and we'll say no more of the matter.'

Biggs stood his ground with the shovel raised in front of him. 'Now you just listen to me, mister high and mighty McKenzie. You bloody Scots think you're above anyone else, but you're really scum. Won't even back the rebellion, will you? But the boys will sort you out before this is over.' He took a menacing step towards Andrew. 'As for you busting in here and sticking your nose into something that doesn't concern you, well, that's really starting to get up my nose. Piss off out of here now, and I'll say no more of the matter, as you put it. Refuse, and I'll lay you out with this shovel.'

'Don't be stupid,' Andy said as he took a step towards him and reached out. 'Just give me that and I'll—'

'Don't call me stupid, you bastard!' Biggs yelled and took a swing at Andy with the shovel, who ducked and took the blow on the shoulder. Driving forward, he knocked his foe to the ground and managed to reef the weapon from his hands. As he struggled to his feet, Biggs picked up an axe and rushed at him. Andy swung wildly with the shovel and felt the shock up his arms as it connected with something solid, and Biggs crashed to the floor, unconscious.

Andy dropped the shovel and went to the girl who was cowering in the corner, crying, with her legs drawn up tight and her skinny arms clutching her knees to her chest. 'You all right, miss?' Andy asked.

A sniffled 'yes, thanks' between the sobs was the only answer he got. 'Come on,' he said, helping her to her feet. 'I'll take you home.'

'Don't have a home to go to,' she sobbed. 'The cops locked my man up and confiscated our place.'

'Well, I'll take you back to my place then. You'll be safer there anyway. God only knows what this animal will do when he wakes up.' He took off his coat and put it around her shaking shoulders, and they stepped around the prostrate Biggs on their way to the door.

But Mr Biggs didn't wake up. Hoping to patch things up with him next morning, Andy was shocked to find him lying just as he had left him the night before. He felt for a pulse, but there was none. He was cold and stiff, and his sightless eyes stared back at Andy when he rolled him over. He shut the door behind him and hurried home.

The three brothers and Jenny Rushmore sat discussing the situation they found themselves in. 'We'll just have to go to the police and tell them what happened,' William offered. 'What other alternative is there?'

'Well, that's the obvious one, I suppose,' Andy replied, 'but I reckon the first thing this corrupt mob would do is throw me in jail. Jenny, too, probably. The law doesn't operate here like back in Scotland, you know. A quick and easy trial, and a lynching is more likely than true justice. And we don't have any witnesses to support our story. Jenny's man being in jail wouldn't help either.'

'Well, his hut's pretty isolated. Do you think anyone saw either of you there?' Scott asked.

Jenny shook her head, and Andy couldn't recall seeing anyone about on the way home. Surprisingly, it was the cautious William that came up with the suggestion.

'I think you're right, Andy. The cops won't believe you, and you'll hang. We've been talking about moving on. I reckon our best bet is to hide his body, get to hell out of here as fast as we can, and hope they never link us to his disappearance. Plenty of people come and go in this godforsaken hole all the time. No one's going to look too hard for a drunken lout like him. They'll just assume he's fallen down a hole somewhere or wandered off into the bush and died. Happens all the time.'

So that's what they did. Under cover of darkness that night, they pushed him down a disused pit and covered him with the overburden. They then tidied up his hut, shut the door, and hoped no one would notice him missing until they were well and truly gone.

In the confusion that was rife in the goldfields, Mr Tobias Biggs was never missed. Newcomers and scavengers eventually stole all his possessions, and the police were much too heavily involved in the Eureka rebellion to worry about looking for missing persons anyway.

A few days after the incident, the McKenzie brothers packed all their gear on a wagon they had purchased and, with Jenny on board, headed north for the new fields being discovered almost daily in the hills around Bathurst.

*   *   *

This district was to become their home for the next twenty years, not as miners but as businessmen involved in servicing the many towns that were springing up in the central west, as graziers and farmers took up the huge areas of available prime land. Andy married Jenny, and they settled in Bathurst where they ran several shops. William married a local girl, took up farming and grazing nearby, and supplied his own butcher shop. Scott ran a string of wagons that plied between Sydney and Bathurst, hauling assorted goods up over the Blue Mountains and returning with wheat and wool.

That may have been the end of the McKenzie story but for a combination of events that occurred in the early 1870s. The first was the insidious advance of the railway system from the coastal ports to the agricultural inland. Scott saw his business gradually being wiped out by the faster and cheaper competitor, and he wondered just where he could go to stay in business. The second event was a disastrous diphtheria plague that swept through the district carrying off many children. William lost his eldest child and only son, leaving him and his wife distraught and also wondering if they wanted to stay where sad memories would haunt them forever.

While Andy, Jenny, and their four girls were happy to stay, as head of the clan, Andy, felt compelled to take his brother's needs into account. He was searching for a solution when news reached him of a big new gold discovery at Palmer River in far north Queensland. He still had gold fever flowing in his veins and suggested to his brothers that they should sell up where they were, load up Scott's wagons with their worldly goods, drive William's cattle ahead of them, and travel overland to the new field. At forty-three, he felt he needed a new challenge. The three brothers, two wives, and six children set off full of excitement and expectation.

*   *   *

Following the tracks and stock routes on the western slopes, they eventually reached the Darling Downs and dropped down to the coastal plain through Cunningham's Gap before heading north through the Burnett district. When they left Gayndah behind them, they entered some wilder and less-settled country, sometimes not seeing any squatters for days. As they entered the scrubby country on the Binjour Plateau, they became aware of a worrisome band of aborigines, who seemed to be following them.

Although skirmishes between squatters and the local blacks had finished in most areas, there still existed semi-nomadic groups of troublemakers who took advantage of any opportunities that presented themselves. They often raided outlying huts and speared any cattle, sheep, and even horses if they strayed away from their owner's protection, but fear of the mounted police and arbitrary justice meant they kept their distance from civilisation and homesteads. The country they now found themselves in lent itself to this kind of activity, and the McKenzie brothers were worried.

For some time, they had caught glimpses of about a dozen of them in the distance, never coming near the camp, and generally only appearing at dusk and dawn. When approached, they melted into the surrounding bush, only to reappear some distance further away. They didn't seem to be too threatening, but their presence was unsettling, particularly as they had been following their expedition for days.

As they gathered together to set up the overnight camp on the banks of a little creek, Andrew left William to ride around the livestock to stop them from straying. Clouds were building in the west, so the other travellers busied themselves putting up tents, collecting firewood, and securing the wagons in case a storm blew in.

No one noticed the two girls following their puppy down to the creek. Nor did they see them follow him as he emerged on the far bank a couple of hundred yards upstream and bounded away into the scrub. Ellen, the elder of the two cousins at twelve, was reluctant to follow him, standing on the edge of the clearing and calling his name.

'Dodger! Dodger! Come on, boy. Time to go home.' He didn't come back, and ten-year-old May pleaded with her to go and get him.

'We'll have to go and get him, Elly. We can't just leave him.' But Ellen, aware of the dangers of straying out of sight of the camp, was starting to lead her back to the creek.

'He'll be all right, Maysie. He knows the way back to the camp, and we really shouldn't be out here alone.' Then they heard Dodger yelping.

'There he is!' May cried. 'He's hurt, and he didn't sound to be far away. Let's just have a quick look.'

'You know, we shouldn't do that, May. Daddy said to never go into the scrub without a grown-up with us. We'll go back and get him to help us.' Elly took her firmly by the hand and headed back. Just then, Dodger let out a plaintive wail, and putting aside all her good common sense and acting on impulse, Elly ran off in his direction. 'You stay here till I go and get him, May. I won't be a minute.'

But a minute passed, and May heard and saw nothing. Staring into the gloom where Elly had gone, she called out to her, 'Have you found him yet?'

No answer came.

She started to panic. 'Elly!' she cried. 'Where are you? I'm scared.'

Still no answer came. Not a sound from the silent brooding bush. Even Dodger was quiet. A cloud moved in front of the setting sun now, and she could no longer see into the trees. She ran off back to the camp, screaming and crying, 'Daddy! Daddy! Come quickly! Elly and Dodger have disappeared, and I can't find them!'

Her father met her at the creek and tried to calm down his sobbing daughter. 'For God's sake, May! Stop crying and tell me what's happened! Where did Elly go?'

'She went into the scrub to rescue Dodger cos he was hurt. We knew we shouldn't, Daddy, but he was crying out, and we were going to come and get you, but then Elly ran off on her own, and I came to get you, and please don't be mad at us!' she gushed.

He picked her up and hurried up the creek. 'Just stop crying and show me where she went. Can you remember?' And he yelled over his shoulder as he ran, 'Scott, bring a lantern! Quick!'

In spite of the gathering darkness, it only took a few minutes for him to find Dodger, lying in a pool of blood. He was pinned to the ground by a spear. Andy's own blood ran cold. His worst suspicions about the natives who had been following them seemed to be all too accurate. He crashed on into the scrub, franticly calling to Elly, but no reply came back. Stopping to listen, the unearthly silence of the Australian bush taunted his ears. Elly was gone, and he could only assume she had been kidnapped by the natives. At least there were no visible signs that she had been killed.

With leaden hearts, they searched into the night without success and tried to track the marauders at first light. They found nothing and never sighted the natives again. They had obviously taken Elly and melted into the rolling hills to the west. By now, they could be anywhere.

Leaving the women and children at the camp, the men searched far and wide for days, but, other than some long-dead campfires, they found no sign of their quarry. There was nothing more that they could do. They just had to treat Elly's disappearance in the same way as they had the death of one of her young cousins not long after they set out on their trek. Then they simply had no option but to lay her to rest beside the track and continue on.

As the sun set on the evening of the fourth day, the whole party gathered around the spot where Dodger had met his death and been buried and erected a cross in Elly's memory. They were all inconsolable but knew that they could do no more and must keep pushing northwards. More to appease Elly's distraught mother than with any hope of having any success, Andy left Scott to ride back to Gayndah and report the situation to the police. He was then to show them where the abduction had taken place and, if possible, join them in their search. Maybe they would know where the natives might have gone.

Sadly, when he caught up with the trekkers three weeks later, he had no success to report. The whole group had simply vanished.

*   *   *

After almost a year and a half on the road, the McKenzie clan finally reached their destination and set about making their fortune. While Andy joined the prospectors scratching in the rivers and creeks for gold, the other two re-established a carrying business and, with the herd they had brought with them, became the first graziers and only butchers in the settlement. Over the next ten years they prospered, and so long as the gold hung out, they were content to stay there. All that is, except May.

She had never got over the trauma of Elly's loss. She still woke at night calling her name and could never rid herself of the vision of her sister disappearing into the gloomy scrub. While the rest of the family had moved on, she could not, and her thoughts constantly turned to that tragic event, and to wondering, *What became of my sister and soulmate?* But what could she do about it?

The chance for her to try came when Scott decided he was tired of the Palmer River lifestyle and wanted to settle down to life as a grazier in a more hospitable environment. While he was trying to help the police track the abductors, he had ridden through some of the best country he had ever seen on the banks of the Dawson River. He had never forgotten it, and now approached his brothers with the idea of using some of their wealth to buy a property in the area. Andy was astute enough to know that the goldfield wouldn't last forever, and eventually they would probably all have to return south too. Scott could establish a base for them all to move to when the time came. Also, still suffering from gold fever, he knew the country Scott was interested in was near Cracow. Gold had been discovered there many years ago. You never knew. It could become the new place to be in years to come.

When May became aware of the plan, she realised this was her chance and pleaded with her parents to allow her to go with Scott. She was twenty now and would be able to help her bachelor brother on the property as well as keep house for him. Realising there was no future for her in the goldfields, they reluctantly agreed to let her go. She and Scott set sail for Bundaberg, he dreaming of rolling plains and fat cattle, while May's thoughts still rested on her sister. The chances of finding her were slim, but she could never settle down to her own life until she had at least tried.

*   *   *

The years of disappointment rolled on. May helped Scott to buy and then manage a grazing property on the Dawson, until he married a local widow with three children, when she started to feel a bit awkward living under their roof. She wondered what else she could do for a living until one day she saw an advertisement in the local paper seeking a governess for one of the large stations further down the river. Her parents had given her a sound education, and her solid Scottish background appealed to her new employers. At the age of twenty-five, she started work in her first paid job.

May quickly became like one of the family, loved by the four children she was called on to teach, respected by their parents who were delighted with her, and constantly the centre of attention of the eight stockmen who worked on the place, especially the only white one of the group, head stockman, Jack Roach. Women were scarce in these remote districts, so it didn't take long for May and Jack to become good friends.

Over the years since she came to central Queensland, May had been constantly on the lookout for clues as to Elly's whereabouts, but to no avail. With nothing to go on, she eventually gave up hope and nowadays seldom thought about her as her own busy life took over. But all that changed when she told Jack the story of the kidnap.

'So that's what happened, Jack,' she said. 'We've never heard from her since. We can only presume they killed her, but until I know for sure, I can't ever stop wondering. I still feel responsible for her loss because I urged her to go and look for Dodger, but I guess I'll just have to get over it.'

Tears rolled down her cheeks as she spoke, and Jack was touched by her obvious grief. He was determined to help her if he could, and, without saying anything that would raise false hopes, he set out with a plan of his own.

He had worked with aboriginal stockmen for years and generally had good relationships with them, but he also knew how secretive and cagey they could be if you intruded on their personal lives. Some of them were totally unresponsive to his attempts to get to know them, but he had become quite friendly with one of the current groups. Over a pannikin of tea at a mustering camp, without giving away too much, Jack started asking about his past – where he came from, where his family lived, and eventually about his parents.

'My old man was a drunken Irish gold scratcher,' Tommy volunteered. 'No good bastard. Filled my mother in and then shot through. The tribe never wanted me, and I ran away as a kid. Been working around the bush ever since.'

'Yair, the tribes don't take too much to you half-white fellas, do they?' Jack asked. 'Many of you around where you came from?'

'Always a few. Some of the girls used to earn a quid with the miners and other layabouts. Always came home when they got into trouble, though.'

'What about the other way around, Tommy? Any white women go with black men?' Jack probed.

'I suppose so, but we wouldn't know, would we? They lived in town and probably took their little piccaninnies home to their tribe,' he said and roared with laughter at the thought.

Jack joined in, and then went on, 'None of them ever lived with the tribe then?'

'Not my mob, but I did hear about a mob out in the Carnarvon Ranges who were supposed to have a white woman living with them. Funny mob of bastards. Never had much to do with them. Years ago now. She's probably gone home to her mob, too, by now.' He smiled, still amused at the thought.

'They still out there, you think, Tommy? Funny they haven't moved into one of the towns or mission stations by now.'

'Not those bastards. Don't trust no one, they don't. Still want to live like black fellas, they do.' And he laughed again at his own black humour.

Jack left it at that, not wanting to appear too interested. He could trust Tommy to a point, but he didn't want the others to hear of his interest.

What he had to do was obvious. Not breathe a word of his efforts to May in case it led nowhere, organise some holidays from the boss, and head out west to see if the suspicious story Tommy had told him lead anywhere. Packing his swag, he headed west, but where to start?

Talking to stations he encountered on the way, he learned of a mission run by the Lutheran Church, which was established to provide protection and education for aboriginal children. They had regular contact with all of the local groups but did not always enjoy the best of relations, as that contact often involved taking neglected and abused children into protection, not always with the approval of their parents. The pastor in charge responded to his enquiries with a degree of suspicion.

'So what is it you are looking for?' he asked.

'Well, it's a long story, but in short, I'm trying to find a white woman in her mid-twenties who may have been held captive by a group of aborigines in the Carnarvon Ranges. Would have been there for many years now, but they're supposed to be a bad lot, so it could be true.'

'Doesn't ring a bell with me, I'm afraid, but I've only been here for two years. We've got over a hundred kids here, who have come to us from all over the place. Sometimes the police bring them in, sometimes their parents even, and sometimes they're just found wandering around on their own.' The pastor pondered the young man opposite him and wondered just what his intentions were. 'Not much point looking at our records either,' he went on. 'Most of them don't know their parentage, or even how old they are. We just try to help them pick up their lives and educate them so they can enter normal society, because, one way or the other, they aren't wanted back in their families.'

Jack was disappointed that his interview hadn't seemed to give him much to go on. The pastor was not aware of any reports of a white woman living with the blacks, so couldn't suggest where Jack could look next. As he left deep in thought, he almost bumped into a coloured girl of about ten as she entered the building.

'I'm sorry,' he said. 'I should be more careful.'

'It's all right, sir,' she responded. 'My fault.'

'Please don't think that,' Jack pleaded. 'I should watch where I'm going.'

She turned nervously away and hurried inside, but not before Jack noticed that, in spite of her dusky skin, she had the most surprising vivid blue eyes, eyes that rang a bell with him. Rushing after her, he called, 'What's your name?'

'They call me Molly here,' she responded, 'but my real name's Molbai.'

Acting on a hunch, Jack asked, 'What's your mother call you, Molly?'

'She's dead now, but she used to call me Elly, when we were on our own and no one could hear.'

Jack felt a tingle run through his body. *Elly.* May's sister was called Elly, and those deep blue eyes were the same as May's. The coincidence was too great to ignore. *This had to be a daughter of Elly, and niece to May.* He hurried back to the pastor's office and told him of his suspicions.

'What can you tell me about Molly?' he asked.

After looking up the records, he was able to say, 'Well, we think she's about ten years old and came from a camp out in the mountains. Officials were concerned she was being abused, so they brought her here about four years ago. Seems she had a younger brother, but he couldn't be found. They tend to do that, you know. Hide the ones they want to keep and let the others go. Surprisingly, she could speak a bit of English when she came here and told staff at the time that her mother had died giving birth. She thought the baby died too. She's a bright girl, well behaved, and will be moved on into domestic employment in a year or so.'

Jack figured it was time to fill the pastor in on the whole story. 'So you see, sir, I reckon this is the missing Elly's daughter. I know May would love to take her in and treat her as her own daughter if you would agree, and her brother too, if he can be found. She would make a wonderful mother for them and perhaps relieve her anxiety and conscience about the loss of her sister.'

The pastor was delighted to be able to play a part in reuniting Molly with her mother's family and promised to get procedures under way. He also said he would do his best to track down her brother and, if possible, get him back with his sister and aunt.

Jack's horse felt the brunt of his urgency as he hurried back to the station with the news for May. He guessed she would be upset at what had happened to her sister, but she had long ago accepted that Elly was probably dead. Now she could transfer her love to her niece and finally put the tragic events of her childhood behind her.

*　　*　　*

The small gathering stood in the clearing in the scrub. Before them lay the scattered stones of a small burial plot and a rotting timber Cross with the following barely decipherable words on it:

In Memory of Elly Mckenzie
Taken 20.10.75

Mrs and Mr Jack Roach stood looking at the sad little epitaph. Jack, Jr wriggled in his mother's arms, while Elly Roach and her seven-year-old brother, Dodger, tried to imagine the terror that their mother must have experienced at being kidnapped by a group of wild natives. Her suffering and eventual death bore down heavily on them, as did the sobbing of their new mother as she finally said goodbye to her sister. They went and hugged her as the frustrations and guilt of the last twenty years melted away with her tears. A bright future stretched ahead for all of them. As the sun settled behind the trees, they stood in the gathering gloom of a late October afternoon, as dusk once more fell like a sullen blanket over the trees.

*   *   *

Epilogue

History has a way of ridiculing the pompous and arrogant members of our society. Now it produced a real doozy for the McKenzie clan.

In 1888, the gay Laird of Lanarkburn had died, leaving no issue, although he had tried marrying briefly in an attempt to create a male heir for the estate. Nobody knew how he achieved it, but his wife did fall pregnant on two occasions. Unfortunately, she miscarried both times, and Hugh lost interest in trying any further. He divorced her and lived out the rest of his life in the company of his friend of many years, Angus.

Now, on his death, the title and the estate passed to the next in line, his adversary of old, the next eldest brother. Andy and Jenny left the Palmer River businesses to William, took their two youngest daughters to Scotland, and assumed the title of 'Laird'. Hardly a day passed when he didn't pay his respects to the graves of his father and mother in the family plot, and as he passed that of his elder brother, he would pause, smile, and imagine poor old Hugh turning in his grave.

What his enquiries had turned up regarding the line of inheritance of family fortunes and titles amused and delighted him greatly. As he had no sons, on his death, the title of Laird of Lanarkburn would pass to the eldest son of his eldest daughter.

Whatever would Hugh think if he knew the next in line for the title was a little ten-year-old half-aboriginal kid with blue eyes, living a carefree and happy life with his adoptive parents on a central Queensland cattle station! Dodger Roach – Laird of Lanarkburn.

'The Laird of Lanarkburn' explained

Some elements of this yarn are true and were told to me by the artist, Tom McAulay. It is vaguely based on the story of his family, who did, in fact, come from Scotland and settled at Queanbeyan before embarking on the big trek to Palmer River. The abduction by natives of one of their girls did, in fact, occur near Mundubbera, and she was never seen again by her family. The semi-happy ending is, of course, fictitious.

One can hardly imagine the despair felt by her family, particularly her mother, when the young girl was snatched from them in such a cruel way. The hard lives and deprivations suffered by the wives of our pioneering families are never sufficiently recognised in the historical accounts of their exploits. They reared large families in primitive accommodation, with no access to medical help and generally living far from their extended family. And maybe the stolen 'Elly' did indeed have some kids of her own living an even more primitive life. We'll never know.

This poem was written for a Mother's Day lunch some years ago. While it refers to modern life, I am dedicating it on this occasion to the mums of our pioneering families. I doubt many of them would have got a nice bunch of flowers and a cup of tea in bed.

MOTHER'S DAY

There is one day, we all agree, no matter what our creed,
It covers all the lands on earth, all colours, shapes, and breeds.
The same day every single year, that day in early May,
When children call to wish their mum, a Happy Mother's Day.

From frozen northern Canada to dry Australian plains,
From foggy streets in Harlem to the coast of sunny Spain,
Wherever people congregate to make their earthly way,
There are mothers, there are children, and a role for Mother's Day.

That young teacher's aide in Brisbane
will ring up her mum in Bell,
Just to say how much she loves her and to hope that she is well.
And the street kid down in Sydney who just had to run away,
Is bound to make one call each year, just one, on Mother's Day.

Religions of the world all claim that only theirs is right.
They preach forgiveness, fairness, love, but all they do is fight.
This hatred for the other side seems, sadly, here to stay,
But they all have worried, loving mums,
and all need Mother's Day.

Each day across the face of Earth, a lot of people die,
But in their place, lots more are born and give that first brave cry.
Another generation comes to grow and work and play.

Another generation to give thanks on Mother's Day.

So on this day in early May, as you prop yourself in bed,
Prepared to eat your charcoal toast, cold tea, and hard-boiled egg,
Accept the adulations, as your kids all say, "G'day!
We love you, Mum, and hope you have a Happy Mother's Day!'

THE TRUCKIE'S WIFE

'Bugger. Bugger. Bugger.' Jodie slammed her palm on to the steering wheel in exasperation. Steam poured from beneath the bonnet of her car and sprayed back over her windscreen. An indicator light on the dash glowed red. Unlike her truck driver husband, she was no mechanical genius, but she knew enough to stop driving, and pulled on to the side of the highway.

What now? she wondered. To add to her annoyance, she remembered leaving her mobile on the charger when she left home. *How stupid!* Now here she was, stuck on the road a couple of kilometres from home, no way to call for help, and Glen somewhere in New South Wales on a trip. *Thank goodness it is daytime. Terrible things sometimes happened to women stranded on highways at night. Ah, well. Nothing for it but to lock up, and hoof it home, or at least to a phone.*

As she gathered up her things, she noticed a large vehicle pull over and park in front of her. Her blood froze, and she hit the button to lock all her doors. A door opened, and a tall well-dressed man alighted from the driver's seat. He came back towards her. He hardly looked like a threat, but you never knew. She kept the windows up and the locks on. He tapped on the windscreen, smiled, and mouthed a question. She tentatively lowered her window an inch or two.

'Hello,' he said. 'Are you okay?'

'Not really,' she replied. 'I think I may have cooked the motor.'

'Would you like me to take a look?'

She hesitated, and he saw the doubt in her eyes as she pondered what to do. He held up his hands, palms out, took a step back, and gave the most disarming smile she had ever seen.

'Look. No gun. No ulterior motives. I just thought I might be able to help you.'

Jodie lowered the window a bit further and returned his smile. 'I'm sorry. Just being careful. I didn't mean to be rude.'

'That's okay. Very sensible these days, but I'm completely harmless, I assure you. If you click the bonnet lock, I'll see if I can find what your trouble is.'

'Be careful. It'll be very hot still,' she warned.

He carefully opened the bonnet, releasing another cloud of steam, and peered underneath, and he then returned to the now-open window.

'Bad news, I'm afraid. Your radiator hose is busted. You won't be able to drive. By the way, my name's Michael. I'm a solicitor.'

'Jodie,' she said, reaching through the window to shake his proffered hand and take the business card he offered. 'Thanks for your help. I don't suppose you have a mobile I could borrow to call the RACQ?'

'Sure thing, but from my experience with them, you might be here for a while. Do you have far to go?'

'No, I live in the next suburb, and I was on my way home, but I'll just have to wait till they come, I suppose.'

Michael could see that she was still quite nervous and worried in spite of his best efforts to make her feel relaxed. He hesitated to suggest the thought that had just come to him.

'Look, Jodie, I don't want to intrude, and if you'd like, you can borrow my phone to call RACQ, but I just had a better idea. I always carry tow straps with me. I could tow you to your place, and you could wait in comfort, not to mention safety.'

'Oh, I couldn't expect you to do that.'

'Nonsense. It's probably not far off my track anyway. It's no trouble. Really.'

Conflicting thoughts were racing through Jodie's mind. *Glen had always stressed that I shouldn't trust anyone in these circumstances. He had seen and heard of so many tragic tales on the road that he constantly worried about my safety. Fair enough too. This very stretch of road had seen the abduction and murder of a young woman stranded by a breakdown twenty years ago.*

But this man seems so nice, and he isn't suggesting I go in his car. Besides, what he said makes sense. I would be at more risk waiting on my own on the roadside. Weighing up her options, she came to a decision and stepped out of her car.

'I'm terribly sorry, Michael. I've been very rude and suspicious of your kindness, but my husband is an interstate truckie, and he tells me all these horrible things that happen to women stranded on the roads. I didn't mean to be unappreciative.'

Michael appraised her as she rose. While not beautiful, she was quite attractive in a comely sort of way and had a beautiful smile, which she now gave him. 'Don't be silly,' he said. 'You acted just like I hope my wife would have in the same situation. You can't be too careful these days. Now what do you say to my suggestion?'

'I say thank you very much, if it's not too much trouble. It's very kind of you, and you must let me give you something for your trouble.'

'Don't be silly,' he said as he searched in the back of his patrol car for a tow strap. 'As I said, I just hope someone would return the favour if one of mine was in trouble. You hop back in, and we'll have you home in no time.'

He secured the towline and returned to her window.

'What have I got to do, Michael? I've never been towed before.'

'Just steer, and watch for my brake lights. I'll drive slowly. Oh, and put your hazard lights on too. We don't want anyone running into your rear, do we? One other thing, seeing as I'll be in front, you'd better tell me where we're going,' he said with a laugh.

*　*　*

The trip to Jodie's modest home proved uneventful, and in no time at all, her car was parked out in the front. Michael had packed his tow strap back in his car and turned to find Jodie digging into her purse.

'You really must let me pay you something for your trouble, Michael. I'm so grateful, and I feel terrible to have put you to so much trouble.'

'Jodie, you're embarrassing me. Please.' He placed his hand lightly on her arm. 'Listen, if you want to thank me, how about a cup of coffee or a cold drink?'

'Of course! I should have offered before. Come on in. I'll make us a sandwich, too, if you like. It's near enough to lunchtime. Unless you're in a hurry to get somewhere, that is. You'll have to excuse the mess in the kitchen,' she gushed.

Michael smiled to himself at her obvious nervousness. His very presence had her flustered, and he was determined to do his best to get her to relax. There was something about her that appealed to him. Was it that she reminded him of the girl he left behind in his teens when he abandoned her in a country town and moved to the city to attend university?

He sometimes wondered how different his life would have been if he had chosen a different path. His mundane life as a city solicitor, married to a society lady, with two kids at private schools was very comfortable but boring. He longed for something different, something exciting in his life, something that would rekindle the memories of his younger days, days when he and his girlfriend had enjoyed the simple pleasures of country life.

Jodie, on the other hand, felt embarrassed as she scurried around the kitchen, tidying up the breakfast dishes, and putting the kettle on. *What on earth would Michael be thinking?* she wondered. *He probably lived in a mansion, where everything would be so neat and tidy. Why on earth hadn't I done the dishes before I went out?*

She and Glen led such a 'normal' life. With their three kids all at school and Glen away most of the time, she seemed to have fallen into a real rut. She should have taken on a job, she supposed, but mainly because of his absence, Glen insisted she should be a stay-at-home mum. Over time, it became so boring. Even asking Michael in for coffee was making her quite excited, and more than a little nervous.

'I'm afraid we only have instant. Is that all right?'

'Absolutely. Milk, no sugar, please.' Without waiting to be invited, Michael took a seat at the kitchen table. Once again, it brought back memories of his old family home. So comfortable and friendly.

'Aren't you good? I have both, I'm afraid. Do you have time for a sandwich? I can rustle up a cheese and tomato if that's all right.'

'Perfect, and I'll bet you use mature cheddar too.'

'How did you know that?' she asked. 'Glen won't have anything else. I keep processed slices for the kids, though. Do you have kids?'

'Two. One of each. Both of them spoilt rotten.'

Jodie thought she detected a note of disappointment in his voice, as if he wished things could be different.

'We've got three, two girls and a boy. Glen won't let me spoil them, though. He comes from the old school. So do I, I suppose.' She handed him his coffee.

'Thanks. You sound like you love him very much.'

'Glen and I have been together since we were in the same class at school,' she offered. 'Fifteen years. I guess, after all that time, you get to know each other pretty well. Too well, I sometimes think.'

She brought a plate of sandwiches and joined him at the table. Feeling much more relaxed in his company now, she asked the question that had been at the back of her mind.

'So what's a busy man like you doing, cruising the streets at this time of the day?' she asked with a smile.

'Holidays. Long service leave actually for six weeks. I'm bored stiff already, and it's only week two. I don't know how you stand being at home all the time.'

'I struggle a bit to be honest. I'd like to go back to work, but, with Glen away so much, I have to keep the home fires burning on my own.'

They chatted on for over an hour. The time flew as they talked of their early lives, finding they had much in common. Jodie was sad to realise just how much his life had changed due to the circumstances of his work and married life. Hers, on the other hand, had morphed naturally into her present comfortable family situation, but as he talked, she started to realise that she too was missing out on much of the enjoyment of her younger days, especially being able to continue with her career in nursing.

'Another sandwich?' she offered.

Michael rose to his feet. 'No, thanks. They were great, but I should be going, I suppose. I've really enjoyed our chat. It's an ill wind, as the saying goes, eh? You'd better get on to getting your car fixed. Just tell them the make and model and to bring a top radiator hose.'

They walked to Michael's car. 'Thank you once again, Michael. You've restored my faith in the human race with your generosity and help.'

'And you have provided me with a little ray of sunshine in my otherwise boring day. And thanks for lunch.'

With that, he was gone, and Jodie pensively returned to her washing-up.

*　　*　　*

As usual, Glen rang in that night, and she told him of her troubles with the car. Predictably, he had been worried at her being stranded on the highway and made her promise never to leave the house again without her mobile. She tried to ease his concern by explaining how careful she had been when a passing motorist offered help but that in the end, she had accepted his suggestion to tow her home. The RACQ had fixed the problem, and sure, she would always remember to take her phone in the future.

She was touched by his obvious deep concern for her safety. He was a wonderful husband and father whom she loved dearly. Maybe that was why she neglected to tell him about having lunch with Michael, or maybe it was to prevent him further unnecessary worry. Whatever the reason, she left it out of her report and spent an uneasy night, worrying about it. *How silly,* she thought. *It was nothing really, just returning a favour.* She would certainly never see Michael again. And yet for some reason, she couldn't get him out of her mind.

*   *   *

Jodie barely heard the doorbell over the noise of the washing machine. Fuming under her breath about annoying door-to-door salesmen, she flung the door open, ready to give whoever it was short shrift.

'Michael!' she gasped. 'What are you doing here?'

'Well, that's a lovely greeting, I must say,' he said, giving her one of his most charming smiles.

'I'm sorry. How rude of me!' she said as she quickly tried to straighten her hair and dress. 'Come in, or are you in a hurry?'

'Not at all. I'm on holidays, remember? I just need two minutes of your time, or two hours if you agree with the suggestion I am going to put to you.' Hope and excitement shone in his eyes, and Jodie felt herself blush for some reason that she couldn't explain.

'Coffee? I'll put the kettle on.' Jodie led the way into the kitchen, and Michael resumed his seat at the table. Mild panic rushed through her mind. *Whatever could he be about to suggest?* While they had enjoyed their little sojourn yesterday, she thought that would be the last she would see of him. And now, here he was.

Michael tried to put her mind at rest. 'Jodie, let me start by assuring you my motives are entirely honourable. If you're uncomfortable with my being here, just say so, and I'll head off.'

'No. Don't be silly. I just wasn't expecting you to come back, that's all.'

'I'm not surprised. I didn't expect to be here either, but, as I sat around killing time this morning, my thoughts wandered to our talk yesterday. It was fun, and I thought, *Why don't we do it again?*'

He watched her carefully to judge her reaction as she placed two mugs of coffee on the table. She looked worried. Cautious. Even a bit scared. He rushed on.

'I called at a deli on the way here and bought some sandwiches and fruit. I owe you a lunch, and I thought we could have a picnic. Have you ever been to the botanic gardens?'

'Not since they moved to Mount Coot-tha,' she murmured, still with her mind in turmoil. *Where is this heading? What is he really trying to achieve? How am I going to handle this?*

'Michael, I appreciate the thought, but you really shouldn't have. You were the one that did me a huge favour.'

'Okay then. I admit my motive was entirely selfish. Talking to you yesterday was a breath of fresh air in my boring life, and I guess I just want some more of it. You seemed to enjoy it too, didn't you?' Another one of his amazing smiles.

'Well, yes. You know I did. It was like a trip down memory lane. Of course, I enjoyed our little talk, and your company, but I don't know that we should go out together.'

'On a picnic in the gardens? Hardly a hot date. Come on. Turn the washing off and shout yourself a break. We'll be back in two hours, tops.'

His enthusiasm was infectious, and she was swept along. Just this once, here was a chance to do something for her own enjoyment. When they came back, she would let him know that he shouldn't call again. It was against all her instincts to deceive Glen in this way, but she had already started down that track last night. Once more wouldn't make much difference, but then it had to stop. He and the kids came first, always had, and always would.

'Give me five minutes to change. You'll find some biscuits in the tin on the bench.'

'Thanks, but I don't want to spoil my appetite. Corned beef and pickles sandwiches no less. For old times' sake.'

Once again, they had a marvellous time, wandering around the gardens and eating their lunch under a giant gum tree. All too soon, they were saying goodbye as Michael dropped Jodie back at the house.

'Thanks once again, Michael. That was lovely,' she said as he opened the door for her.

He walked with her to the front door. 'What have you got on tomorrow?'

'Plenty, and Glen will be home before lunchtime. Really, Michael, I honestly think you shouldn't call again. Someone will notice.'

'Too bad. Just tell them you're seeking legal advice,' he joked. 'Surely we're not doing anything wrong in having a bite to eat and a chat.'

'We are when we're doing it behind people's backs,' Jodie said, as she stood in the doorway to prevent him from following her inside. 'Goodbye, Michael, and thanks for everything.'

With that, she closed the door and left him standing forlornly on the doorstep. She watched from behind a curtain as he slowly returned to his car and drove away. Her initial feelings of discomfort at what she had done were fast turning into a state of mild panic. She had never done anything like this before, and while it might be totally innocent, even carrying on like this behind Glen's back made her feel ashamed of herself. When he came home tomorrow, she would have to tell him about Michael's visits.

*   *   *

But when Glen returned next day, she didn't. As usual, after one of his interstate trips, he was so excited to see her and the kids that she couldn't bring herself to mention the subject, knowing as she did what he would think. It was finished anyhow, so there really was no reason to worry him over nothing. She soon put it out of her mind as they enjoyed a few days as a family before he left on his next four-day trip.

All too soon, it was over, and his mate came to pick him up on the way to the depot. She handed him his spare clothes and thermos, kissed him goodbye, and returned to her jobs indoors. An hour later, the doorbell rang.

'Michael! I told you not to come again,' she said, once again barring the door. 'Glen might come home.'

'Hello to you too. No chance of that happening, though, Jodie. He left in his truck half an hour ago.'

Cold realisation chilled the blood in her veins. What had been a disarming smile last week, now appeared as a lecherous sneer. For a moment, she thought of slamming the door in his face and locking it, but then realised that would solve nothing. He would probably stand there knocking and calling until some of the neighbours heard him. Somehow, she had to put an end to this whole sorry episode. She stepped aside, and he followed her inside.

'No chance of a coffee, I suppose?' he asked, completely unaware of her obvious discomfort. 'You relax. I'll make it.'

He walked past her towards the kettle, but she beat him there and put a hand on his arm to stop him. She swung him around and confronted him.

'You've been stalking him, haven't you? You watched him leave and followed him to work. How could you?'

Michael was taken aback by the vehemence of her accusation. 'Well, hardly stalking, but sure, I wanted to know he wasn't coming back. I've been looking forward to our talk for days. I've really missed you.'

He took her hand from his arm and held it in his own, searching into her eyes for an explanation of her agitation. She pulled it free and turned away from him, her heart pumping and terrified thoughts rushing to her head.

'Michael, this has to stop,' she said. 'I think you've taken this too far. We're both married. You may be prepared to risk your family, but I'm certainly not. I think you should leave now, and not come back.'

She waited for his response as the seconds ticked by on the kitchen clock but was completely unprepared for what happened. Michael moved up behind her, put his arms around her, and whispered in her ear, 'Come on, Jodie. You know you want this to go further as much as I do. Don't be such a prude.'

She wrenched herself free and swung to face him. 'Prude?' she screamed. 'Prude? I'll give you prude, you lecherous bastard! Now get out of my house!' She pushed hard on his chest, and he was sent reeling backwards to crash on to the floor. Hovering over him, she snarled, 'Get out, before I call the cops!'

The initial look of shock and surprise on his face was soon replaced by one of frustration and disappointment. Without taking his eyes from her, he climbed to his feet and stood forlornly in front of her. Neither of them spoke, and a strained silence hung in the air. Eventually, he broke it.

'What's gone wrong with you, Jodie? We seemed to be getting on so well together. Why don't you want to see me any more?'

Jodie turned away from him and stared out the window while she composed herself and considered her reply. Perhaps it was partly her fault that it had come to this. She should never have agreed to go on his picnic, but she had felt so grateful for his help with the car that she had felt obliged to be nice to him. And, she had to admit, she had enjoyed chatting to him. Perhaps if she had more experience with men in her younger days, she would have seen that his intentions had gone beyond that. Now she would have to find a way out of this mess. Finally, she turned to face him.

'Michael, please forgive me if I've led you to believe I wanted anything other than to show appreciation for your help. Okay, I admit I enjoyed talking to you, too, but that's all. We're both married people with families, and I love mine with a passion. I wouldn't do anything that might break it up. That's why I want you to go now and not contact me again. Please.'

She didn't like the look that slowly spread across his face – embarrassment, followed by disappointment, and finally anger as he realised how determined she was. When he eventually spoke, he could not hide the venom he felt at being rejected like that.

'There's only one way that your husband will find out, and that's if one of us tells him. You obviously don't intend to, but I might. You may have a lot to lose, but I haven't. The sooner my stuck-up bitch of a wife takes her snotty nosed kids and pisses off, the better. I've had a gutful of the lot of them. And you too.'

By now he was ranting around the room, and Jodie was becoming terrified. She retreated to the corner of the bench and waited for him to calm down. Finally, he pulled himself together, gave her a long baleful look, and turned to leave. At the door, in a voice that sent shivers up Jodie's spine, he left her with a threat that was to prove ominous.

'Don't think you've seen the last of me, Ms Prude. I just might have to tell your marvellous Glen about our little interludes, seeing as you won't.'

With that, he took off, slamming the door hard and leaving Jodie trembling and in tears.

*   *   *

But the relief she felt was not to last. Next morning, after she dropped the kids off at their school, she was sure she saw his car pass the end of her street. *If it was him, what was he doing around here?* She hurried inside and locked the door but saw no more of him all day. *Perhaps I had been wrong.*

Next day she went to the shops to do the weekly buy and had virtually forgotten about Michael and his tantrum. Then, as she waited at the lights to turn off the main road, there he was beside her in the right-hand lane. She snuck a sidelong glance at him as the lights changed and was aghast at the sneer he returned. She hurried home but saw no more of him or his car. *Was this another coincidence, or was he actually stalking me?*

Her question was answered the very next morning. As she went to retrieve her wheelie bin from the footpath, she was halted in her tracks by the sight of him standing beside his car fifty metres up the street – just standing, motionless, and staring at her. She abandoned the bin and hurried inside, once again checking that all the doors were locked, and then waited beside the phone for the dreaded knock at the door.

It never came. For half an hour that felt much longer, she went over in her mind the whole sorry episode. Finally, she peeked through the front curtains. The street was empty. He and his car were gone. *Thank God! Glen would be home before dark. I would have to tell him before he went away on his next trip.*

*   *   *

On Monday morning, Glen's mate picked him up as usual and drove him to the depot where he picked up his rig and headed out of town. An hour later, Jodie wasn't at all surprised to see Michael in his familiar position beside his car, staring at the house. She went on to the front patio and returned his gaze. Neither moved. So transfixed was he that Michael was unaware of a car pulling up behind him. Two men with goatee, tattoos, and plenty of muscles hopped out and quietly walked up behind him.

The bigger one broke the silence. 'G'day, Michael. Waiting for someone?'

The blood drained from his face, and he almost collapsed. 'My god! It's you! What are you doing here?' he said.

'More to the point, what are *you* doing here, you arsehole? That's what my mate and I are here to find out.'

Before they could grab him, Michael dived into his car and shut and locked the door. Fumbling with the key, he fired up the motor and roared off down the street at top speed. As he searched in the rear-view mirror to see if they were in pursuit, he failed to negotiate the T-junction at the end of the street and, with a tremendous crunch, ploughed into a huge tree on the footpath.

The two men drove up and raced to his aid, but it was a waste of time. With no seat belt on, he had been pitched headlong through the windscreen and was probably dead even before his body hit the tree. With shaking hands, Glen dialled 000.

'The Truckie's Wife' explained

Hardly a day goes past without a story in the news where someone suffers a terrible fate after being conned into doing something that they should have steered clear of. Abductions from roadsides, alcohol-induced rapes, drug overdoses, and burglaries are all too common, and all start with a misplaced trust.

We are probably all guilty at some stage of putting too much trust in the wrong people, in the forlorn hope that that trust will be returned. Sadly, sometimes it is not, with dangerous or even deadly consequences.

Fortunately, Jodie recognised the danger in time and was able to extricate herself from an awkward situation. Not all perpetrators get their just desserts like Michael, however, so heed the warning. Just be careful in placing your trust in a stranger.

SUCKED IN

The predator stood on the corner, with a
lolly bag gripped in his hand.
His location, approach, and timing were
all very carefully planned.
The smile that he gave to the girl, who came
by, was friendly, benign, and nice.
He seemed such a kind man. She fell for his
line, and forgot her mother's advice.

The party was rocking, and he was too,
as he swigged on an alcopop.
Friends had invited him into a group
who didn't know when to stop.
It all seemed so innocent at the time, as
they conned him into a ride,
But the drunken youth behind the wheel,
meant this was the night that he died.

She'd known him now for a month or two, and love was in the air.
A night on the town with a drink or two,
and she followed him into his lair.
The coffee he made knocked her out cold,
and she woke next day from a dream,
Taken advantage of, time and again, by him, and half of his team.

The pressure of work was taking its toll, as
he toiled until late in the night.
The wife and the kids all hassled him too.
Every day seemed to end in a fight.
Then a mate in the office suggested a cure,
and gave him a shot of cocaine.
In a month, he was hooked. In a year, he
was dead. A family destroyed again.

The old lady stood behind her front door,
the safety catch still in its place.
She'd always been careful in answering the
door. She was cautious, just in case.
But this young man seemed so lovely, well
mannered, and in need of a phone,
To call up his mum, let her know he'd be
late, so she let him into her home.

How often we hear the sad stories, of
good people sucked into strife,
That leads them towards unspeakable
crimes, and eventual loss of life!
It's so easy to take that first step on the road,
go along and fail to see danger.
But better by far, to be wary and wise,
whenever approached by a stranger.

WITNESS FOR THE DEFENCE

It had been a long shift for Gary, and he had decided this would be his last fare of the night. He had been on the road for eight hours and was due to hand over to another driver at four o'clock. Just one more handy fare would do him, and he hoped it wouldn't take him too far from base. Then it would be home for breakfast with his partner, Chris, and to catch up on some much needed sleep.

As he trawled through the streets in the nightclub district, his gut tightened, as it always did in this area, at this time of the day. Too many bad things happened when booze, drugs, and testosterone combined to create lots of unruly and boisterous revellers, and he tried to avoid this crowd whenever he could. But his last customer had landed him there, and it was about the only place to find a job at four o'clock in the morning.

His luck was in. A lone young female was flagging him down. Obviously, she was well under the weather, and there was a chance that she might throw up in his cab, but that was better than a gang of males, who could be a much worse risk. Only a few days before, a mate of his had been mugged and robbed by three kids, who took his day's earnings and put him into hospital for a few days. At least she would be safe. Out of habit, Gary cast a wary eye around the street near her, in case she had someone with her, but saw no one, so he glided into the kerb.

She opened the door and slid into the back seat. 'Where to, miss?' he asked.

'Kelvin Grove, please,' she responded. '124 Gilchrist Avenue.'

How lucky could I be! Gary thought to himself. *Right on my way back to base.* He eyed her off in the rear-view mirror. She didn't seem too bad. He probably wouldn't have to spend half an hour cleaning up vomit. *You should be able to levy a surcharge for that,* he thought, *but good luck trying to get it out of some belligerent drunk.* Perhaps he should use his usual ploy of getting her talking to keep her mind off how crook she was feeling.

'Have a heavy night, eh?' he ventured.

She started as he brought her back from her private thoughts. For a moment, he thought she was going to ignore him. They did that, too, a lot of the time, ignorant and rude. Always demanded that drivers had to be civil but felt no compunction to return the favour. Still, it was probably only the grog reacting, but he reckoned it was part of their character nowadays. He could still remember his youth when they would laugh and joke all the way home after a night out, which admittedly didn't last until daylight, and everyone thought drugs were what the doctor gave you when you were sick.

It was her turn to bring him out of his reverie. 'I suppose you could say that. No worse than normal, though.'

Gary guessed it was none of his business really but decided to fire ahead with his thoughts anyway. 'You run a bit of a risk being on your own in that area, don't you? Some terrible things happen these days.'

There was another long pause, and Gary was starting to think he must have offended her. Then he saw her rifle through her bag for a tissue and blow her nose, and catching his eyes on her in the mirror, she said, in not much more than a whisper, 'I broke up with my boyfriend.'

Gary thought he could hear real despair in her voice. 'I'm sorry. I didn't mean to stickybeak.'

'It's all right. He was a real bastard anyway. I'm better off without him. Now I'm free as a bird. I can crack on to anyone I see now, just like him. I'll teach the two-timing little prick a lesson. Two can play at that game.'

By now her voice was becoming shrill, and Gary thought he could detect the glitter of more than tears in her eyes. If he had learned anything about the drug scene, it was how to pick someone who was high, and he now came to the conclusion that she was full of more than just alcohol. Maybe he had better let her settle down again, so he said nothing. But she was fired up now and leant forward over the seat beside him.

'Why is it you guys think you can pick up anything with a skirt and a big come-hither smile, while we're supposed to just be there when you want us? Bloody men! Well, I'm going to show him. Two can play at that game. From now on, it's open slather for me.'

Deciding that discretion was the better part of valour, Gary said nothing and concentrated on his driving. It worked, and she slumped back in the seat. He searched the passing houses for numbers and eventually found 124, doing a U-turn in the deserted street and stopping in front of the house.

'That'll be fifteen dollars, near enough,' he said, turning to watch her leave the cab. She searched in her purse and then, with a strained giggle, said, 'Guess what. The bastard must have cleaned me out when I wasn't watching him. What a mongrel! I've only got a bit of silver on me, I'm afraid.'

Just what Gary needed – a fare skipper. 'I'll wait here while you get some from the house,' he offered, having been forced to do that many times over the years. He hopped out of the cab, ready to go with her to the front door in case she did a runner. She stayed huddled in the far corner of the seat, and he thought he could hear her giggling again. He opened the back door on his side and stuck his head in.

'Come on, I'll help you to the door,' he said. He was becoming increasingly concerned at her antics, but he couldn't afford to walk away from a fare. It looked like he was going to have to help her out. He reached in towards her and then froze, as she asked in a contrived sexy voice, 'Have you ever let one of your customers work off a fare?' Again that giggle.

Gary had heard fellow drivers boasting about offers like this, and believed some of them had accepted, but it had never happened to him before.

'Now don't be silly,' he said. 'You've had a few too many, so just let me help you inside so you can pay me, and then you can sleep it off.'

'I don't want to sleep it off. I want you to hop in here with me, and I'll give you more than fifteen bucks worth of fun. Come on. Don't be a meanie.' She reached towards his outstretched hand, and before he could draw back, she had pulled him through the open door. 'Come on. Hop in and shut the door. It'll be daylight soon.'

Out of the corner of his eye, Gary had seen a police patrol car slowing as it passed them, and as he looked up now, it was pulling into the kerb in front of his cab.

'Now listen here, miss, I'm not interested in your offer. I just want my money. Let me go, or I'll call out to the police, who are watching all this. Then I'm going to come around and open your door, and we'll go and get the money, eh?'

She sat up enough to see the patrol car and the police woman getting out of it.

'No, you don't!' she snarled, holding on to Gary's arm and pulling him closer. He could smell alcohol on her breath and was now sure she had been popping pills too. Her face was distorted with anger as she hissed into his, 'I'm not good enough for you. Is that it? You think I'm just a drunken little slut, eh? Well, I'll show you that you men can't get it all your own way! We can play games too. Just watch this.'

With that, she let go his arm, ripped the front of her dress down to her waist, and flung her door open. Half-falling on to the footpath, she shouted, 'Leave me alone, you lecherous old bastard! I told you I'm not interested in working off a lousy fifteen dollars. And look what you've done to my dress!'

'Hold everything! What's going on here?' Constable Leanne Peters helped her to her feet. 'Are you all right, miss?'

Sobbing uncontrollably now, she clung to the officer. 'He tried to rape me. Just because I didn't have enough money for his rotten fare. I told him I'd get it from the house, but he said I could work it off. Can you imagine that, with an ugly old fart like him? And then he tried to rip my dress off.' By now, she was wailing hysterically, and Constable Peters called for assistance from her fellow officer.

'Andy, you'd better come and give me a hand. We've got a serious incident here. Shut the door, driver, and move away from your cab. You look after him, Andy, while I take this poor girl inside.'

Gary turned to see another officer unclipping his holster as he approached. He couldn't believe what had just happened. *That conniving little bitch! Surely they aren't going to believe her.*

'Look here, Officer. This isn't what it looks like. She set me up.'

'Well, you're going to have to explain that back at the station, I'm afraid, sir. Just hold your wrists out in front of you, please.' The handcuffs clicked shut; he was under arrest.

$*$ $*$ $*$

The court case

'Order in the court. This case is The Queen versus Gary Thomas Worth. Judge Margot Crawford presiding.'

The sonorous tones of the court official filled the room. Gary sat beside his barrister, still unable to comprehend what had happened to him. The police had believed the story that his passenger had spun to them, and he had been charged with attempted rape. In the absence of any witnesses, he wondered how he would ever be able to prove his innocence. That the judge was renowned for her feminist rulings, and the prosecutor was also a woman, was not going to help his case.

'The prosecution calls Ms Caitlin Forbes to the stand. Take the Bible in your right hand and repeat after me—'

Gary gazed at the nervous young woman in the witness stand. He had only seen her in the gloom of the cab before. Now as she took the oath in a timid little voice, he could understand how her complaint would have been very convincing to the investigating officers. *No wonder they believed her version of events and rejected mine, but surely the truth would come out in the end.* He forced himself to listen as she told of the trip from the Valley to Kelvin Grove.

'And then, when I discovered that I didn't have enough money to cover the fare, he suggested I could work it off, and he started to climb into the back seat with me.'

Gary found himself wondering if she was a professional actress; so well she played the role of a sweet innocent young thing. Having started playing the game while full of grog and drugs, she now obviously intended to keep it going. *She'd be in trouble herself if she told the truth now*, he guessed.

'And what did you do then?' the prosecutor asked.

'He kept coming at me, but I pushed him away. He forced his way back in and ripped my dress. Then I managed to open the door and escape.'

Gary glanced at the jury and thought he could detect pity on most of the faces. 'Can you offer any reason why he attacked you, Ms Forbes? Perhaps you gave him some encouragement?' the prosecutor continued.

'No way. He must have thought he had me where he wanted because I was a few lousy dollars short, but I certainly didn't lead him on,' she said in an offended tone.

Her evidence went on and on, one bare-faced lie after another. Eventually, the defence barrister had his chance to cross-examine but made little headway. She claimed to have had only a few drinks, had never taken drugs in her life, and had given Gary no encouragement at all to think she wanted to supply favours in payment of the fare. Quite the contrary, she said, as she had offered to get some money from the house while he waited. *What a bare-faced, conniving little liar!* Gary thought. Things were starting to look pretty bad.

Finally, after the two constables basically supported her claims, the prosecution case was completed, and it was the turn of his barrister to mount his defence. He had not confided fully with Gary on what his approach would be but did say he had an ace up his sleeve. It appeared straightaway when he called his first witness.

'Calling Christopher Charles Dawson to the stand,' droned the court official.

Gary's mind was in turmoil as his lifelong partner took the stand. It was a big deal for Chris, who had never openly admitted his homosexuality in public before. He caught Gary's eye and gave him a wink.

'Mr Dawson, I notice your address is the same as the defendant's. Do you know each other?'

'Yes. You could say that, sir,' he replied in that deep baritone voice that Gary loved so much.

The barrister gave the jury a searching look to make sure they were paying attention and then continued, 'Would you care to tell us, Mr Dawson, exactly in what capacity do you know the defendant?'

The loving gaze that passed between Chris and Gary could not possibly have been missed by the jury, who were now rapt in the proceedings. Again that deep melodious voice. 'We've lived together for about fifteen years now.'

'Lived together, Mr Dawson? Would you care to expand on those arrangements for the benefit of the court?'

'Gary and I discovered our homosexuality while we were at school together, sir. We have always been great friends, and became lovers when we moved into the house where we still live.'

The barrister paused to let this sink in with the jury and then continued, 'So in all that time together, Mr Dawson, have you ever known, or even suspected, that Mr Worth might have had sexual relations with a female? In other words, do you think he might possibly be bisexual?'

'Good heavens, no!' Chris said. 'Both of us are totally repulsed at the very thought of such a thing. Right from when we accepted our homosexuality as teenagers, we have never even looked at girls. Besides, ours is a faithful and monogamous partnership. There's no way he would ever try to have sex with anyone else, let alone a female.'

The proceedings continued for another few hours, but the rest of the evidence had been made largely irrelevant by the testimony of the star witness. Finally, Judge Crawford intervened, calling both parties' representatives to the bar.

'I think this farce has gone far enough, don't you think?' she whispered to them. 'In the absence of any third-party witness, it is a case of one person's word against the other, and I am inclined to place a lot of weight on the defence's first witness. I am at a loss as to what caused the incident, and in an attempt to get to the bottom of this, I intend to recall the complainant to the stand. You can both ask her more questions.'

Under the pressure of further cross-examination, she broke down and admitted that her story had resulted from her intoxicated state, her busted relationship, and Gary's refusal of her offer.

'I was in a fragile state, Your Honour, and when he kept refusing my advance, it was the last straw. I just cracked. I didn't mean it to go this far, and I'm sorry I started it now.'

Judge Crawford delivered her the severest warning possible, stopping just short of charging her with contempt of court but ordering her to meet Gary's costs, including fifteen dollars for the fare, and payment for the time he was not permitted to drive while awaiting trial.

Gary and Chris shook hands with the barrister, gave smug looks at the plaintiff, and headed out of court, arm in arm.

'Witness for the Defence' explained

Every major city has its sleazy precinct, where fun-seeking young people congregate to get their thrills. Unfortunately, many of them overdo it and end up getting into all sorts of trouble. Drugs, prostitution, and all-night drinking sessions provide many opportunities for bad things to happen, and they do, quite regularly.

Taxi drivers helping to clear the streets of these revellers in the early hours are often the target of their inebriated state. Who'd want to be a cabby?

The Valley

Lurking in the alleys stark and bare,
At the corners, doorways, everywhere.
Hiding, sidling, with a furtive glance,
Waiting, hoping, for a lucky chance.

Lurking under streetlights for a job.
Lifeless, listless, daughters of the mob.
Flashing, garish, touting fun for cash.
Amber, Candy, Donna, Madam Lash.

Lurking in the nightclub bars till dawn.
Browsing through the sex shops selling porn.
Brawling, bashing, kicking fallen foes.
Broken ribs, black eyes, and bleeding nose.

Lurking in the cells, awaiting calls.
Stinking, scary, cold, grey prison walls.
'Why? Oh why?' becomes their plaintive cry.
Will they never learn until they die?

ABOUT THE AUTHOR

In 2002, I wrote a book entitled *Pass the Ball,* a sort of an autobiography, which started with the arrival of my ancestors to Australia in the last half of the nineteenth century. At the time, in the 'About the Author' section, I stated, 'This is the first, and probably the last, book to be written by this author.'

Well, I was wrong, it seems. Here is a second one, and, you never know, maybe not the last either.

Having read hundreds, if not thousands, of novels over the years, I wondered if perhaps I could write one. When I tried, I soon attained a great respect for those who can, and realised at the same time that I probably can't – too impatient, by far. I'm sure someone more talented than I am could have turned one of my yarns into a four-hundred-page novel, but I found I could tell the tale in a dozen.

That being the case, I have tried to create my book from twenty of them – some serious, some funny, and some philosophical. Most are about down-to-earth country folk. Some, like 'Rusty' and 'A Farmer's Wife' have a lesson in them. Others are even a bit romantic, for example, 'Blind Love' and 'Best Friends'. In a number of cases, the story is inspired by a poem already written, and in other cases, one is written specially, but in any case, all are accompanied by a poem or two and an explanation as to how it all came about.

Primarily these yarns were written with an Australian readership in mind, most of whom would understand and appreciate the slang words and phrases used, particularly by unsophisticated bushies. However, I imagine some of the terms may leave non-Australians a bit perplexed. Stick with it, and by the time you've read Witness for the Defence you will have probably worked out what a "sheila' is, along with all the other words and expressions that are uniquely Australian country in origin.

I hope you enjoy the adventures of the 110 characters who play some role in these yarns. As an author, I feel I know these people – how they look, how they speak, how they would react to different circumstances, and so on. If you, the reader, can similarly identify with them, then you will probably get some satisfaction out of this book.